THE
SANCTUARY

Also by Andrew Hunter Murray

The Last Day

THE
SANCTUARY

ANDREW HUNTER MURRAY

HUTCHINSON
HEINEMANN

1 3 5 7 9 10 8 6 4 2

Hutchinson Heinemann
20 Vauxhall Bridge Road
London SW1V 2SA

Hutchinson Heinemann is part of the Penguin Random House group of
companies whose addresses can be found at global.penguinrandomhouse.com.

Penguin
Random House
UK

First published in the United Kingdom by Hutchinson Heinemann in 2022

www.penguin.co.uk

A CIP catalogue record for this book is available from the British Library

ISBN 9781529151572 (hardback)
ISBN 9781529151589 (trade paperback)

Illustrations by Jessica Pilling

Typeset in 11.75/17.25 pt Times New Roman
by Integra Software Services Pvt. Ltd, Pondicherry

Printed and bound in Great Britain by Clays Ltd, Elcograf S.p.A.

The authorised representative in the EEA is Penguin Random House Ireland,
Morrison Chambers, 32 Nassau Street, Dublin D02 YH68.

Penguin Random House is committed to a sustainable future for our
business, our readers and our planet. This book is made from
Forest Stewardship Council® certified paper.

To M.M.F.L.

Prologue

He has heard for years that this day would come. He always dutifully believed it, repeated the words with the rest of the congregation, but he didn't seriously imagine it, nor that he would feel such strange pleasure when it did.

He doesn't have a gun; he's only fourteen, and slight. His mother has explained that the recoil alone would knock him flat. He was always told there was no need to rush his training. Except now – with the firing outside, and the sand-coloured armoured vehicles crawling forward, the cowardly troops shielded by them pressing ever closer – now he wishes he had one.

Still, he has the next best thing. He's been down to the kitchens. A knife won't be missed now, not in the middle of all this. The older men and women are running through the corridors, finding the best positions to return fire, but he has his own labour to fulfil. He walks calmly, with it balanced in his hand.

Back upstairs, he sees the great man. He's standing behind a column, holding a rifle and glancing outwards, coordinating, shouting. He is alone; there is something about him that is always curiously alone.

If *he* ran the place, the boy thinks, he doubts whether he would make all the same decisions the great man did. He is not sure, if he was the great man, whether he would hit others so enthusiastically, nor for so long. Although these thoughts are heresy, of course, and the great man is simply acting on instructions from the highest power of all.

The gunfire is much closer now. It has made the day hotter; the individual bullets have warmed the air, agitating it like wasps as they slap the walls. The men approaching the compound are gaining, but the battle is in the balance. Beyond the outer wall, something explodes.

When you are small, and weak, a knife simply requires a sharp point. His mother has shown him this in the kitchens, how a little pressure exerted in the right place can create a great rip in an animal's side. All you need, she has explained, is the courage to create the first incision, and the rest will follow on. It's a lesson he likes far more than any the great man has taught him over the years. She has explained, too, how to recognise a moment of opportunity.

The great man is distracted, facing away and glancing out of the window. He laughs as one of the uniformed men outside falls, and bellows to his own followers that they are winning.

The Sanctuary

It is so little effort, just a few steps, to cross the room towards him, find the right point in his side – free of ribs, just like on a pig – and, with a quick gesture, to bury the blade. One, two, three.

The great man looks down, and drops his gun. He stumbles into the window's light, and is immediately cut down by bullets from without. His eyes rest on the boy, but they are glazing already, and the boy cannot tell whether the great man sees who did this to him. He hopes he does.

The gunfire from within the compound crackles on, but without the dominant note of its leader, it will not last long. The boy pauses only to wipe a rough cloth over the knife's handle, removing the fingerprints, then leaves the body and returns downstairs. He walks calmly once again. His mother will be proud.

Book I

Mainland

Strait is the gate and narrow is the way which leadeth unto
life, and few there be that find it.
Matthew 7:14

The week I travelled to Pemberley's island was the week the old king and the last elephant had both died, and although any connection between the two deaths seemed too glib to make, for several days one was hardly mentioned without the other. Two exemplars of their respective species, two mighty symbols of venerability and distinction, that sort of thing. You could write it yourself in five minutes, if you were fool enough or had news to sell.

They died days apart; the elephant went first. Accounts of them drawing their last breath at the same moment were later revealed to be nothing but sensational fabrications, the fevered work of journalists who should have taken up fiction instead. Although looking at what followed, perhaps the double extinction was significant after all.

Once the king went, the eradication of the earth's largest remaining species was immediately relegated down the news order. Our country had been elderly for decades, and the death of our leader after years of stodgy, comforting inactivity felt important. It was another nudge of the wheel, another change of course sending us off the road into unknown country. Our national subconscious muddled the two; across the country people dreamed of elephants in crowns squeezing through palace gates, or of the old king himself, his skin grey and rugose, his nose warping into a trunk.

I forget the king's name now, but the elephant was called Nala, and she had been the last of her kind for over a decade. There had been thousands of other extinctions by now, of less memorable creatures, but Nala seemed to be the perfect example of our great carelessness. Some had suggested breeding from her, but the notion seemed freakish, and the proposal was treated as the folly it was.

That was one clear difference between Nala and His Majesty – the old king had his replacements, the glassy-eyed children he had produced late in life. To see a facial feature – a look in the eye, the twist of a smile – repeated from one generation to another is greatly comforting. It tells us our ancestors have survived, if only in ghostly, half-glimpsed fragments. The young princess who took the old king's place had the same smooth manner as her father, the same high cheekbones, and that was good enough. And so the country stumbled on, surveying its dimming reflection in the mirror with anxiety and vanity alike.

I didn't pay much attention at the time. I was working that week. My notebook, left in the city, will have a one-line record of the fact. It has probably been torn or burned or mulched by now, but if not, the week will appear on the final page: two dates, a sum of money, a phone number, and a name. *Bywater*.

I finished the Bywater commission in five days flat; more fool me. Another day would have paid for a week's living back in the city, but I couldn't bear to drag it out any further than necessary. Apart from anything else, I was coming home to Cara. I even found myself hurrying over the final brushstrokes, and heard Anthony in my head chastising me for it. As it happened, that wasn't the reason the job ended badly.

The Bywaters' Village was one of the most exclusive in the country: a huge service settlement outside the walls, great beauty on display within. The sittings had taken five days; days that stretched out even as I sat through them, trying without success to lose myself in my work. I'd offered the family the option of working from photographs, but I could tell in my initial inter-view they would be the kind of clients to insist on what they considered the full experience.

They were a family of three – father and mother, him a decade older than her, and their son. The father was a type common in these places: tall, broad and vicious. He was wide-shouldered, with a breadth just on the turn, a suggestion of jowl beginning to make itself known above the collar of the shirt. The kind of client who makes you relieved you've brought enough paints to mix a decent quantity of pink. His work was something in the city. I loved that phrase. By then, most people who worked in the city didn't.

It was Mrs Bywater who'd come up with the – to her – rather daring idea of having the family painted. My work was not exactly fashionable, but it had somehow outlasted the new technologies, as faith in them waned. There was an eternal quality about my medium, or so most clients thought, and I was loath to remind them of the thousands of portraits lost across the centuries, torn or binned or carelessly dismantled, their frames used as firewood. The older way of doing things had somehow survived into our own age, and I wasn't going to correct anyone deluded enough to think my work might last.

It was more often the wife than the husband who commissioned me, but it was closer to half and half than you would think. It did, however, tend to be mostly groups of at least two. The few single people I painted tended to be receiving their portrait on behalf of an institution, and usually there was a bit of awkwardness about the process.

I preferred single portraits despite that tension; maybe because of it. They produced an agreeable sense of struggle – the subjects' resistance and awkwardness matched against my determination to capture their features, and the slow process of making sure it happened, stroke after stroke. Pemberley, of course, my final portrait, was the perfect example.

The Bywaters, though, had presented all the difficulties I least enjoyed working with, and none of those I treated as a challenge. Mrs Bywater was the opposite of her husband, physically. It was as if two average people had pooled their assets – the size, the colour, the movement – then divided them unequally. Where he was broad, she was slight. Where he was pink, she was pale; and while he treated the sittings with a bovine stolidity, she made the constant quick movements customary to the unnerved or the disappointed. A difficult client.

The Sanctuary

The son was sixteen, and clearly was at the exact age where he simultaneously craved his parents' approval and wanted nothing to do with them. He hunched himself in the foreground like a folded deckchair, and looked off to the side.

After each morning's sittings, I withdrew to a small timbered office at the end of the garden to work on the details. I was in the office when Mrs Bywater brought me tea and the news of the old king's death. It hadn't been unexpected, but it was a shock nonetheless – a storm wave glimpsed from a distance, no less destructive when it hits. She asked me what I thought would happen, and I childishly replied that the family would probably just carry on with the next generation, an option not open to poor Nala.

Mrs Bywater pursed her lips, and for the rest of the week her expression in the sittings as she looked towards me was one of mild distaste. I allowed a little of that look into the final painting; not enough to lose my fee, but enough for honesty.

I'm sure they were a family like most others. But the root of their urge to be painted – not for the sake of art, not to engage with the process, but simply for another image of themselves – gave me the feeling I had in all my least happy commissions, the feeling of sheer unimportance from the wrist upwards. I may as well have just bought them a mirror.

On the last morning, I came into the studio at the end of the garden to see the son trying to prise off the cover I had fitted over the canvas, to keep clients from looking at work before it was complete.

'Excuse me. Please don't do that.'

'Why not?'

'Because the picture isn't ready. I still need an hour or two to finish it.'

He gave me an impassive look just like his father's, then moved to the next corner of the cover and started working it free.

'Could you please stop that?'

He paused, and looked at me with amusement. The precious artist, in his home, telling him what to do.

'How old are you?' he asked.

'Thirty-three.'

'My dad says you want to live in a place like this. He said you never will. If you're not here by twenty-five, you'll never make it in, he says.'

That made me angry. 'Well, I certainly wouldn't want to live anywhere near a young man like you. Will you just leave it alone?'

He wasn't quite confident enough to challenge me physically, and as I stepped towards him, my fists balled in annoyance, he moved back, wide-eyed, raising his hands in innocence. A pantomime gesture.

'What's this?' The boy's mother was behind me in the doorway.

'Your son was interfering with my picture.'

'He threatened me, Mum. He said I'd better leave it alone or else.'

All of which explains how I found myself leaving the Bywaters' compound, unpaid, and escorted by Village security to the gate.

If they could get over the row, I thought, the family would be happy with the result. They would get what they had asked for, barring the finishing touches – a glimpse of their younger selves, a sliver of eternity to hang in their front room. No matter what joys or sorrows followed, the painting would keep them fixed in a time of relative youth and possibility. The pictures I produce are not meant to be nostalgic, but they almost inevitably end up being so for their subjects. 'How young I was,' clients would say to me, the few times I saw them again. 'How little I knew.'

These were the thoughts that occupied my attention as I made my way through the Village's gatehouse, bid the security team farewell and passed onto the service road outside. They faded to insignificance as a new thought replaced them: I was finally free to return to Cara. Our life together was about to begin.

It was a morning of crystal skies and unwarranted warmth, the latest in a long line of such mornings, and each new day dawned with no change in the blue colour of the sky. Only the land beneath it changed, the open grasses yellowing to straw and the trees bowing their branches in mourning for their dearly departed friends, the clouds. A hot spring.

The queue outside the Village this morning was long, even though I left after ten. Seeing it gave me a feeling of relief at having been in the Village's hostel – some clients would have kept me outside the walls in the service hub. Like the majority of my subjects, the Bywaters had seen me as an artisan, which earned me a little more respect than the average support worker.

The line looked much the same as all the queues outside these places: the young outside the walls, waiting to serve the old (plus their occasional fortunate brats) within. Building teams in their hi-vis jackets, smoking the final guilt-free fags of the day; a cadre of tired-looking women I guessed must be cleaners; a huddle of chefs with tattoos on every spare inch of skin. Half a dozen schoolteachers, smartly dressed, kept themselves apart.

One of the builders, a thickset man in his thirties, had sat down against the wall to sleep. He could have been hungover, but it's likelier he was overworked. He looked beaten. If I'd had more courage or creative impetus, I'd have stopped to sketch him. But I was suddenly in a hurry, and didn't want to risk a confrontation. Cowardice always was a weed scattered through the underbrush of my character. Anthony told me it would stop me becoming a great artist, although if he could have seen my final painting, he might have recanted.

Neither the queue nor my cowardice nor the Bywaters mattered, though, because I was on my way home to Cara, and she was on her way home to me. I knew when her coach was scheduled to arrive back in the city. I would be there two hours earlier – long enough to tidy our home until it looked as good as the day before she left. I would have something cooking by the time she got back, something full of comfort: a stew with crusty bread on the side, or the better brand of chicken. I wanted her to know we would be comfortable together, that she could safely imagine growing old with me.

The coach to the city was a cut above the usual. It served the Village itself, not the satellite dwellings of the workers, which meant better seats and suspension, a more amiable driver, a happier experience in every way. I took out Cara's last letter to me to read. It had come through two weeks ago, before the

Bywater trip, and although it was short, I could not help taking it with me to reread in the evenings. It had ended:

I'll be back on the fourth, sometime in the late afternoon. Knock off work in advance, won't you. I want to have your full attention when I tell you about this place. I think it's on the brink of something entirely new. I think I am too.

I wasn't concerned by her brevity, of course, but it was a noticeable change. Her first notes from the island had been several pages each: long paragraphs interrupted by sketches, extra observations and footnotes crammed in at the sides, the ink blotching here and there as though too eager to get out of the pen. Even in those letters, and in her one phone call, she hadn't told me too much about her work on Pemberley's island – commercial confidentiality – but her first notes had been full of life, and love for me. That seemed to have been draining away.

As I say, I wasn't concerned. She would be coming back to me shortly, and we would be free to marry at last.

The journey back towards the city was the same as always. First we were in the rough ring immediately surrounding the Village, and still felt the glorious glow cast by all that money behind us, like a patch of sun. The crops waved in the fields, and there was an atmosphere of life and purpose in the people I saw. The few lone buildings we passed looked clean and somehow contented.

Then the aura of money disappeared from the land, ray by ray. Tiles absconded from rooftops; beams sagged. The buildings we passed took on a lowering aspect, their windows transformed to ranks of bared teeth interrupted by gaping cavities. Any lone houses had windows edged with mould and thin, bedraggled curtains. Behind those windows were shadows, punctuated by dim figures that moved in the darkness like lost souls. The road itself coarsened, and the coach swayed as the driver avoided potholes. Across the fields and the stubble, shreds of plastic danced a fitful tango with the crows pecking uncertainly at them. This was how the country was broken down.

That day, I paid little attention. I was interested in nobody but myself and Cara. I looked only at the seat in front of me, and dozed, imagining reunion scenes in films, transposing us into them. Cara, Cara, Cara.

For some time now I had avoided using the word 'fiancée'. It seemed so childish somehow, the remnant of a bygone age of courtesy. The word evoked brides-to-be petulantly rejecting a dozen dresses in a row, bluff grooms visiting their tailors, worries about canapés. It seemed a pure archaism in today's world – something Village-dwellers might like to play at and normal people could not. Cara felt just the same way, whenever we'd discussed the matter. But now, on the brink of her return, I could think of the word with joy.

I was nearly asleep by now, but one more troubling thought struck me as I drifted off. For a couple who so disliked the idea of the 'fiancée', we had spent two years in that temporary state, without actually taking the final step to bring the condition to an end.

I woke at the outskirts of the city, and an hour later the coach reached its destination, a private station near the centre. This was designed for people who might be visiting another Village across the country and who wanted to break the journey, or who had business to transact here. High fluted columns, fashionable seating, attendants with braided caps; it was a salubrious enclave of Village life at the city's heart. I passed my papers through the grille to the rep on the other side, a bored woman who kept a finger in her book even as she glanced over my documents, and left as quickly as possible.

There had only been four of us on the coach by the time we arrived. Two of the others were teenagers clearly out for adventure; I wondered what they had told their mothers. The third was an older man. He had appeared respectable when I had boarded but had somehow changed in the city's light to look distinctly raffish. I guessed he was there for exactly the same reason as the teenagers.

It was only an hour's walk from the station to my home, but carrying a week's clothing and my painting roll became tiresome, and the heat of the quiet city made me sweat. Even so, all my spare money was already mentally allocated for celebrations with Cara, and I had nothing else to do.

As I went, I remembered my half-wakeful anxiety from the journey, and saw now that it was absurd. Cara's work routinely took her away for weeks or even months on end, as did mine. It was hardly surprising we had not managed to arrange a wedding yet. Tonight we would discuss it properly, would fix a date and build the next year around it. And thirty-three was still young to be married these days, after all.

The city showed me its usual sights as I went. At this time of day, in the heat of the spring afternoon, it seemed at its greatest and most stagnant all in one. Cara and I had lived together here for a decade now, since I came back from Florence and she from university. It was still magnificent from the right angles. But like the countryside I had just come through, no matter how splendid it might sometimes seem, there followed the constant shadow of its physical corruption.

Even on special occasions, when the place remembered it was meant to be one of the great cities of the earth and temporarily made itself presentable, another current whispered beneath its surface: the knowledge that these gains would pass. It still functioned as normal from time to time, but the prospect of imminent collapse was palpable. Here a team of workmen stood in blank dismay around a thirty-foot puddle of stagnant water; there the facade of a grand old building was pinioned in place, no building behind it, no substance behind a crust of former glory.

We lived not in one of the newer – now ageing – residential estates, but in the great swirl of houses surrounding the city, built two centuries ago. These houses had seen the nation collapsing, triumphant, collapsing again. Our home was pleasant enough: the upper floor of one of these buildings, accessed by a mean and badly lit stairwell, but fresh and clean within. It was about right for a couple with aspirations but with no real prospect of ever leaving the city and making it to a Village.

The place had two tiny bedrooms. Cara kept her clothes on one side of the second bedroom, and I kept my paints and canvases on the other. If I stood halfway across the room and faced in one particular direction, I could pretend I had a proper studio. I loved it there.

I remember being in a hurry that day. The people Cara worked for often spent their time moving from one pleasure-dome to another with her in tow; they owned yachts, or aeroplanes, or more houses than they knew what to do with. God alone knew how luxurious her latest billet had been. I had a powerful sense of anxiety on the days when she was returning home, because I knew that at some level, she wouldn't be able to help comparing what we had with what she had left.

I moved sketches from the kitchen table; I emptied the bins, stinking after five days of spring heat; I cleaned the floors two different ways, even fixed a shelf. After all that, it was past five and I was sweating. There was just time to run to the shop on the corner and buy some ingredients for supper. Cara was never used to cooking for herself for a few days after a job ended.

Six o'clock came and went, and seven. The hours were long, and I spent them in constant restless motion. I would stand before an easel for a few minutes, improving a sketch; I arranged the books on the newly stable shelf; I looked over the ingredients and saw that they were good. I realised later, of course, that I had simply been arranging myself into a series of positions to remind her of my assets as a partner: creative, provider, lover. After a while, I felt as if I was acting in a dumb-show for an audience who were late to their seats on the opening night.

At eight o'clock, I remembered the postbox in the hall, and hurried down to it. Inside were four letters; three typed, one in handwriting I knew well. I saved that one to open last, because I had the feeling it would change my life somehow, and I felt certain the change it brought would not be welcome. So I decided to stay living as the person I was, just for a few minutes longer.

The first two were inconsequential updates on forthcoming jobs. The third informed me that my regular post, teaching on a Monday at a nearby school, could no longer be reconciled with their budget, and this would be my final term of employment there. I didn't even read it in full because of my worries about the fourth letter. But even as I skimmed the ritual expressions of regret, I reflected that I now had one fewer tie to the city.

The Sanctuary

The final letter was from Cara. It was even briefer than her previous one, which had barely made it over onto its second side. There was a little preamble here, but not much. The paragraph I was looking for was the third one.

I'm not coming back. The work we are doing here is at such a critical point, and I have a vital part to play in keeping it on time. I have been trying to solve this problem for so long; how to please you and myself. I haven't worked it out, but the upshot is: I'm going to be here a while longer, I don't know how long. I really am sorry. You deserve much better treatment than you've had from me. I do miss you terribly, for what that's worth, but this place is much more important than that. Than us, is what I mean. This is the most important place in the world.

There was a little more, but in short, that was the message. She would not be returning; her work on Pemberley's island was too important to her, possibly to Pemberley himself. The question of whether we were still engaged was left decorously open, as though it would have been vulgar to bring it up. In the circumstances, it was wise of her not to mention our forthcoming anniversary this weekend.

I stared at the letter for a while, then folded it and put it with her others. They told their own story. The long, rambling missives of her first weeks, enthusing about the place and her role there, full of amusing details and indiscretions about the people, had slowly shrunk, had grown faded and distant. And now this.

The evening sky from the studio window was dark, but the oppressive heat of the city was still rising off its surfaces. The land was exhaling again, having lasted another day.

At about ten o'clock, I turned on the television. I wasn't hungry yet; the ingredients for dinner sat abandoned on the worktop. I forget what show was on, but the very first advertisement break contained an advert for one of the Villages. This one had been running for a few weeks; I had caught the edge of it before. This is what it showed:

Shot. A couple in early middle age out walking together, sensibly dressed, and looking up at the hill path rising before them. As their golden retriever races off ahead of them, they begin their climb.

Shot. We pan across a gleaming restaurant kitchen with fittings of shining chrome, where chefs in pristine whites are preparing meals. At the dark hatch behind them, waiters and waitresses come by to collect the food, like bees to a flower.

Shot. An elderly couple sit in a wicker gazebo overlooking a beautifully tended garden. They address a small white microphone, and smile at the responses they hear. There is no sign of any gardeners.

Shot. Two happy parents and their son sit in a theatre, laughing in delight; a counter-shot of pantomime actors on stage, looking out at the audience, laughing along too. One of the actors grins, happy in his work.

The Sanctuary

Shot. A small classroom of well-dressed children, boys and girls, being shown a magic lantern. We recognise the boy from the theatre, and we see in his eyes the same joy we saw before.

Shot. A friendly security officer at the gates welcomes a team of workers, carefully examining their paperwork before letting them in. The shot dissolves into another: the same officer, shaking his head at someone else who wants access, sending them away, keeping the place safe.

Shot. The middle-aged couple from the first shot have crested the hill. They look round at the view, then back to the village below, a perfect oval ringed by a sturdy wall. He puts his arm around her; even the dog returns and sits at their feet. They blur, and a swirled logo appears in the foreground, along with the company name. *The Tomorrow Trust*.

I thought back to where I had woken up this morning, the Village where the Bywaters lived. I had never liked the places, even before Cara went to work for Pemberley. They were obviously a drain on the landscape, an institution that excluded millions even as they provided me with most of my work. But now, as I watched this advert, I found them malevolent.

As I sat and watched the logo fade, with Cara's letter before me on the table, it seemed the advert had been transmitted as a personal challenge. These places were the creation of Sir John Pemberley, the cause and result alike of his wealth. He owned the land they sat on, the land around them. Now that Cara had decided to stay with him – perhaps permanently – on his island, the ultimate Village, he was reminding me via this advert of the power he held in this country, and over me. This seems absurd with hindsight; all I can tell you is how I felt just then.

That was the moment the idea first occurred to me. There was little keeping me in the city: I had made sure I had several days clear of work so Cara and I could grow close again after her return. There was at least a month's money in my account. And I loved her.

I turned the television off, went into the studio room and sat in the low chair, looking at the work of my life so far, the city's distant clangour occasionally breaking the silence. It seemed to me I was looking at it from a great distance, even in a room just a few metres across. But the idea stuck in my mind, overwhelming and obvious. I would go there, to the island, and I would save her from Pemberley. I would bring her home.

Cara and I had never been what you might call a perfect couple. If we were shuffled into a crowd of people being paired off by some great Cupid, we might not automatically be selected for each other. To put it at its crudest, the sorting mechanism might pick someone more creative for me and someone more ambitious for her. I always found it reassuring that we didn't have the neatness of shared interests. It proved to me that what we actually loved about each other was each other, rather than the pale reflection of ourselves we saw in the other's eyes.

We met in Florence. I had been there about eight months by then, studying with Anthony, drawing to the end of my first year. She had only been there two weeks. She was visiting with her guardian, her aunt – like something out of E. M. Forster. But there she was, taking a break between years of university.

I was in one of the little cafés overlooking the Duomo. I had worked out I could supplement my tiny income by listening in the cafés for the sound of my native language, and introducing myself to the people who spoke it. I would slowly turn the conversation to the city's artistic heritage, the glories of the Uffizi. Then, when they asked what I did, I would reveal I was training at Anthony's studio.

In the early days, I neglected to mention that, studying under Anthony, I was not even allowed to paint yet, that we had to spend a year working in charcoal first, until our eyes reached new heights of accuracy. Nor did I mention this extracurricular work to Anthony, although I think he understood I had to stay alive while I learned.

More often than not, the marks suggested I paint them, but if not, I carefully introduced the idea. When they asked my rate, I would demur, before naming a figure roughly double what I would have been happy with. Once they had made a counter-offer, it was really only a matter of haggling. I had rented a tiny studio, an upright coffin with a skylight at the top and lime-washed walls, and took them there for the sittings.

I marvelled in later years at how confident I must have been to spend my days trying this trick. It amused the café waiters when it didn't work, but it got me a lot of unofficial commissions – all doubtless painted before Anthony would have said I was any-where near ready. That was my whole life, really, before Cara. There had been women, sometimes, but very few, and in any case I thought of love as a frivolity. The work didn't allow it.

One day, I approached a girl about my age, the companion of an older woman. The girl was good-looking, although there was something about her I recall finding too smart, too scrubbed with propriety. I was wrong, of course. Her eyes were hazel, her skin light brown.

When her aunt had left the table, the girl asked me bluntly what I wanted, and I told her in a moment. That surprised me: I didn't usually share the game with anyone while I was still playing it. She told me I could pay for the drinks, and I understood the game she was playing with me – I had tried to deceive her, so I had to make a sacrifice to balance the account. I didn't mind. I asked her name and for some means of contacting her, and she wrote the name of the hotel she was staying in – Diodati – on a napkin, with her name beneath: Cara Sharpe.

So it began.

I never painted her during her time in Florence. An inchoate superstition of mine told me that once I had painted a person completely, I would have no further need of them in my life, nor they of me in theirs. So I did not paint her, neither then nor later. The only depiction of her I ever made was a small pencil sketch, the morning after our first night together. That did not break my arbitrary, self-imposed rule, and anyway, for the first time in my life I felt as if, in drawing her, I was depicting a newly discovered part of myself.

I woke in bed, and realised I must have transferred myself there from the sofa in the night. For a pleasant moment I was empty, remembering nothing except the feeling of being home, and enjoying the sight of the light sidling around the curtains. Then I saw Cara's letter on the bedside table, and the evening before returned to me.

It wasn't surprising that she had chosen to do it by letter, of course. We had both grown up as the old networks were breaking down, failing a little further day by day. Even if I had been able to afford one of the rare devices to receive messages through the ether, she might not have been able to send one; Pemberley's island was almost completely disconnected from the world. She told me that in an early letter – another of her new employer's wonderful eccentricities. She still could have called more often from her posting: we had a phone attached to the wall, after all, and the fact that she had rung just once in six months was bad enough.

My principal memory of that morning was the ease with which I acted on the previous night's decision. I emptied my bag and packed a week's clean clothes, two empty sketching books and pencils; I prepared some food too, in case I had to sleep out. The country was more unreliable than usual lately, and I knew I might have to throw myself on some uncertain rural places at night. Taking extra food was sensible, even if it made you a target to anyone who knew you had it.

As these preparations occupied me, I was aware of another current of thought running through my brain, studded like a hangover: Cara did not want to see me. That much was clear from the letter, wasn't it? She had had the choice over whether she would stay on her island, working for her potentate, or return to me. The fact that she had decided on the former course should deter me from going.

The Sanctuary

I dismissed the notion. Perhaps her letters were being observed; perhaps she was not able to say how unhappy she felt. I read it again, and sensed she really would like to see me, although her duty came first. Well, I would solve that problem.

On and on the doubts came, and just as quickly I dismissed them. I kept from my mind the glaring omission from the letter – the fact that Cara had provided no information at all about when she might eventually return. The only other thought I had was about Pemberley. This was his fault, I knew. At some level he was the author of this change in her, and of my misfortune.

In under an hour I had two bags ready; the first containing my clothes, food, a book or two, and a compartment for cash. The other was my painter's roll, stuffed with as many brushes and implements as I could fit. It seemed silly to take it, but it would have crippled me to leave it, so it came.

In the front pocket of my main bag I packed all Cara's letters. I wanted to take them with me, as if they might act as a passport to get me onto the island. After some hesitation, I carefully flattened and packed my pencil drawing of her too. I had the feeling of carrying a household god.

My journey was going to be easier than anticipated. The Bywaters had inadvertently let me travel across the country as I wished; with the lazy indulgence of wealth, they had bought me a monthly permit, rather than merely a week's travel between their Village and my city. I was suddenly grateful to them for their carelessness.

The most important thing was to know my destination. This was difficult – perhaps the most difficult thing – as I already knew the place she was living was not listed on maps. Cara had told me that before her departure, and set me the challenge of finding it. She knew I wanted to write to her, and told me that if I succeeded in locating the island I'd be able to do so direct; if not, I could address my letters to the firm's head office in the centre of the country, and they would forward them on. I wanted to contact her directly, disliked the idea of even our casual communication being intercepted by Pemberley's staff. So I found it.

It was off the west coast, up in the high north of the country. There was a range of inhabited islands there; Pemberley's was further up the coast from them, and further out. The closest point on the mainland was a village called Freborne. I found all this information in an article from twenty years ago, which took a great deal of tracking down. When you searched for the island in an old atlas, its location was plain. These days, when you looked for it on a newly bought map, there was nothing. If you looked very closely, there was the faintest wrinkle of ocean around its former edge, as if something had been scrubbed away, and the ghost of a letter S where the name had been. Its name was Sanctuary Rock.

I asked Cara about this, and she laughed, and told me perhaps she was moving to Atlantis. When I persevered, asking what kind of person wiped their home address off the face of the earth, she became irritated, telling me I didn't understand Pemberley's business, and there were dozens of reasons he might be concerned about security.

Such as being a billionaire, I remember saying. I was hoping the use of the ugly word might rattle her, but in her line of work 'billionaire' was merely something to aspire to, and carried no negative connotations. She simply looked back, imperious, and said, yes, such as being a billionaire. And at that point I could not help laughing, and forgiving her, because of her hauteur, and the ways she was different to me. And the argument was solved, as a thunderstorm solves a humid day.

My two bags were by the front door of the flat by now. I parcelled up last night's ingredients and left them for our neighbour downstairs. Before leaving, I took one last look behind me. The lights and the two-ring cooker were off, the windows bolted, the curtains drawn against the sun. If I had known what was to happen, would I have stayed longer, going through my few possessions, thinking of the time we had spent there together? I am not sure I would. I wanted to be gone.

The city was too hot, and the country was still flooded. The news reports could have been exact repeats of last year's. Men and women wearing waist-high rubber and wading through the streets, towing frightened grandmothers in dinghies. A dog at the prow of one boat; an aerial shot of children on a roof. Then, a few days later, the next video package, the return to assess the damage, the maroon tidemarks halfway up newly-weds' walls, the ruined furniture elderly homeowners had lacked the strength to salvage.

None of Pemberley's several hundred Villages had ever been flooded, of course. He had arranged their locations cleverly. They were simply anchored higher, so when trouble came or rivers burst their banks, they would be the last to know about it.

I made no stops to bid anyone farewell as I left. There were no friends close enough to miss me, not for the few days I thought I would be gone. As for family, my parents were no longer alive, had not been for a decade. They had died separately in place – they left each other when I was ten – but together in time, within six months of each other. There was no link between their deaths – one illness and one accident – but it made me think of them as a unit even after their death, as though their years of separation had been just a quirk of the living.

My father was not a large part of my life once his marriage to my mother ended, although with hindsight I am not sure how closely involved he was before that either. He and my mother were so different that it seemed miraculous they had ever come together in the first place.

My parents had had me young; very young, in my mother's case. From her comments it was clear she thought of my father as a bad influence on me, and she ignored the fact that half of me *was* him. I never knew how he actually made his money; it certainly wasn't through anything as tiresome as a job. He would not hurt anyone, but the mere fact of criminality would not have put him off any work in itself; minor frauds seemed to be his speciality. He was the one who died in the accident. The coroner noted that, for all of the occupants of the car he'd been in, 'drink had been taken'. That was my father.

My mother, Jennifer, had wanted the best for me, and after my father left, she set about making sure I got it. Her faith in my abilities was total. I was educated at one of the country's best schools, thanks to her. Her brother, my uncle, had paid – he was a wealthy man, rich from oil, and he supported my mother's attitude to elite schooling as the way out of common lives. From the age of eleven until eighteen, I spent nine months of each year at Hillcrest, a school across the border in the north of our country.

In the end, I disappointed her. To my mother, my declaration of a career in portraiture was a waste of the schooling she had worked so hard to secure, the sort of thing my father would have done. Conversely, my father was delighted by the choice. It was quixotic, archaic, the perfect job for someone who wanted to know a thousand people but none of them too well. If it didn't require discipline, he might have taken it up himself.

The most illustrative difference between the two of them was in their attitude to Pemberley's Villages. My mother thought they were wonderful, and even though my uncle could have bought her a place in one, some instinct within her, some innate modesty, kept her from asking. My father never set foot in a Village unless he could earn some money by doing so, and insisted they were 'mausoleums for the living'. But he always was out of step with the national mood.

Despite the fact that we didn't live in a Village, we visited. I must have been about nine. Uncle Julian himself – I loved the synchronicity of their names, Jennifer and Julian – was travelling, or indisposed, I forget now, and we never actually saw him, but we did stay in his house.

The Village was on a hill, and my first impression was the glorious sight of it as it was revealed to us through slowly lifting cloud, as if God the magician had whipped the tablecloth away at just the right moment. I remember a few other things: cakes with our names iced on, ramparted walls, the beautiful parks … I must have been too young to notice the queues of workers outside, the service quarters and so on. Either way, it prompted a sense of avarice in me that took years to unstitch.

The next time I saw my father after this visit, he asked me about it. I answered in rhapsody, telling him about the ice creams, the entertainments, the lush wide lawns you could play on all day, if you chose. I remember he gave me a long, cool glance, and said, 'Well, you're definitely your mother's son.' I had no idea what he meant, and a confidential smile crept over his face as soon as he'd finished speaking, but his reaction gave me a little shard of unease. Perhaps that was the seed from which my later dislike of the Villages grew.

I never asked my mother why she and my father had had no other children – she was young when she had me, after all, and he not much older than her. I assumed later that their relationship had declined so soon after my birth that the thought of an extra child to tie them together was anathema to them, but that was only a guess. There was little time for me to ask with an adult mind. When my mother's illness struck soon after my nineteenth birthday, its progress was so sudden – a matter of weeks – there was hardly time for even my uncle's wealth to palliate it. We failed to trace my father, and Jennifer herself seemed quite at peace with that in her last days. His own death in a traffic collision, a few months afterwards, closed me off from my early life quite conclusively. It was as if the world had provided a definitive answer to any questions I might have still had about myself: an enormous *no* whenever I looked back over my shoulder, propelling me away from it into the future.

4

My first step was the public coach station in the city centre; the trains were down, as usual. The building had been handsome once: halfway up the walls was a beautiful frieze, a century old, now almost totally concealed by a jammed-in mezzanine. The scent of the food shacks up there arced high into the roof and then down onto the crowd, a great spiced wave of heat.

The station had only reopened the previous day, after four days of public mourning. The livery of official grief was everywhere: the four large government boards overlooking the station showed a diptych of the departed king's face beside that of his cool, self-assured daughter. The city's principal newspaper, never far from full self-abasement, had edged its stands in black crêpe, and the bazaars around the ground floor had produced official

keepsakes with amazing speed. Nala the elephant had been relegated to the higher shelves.

Almost everyone I saw in the station seemed to be in mourning too. To me they resembled a huge company of ageing crows,
bereft of their leader, uncertain which way to fly next. The people
around me – overwhelmingly older than me, most by more than
twenty years – would have seen the king grow, shared his sorrows
and joys, felt themselves part of his life. Of course they mourned;
he was more part of them than Nala had ever been. The fact that
he too had lived in one of Pemberley's most exclusive Villages
for several months each year, had effectively struck the national
colours for private land, had gone unmentioned, and part of me
felt disloyal for even remembering it.

I would be travelling up the country on the east side – a
journey I used to make a great deal due to a glut of commissions I had in the north-east a few years ago. That was how it
went sometimes: you found yourself temporarily in fashion. The
coach I was booked on was a non-Village service; crowded and
uncomfortable, but it would carry me to the northern border by
night. Tomorrow I would cross and head north-west, towards the
thumb of land poking into the sea closest to the island itself. I had
already marked the coastal hamlet I was aiming for – Freborne.

Before leaving the flat, I had dug through my old research
from before Cara left, and found a fifteen-year-old article about
Pemberley I had tracked down at the time. It was closer to a
press release than a news story; it simply said that a biography
of Sir John was being written that would lay bare his first years

in business. In particular, it would reveal how he had started out: how he had come by the enormous fortune he had arrived with in public life, and which he had used to begin his ascent.

The book's prospective author was a journalist called Kevin Ladd, who had already written several other biographies of plutocrats, though none as rich as Pemberley. It was to be called *The Man Who Bought a Country*.

That was the first and last I had found about the book. My library had no record of it. I had even phoned a few second-hand booksellers, asking for any evidence of it – a pre-publication copy, a leaked draft. Nothing. Perhaps it had never been published, or perhaps it had been pulped.

I had not told Cara I was researching Pemberley – I was embarrassed to admit I wanted to know more about him. Nor had she wanted to tell me anything herself. It had taken a fortnight after she got the job before she revealed her new employer's identity. Normally when she took a position as an executive assistant she would tell me with glee about whichever monster she would be working for next. Not so this time.

In fact, this job had been different from the start. The interview process had lasted several weeks, with Cara speaking to progressively more senior officers in the organisation before she was offered the post. And she attached great significance to it, too. She said she had finally found work that married her keen ambition with the prospect of improving the world.

The coach station had a row of phones under plastic hoods, and the fourth one along worked. I had the company's mainland phone number on me, etched into the front of my sketchbook.

This breached one of my rules – nothing in the sketchbook but sketches – but I was glad I had broken it now. I would give Cara a chance, try to let her know I was on my way.

'Tomorrow Trust, this is …' – a vague noise, one I couldn't identify as a name – 'speaking. May I help you?' The voice was pleasant and curiously unidentifiable, as if our country's hundred accents had been shaken together and smoothed into a paste.

'My name is Ben Parr. I'm ringing to try and get through to Cara Sharpe. She's working on the island at the moment.'

'The island, sir?'

They did this thing where you had to mention the place specifically. I don't know why. Maybe there were a dozen islands. Either way, I named it.

'Cara Sharpe is working there in an executive role and I'm trying to contact her.' I thought about it and added, though I knew it made me sound desperate, 'She's my fiancée. It's important.'

'I'm sorry, sir. It's not possible for you to be put through today.' Even as I heard the lie, or the evasion, I admired the passivity with which the woman spoke, and imagined the inside of her head: a smooth place, probably, free of the jags of action and responsibility. A calm place.

'Why not?'

'There's a problem with the cables at the moment. The situation is under urgent review, of course, but contact has been very limited for some hours now.'

'I see.'

'I can attempt to put a message through for you, sir, if you let me know where you're calling from. What is your location?'

I didn't want my message to Cara to come from her employers, mediated through the company, and I certainly didn't want to tell them where I was. There was only one other thing I could try: an appeal to rank.

'She's actually working for John Pemberley himself at the moment, so it really is important for me to speak with her.' I don't know what I had expected as a result of this little act of desperation, but it didn't work.

'Everything possible is being done to repair the situation, sir. If you let me know where you're calling from, I can put you through to our nearest office.' It was as though she had never heard of Pemberley; perhaps that was part of their training. Lots of unhinged people probably phoned claiming a close personal connection with him, after all.

I declined, and thanked her, and hung up.

The number of the coach I was waiting for was shouted across the coach station; a long queue at the gate had formed almost before the manager had finished speaking. I felt in my pocket. Enough coins for another call or two.

First, to the enquiries line, to find out how many Kevin Ladds I might need to ring. Just two, I was told. For a few years the man I needed had been writing for a local newspaper based in the country's east, deep in the broad, flat zone now flooding twice a year. I asked for the location of each number, and one of them was in the right area.

'4291.' It was a woman's voice that answered; in the background, I heard a television set muttering. I could even match the voices from the set with the screens overhead in the coach station.

'Is Kevin Ladd available, please? The journalist.'

'Who is this?' A note of caution entered the voice, and the noise of the television snapped to nothing.

'My name is Benjamin Parr. There's something I'd like to speak to him about.'

'I'm afraid he's passed away, two years ago now. This is his wife. Widow.' I mumbled condolences, and the voice replied with impatience. 'That's quite all right. I keep telling them to remove his number. Clearly they haven't managed it yet. What are you calling for, Mr Parr? Perhaps I can help.'

'I'm trying to find out about one of his projects. On Sir John Pemberley.' There was no reply. 'It's of interest to me.'

Still she said nothing, and I watched the clock in the middle of the coach station ticking round for ten full seconds before I spoke again. 'It seems like he never wrote the book in the end, but I just wonder—'

The voice cut across me then, its tone now one of brittle fury. 'When will you people give up?'

'I'm sorry?'

'When will you stop? My husband is dead. I've burned his papers. Nothing remains of the work. For Christ's sake.'

'Please, I think there's been a—'

There was no stopping the voice. 'Years of his life taken away from him. You can't take anything else away from me, because you already took him, and I only regret that I followed his wishes and burned his papers, because if I could do anything to you in return for what you did to him—'

'Mrs Ladd, please. Please.'

It was no use. The voice started swearing, and then the phone was slammed down with extraordinary violence. I called back, but I was met only with the engaged tone. I noticed, as I hung up, that the hand with which I held the phone was shaking.

The queue for the coach was somewhat diminished, but from where I stood, I could see a group of workers at the front holding it up. Some query over authentication. I had time for one final call. After some confusion, I got through to the woman who had been named in the news story as the editor of Ladd's forthcoming biography.

Abigail Turner was her name, and her voice was warm and deep, starting to crack with age. From her voice alone, I knew she would be enjoyable to paint. I pictured her in a corner office, now nearing the end of a long career and enjoying all the indiscretions of her trade as her right – like a barrel of wasps, or an undetonated piece of ordnance, just waiting for the excuse to go off.

I described my call with Kevin Ladd's widow, and got a theatrical moan in response. 'Did she really say all that? My goodness. Just extraordinary. Grief, you know, it deranges us. Deranges us completely.'

'I'm just trying to find out why the book wasn't written.'

'Of course, of *course*. Kevin Ladd, that bad man. Let's see.' She paused, as if searching her memory. I suspected she could have told me immediately but wanted to inject a little more drama into her day. 'Yes, that's it. He got in touch one day, he wrote to me, Mr … *Could* you remind me of your name again?'

'Parr. Ben Parr.'

'… Mr Parr, and he said he wouldn't be writing Sir John's biography after all. He didn't give a reason, and he enclosed a cheque for everything we'd paid him so far. I can assure you it was a very reasonable fee, because we liked him a lot. I don't want to name a figure, but it was a *handsome* amount. We would have published the book and stood by him through any trouble – in a legal sense, you understand. But you can't do much when an author pays back their advance and stops answering the phone. It would have felt vindictive to sue. It was embarrassing, of course, but such is life. Embarrassment fades, after all, and all we are left with is our conduct.'

'Had Mr Ladd done this before?'

'Not once. I hate to say this about him, because we washed our hands of him – professional pride, a terrible thing. But the thing is, he truly was among the best. Dogged, never afraid to go to court … in forty years I never saw him caught out on a matter of fact. It was a complete surprise. A *shock*.'

'Was there a legal challenge?'

'Not at all. Anyway, Kevin had had the frighteners put on him before and always remained pretty unmoved. So either Pemberley managed to find a longer and more powerful lever for his leverage, if you like, ha ha, or the reason was something else. But he never contacted us again. That was his last work, as far as I know.'

'Could Pemberley have contacted Ladd directly?'

'I doubt it. If Sir John had been planning any legal scare tactics, his lawyers would have sent them to us, rather than to Kevin. He's not eccentric, as far as I can tell – or at least not in that way. He would do it all as scrupulously as possible. He's reputed to have quite beautiful manners.'

I thought of Cara, working for this man she thought was the greatest in the world, a man with beautiful manners who could stop enquiries about him with a wave of his hand. Abigail Turner interrupted my thoughts to ask me the same question Ladd's widow had done.

'Why do you want to know all this, incidentally?'

I told her I was a journalist looking into Pemberley for a story. She seemed convinced, and gave me a florid farewell, telling me to ring any time, any time day or night, if I needed help again. Then she rang off.

The queue for the coach had died down now, and the low murmur of voices echoing around the chamber had diminished too, replaced by the grinding noises of the huge unknown machines that ran the place. I shouldered my bags and walked to the gate.

The northern outskirts of the city prompted a strange calm in me. Here, the street containing our first grim basement studio after my return from Florence; here, the parade of shops Cara and I had lived above until her first well-paid posting. My work and Cara; the only two elements of my life that mattered.

We had argued a lot before she left for the island. The first row was because she had been back from her previous job just six weeks before she went away again. I knew her work as an executive assistant demanded agility and compromise. But we had agreed we would spend more time together after her last job had come to an end. When, after two weeks back, she told me she was interviewing for a post starting in just a month, I lost my temper. I accused her of valuing her work above our life together, and she said her work was what allowed our life together, and the prospect of a better future.

She was right, of course. But in her anger she also brought up the one subject guaranteed to hurt me most. She asked me when I would know it was time to give up art and take more reliable employment.

We had discussed the matter before, but I had always been the one to bring it up first, in the middle of some crisis of confidence, and she had always encouraged me. This time she did not. She told me that if recent years were anything to judge by, I would live out my career producing substandard work, growing unhappier all the while, neither following what I thought was my calling nor earning enough to justify ignoring that call.

We made up, of course, but it took several days for me to feel calm when I looked at her. Clearly, I still hadn't forgotten her words – because, in their own way, they were true. She had spotted the fact that for years I had not been producing work of the quality I knew – somehow – I was capable of. I tried to conceal it, but I knew I had still not painted anything I could be proud of, not yet, and that time was running short.

I knew where the compromise came from. We both worked for the overclass, for the small percentage of people who lived in Villages. No matter how much time I might give to schools in the city, my money came from private commissions for Village-dwellers. Pemberley, entirely unwitting, was the facilitator of the way I lived now. Cara, of course, worked for an even smaller subset of my clientele, the ones who ran the businesses that owned the world.

A vision occurred to me now and then: of a walled citadel on the side of a hill, fashioned of pure white stone glinting in the sunshine. The streets and courtyards and porticos of the city contained nothing but statues, beautiful, flawless statues of crystal people, and all of these required maintenance. Cara and I both spent our days in this city, scurrying from corridor to courtyard, through alleys and up staircases, in the service of these statues, never resting. Where we disagreed, of course, was on why we did it. I did it to build a life for myself elsewhere, somewhere vital, and messy, and difficult. Cara dreamed of elevation to the citadel itself. She had a pedestal in mind, and one day she would ascend it, take her pose, and be frozen in place for ever.

I lacked the heart to tell her we would never make it. The citadel almost never took new members; the principal qualification for entry was to be made of crystal already. And I feared her reaction when this unstated difference between us became plain to her. Perhaps it already had done, and that was why she had left.

These were the thoughts that occupied me on the journey from the heart of the city.

The initial stages of the route were drab. Sprawling miles of concrete interspersed with weeds; high streets of poor, bare shops huddled in short parades, banding together for security. Further out we passed the huge boxy stores defended by their ramparts of tangled metal. I found myself wondering idly how much the whole display weighed, the thousands of miles of tarmac and concrete and shaped steel, all connected to make a great complicated hieroglyph on the ground, projecting into space the message: *We have been here, and these are the choices we made along the way*.

And as we went, I saw the country's dreadful collective age. I felt a kind of breathlessness to realise again how the nation had let itself grow so old, how the generations above me had forgotten to fill up the population again as carelessly as running out of milk. There were so few young people on the streets we passed, it felt as though they had been spirited away by a Pied Piper lax enough to take anyone under thirty. A few children accompanied the aged; even they looked tired already.

It was not just this country, of course. The whole world was like a dowager duchess tottering along a dark alley, clutching her standards and her values like so many precarious strings of pearls. The planet was winding down, and every day its spring grew a little more slack.

I reached up and retrieved one of Cara's early letters from my bag, from a few weeks into her stay.

Ben. I'm going to get you here somehow, because I think it might do you a lot of good. The faces on display here! You could get ten exhibitions out of them. Not that they all deserve immortality – one or two deserve only obscurity if you ask me. But most are just wonderful. This place and its people – this is what he has been trying to do all along. The Villages, everything on the mainland: they were all just steps on the path here.

It is so *green. JP says that in a century's time we will grow so much more here than we can now. It's almost impossible to believe there being more life here than there already is. God, I wish you could see it. They are extremely strict on outside visitors, that's the annoying thing – that's Angela's fault. She's one of the ones I could happily forget about – she's Sir John's mentor, as far as I can tell, or guru, or something. She's a key part of the business, apparently.*

You should see the Devil's Chessmen too. They're these sea stacks out on the western coast, and they have formed into these incredible banded shapes. You can see a rook, definitely, and a bishop, although the knight is a bit wonky. A lot of the island is gneiss – a kind of rock they have up here. It's 300 million years old, Ben. Can you imagine? Deep time, JP calls it. My whole sense of the world is spreading out.

As the months had gone on, her desire to bring me over for a visit had waned. The other thing she dropped was mentions of Pemberley – it was as though she divined I was threatened somehow by his presence, as if he stood behind her shoulder as she wrote. I *was* threatened, of course, and also perhaps a little jealous. I took pleasure in not mentioning him in any of my letters, staying deliberately incurious, knowing that was somehow stifling her desire to show off about him.

Cara was quite brilliant at her work, of course. That was why she'd made it so far so young. She'd been working in different bits of the estate management industry for a while, and had then become chief assistant to Pemberley's main building firm, before she was even thirty. I suppose that was why she'd eventually caught the eye of the man himself. The firm, she liked to say, was good at spotting potential.

Normally we would laugh about her employers and their characters, misshapen by wealth; although she sometimes admitted she felt sorry for them too. She even had her own set of rules to ensure she didn't work for anyone too awful. No inheritors unless they'd done something useful with it; nobody in repugnant fields like arms; no tax avoiders, although this rule was harder to observe than she had first imagined.

Her final rule was that she would not run her employer's private household. No picking up the socks, the children from school or the abandoned mistresses from the doorstep. She had resigned from very lucrative jobs before bending the principle. She wanted something of worth; and now at last it seemed she had found it.

As I remembered that, a worm of doubt gave a wriggle behind my eyes. *She's made her position clear, and I'm showing I can't take a hint.* I found the worm and pinched it. Her letters had changed, and if she wanted to end things between us, she could do it face to face. But my thoughts turned once more to Pemberley, the perfect employer with beautiful manners, and fear rose in me again.

We were leaving the city now, along a stretch of road elevated above the houses. I looked out across them, and thought of the man who bought a country.

5

Pemberley established his first Village nearly three decades ago, when he was twenty. Absurdly young, impossibly rich. He seemed to have more money than anyone else on earth had ever seen, yet nobody knew a thing about him. All these years later, the world was little wiser. He had never given an interview, had hardly been photographed. He could walk past you on the street – him, the architect of the nation – and you wouldn't give him a second look.

His first Village had been experimental, an attempt to lure some of the wealthy middle class from the cities to a better way of life. In a world where the cities were already dying like huge cephalopods, sprawling over the land and reeking as they did, it was an instant success.

Crucially, Pemberley's Village was exclusive. Outside his first site he built a service hub, for the young workers who would keep the place running. There were stipend programmes for people who would be useful enough inside – teachers and doctors – but menials were kept outside. Even they, though, were treated to decent communal living in the satellite homes.

His first attempt was treated as a curiosity, like the model villages of old. The next five were seen as exciting opportunities for wealthy families to slip away from the old world, to gain tranquil and stable lives without sacrificing their comforts. And the next twenty, fifty, hundred were oversubscribed before they were even announced.

The Villages had a van system, which meant you could visit friends or family in other Villages almost free of charge. Their ecological credentials gave residents a warm feeling without requiring any sacrifice, and they were so safe you could persuade yourself you were buying in for your children's security. Plus the inheritance system meant you could pass your wealth on when you died. 'A slice of eternity', the adverts said.

There were investigations into the company's ownership structure, the Russian-doll shell companies used to operate them, the employment status of the workers; none of them damaged Pemberley. These days, a third of the country's elected representatives owned property in one or another of his establishments. The land had been captured by them, and those who didn't live in a Village either aspired to, or worked on the edges of one; or they turned their back and tried to make their living in the cities. And the man who made it happen had drifted away like smoke from a chimney.

The chief spokesperson for Pemberley was the woman Cara had mentioned, Angela Knight. Whenever challenged, she described the Villages as 'the link between the world we know and the world we need'. It sounded impressive, without leaving the listener any wiser.

The coach stopped for fuel. I used the service station's bathroom, watched over by an ancient attendant, then found a payphone and rang the company's headquarters again. Another pleasantly spoken young woman assured me there was a problem with the communications. Her excuse was different this time, something to do with a transponder. She asked me where I was calling from too, and I shuddered. They had heard my voice twice now. Could they find my location from my payphone calls and track my trajectory from that? Surely not.

It was baking hot on the tarmac of the coach station, even though it was still spring, and even though parts of the country not far away were flooded. There were disordered symptoms everywhere.

Here was I in my dying world, not knowing how to live or what to live for; and there was Cara, on her island, working for someone she thought was solving the problem. Again, the treacherous thought occurred to me that I would make a fool of myself turning up unannounced, but I took her letters from my bag and looked at the way they shrank, became impersonal. She had grown strange in this place, and I would find out why.

We were heading up the main road north on the country's eastern side; a colossal statue of an angel by the side of the road, with *NOTHING NOTHING* daubed in white across its broad, boxy wings. Then we were through most of the cities and the countryside grew wilder. We passed the occasional hamlet, abandoned or nearly so. It seemed to me there was a drain at the heart of the land, and everything good had slipped down it.

Further north still, the road was surrounded on either side by sodden marshy fields. There were diggers right by the road at one point, building an apparently purposeless rampart; the men in the machines and their colleagues on the ground were equally spattered in mud, their eyes unnaturally white against the soil smeared on their faces. They looked like exhausted golems.

We passed a mass planting of trees, sickly-looking things held up by plastic tubes and mocked by the half-foot of water they stood in. On a side road disappearing into the would-be forest there slouched an abandoned car, its tyres buried three inches deep in tarmac that had melted in some previous heatwave, then congealed together once more when the bubbling mess cooled.

Out of the marshes, we entered hill country, the ground rearing and carrying us with it. The fields lasted a while: in one, children had been hired as live scarecrows. They exploded from their hiding spots in furrows, prompting the birds there to flap away, half-scared, half-lazy. And then we were too high for fields, and the stone walls fell away too. The air felt newly washed suddenly, and the hills were dotted with sheep; I saw a lamb, standing uncertain and nudging a larger clump of dirty yellow that lay prone before it.

I spotted a few of the Villages as I went. They were easy to differentiate from normal villages in two things: the telltale ribbon of wall around their edges, and the surrounding service quarters, always low and discreet enough to preserve the residents' view.

I didn't remember seeing any service quarters in the advert I had seen last night, but they would have been there, providing the endless and constantly shifting rota of cooks, cleaners, guards. Perhaps Pemberley's island would look exactly the same, only on a larger scale. Perhaps that was why Cara was so happy; she'd finally found herself on the right side of a barrier.

By night we had reached another city, this one in the northwest of the country, close to the border. I secured a lodging near the coach station, in a house with *ROOMS* painted above the door – presumably the place was never full enough to make the sign inaccurate. On closer inspection it was easy to see why. Four flocked walls all seeming to lean inwards, a mattress resting on half-broken planks of wood, and corners doubly darkened by shadow and mould.

The lock on the room's door didn't work, so I took my possessions out with me to eat. On the way back, I withdrew as much cash from the late-opening bank as I could, and packed it with the rest of my things. I returned to the lodging to sleep, one arm through the loop of the bag with the money, the other holding my painter's roll.

I should have guessed Cara might stay longer on the island, because of what I heard her saying in her final interview for the position.

It was the fourth interview she'd had. The previous ones had been face-to-face, and although she wouldn't tell me who this one was with, the fact that it was on the phone suggested it was someone outside the city. She had spent days preparing to receive the call – surrounded by notes, thoughts on her previous interviews, books of aspirational advice. When the time came, she even wore professional clothes, to get herself into the right mindset. I had not teased her, even slightly; I knew how badly she wanted the job.

She had asked me to be out for an hour to make sure she had the space and time she needed. I spent twice as long out; there was a café on the corner that was always empty, and where I felt no guilt about making a coffee last. It was no hardship; I had a book to study on the temperament of artists through the ages. When I eventually returned, she was still on the phone. As I opened the door, I could hear the other voice too, on speaker. It was warm and male with an American undertow somewhere beneath it; I knew, without knowing how, that it was Pemberley himself. They were laughing together, and after that, the first words I made out were:

'... very demanding.'

'Yes, of course. I understand.' Cara sounded pleased, flushed; it must have gone well, and I felt a jolt of pride, mixed with sadness at the prospect of her leaving again.

'So I hope it's not surprising to you for me to say this: we may ask you to stay longer. We may ask for more of your time, of your life, than you had anticipated. A lot of people find themselves wanting to extend their stay and we try to accommodate that. But mainly we need to know you yourself are ready. So: is there anything at home that might keep you from devoting yourself to life here?'

Almost before the question was asked, she had replied. 'No, nothing at all.'

'You're sure about that?'

'I'm quite sure.'

He carried on speaking and I withdrew, easing the front door closed behind me to prevent it from slamming. I let it rest and sat against the wall for a few minutes, until I heard the murmur of voices stop; then stood, put my key back in the lock and asked how it had gone.

The interview had been a success, Cara said, glowing with pride; she had been offered the job. And when she got back, we would talk properly about when we could get married.

I lost my temper at that. I told her I had overheard what she had said – completely by accident, of course – and asked what she had been playing at, implying there was nothing to tether her to the mainland. She, in turn, became immediately angry with me for eavesdropping on a private conversation, and in the ensuing row the central point got lost. But I remembered it, and worried for weeks until she left that Pemberley was already exerting a malign influence on her.

And now she was on his island, refusing to return, turning away from the world.

I woke early, whether due to the light coming through the thin curtains or the pain in my back from the mattress I couldn't tell. I handed over the key to my room, bought some steaming, tasteless tea from a kiosk, and looked at the headlines. The death of the king was still pre-eminent, but there was enough room on the front of the papers for other stories. Wars still stretching across the continent; the next approaching heatwave, coming on the heels of the last one; a new city being built overseas for displaced children, funded in large part by the philanthropic Pemberley. Four more suspected extinctions – three amphibians, one mammal.

The northern border was fifty miles away; I found a coach going in the right direction. This one, then another would take me to Freborne, just south of Pemberley's mainland estate.

This morning's coach was a beaten-up thing, with fewer than twenty seats. The upholstery was torn here and there, and stuffing sprouted like mushrooms from the gaps. There were only a few other passengers, so I secured a comfortable spot, away from the wheel arches.

The skies were clear now. The road we were on followed the coast in a wavering line, so glimpses of the western sea approached then withdrew again in a flirtatious little dance. The border must have come and gone, because this looked like proper northern country. I found myself suddenly familiar with my surroundings, and realised with a shock – surprised I had not thought of it before – that we would pass within ten miles of my old school.

My time at Hillcrest had not been unhappy. It was strange, yes, but it's hard to say something has really been bad for you when it provided you with the work you do, gave you the room to imagine being different and the time to actually become that different person.

It had been my mother's idea to send me there. Uncle Julian was wealthy and childless, and I suppose wanted to find a means of speculating on the future in a limited way, a hedged bet. Even then, over two decades ago, it was clear Pemberley's Villages would be the future, a locus for the country's smartest and most successful residents; they wanted me to have a fair shot of getting there.

So: Hillcrest. Imagine a ruined castle where the collapsed stones have been cleared, replaced by glass structures linking one block to another. A place both old and new; old enough to inspire veneration, new enough to equip children for the uncertain world to come. That was the pitch.

I remember more dead languages and cold sports fixtures than equipment for the world of tomorrow, but the teachers were humane and there wasn't much bullying. We were widely assured that conditions were much less comfortable forty years ago, when some of our teachers had been pupils and all of them had been boys. By the time I went, the school was mixed, at least.

I sometimes found it dizzying to consider the link between the raw stuff of my uncle's work – the fossil fuels he extracted from the ground – and my education. I thought of the countless ancient life forms across the world dying and pressing down on each other, the mosses and crawling things and blind striving bits of matter, all in a heap, unaware of even the moment of their death, then spending millions of years in unimaginable heat and pressure, until their gummed remains – trillions of minute corpses – were disinterred and sold to pay for my education at Hillcrest.

The Sanctuary

The sheer accident of it baffled me. The great storehouse of the earth was being cracked open, its contents raided, never to be restored, and for what? So I could feel like an outsider at a first-rate school? It was baroque, ludicrous. The other pupils appeared to feel no such pressure at all. They looked out across the fields surrounding the establishment and knew that whatever sacrifices had been made to send them here were worthwhile.

It wasn't an unwelcoming place, though. And without it I might never have learned to love art, and I certainly wouldn't have built a career from it. The walls of the school were hung with paintings picked more for their acreage than their merit, but I found myself trying to copy them in my spare time, sitting in corridors attempting to unlock the secrets of perspective, or shadow. The art teacher at the school, Dr Fentiman, noticed, and encouraged me.

Successful people are often asked in interviews if there is a particular teacher who changed their life. Sarah Fentiman changed mine. She had been teaching there for thirty years by the time I arrived, knew the place intimately, but kept herself somehow apart. She lived alone in the small hamlet where the teachers' residences were kept, and seemed always to be enjoying a private joke or in conversation with herself.

Fentiman had two gifts that made us adore her. First was a raw, powerful sarcasm, employed only occasionally but to devastating effect. The second was that she was willing to abandon a lesson plan for an impromptu lecture. She would cheerfully ignore the week's topic to discuss mink in portraiture, or why medieval pictures of babies looked so odd, or the symbolism of the lemon. We loved her for it, and she accepted that love while knowing perfectly well that at least half of it was due to an unexpected lack of work.

She was honest, too. Even while encouraging me, she offered me no bromidic illusions about the odds of making a success. She let me know the world didn't need another portrait painter and wouldn't fall over itself to pay for one. In fact, she told me, I ran the risk of ending up a street caricaturist, or (here she would smile) a teacher at a good school, providing tomorrow's Village class with a patina of culture. The honesty with which she presented the pitfalls made me only more determined to succeed – which may, of course, have been her intent all along.

My first commissions, as a teenager, were for the parents of friends, and it was during that final year of school that I saw clearly for the first time the gulf between my classmates' parents, with their sprawling Village homes, and my mother, respectable yet not rich in her suburban house. But it was also the year I started to learn my trade, and the emotions that persuade people to pay an artist for their work.

It was all thanks to Fentiman. It was thanks to her, too, that I went to Florence to study with Anthony – I suspected a former lover of hers – and to meet Cara. I stretched my aching legs in the cramped space beneath the seat, remembering it again now.

I hadn't contacted Fentiman since my schooldays. She couldn't possibly still be at Hillcrest today, I knew, but I liked to imagine it regardless. I pictured her as she was in my time there, unaged, surviving yet, and still distracting her pupils with unplanned lessons on galleries, on clouds, still converting people to the beauty of the human face.

I changed coaches in the first town across the border, muddled the timetables, sprinted for a service that ran only once a day, and made it onto the little twelve-seater heading for the village of Freborne, eighty miles north and west.

Two hours later, the land around me was completely wild but for two things. The first was the road. It had been appalling for hours, gashed at the sides by roots and as pockmarked as the moon, but for the last twenty miles that had been replaced by beautiful tarmac, almost eerily smooth and silent beneath the wheels. The second was the double fence running alongside us to the north, two metal barriers with ten metres clear between them. Beyond the far one was nothing but thick forest; the nearer one was knotted at intervals with short concrete towers. I got the sense of movement or intelligence within these, and the impression I was being watched.

Not just from the towers, either. For some time I had been the last passenger aboard, and the coach driver gave me long, curious looks in the rear-view mirror as we went. The double border fence was only interrupted once, as far as I saw – by a pair of huge gates consisting of iron slats, completely hiding whatever lay within. The metal looked brand new; the stone gateposts on either side seemed practically Jurassic in their age and bulk.

A couple of miles after that, the coach slowed suddenly. I looked out ahead and saw we were coming to a halt just before a strange block on the road. Three men guarded it, dressed in black, and I saw metal gleaming at their hips.

The door creaked open. They had a word with the driver, who nodded, keeping his face to the road ahead, and the three of them sauntered along the aisle towards me.

'Identification, please.' The man in front was bulky, with the muscles of the perennially bored. There was no malice in his small eyes, but perhaps a suggestion of mischief: a telltale crease at the corners that hinted at a love of diversions, innocent or not. He and his colleagues wore hunters' vests, or military vests, all pockets and pouches, and as the man in front waited for me to reply, the pair behind him gave each other a little smile.

I still felt confident enough in myself to challenge him. 'Who are you?'

'Estate security.'

'Estate? This is a public road.'

'I'm afraid not, sir. My employers own a large, you might say a substantial stretch of it' – he gestured lazily up and down – 'and that gives us the right to check who's passing through. It's all company territory.'

'I don't believe you.'

'You're welcome to wait for your lawyer to turn up. Identification.'

I fumbled in my pocket for my papers.

'Where are you visiting today?'

'Are there many villages at the end of this road? I'm going to Freborne.'

He ignored my sarcasm. 'Purpose of journey?'

'I want to paint the coast.' I had enough equipment on me to prove it, and as I hadn't named anyone I was on my way to meet, they couldn't test the lie. He gave me a long look, tapping my documents into the flat of his hand.

'We can't let you through, sir.' He raised his hands like a magician, shoved my papers into my lap, then pushed his thumbs back through the loops of a security belt and smiled.

'You're joking.'

'Sorry, sir. So much regulation these days. You'll have to turn back.' That was it, then. The company had been tracking me, knew I was here. Was Cara in on this? Could she see me approaching across a screen; was she making sure I got nowhere near her?

The guard continued. 'There is, of course, a local toll you might be able to pay to rush things through.'

He was asking for a bribe, bare-faced.

'Bullshit. You're on the take.' I stood, and met him eye to eye. It felt very cramped, suddenly, in the little space at the back of the coach.

'That's not polite, sir.' He slid one hand around to the baton at his side, unclipped it and gently raised it to push, ever so softly, on my shoulder. His smile had melted away, and the creases round his eyes had lost their humour. 'I suggest you sit back down.'

By now I was afraid, and I knew things were coming to a head, but I thought I had as little to lose as these louts. With my right hand I pushed his baton off me, and spoke as calmly and confidently as I could manage. 'Don't you dare touch me again.'

Things sped up a little after that. I saw the baton coming towards my stomach, but not quickly enough to do anything about it, and when I was doubled over, the man in front gripped the side of my head and rammed it into the side of the coach, then forced me onto the seat. He was shouting, too, and a few more blows hit my head, my shoulders, my ribs. I stayed like that a few seconds, trying to find his legs to kick out at, but they were defended, and there was nothing to do but swear.

Then one of them was saying, 'Got it, I've got it,' and they were off the bus again. My main bag was ripped, the compartment with the cash gone. The leader had taken my identification, too, as a little extra. That left me in big trouble if I wanted to head south again.

They hadn't touched the food. Pemberley clearly fed his men well.

The Sanctuary

Through the window, I saw the three of them sauntering back towards the wooded area to the north, and almost as a joke, one of them pressed the button that hauled the barrier up.

The driver was eyeing me in the mirror until I met his gaze and he quickly looked away, as if I had embarrassed him. The coach inched forward.

The rest of the journey was quiet, and I took stock. When the forest was near enough to show me my reflection against the dark of the trees, I saw my face was bruised on one side, grazed from where I'd hit the side of the coach. There was a lump at the back of my skull, too, and I could taste iron – I had bitten my tongue, perhaps when I first fell backwards. But my teeth were intact, and my ribs seemed to have stood up against the baton. My financial situation was more pressing. Now that the money pouch was gone, I had nothing but a couple of notes in my pocket.

But they hadn't bothered with the painter's roll, and the drawing of Cara was secure, thank God.

After a few more miles, we pulled up in the central square at Freborne. As I gathered my bags, the driver waited in his seat, and I turned to him at the door.

'You getting your cut on the way back, I suppose?'

'They don't always come. There are so few visitors that they normally don't bother with the block. But they know who the locals are, sir, and if you aren't from round here you get a hard time.' He paused, then added: 'If they don't like the look of you.'

'You might have warned me.'

'I am sorry, sir.' I was on the tarmac by now, looking back at him, and his face was blank with the fixed resolve not to care. 'If it's any consolation, I've seen worse.' He pulled the doors to, turned the vehicle in a broad loop and moved off.

The town consisted of a few dozen stone houses, plus the square I was in and the civic buildings around its edge: a church, squat and uncompromising, a shop, and a low-doored pub. But that was only the landward side. The other half of this place was the sea.

The land did not curve outwards around us; no protecting horns of rock or turf shielded this place. Even on a day like today, with the sea undisturbed and a mackerel of clouds overhead, it was bleak and magnificent. I could only imagine how it might look in a storm. The seafront was dominated by a large stone harbour, recently built by the look of it, with smart little fishing boats bobbing on either side. Despite its new appearance, the weather had already buffeted the harbour savagely, and I could see score-lines across it from storms like the claws of a giant beast. North of the town, the wire fence marking Pemberley's mainland estate ran all the way into the water. Kelp clung to the wire diamonds at the waterline.

I picked up my bags and headed towards the pub.

The interior walls were smoke-marked, as if the place had been scorched by a fire and never refurbished, and the ceiling was low. More surprising still, the place was full – far too full, for early afternoon on a weekday. The volume dropped as I entered, and several drinkers turned to look at me. I tried to keep my expression neutral; I have never enjoyed being the centre of attention, and looking as dishevelled as I did didn't help. But I could not help noticing the faces of the townsfolk with professional delight. There were lines of guile, of mirth, of pride scored into them, yet each person I saw surveyed me with the unmoving hauteur of a house cat. I would have painted any of them for free.

The place seemed unusually crowded, and I reasoned they were marking some occasion – not a festive one, by the look of things. The buzz of conversation had resumed by the time I reached the bar. The only patron at the counter itself was a shrivelled old man in a dark suit, who sat wordless, facing inwards. He hadn't turned at my entrance, and did not acknowledge me now.

The barman was younger than his clientele, perhaps in his fifties. He wore a dark suit too, and a tie sombrely pinned to his shirt. Behind him, in the gloom of the doorway to the pub's back rooms, was a small boy, I guessed the proprietor's son. He was too young to be wearing a suit, but was dressed in what must have been the darkest clothes available to him: a navy jumper and black jeans. He gave me a little smile and a timid gesture, not quite a wave. I waved back. He seemed to be the only child in town.

I waited for the barman to finish filling two glasses with beer and send the boy out with them before I ordered a drink. As he poured it, I spoke.

'Feels busy today.'

'A wake.'

I gave him one of my last two banknotes, then wiped my mouth with the back of my hand and was embarrassed to realise it had started bleeding again. He passed no comment on how I looked.

'Sorry to hear that,' I said.

'Happens.' He cast a look at the man at the end of the counter.

'I can leave, if you'd prefer. Or if the family of the deceased would prefer.'

'And go where?' He snorted. 'No, you're fine here. Nobody will be bothered by a stranger. Good luck to have a stranger at a wake anyway. Old life leaves, new one arrives. You staying overnight?'

'I don't know yet.'

'Long way to come without plans for what you'll do when you get here.'

I mentioned Pemberley's name, as casually as I could.

'Ah, yes. Our benefactor.'

'Popular man here?'

'He's invested a lot in this place. But for him, most of these people' – he nodded around the room – 'would be in some home, being cheated and mistreated like enough. Nobody likes wealthy people interfering. But he paid for the harbour and he's the reason there's still enough of us to bring a catch in.'

'Universally popular, eh?'

'I didn't say that.' He glanced again at the shrivelled man along the counter.

'Why pay for your harbour?'

'I believe so we'd think well of him when scruffy young men came around asking stupid questions, and maybe tip him off about it too.' He looked at me pointedly. 'I take it you have no actual business in the estate.'

'Why do you say that?'

'You would have gone there. Not like there isn't a proper entrance.'

'I do have business there. I'm going to see somebody.'

'And they know you're coming, do they?' He smiled, and I felt I had been trapped into the lie.

'I was hoping to surprise them.'

'I wish you luck in that.'

I felt stupid asking my next question, but I couldn't see any other way of learning what I needed to know.

'Is there anywhere here I could hire a boat?'

He shook his head. 'Fishing boats don't go within ten miles of the island, as a courtesy. So no, I'd say you're out of luck.' He paused, then continued, rather louder, 'And if you want a bit of sensible advice, you'll drop whatever your idea is and talk to the men on the gates at the mainland estate.' He glanced yet again at the man to my right. 'They're reasonable people.' Then he turned and walked into the gloomy passage beyond the bar.

So that was it. I could go from house to house asking people how near the island they could take me, but the very idea was already sending mortification creeping across my scalp. I had wasted two days of travel and not thought of what I would do once I was here. For all the planning I had done, I would have been better off walking to the gates we'd passed on the road to Freborne and begging for admittance.

No. I had come this far, and I was going to get onto the island somehow, even if I had to swim.

The old man at the end of the bar shifted on his seat and angled himself towards me. He was small – his feet barely reached the footrest of his stool – and his spine had bowed him so far forward he had to strain his neck to look directly at me. His eyes were veiled and hooded, but they were the mild blue of a baby's, and wild hairs sprouted from his nose and cheeks. He was a curious mixture of age and youth.

'You have business on the island?' His voice was not yet cracked, although he must have been nearing eighty. He spoke with the accent of the region, running the vowels together.

'I do. Yes.'

'Tell me what takes you there.' I must have looked uncomfortable, because he added simply, 'You won't get there unless I know.'

I briefly told him about Cara, about her letter, and that I was worried about her. As I stumbled to a close, he nodded.

'Course of love, ah?'

'I hope so.'

He nodded again, then seemed to come to some decision. 'All right. I'll get you there. Well, not myself, but I'll help you get yourself there, if you see what I mean.'

'How?'

'Finish your drink.' He hauled himself from the barstool to the ground, wincing at the step, and moved to the edge of the bar, taking a hat from the stand by the door as he did so. The eyes of the locals followed us as we left. I looked back and saw the barman standing in the gloom, talking to someone on the wall phone and watching me all the while.

Outside, the old man turned not towards the harbour, but north, towards the row of houses directly facing the water. His was the third along, a one-storey bungalow of breeze blocks, with a roof of slate. He led me down the side of the building to a garden on the seaward side, covered in low mossy turf. The windows facing the sea were tiny; suspicious eyes in a weather-beaten face.

There was an object in the garden covered in tarpaulin. He gestured to me to help him uncover it, and slowly we pulled the tarp back. Beneath it, balanced on a wheeled trailer, was a boat. It was small – bigger than a rubber inflatable, but not much. The steering system was a salt-bitten rudder, which trembled in the breeze.

'Hasn't been used for a while. Should still work.'

'I'd use it on my own?'

'If you want. I'm not getting in it.'

'I'm no sailor.'

'I wouldn't suggest a sailor lower himself to this. This is simple. You point it and twist the throttle.'

'How long has it been out of the water?'

'Couple of years.'

'Why hasn't it been used for so long?'

He looked at me. 'My son died in it.'

'Did he die because of something wrong with the boat?'

'Nothing was wrong with the boat. Nor with him, for all that.' He coughed. 'Do you want it or not?'

'How long will the journey take?'

'You've time to get there today, if you start now.' He looked at me, expectant.

The thought of spending a night in this place – perhaps in the rooms above the bar, if they would let me stay on credit, or sheltering from the wind in the lee of the church – did not appeal. If I was still here tomorrow morning, I might well abandon the attempt and go home. I thought of my flat in the city, of living there by myself, eking out money between commissions, and then I thought of Cara, so close to me across that calm water, and grew determined once more. I looked back at him, and nodded.

He sent me to the shed, where there were several ten-gallon drums of fuel. I slowly rolled one out and managed to fill the boat's tank. Then I took up the trailer's end and began hauling. We moved back through the empty village, past the inn. The wind pushed us as we moved, and the boy in the bar watched us from its window.

After thirty agonising minutes, I got the trailer to the water. I was sweating with the weight; it was a job for two men, but the old man was in no position to assist me, and sensibly did not try. But eventually the boat was on the water, and he pointed out the principal controls.

Leaving him standing guard, I went back to his garden and picked up my clothing bag and the painter's roll. He was still beside the boat when I returned; I clambered in, gingerly, and looked back at him.

'Why are you helping me? The barman said nobody would.'

In response, he nodded northwards, towards Pemberley's fence. 'I don't know what you want with him, but you don't seem minded to befriend him and I suspect your being there will hinder him. So it's no hardship to me.'

'Excuse my asking, but is it anything to do with your son?'

He carried on speaking as if I had said nothing. 'I'm not going on the water in this again. It may as well get one more trip. Bring it back if it's convenient, but don't if it isn't. Nobody round here would buy it.'

I nodded. 'Whose wake was it in there?'

'My other son's.' He said the words quietly, but without shame, and as he spoke, he looked at me until I dropped my eyes.

'What if something goes wrong with the boat?'

He shrugged: *you should have considered that*. But he answered anyway. 'It was in good condition two years ago and it's in good condition now. It won't get you to America, but we're not trying to get you there. You're trying to get forty miles offshore. You do know where you're going, I presume?'

'I have a map.' I drew it from my bag, showed him where I had marked the island's location from the older maps I'd found.

He looked at it with disdain. 'I'd better give you the bearing from here. You have a compass, don't you?'

'I ...' I looked around me, as if I could summon one up.

'Lord in heaven. You really did come on impulse, didn't you?' He gave a fraction of a smile. 'Stay there.' He hobbled back towards his home, leaving me in the boat.

I was glad of the moment's pause. This was my last chance to stop. Cara might finish her work unexpectedly. Maybe she would fall out of love with the place; maybe she and Pemberley would argue. Then she would come home, we would celebrate our anniversary late, and she would never need to know about this mad journey I had made.

Even as I thought it, I knew it wouldn't happen. And in that moment I realised I wasn't especially interested in resuming my old life without Cara around. I loved her, and she loved me. Would love me again once she saw me on the island. Resolved once more, I sat in the boat waiting for the old man to return.

After about ten minutes, he came shuffling back towards me. He held a bag, which he proffered as he got closer. The compass was in there, on a cord so I could wear it around my neck. In the base, bundled tightly, was a bright orange lifejacket, which looked waterproof and was far more practical than anything I'd brought. I put it on and tied the loops around myself. There was also a half-loaf of bread, a piece of cheese wrapped in plastic, and a thermos flask that sloshed as I took it.

'Thank you.'

'Take you a few hours, I reckon. Don't want you starving before you get there. I take it you know how a compass works?'

I told him I did, and he gave me the bearing I needed to follow and told me to look for the island's only harbour, which lay on its western side. Eventually we ran out of practicalities to discuss.

'Your son. Your first son. Did he die on Pemberley's land?'

'Not according to them.' He nodded and repeated it, although I had understood his implication the first time.

'What was his name?'

'William Steensen. Bill.'

'How did you get the boat back?'

'Was found a few days later, tied up in the harbour. Like it had never been out at all.' He looked around. 'Right. I think you're set. Anything else?'

'I don't think so. But thank you for all this. I wouldn't have been able to get there without you.'

'That much is clear.'

It was too late really, but I asked if there was anything I could do for him in return. He looked at me from his spot.

'You're going to see Pemberley?'

'I might see him, yes.'

'Make his life difficult. If you get there, that is. Make it hard.'

'Why?'

'Because he's the devil.'

He spoke plainly, unembarrassed, then turned and started back towards the village. I shouted some further question over the noise of the engine, but he merely gestured with his hand as he went, a wave of blessing and dismissal. I don't know why he didn't turn. Maybe he didn't want to see me sitting in his son's boat.

There was a small compartment near the rudder seat, like a glovebox in a car. I opened it. It was pristine. No crumbs, no scraps of paper, nothing. I stowed the food in it, made sure the rope was free, and gently turned the throttle. As I left the harbour, only two figures were visible. The old man, walking towards his home, and the boy from the pub, standing and waving.

I think I could have made it all the way there if I'd had a little more experience with boats.

The first hour was uneventful. My eyes were streaming to begin with and I was chilled to the bone, but the boat was swift, and by the time my eyes had recovered the village of Freborne was nearly invisible behind me. The sea was smooth.

I was surprised only once, a couple of hours in, when I spotted a sleek object in the water, grey and gleaming between one wave and another. I saw it for only a second before it disappeared again. I strained my eyes in its direction, my mind full of worries about torpedo tubes or periscopes or other unknown defences Pemberley might have in place. When it appeared once more, I saw it was nothing but a seal.

The Sanctuary

There was something ahead of me, a smudge on the horizon, and within another few minutes it had grown clear. This was it. Pemberley's island: Sanctuary Rock.

It looked like it had burst through the sea, a single malevolent molar erupting from a gum. The southern side was a long, sheer wall of rock, rearing up perhaps a hundred metres and stretching for miles in either direction. It shimmered with dots that slowly resolved themselves into the shapes of birds, moving back and forth from one white-speckled ledge to another. The top of the island was lincd with a thick band of green.

I came closer, closer still. I was perhaps half a mile out now, and realised too late that I should start steering to the left, towards the western harbour – the only safe place to land a boat, the old man had said. What would I say to the people manning the harbour? It didn't matter. If I got ashore, I would see Cara. That was all that mattered now.

I sped up, now only a few hundred metres from the base of the cliffs, and started pushing the rudder. I could almost hear the birds' cries. I was here. I had made it.

Then the boat struck something beneath it in the water.

My only memory is of seeing my two bags arcing into the air, and of starting towards them as if to catch them – but I was probably just being thrown from my seat by the collision. The sound it made was a screeching tear, and it took the engine's noise with it. In a few seconds the boat was motionless in the water, and once the scream of the hull had died away, all I could hear was the waves ahead of me being dashed on the rocks around the island's base. A terrible feeling of stillness settled around me as the boat bobbed there; stillness and a kind of numbing cold.

One of the bags had gone overboard, the one containing my possessions – *the drawing of Cara*, I thought, leaning over the side to look for it before realising it would be soaked through anyway by now. The other, the painter's roll, was perched at the front, snagged on a hook. I stepped forward to retrieve it, and noticed my foot was wet. Water was pooling in the base of the boat.

I leaned over the hull at the back, and saw with horror that the rudder had been torn away by the collision; the engine itself was loosely attached, sickeningly precarious. That would be where the water was coming in. It felt icy, soaking through my shoes. I remembered reading somewhere that seawater was coldest in the spring, and I could believe it. Swimming in this would kill me in ten minutes.

The water was above my ankles now. I opened the cupboard by the rudder seat, then looked in the other compartments, hoping for something to bail out with. There was a bucket, and I started working. My hands were shaking, I couldn't tell whether from adrenaline or cold. If I could clear it fast enough, I could keep the boat afloat until I was past the island's southern edge, and I might be in reach of the harbour. The harbour would be manned, and they would come and get me.

I looked ahead at the southern face of the island, and saw how far it stretched away. It was no good. I couldn't make it to the western side by paddling. I couldn't fix the boat. I couldn't bail and paddle at the same time.

The Sanctuary

The waves might carry the boat to the southern cliffs, though. Maybe there would be a spot at the base I could cling on to. Yes, that was it. And the boat could still be useful. If I rolled it, it might just float with the air trapped under it. If I could only roll the boat and get astride it somehow, then I'd be safe. I know I wasn't thinking straight at this point, but it seemed better than nothing.

I started to rock the boat. It wasn't easy due to the water pooling in the base, and I found myself yelling and swearing as I threw my weight from one side to the other. Eventually it started working, and the boat tilted further and further until the water started pouring over the side I was tilting to. Slowly – very slowly – I got it inverted. I think I shouted again as my legs met the sea.

The tear in the boat's side was longer than I had thought. Narrow, but long enough to let in a lot of water each second.

I tried to haul myself up the side, thinking I had turned it into a raft, but the only place I could gain purchase was the rip in the hull, and the edge of it bit into my hand as I tried to drag myself up. I remember thinking it would have been agony if I could feel my hands any more, and it was lucky I couldn't; and then thinking that would make painting difficult from now on. I'm certain I wasn't thinking straight by then. I relapsed halfway back into the water, my bleeding hand wedged into the gap, my head and chest out of the water.

I imagined what might be swimming below me, what was seeing my legs kicking from beneath and deciding to investigate. Did sharks live in water this cold; did seals prey on mammals?

I didn't know. I had got the boat inverted. I had to climb onto the boat. I had no strength to do so. My thoughts were looping back on themselves by now. I felt like a simpler machine with every passing second, being reduced to one instruction: survive. Survive.

Soon before unconsciousness, a moment of hysterical clarity struck me. Would my body be pulled onto the island; would Cara hear the name of the corpse once it was identified and realise it was me? I thought with a kind of satisfaction that the riddle would annoy her for the rest of her life.

I couldn't even tell if the current was pulling me towards the western harbour or not. I might be dragged away east, might wash up nowhere, just stay drifting here, my hand wedged in the gap in the boat's hull until eventually it was the only bit of me left. A severed hand in a boat. Nice start for a story.

But that didn't matter now: I was going to die here, dead in a stupid collision, just like my father. I thought of the words of the coroner, *drink had been taken*, and then realised I had had a drink in the pub before boarding the boat.

It was a struggle to stay awake in this cold. I sensed a wave of nothing moving up my body, and then a sudden rush of heat, as though the water around me was boiling.

The last thing I saw was the cliffs ahead of me, sheer yet welcoming somehow, stretching to gather me up. And then I knew no more.

Book II

Island

We may hope, moreover, that with the increase of wealth, knowledge and refinement, which happily seems a secure prospect ... man will endeavour to preserve the equilibrium which exists in the meteorological forces and vital conditions of countries ... and thus save from extinction the myriad beauteous forms of life which have shared with him the inheritance of this wonderful earth.

Mary Somerville

Nobody nearby; no voices. Just a room. Sleep again, maybe. Yes, why not. Better idea.

Nobody before me, but a voice at my ear. 'You're doing well.' It doesn't feel like it. Burning sensation all over me. Too hot. Must get these bedclothes off. I have to paint. The Bywaters will be angry. They paid extra for sittings at home, and I'm still in bed.

'Shh. Stay where you are. Sleep. Here. Drink this.' No energy to fight. The voice is soothing, although I don't know where it comes from. I think part of me is in bandages. The drink tastes of strawberries.

Cara must be here. I'm here to see her, after all, but there are twenty phones in front of me and only one of them will get through to her. The old king is here too, and he's brought someone to see me: Nala, the size of a shrew, dancing on my chest. I need to spit because I've swallowed the sea by mistake. Another voice is speaking.

'Can he hear us?'

'He won't remember even if he can.'

'Is he a candidate for human trials?'

'No. We don't need any more.'

'All right. We'll deal with him in the standard way. Check out everything in those bags too.'

But I'm busy. Dr Fentiman has challenged me to paint her and Anthony together, and I don't have time to listen to these voices off.

In this manner, two days passed.

There was a cupboard to my left, and a window to my right. From where I lay I could only see a patch of sky, where a small, lone cloud was about to be enveloped by a much larger one. I was in a wooden bed, covered with sheets of white.

There was a door in the far corner with a low murmur of voices beyond it, and I noticed at my elbow a button engraved with a bell. I pressed it, more experimentally than anything else. Nothing.

The bedclothes were heavy, but I worked them free and sat up. Someone had taken my clothes and dressed me in a loose, papery gown that rustled dry against my skin. There was a mirror in the corner on a chest of drawers, and after testing out my legs,

I hobbled slowly over to it. I looked terrible. My left hand – my painting hand – was swathed in bandages, and for a mad, paranoid second I doubted I still had a hand under there. My eye was badly bruised, and my hair had been clipped shorter. I saw why when I turned my head: a nasty-looking cut, stitched up, along one side of my skull.

'I think you'd better lie back down.'

The woman standing in the doorway was perhaps seventy; short, and round, with iron hair in a bob. Her clothes were rural, faintly formal in appearance, not medical at all. I returned to the bed and eased myself into it. The woman sat in the chair in the corner by the door, took a tiny notebook and stub of pencil from her pocket and began writing. She seemed in no hurry to speak.

'Who are you?'

She kept writing for a moment, then looked up at me. 'Who *you* are is a more pressing question. Your name?'

'Ben. Benjamin Parr. Where am I?'

She answered as she scribbled. 'You're in a clinic on the island you were trying to trespass on. Were you expecting to be somewhere else?'

I had made it. I could think more clearly now. 'I didn't expect to arrive like this.'

'Not a lot of boats pass round the southern side. Highly stupid way to approach, due to the rocks. If there hadn't been a daydreamer up on the cliffs who contacted our security chief at the harbour, you'd have been a goner. You're lucky you weren't shot. I'd have shot you.'

I didn't say anything to that for a moment, and she sighed, impatient.

'How long have I been lying here?'

'Two days. You've risen again on the third. And now we come to the more important matter: why are you here, Mr Parr?'

'I know someone who lives here.'

'Very likely.'

'I do. Cara Sharpe.'

'You know Ms Sharpe?' She blinked with surprise as I nodded, and it took her a few seconds to recover. 'How typical. So you approached in a boat, I imagine stolen ...'

'It wasn't stolen.'

'Was it yours?'

I thought of the old man and determined not to give him away.

'I borrowed it.'

'From whom?'

'I'm not telling you that.'

'Did you have accomplices?'

'Did you not find the crowd of people I came with in my little one-man boat? About twenty of us.'

She grimaced. 'And you came to see the lovely Ms Sharpe. Did you consider using the proper channels?'

'I did. They were shut.'

'If they were, it was for a reason.' She frowned. 'How do you know Cara, then? Family? Friend?'

Something held me back from saying it at first, some instinct of pride or determination that if she hadn't mentioned it I wouldn't either. It didn't last, of course.

'We're engaged to be married.'

'Really?' There it was again, distinct surprise. I nodded. Her smile in response was silky, like she'd caught a fly. 'She never mentioned you.'

I realised in that moment how easy it would be to underestimate this shabby creature with her unfashionable haircut. But I was stung, too, and reached for the only thing I could think of then, the only bit of tangible evidence I had of the corruption of this place.

'You know your men on the mainland are running a little extortion racket?'

'I highly doubt that.'

'It's true. They've got a private operation on the road to Freborne. When I didn't pay them off, they beat me.'

'Absurd. We only hire professionals. And I'm quite sure you wouldn't be able to provide proof.'

I wanted to stay on the subject, but something else was worrying me more. I waved my bandaged hand. 'Am I badly hurt? Under here?'

'I'm not a doctor. I believe the staff here have predicted little long-term damage. You will paint again, I'm sure.' My turn to look surprised. 'Your bag survived the trip.' She nodded to the corner, over my shoulder; the painter's roll was there. I couldn't believe my luck.

'Was that all they found?'

'It was.'

So my clothes were gone, and my notebooks, and Cara's letters, and the drawing of her. I had no record of what she had looked like when we met, no way of checking the Cara of the island against the woman I had fallen in love with. I felt suddenly untethered.

'What should I do now?'

'You lie here while we prepare to send you back to the mainland.'

'I want to see Cara.'

'I'm sure you do. Life's not so easy.' She rose from her seat and looked down at me. 'Good morning.' She turned and left.

When the door was closed, I moved across the room and brought the painter's roll back to the bed. It had long stains of salt arcing across it, and the canvas crackled when it moved, but the contents were intact. The brushes, the blocks, the bamboo mat, all of it. I buckled it, tucked it beside me, and slept again.

She was moving ahead of me, in my dreams, through a series of rooms: a party, a long, cool veranda, into the darkness of a forest. I knew it was Cara, of course. It had to be her. But she never turned her face.

9

I woke to a rhythmic tapping, which became a knock at the door. The bar of sunlight through the window had slid from one wall to another; I must have been asleep a while.

'Come in.'

The door opened a little, and a head and shoulders appeared around it; a young woman. 'Are you Ben?'

'Yes. I ... arrived here a couple of days ago. So I'm told, anyway.'

'You're *famous*.'

'I guarantee I'm not.'

She laughed, and moved into the room, closing the door behind her. 'Don't be so modest. Your arrival was pretty much the most exciting thing that's happened here ever. You are now an island celebrity, I'm afraid.' Wonderful. Cara would doubtless be delighted, when I caught up with her.

'I don't think I heard your name.'

She stuck out her hand. 'I'm Bianca. I live here. Work here. Same thing, really.' She was tall, and slightly built, with hair so dark it was almost black, framing a long, open face. I guessed she was my age, more or less.

'Someone came to see me before.'

'Can you describe her?'

'Older than you. Angrier, too.'

She made a little moue of distaste. 'Sounds like Angela.'

I remembered another Angela, one Cara had written about in an early letter home. 'Angela Knight?'

'That's the one. I'm sure she gave you a friendly island welcome.'

'I'm here to visit—'

'Cara Sharpe, yes. I know that too.'

'News travels very fast here.'

'Does when it's a shipwrecked sailor. Are you able to walk?'

'I suspect so.'

'Good. I thought you might want a tour of the place. Only if you feel like it.'

'Would anyone object?' I wasn't sure of my status here, and I suspected going on the run with this woman wouldn't do much to improve it.

'Not if you're with me they won't.' She smiled, conspiratorial, and I joined her, until I looked down at the gown I was in.

'I don't know where my clothes are.'

'They'll have provided fresh ones. Check the drawers.' I paused until she realised why I was unwilling to get up, and laughed. 'I'll wait outside.'

The Sanctuary

She was right. The chest in the corner held clothes – a pair of trousers, dark blue and thick cotton, a plain white T-shirt with long sleeves, and a thick woven jumper, also dark blue. I might have blended in anywhere. My legs felt strong as I dressed, which was a relief, but I still spent a couple of minutes going over my body, checking for any injuries apart from the one on my hand. What exactly I was looking for, I wasn't quite sure. The stitches on my skull felt huge, and the skin beneath them was throbbing.

Bianca was still in the corridor when I emerged, picking at her nails.

'Very smart. Come this way, then. We'll spring you out.'

The clinic was far more pleasant than the average city hospital: large windows, light wood lining the walls, and a tang of lemons in the air. The open doors we passed showed us the ends of empty, made beds. They didn't seem to have many patients. We walked past a nurse at the front desk, a young woman in a rich blue uniform, and she gave Bianca a nod and a smile before sliding her glance to me and making a note in her ledger.

The hospital opened onto a circular tarmacked area, with a few white carts hitched to chargers around the edges and a huge tree rearing up at its centre. There were a few other buildings to left and right – one with a pharmacist's sign – and behind them a few dozen more, which looked like cottages. Beyond those there was only thick woodland all the way round. The air was warm, rich with the aroma of the forest.

Bianca gestured around her. 'What do you think?'

'I don't know what it is, but it's nice.'

'First right answer of the tour. The questions get harder from here on, of course. This is the medical hex.'

'Hex?'

'A hex is just the way this place is split up. Hex like a beehive, you know? Hexagonal cells. There are forty hexes here. Each of them runs a different bit of island life. All the doctors, pharmacists, surgeons, midwives – lots of midwives – live and work here. There are hexes for food processing, clothing, construction, road-mending, sanitation ... all sorts.'

'Does everyone spend their time in their own hex?'

'Not at all. Some hexes are purely residential and some are half occupational, but in general people spend as much time as they can communicating with other disciplines. There's a lot of mixing in the evenings. Half the innovations here are thanks to an electrician talking to a seamstress or a vet speaking to a solar engineer. And, of course, they frequently marry each other, which is another plus.'

'Clever.'

'Oh, believe me, the cleverness of this place surpasses the understanding of man. Come on.'

She walked over to one of the little electrical vehicles and spoke to the young man standing next to it, a tall boy barely out of his teens in blue overalls, then beckoned to me.

'George is very sweetly going to let us take his cart. Aren't you, George?' The boy nodded and smiled, bashful, as he stepped away from the vehicle. 'Hop in.' I did as I was told, wondering at the power Bianca seemed to exert in this place.

The Sanctuary

The road she drove us along was lurid with life on either side. Dozens of different species of tree, low thickets of shrubs, the occasional hut half overgrown with the greenery climbing across it ... It was very soothing. The vehicle's engine was so quiet, and the road so smooth beneath the wheels, that she hardly had to raise her voice when she spoke.

'Right, next question. Do you want to have dinner tonight?'

'Like ... you and me?'

She laughed, and glanced at me sideways. 'Yeah. Intimate dinner date. Plus another few thousand, if you don't mind. Everyone here eats together.'

I blushed. 'Of course. Sorry.'

'No, I phrased it wrong. That probably sounds different on the mainland.' She sounded almost sad as she spoke, but her brow cleared in a second and she continued. 'There's a huge hall in the central hub and a few supplementary ones elsewhere. Almost all of us eat in one of the four main venues each night. I'll try and get you close to John's table.'

'Me?' The thought startled me. 'I'm really just here to see Cara, talk to her. Try and bring her home. I didn't mean to trouble the boss.' Nor did I trust myself not to hit him if we were ever introduced.

'Ben, about that ...'

'About what?'

'About why you're here. To see—'

'Cara, yes. What about it?'

She frowned through the windscreen for a few seconds before she answered. 'Angela didn't say anything to you?'

'About what?'

She sighed. 'Guess it's my job to tell you then. She's not here at the moment.'

'What's that supposed to mean?'

'Cara's not on the island.'

'Stop the cart, please.'

'Ben, I'm sure it's fine, it's just—'

'Please stop the cart right here.'

She pulled us over into a little extra curve of tarmac at the side of the road, and I stood, got out, looked one way and then the other, along a tunnel of green in either direction. My breath appeared to have shortened, and I leaned over towards the driver's seat where Bianca sat.

'Where is she?'

'All I know is that she's left. She hasn't been at the top table at dinner for a while now.'

'How long?'

'I don't know. A few weeks, maybe.'

'Where is she?'

'Ben, I think you should calm down. You look very distressed. Do you need a tissue?'

'I'm fine.' I wiped my face with my sleeve. 'Where is Cara?'

'I don't know. This isn't the only place John owns, Ben. She could be on the mainland estate, the one you would have passed by on your way up here. It has thousands more employees. I'd guess she's there. She'll be completely safe, if that's what you're worried about.'

'Then why would she have stopped writing to me?'

Bianca gave me a look and I wondered if I was losing my grip. 'That's kind of between the two of you, Ben, to be honest.'

'But she has to be here.' My voice was high, and I heard it as if it was someone else's; *whoever that is, he sounds terrified.*

'She's not. She was on top table with us almost every night until a few weeks ago, and then she wasn't.'

'Did you see her leave?'

'No. But I think I remember her saying something about the mainland. Or John saying something to her.'

I looked out at the thick woods on my left. 'I nearly killed myself getting here to see her.'

'I presume you told her you were coming?'

'I wrote letters ...'

'They'll have been forwarded to wherever she is. She won't have missed any letters, Ben.'

So Cara had been on the mainland all this time. There was no need for me to be here. I felt like a fly that had blundered into a great grotesque web. This was all thanks to my stupidity. If I'd told her I intended to visit, waited for her to reply ... No, she wouldn't have come back anyway. She'd made that clear in her last letter. That didn't change the fact that I had half killed myself coming here for no good reason.

'Ben, I'm going to start the cart now, and take you where we're going. Come on.'

I slowly resumed my seat, and she pushed a button. The engine muttered into life and the cart rolled quietly along for a few minutes. I realised Bianca was waiting for me to speak first.

'Sorry about that. Just a shock to hear.'

'It's all right. I think it's wonderful that you came all this way. Anyone would be distressed, even without waking up to Angela Knight.'

'She seemed pretty strange.'

'That's absolute power for you. She's John's original right-hand woman. The proto-Cara, if you like, although she would hardly take that as a compliment. John and Angela have worked together since the first Village, but these days she's getting closer to stepping back.'

'She didn't give me that impression.'

'Well, shrinking kingdoms often have the fiercest guards.' She laughed. 'She'll warm to you in no time.'

I thought of the iron-haired woman. *I'd have shot you.* 'Perhaps.'

We drove through a few more of the hexes. Several people in each waved as we passed. By now I had no idea which part of the island we were in. As soon as we left a hex, the thick forest closed in again, almost to the road. I didn't notice much, wrapped up in how stupid I had been to come here without knowing for sure whether Cara was here or not, but eventually a thought occurred to me.

'I thought there were no trees on these islands. Not this far north.'

'There normally aren't. The first inhabitants chopped them down when they got here for their houses, boats, that kind of thing. Then they introduced livestock, which ate any new shoots. So you get these bare landscapes on almost every island off the coast up here. Dreadful, really, when you think they could all be like this.'

'How come this place has so many?'

'We had a benefactor two hundred years ago. Henry Fellingham. Made his money overseas, doing unpleasant things to unarmed people. But a trader too, and a successful one. He became obsessed with this place. Bought it wholesale from the Crown, then spent his fortune reforesting it. Paid the handful of previous residents off, found them better homes on the other islands. He turned it into a forest again, but he beggared himself in the process. This island has form when it comes to wealthy men spending all their money here.'

'Why did he do it?'

'He wanted to re-create the Garden of Eden.'

I looked around at the thick foliage, breathed in the fresh island air. 'I'd say he managed.'

'You won't be saying that if you're still here in winter. But the trees give a good amount of cover from the weather, at least. And with the way the climate's changing, John reckons this place will be one of the most fertile on the planet in fifty years' time.' Again I noticed how she referred to Pemberley. *John*. As if he was a friend, or something closer than that.

We drove in silence for a little while.

'Where are you actually taking me?'

'Thought you'd like to see the hub. And behold, here it is.'

The 'hub' was a larger area reclaimed from the forest. There was a grand hall on one side, a huge red-brick structure topped by a steep slate roof. There was something unusual about it, something uncanny in its lines and shape. I couldn't identify any particular unsettling feature; I just knew it was oddly familiar, although I couldn't tell how. There were smaller buildings on either side, more utilitarian in their form; and in front of the buildings a small fleet of carts like the one we were in, like paper boats with their white canvas tops.

These buildings were spread around a huge green oval, the only manicured space I had seen so far. It was sunken in its middle, and carpeted with grass like a new meadow. On its far side was a plantation of thin young trees, with silver trunks and drooping leaves. A small troop of gardeners moved back and forth with barrows of earth. I turned back to the main hall.

'Can we go in?'

'They'll be laying out for dinner. But yes, of course.'

Bianca led me up the steps, opened the doors, and I stepped into my own past.

It was larger, but the design was identical. The beams, the bricks, the alcoves, the benches, even the fireplace halfway along. The only thing missing was the lectern – no, there it was, tucked out of sight. It was so disorientating, I stopped dead, and Bianca asked what was wrong.

It was Hillcrest. The room I had come to three times a day for seven years. Where I had sat through meals, assemblies, lectures, plays staged on the dais … All of it returned to me in a moment.

The only change was at the back, where the entire wall had been covered by an enormous and grotesque mural. The left-hand side was a huge round shape, the upper half of which resembled an island, or a bank of mud and earth covered in weeds. Beneath the shoreline, though, the island was a beast, an enormous fish adorned with all the monstrous accoutrements the artist had been able to imagine: drifting tentacles, a beak, horns and nodules, and unknown slits and orifices from which more tendrils blindly groped. The limbs stretched up to the waterline, where they were transformed into trees.

The right-hand side of the mural showed a ship moored to the island. A group of travellers were halfway through disembarking onto its surface, fanning out across it, knowing nothing about the ground on which they stood. It was a grotesque image, a sailor's nightmare.

Bianca was speaking to me. '… Ben?'

'Sorry. This place is … I recognise it.'

She looked at me, interested suddenly. 'How?'

'I went to school here. I mean, this is a replica of the school I went to. It was – is – called Hillcrest.'

'You're joking.' Her eyes were wide. It was as if I'd confessed to a crime. No, happier than that – as if I'd told her where there was buried treasure.

'I'm not joking. The lamps, the floor, all of it. It's the same. He – Pemberley, I mean – he went there himself, then?'

'I don't know.'

'He must have. That's extraordinary. Well, there's something for us to bond over.'

'No.' Bianca said the word violently, then lowered her voice, even though there was nobody near us. 'A warning for you, Ben. Don't tell him. John, I mean.'

'Tell him what?'

'Don't say you recognise this building. That you went to the same school. I'm serious. Don't say a word about it.'

'Wouldn't he like to meet someone else who went there?'

'Not at all. He'd probably evict you immediately. Or worse.'

'Why?'

'Just don't ask.'

With that, she turned and left, leaving me standing alone. I felt uneasy once again. No, that wasn't quite right; I had been uncomfortable since I woke here, despite all Bianca's kindness. I saw no choice but to follow her.

Once we were out in the open air, Bianca resumed her previous mood, apparently without effort, and the tour continued. Next to the grand hall was the library. She told me it had several miles of shelving beneath the ground, enough to store almost every book ever printed.

'Archives of newspapers too, every single one, although nobody has time to read them. Imported wholesale. I arranged that. Sorted a deal with a huge national library that was closing down, and they finished bringing them in a few months ago. All on microfilm. You can store an entire world in a cardboard box.' She seemed completely enamoured of a technology I would have thought of as ancient – although as a portrait painter I could hardly criticise her for that.

I was starting to enjoy Bianca's company, although I couldn't work out why she was paying me quite so much attention. I asked her whether I was distracting her from her work, and she shook her head.

'No. Today is a quiet day for me.' She spoke with the same sadness as before, when she had asked me to dinner, and I felt embarrassed somehow, as if I had unwittingly pointed out a deformity of hers. I tried to explain that I was simply anxious not to be a burden, that I'd be leaving the island soon in any case, and she brightened. I asked almost as a distraction where we should go next.

'Want to see the harbour?'

'Of course.'

We returned to the vehicle, and she started driving south and west, into the light of the sinking sun. As we went, we saw a few more of the hubs, one of them quite industrial, like a factory, and I realised something about the workers there too – about all the workers we'd seen.

'Everyone's so young.'

Bianca nodded, her eyes on the road ahead. 'John's obsession. He and Angela are just about the only people over forty. He wants to make the world young again.'

'Sounds deranged.' I meant it, thinking of the millions of people I'd left behind, but I must have spoken badly out of turn, because she snorted with laughter.

'Oh, he's going to have a lot of fun with you.'

'Forgive me. Mainland manners.'

'Life on the mainland sounds pretty rough these days.'

'Not if you're in one of the Villages.'

'The thing about John is that he's a provider. Half the people here are having children.'

'You?'

'No. Not my thing.' Another little pause, another odd lurch in the conversation.

'Have you been here a while, then?'

'Yeah, a while.'

'How long?'

'Oh, ages.' She changed gear and swung the electric vehicle round the corner, rather sharply, pointing out something else to me, one of the rarer trees they had here, an aspen personally planted by Fellingham himself.

A few minutes later, we pulled up in another enormous clearing. This one had a couple of buildings in it – long, low barns that looked industrial somehow – but they weren't the most impressive feature. The clearing was dominated at one end by a huge heap of rocks a couple of hundred feet across. It was as if a set of giant's building bricks had been scattered carelessly. Some were the size of a car, some as big as a cottage.

As we walked towards it along the ribbon of tarmac, I realised there was a void in the middle of the rocks – a gap fifty feet wide. It was the mouth of an enormous, gradually descending tunnel. Weak bulbs lit the interior, and the rock floor had been smoothed and tarmacked. A set of rails sloped away into the murk.

'What is it?'

'This is the road down to the harbour.'

'Is it natural?'

'Mostly. There were bits of clearing and blasting, but it was basically perfect when Fellingham got here a couple of centuries ago. Come and see.'

I followed her, and as we entered, my eyes adjusted to the gloom. There was a track for pedestrians, marked off with clean white paint. The metal rails ran down the centre between two broad traffic lanes, and the path beneath us glowed slightly. The ceiling was almost invisibly high in the darkness.

The place gave me a church-feeling, and even though I lowered my voice, the echo still whispered above us for seconds before fading.

'Is this the only way down to the harbour?'

'Pretty much. Impressive, isn't it? John calls it the eye of the needle. Although he points out that he's already in, and he doesn't want to leave, so as far as he's concerned the rich man has already got to the kingdom of heaven. Everyone who comes to the island passes through here. You did too.'

'Everything on the island comes through this one tunnel?'

'Everything and everyone. The Neolithics, the Victorians, us ... You see those tracks?' Bianca pointed to the twin rails. 'There used to be a kind of funicular running up and down carrying loads. John revived it.' I imagined the tunnel for a second as a huge umbilical cord. 'When Fellingham was here it mostly took his foresters up and down. I think John is probably trying to beat Fellingham's vision on top of creating his own.'

'Bianca, can I ask ... what is Pemberley trying to do here?'

'How do you mean?' She sounded wary.

'He must be one of the wealthiest men on the planet, but he's never been interviewed. Hardly anyone even knows what he looks like. And now he lives here, building Villages on the mainland for the old and this island kingdom for the young. Is he a genius? Is he mad? Is he safe?'

She didn't answer for a long minute, and I could not see her face as she walked downhill before me.

'Bianca? I'm serious. Is he unhinged?' I must have sounded angry; I didn't care. 'Cara is ... she's completely in the grip of this place. I need to know the truth.'

Bianca stopped walking, and kneeled to retrieve from the rough floor a small tangled object of metal and wood.

'You ask if he's mad. Here's an example.' She held the object out to me. 'When he got here, the island was overrun with rats. The Victorians introduced them by mistake. They had ships big enough for the rats to stow away, and all you need is one breeding pair. By the time John arrived here, they had killed almost every seabird on the island. The birds were reduced to a tiny fringe on the rocks that the rats couldn't get to. They ate the eggs, they ate the chicks in their nests.'

She spoke low and fast, and although we had only been standing still for a minute, I felt the cold and damp of the tunnel walls around me penetrating the thick jumper I wore.

'He laid poison, hundreds of thousands of dishes, and traps' – she waved the tangle she held – 'and killed the rats. Wiped out every single one. And now there are more seabirds on the northern plateau than anywhere else on the mainland.' She looked at me, and under the feeble lighting from above, her slender face looked hollow. For one indecent second I saw the shape of her skull. 'It's mad and it's genius. It would be mad if he couldn't do it, but he can, so it's both. Does that explain him a bit better?'

She must have seen the expression on my face.

'All I'm really trying to say is, if he can identify a problem – a problem in the natural world – he fixes it. And he has a longer vision than most people. He's thinking about the problems of the next ten thousand years, not the next ten.'

'He wiped out every rat on an island this size?'

'It took him years. He kept at it, though. The seabirds were almost extinct. If he had arrived ten years later, it would have been in vain.'

'It still sounds almost impossible.'

'The phrase "almost impossible" is music to him. I think that explains him too. He's the will made flesh.' She threw the trap to one side. 'Anyway, there's another reason I'd prefer to say he isn't mad.'

'Which is?'

'He's my father.'

I took a second to digest that. All the people greeting her, the way she'd been allowed to just take me out of the hospital, to take the cart . . . Of course she was his daughter. What a fool I had been. I thought of Cara again. Why wasn't she here to stop me blundering into these mistakes?

'I'm so sorry. I didn't mean . . .'

She produced a smile from nowhere, and shook her head. 'Don't be. It's actually a pleasure to meet someone who's not a paid-up member of the Pemberley fan club. Come on. It's a way yet to the harbour.'

She started walking again, this time in silence and briskly enough to discourage further conversation. I followed in silent mortification.

We kept going for about fifteen more minutes. Ahead of us, a point of light grew to the size of a thumbtack, then a headlamp, then a floodlight: the outside world.

'The harbour.'

We were on the island's western side. The harbour before us looked like it had been built around the mouth of the rock tunnel. There were cranes on the dock, and a concrete apron around its edge. A huge cartridge loaded with shipping containers waited on rails near the tunnel's mouth, and two cargo ships sat squarely on the dark water before us.

This part of the coast had horns. Two huge peninsulas curved some miles out on each side, the forest stretching almost to their tips. The bay itself looked like the crater left by an enormous asteroid, some titanic act of violence millions of years ago. I imagined the precise moment of impact: the air and soil inverted, the rocks rumpling like bed sheets in a gale. It was a momentary vision of a cosmic evil – no, not an evil, not even a malignity. Just the uncaring laws of nature, showing their precedence over the thin layer of civilisation we had since sprayed on the planet's surface.

Bianca had said nothing for some minutes, but she spoke now. 'This is where they brought you in.'

I looked at the dark water, and realised that nobody on the mainland – no friends, certainly no family – knew I was here.

The islanders could have let me die out there with ease. I shuddered, and took refuge in conversation. 'What happened to the boat I was in?'

Bianca gave me a curious look. 'Disposed of.'

'Did he build all this?'

'John? Yes. The whole dock infrastructure. He carved out space underwater so even the biggest containers can dock nearby. But we haven't needed much extra really. He has a saying: whatever we need, the island will provide. If we don't find it, it's a sign we don't really need it.'

'I'm sorry if I was rude about Sir John back there. I didn't mean to pry. He seems like a good employer.'

That made her smile, for some reason I couldn't identify. 'Oh, he's a very good employer. A very good employer indeed.'

The sun was dipping behind the lower horn of trees out towards the horizon, and she swung her arms in the chill. 'Want to go back to the hospital? We should get you some formal clothes for dinner.'

'You dress for dinner here?' I must have sounded completely appalled, and completely credulous, because she threw back her head and cackled.

'I'm joking, Ben.' She gave me a look almost of fondness, the corners of her mouth still twitching.

'Got it.'

As we turned back towards the mouth of the tunnel, I noticed two squat towers built just inside it on either side, like those I had seen on the mainland, and a couple of figures standing in each. One of the figures lifted a lazy arm to Bianca and she returned the wave.

The Sanctuary

'Security?'

'Yeah. Just waiting for the mainland to collapse, I guess, at which point they'll close the tunnel and we'll wait out the world.' The figures and the buildings alike seemed somehow ancient in that instant. I envisaged the towers overgrown and decayed, covered in creepers, yet still with the guards standing there, keeping others out.

'Are they armed?'

'There are a handful of guns on the island. Don't worry, all very secure. Military standard. The guards, too, all ex-special forces. John went on a hiring spree a few years ago. I'm not sure you could invade, though. This is the only point of access, and you'd have a job scaling the cliffs.'

I imagined the tunnel collapsing, the building-sized rocks rearranging themselves, the cord between the island and the rest of the world folding itself shut for ever. It would take all the dynamite on the planet to clear a path through those stones.

Back at the hospital, Bianca escorted me to my room, and told me to make my way to the hub for dinner in an hour. I sat on the bed for a while, trying to move my hand beneath the bandages, and then set off.

The medical hex had four tarmac paths leading off it, signposted with the destinations they led to, and how long the journey would take, either walking or by cart. Darkness had fallen, and the way was lit by elegant curved lamps. The paths glowed with the same blue light as the harbour tunnel, as though they had sucked up the sun's rays during the day and were emitting them now. I decided to walk. Every so often, a cart appeared behind me. The drivers saluted as they passed, and one or two offered me a lift, but I declined. I needed time to think.

The Sanctuary

I had come here to get Cara back. But Cara had left without telling me, without any indication. The last I had heard from her, she was happy here and not coming home. Why would she have gone? She couldn't have taken another position voluntarily. I remembered a phrase from one of her letters. *It's paradise, darling*. But she hadn't known I was coming. My timing was wrong, that was all. I would have to find her, wherever she was, perhaps on Pemberley's mainland estate. When she saw me, she would remember her love for me, and we would return to the city, to life as it was before all this.

The great hall's lights radiated out across the hub, and hundreds of people were arriving, streaming in through the doors. White-clad assistants moved the emptying carts out of sight. I explained myself to a helper at a lectern outside the hall, who said she would find me a place right away. She consulted a list, left for a minute, then returned to shepherd me inside.

The room was full of long benches, stretching out either side of a central dais, and the benches were full of men and women, all dressed more or less like me, plus dozens of children running between the tables or sitting on their parents' laps. They were a diverse group – every ethnicity, every shape and size, but not every age. The very oldest people I could see looked to be in their late thirties.

On the central dais was a round table, laid for a formal dinner, and as I followed my guide, I realised with horror that she was leading me there. Two of the seats were already occupied; a young couple looked up at me briefly, then returned to an anxious conversation in low voices. Each seat had a place card – one read simply 'Bianca', as though she was the only woman with her name on the island; elsewhere, 'Angela Knight', and sitting before a short, muscular man a few years my junior, 'Alun Munro'.

There were two more names around the table. The first was 'Ben Parr', scratched in copperplate on a perfect square of card. It looked intended somehow, as if I'd always been going to end up here. Next to it, the final card simply read 'John'. I was going to be beside Pemberley himself.

'Ben.' I started, and turned to see Bianca. 'You ready?'

'Of course.'

'Don't be intimidated by him. He's very bored of meeting people who quiver as they shake his hand. That's why I've placed you beside him.'

'I meet important people often enough. I'm sure I'll cope.' I wasn't sure of it at all.

The benches on either side of the central dais were full now. Suddenly a ripple of silence stretched across the room, broken only by the scrape of benches as people stood. A procession was moving towards us, raising a buzz of conversation in its wake. A voice at the front was saying something: 'Sit down, sit down, that's enough of this.'

With that, Sir John Pemberley was at the table. He turned to one side to speak to an attendant, and I had a few seconds to observe him. I should have enjoyed them more: the last moments of my life free of his personality.

I had somehow divined from Cara's letters that he would be physically broad, that he would have spent his free time exercising, like a lot of other plutocrats. I had even correctly predicted a shaved head, polished and gleaming under the lights of the hall. But his muscles did not look gym-built. His whole bullish frame had a kind of practicality about it, matched by the clothes he wore – a plain white shirt, and trousers of dark blue.

Despite his bulk, there was a sense of energy about him. He was fast without being agitated, present without being frantic. He seemed to pick up on everything about him without losing focus on whoever he was listening to. He was balletic, in a way. He moved to his seat and slid sideways into it.

'So. Who do we have tonight?' He looked around him, to his right at first, greeting the people sitting there – Knight and the man Munro, then the young couple I guessed were the 'ordinary' residents of the island attending as a privilege. They looked like they were about to faint. Bianca was on the other side of them, then me. Pemberley's eyes settled on me as we sat down.

'Who's this?'

Bianca answered him. 'This is Ben.'

He frowned, and Knight spoke to help him remember. 'The intruder.'

'Why's he at my table?' He looked at Bianca, and she stumbled over her answer.

Eventually she managed to speak. 'I arranged it, John.'

'And why the hell would you do that?'

'He explained to me why he's here. It's a funny story really.'

'Is it now?'

'Yes, Father, it's—'

'Perhaps he could tell us himself.' He turned his attention to me, and his eyes were very calm.

'I don't know how funny it is, Mr Pemberley.' I certainly wasn't going to call him *Sir John*. 'I was coming to see Cara Sharpe. Obviously I didn't arrive quite as planned. I'm very sorry for causing so much difficulty.'

He kept his eyes on me. 'You came all this way to see our Cara?' *Our* Cara.

'Yes. We're engaged.' He blinked. 'It was meant to be a surprise.'

'Certainly has been.' He kept his eyes on me and nodded slowly. 'Quite intrepid.'

'Quite stupid.' That was Knight, on his other side.

'Well anyway, Ben, she's not available.'

'I ... Yes. Bianca informed me of that already.'

'So why are you still here?'

'I believe my departure is being arranged, although I'm not sure ...'

'Fine.' He nodded, and I left my thought unvoiced: *I'll find her, and take her from you when I go.* He gestured at my bandaged hand. 'Need your food cut up for you?'

'I'll manage.'

'Well, as we have you for a meal, you may as well know who's here. On my right here, Alun Munro, head of security. He's the one who should have stopped you getting in.' Munro simply jerked his eyebrows, as if to show me how little he thought of my presence at the table. 'Angela Knight, geneticist and ecologist, also management genius, has run bloody everything since the year dot.'

'We've met.' Knight smiled with half her mouth.

'Here we have' – and he paused almost imperceptibly, retrieving the names of the other two guests – 'Francis and Joanna, who work in food. And a baby on the way too, yes?' They nodded, bashful but delighted by his attention. Joanna's hands moved to her proud stomach, almost instinctively. 'You've met Bianca already. And I'm John.'

A steward was at his elbow. 'They're ready for you.'

Pemberley nodded, and looked back at me. 'Don't do anything else stupid for the next few minutes.'

He left his seat and crossed the dais towards a slender wooden podium that overlooked the whole hall, left and right. I sat back. My cheeks were hot. His delivery had been fast, confident. Almost everything he'd said had left me stumbling along after him. But on my other side, Bianca gave me a little smile, conspiratorial. Perhaps I hadn't done as badly as I thought.

The room had fallen quiet now. Pemberley was at the podium, and I swivelled in my seat.

'All right, everyone. Not much from me tonight. Just a few quick thanks to some people who've gone above and beyond. Donald Matcham from sanitary, who has been doing some heroic things in the septic tanks. Extra showers for Donald, please.' A laugh. 'All of you working in food, because you've just got our fifth harvest of the year in. Tonight's meal was ninety-eight per cent produced here, in the fields and tunnels. Everything but the saffron.' Applause at that. 'And lastly, Samantha and her gang in the engineering hex. Sam informs me the turbines are working again thanks to their efforts, meaning we won't die of cold when winter comes.' He nodded at the half-ironic cheers from around the room, and grinned. He was charming under those lights, unrecognisable from the thug who had sat beside me. 'So enjoy tomorrow. We're building it.'

At that, the entire room responded, echoing his final words: '*We're building it.*'

He looked as though he was about to step down from the podium, and the conversation was starting to build again, but he leaned back towards the microphone. The room fell silent in a second.

'Just one more thing. I've told you all this before, but I want to remind you: however you came here, you chose to be here.' He glanced towards us, but I could not tell from his hollow eyes if he was looking at me. 'And not only did you choose, you were chosen. Whatever the choice that brought you here, the fact that you are still here means you were chosen in return. Never forget it.'

He stepped down, out of the discreet spotlight from above into shadow, and crossed the room towards us once more as the buzz of conversation spread back through the hall.

Plates were brought out from the kitchen. It wasn't luxurious food – a kind of vegetable broth, with bread on the side – but it was delicious.

'So. Ben. Got another name?'

'Parr.'

'Par as in average?'

'Two Rs.'

'Not a very average way to behave, coming here, creating such a bloody fuss.'

'As I said before, I'm sorry for the trouble I've caused.'

'You're just lucky I was walking the cliffs. Spotted you just as you hit the rock. Bloody great bang you made.'

'It was you who saw me?' I glanced at Bianca for confirmation, and she nodded. What had Knight told me? A daydreamer, she'd said.

'Thought you were the revenue. Revenue don't normally capsize their own boats, though.' Pemberley laughed and I tried to join in, still unsettled, picturing him witnessing my accident from the cliffs above, weighing up whether to intervene.

'Tell me about yourself.'

He ascertained my profession and parentage in what felt like a few seconds. I had the sense of being rifled through, of the most salient facts about me being noted for future reference.

'Age?'

'Thirty-three. The same as Cara.'

'Not very young.'

'Still just about young enough, I'd say.'

'For what?'

'To leave a mark.'

He glanced at me, then returned to savaging his food.

'Siblings?'

'None.'

'Why not?'

'I couldn't say. My mother had me very young.'

'Perfect time to have more, then. Something wrong between her and your father?'

I felt for a strange moment as though he was pulling me along over stony ground, territory uncertain to me but which he already knew well. 'You'd have to ask her, but she's passed away now. They both have.'

He nodded. No condolences. 'Your education?'

'A little school in the south. St Christopher's.' My first lie. Bianca's fork slipped and squeaked against her plate. I think I told it naturally enough, though, because he grunted, and asked me about my training. I told him about Florence.

'You strike me as being pretty serious about your work.'

'You have to be if you want to make a living at it. There's hardly an infrastructure to support my kind of art any more.'

'What's your style?'

'Portraits, in oils.'

He nodded. 'Who do you paint?'

'Quite a lot of people in the Villages. Your ones, I mean.'

'Obviously. How are they, as subjects?'

'Some are really interested; they understand it's a process of collaboration between artist and sitter to get to some kind of ...' I paused. 'Some kind of truthful representation, I suppose. If we're being pretentious.'

'And the rest just have a bit of blank wall going spare and too much money on their hands?'

'Sometimes, yes.'

'What do they get out of it?'

'Some of them just want to be looked at for a few hours, and they don't even care whether they get a painting at the end of it.'

'You're their niche therapy.'

'If you like.' He was needling me, trying to find a way in, and I was determined not to give him one. 'But a few are looking for something a bit more permanent.'

'Elixir of youth.'

'If you like. I can understand the appeal. I'm sure you've been painted in your life.'

'Me?' He snorted. 'Don't even like being photographed. Wouldn't let someone look at me for a month, or however long it takes.'

'You should consider it.'

'Why?'

'Well, you clearly have an interest in legacy. You want this place to last.'

'Exactly. The place, not me. It doesn't need a picture of me hanging around like Dorian bloody Gray. No, that's not the way to immortality.'

'I don't think there's any way to that.'

'Then why bother painting anyone at all?'

He had asked so casually about the core of my life's work that it took me a few seconds to reply.

'Like I said, it's a way of capturing the reality of a human life.' I spoke slowly, feeling my way. 'There are so many different versions of ourselves possible in our muscles. But when I've done my work well, most of those temporary versions are stripped away, and you see a little of the subject's inner life.'

'I thought there was no art to find the mind's construction in the face.'

'You can't tell what someone's planning. But you can tell what they are.'

'Sounds mystical.'

'Slightly.' Talking about my work had always felt like taking off a layer of skin, and Pemberley was better at creating the feeling than most people. I changed the subject. 'Do all the people here come from the Villages?'

Pemberley glanced at Angela Knight, and she gave me a patronising and confidential smile, as if I had said something impossibly stupid.

'We pride ourselves on taking people not from the Villages for the most part,' she said. 'The only people here who have spent much time there were in the service hubs. We want talented people from the whole spectrum of life.'

Pemberley cut across her. 'Joanna. Francis.' The young couple had been watching us like rabbits, and they snapped to attention now. 'Mind telling Ben how you came to be here?'

The pair told what I felt was a slightly sanitised version of their life before coming to the island. Joanna had been in a service kitchen, working across several Villages, and Francis had been an arable farmer. They had been allocated to the same cottage on their arrival, as all the cottages on the island had two rooms, but were now living together in one half of it.

Pemberley waved his fork. 'You see? People who have the skills to work in the Villages but can't afford a place there. That's who you'll find here.'

'You speak as though you like them more than the people who've made you rich.'

He shrugged. 'Villagers are fine. But you'd have to be stupid not to see that the Francises and Joannas of this world are worth more.' They looked like they could float from their seats with happiness.

Empty plates were taken away, fresh ones brought.

'So. What do you think of it?'

'Of the place?'

He rolled his eyes. 'No, the stew. Of course the place.'

'I don't quite understand the purpose of it. It feels like a world-in-parallel. And I don't understand the need to be all the way out here.'

Pemberley sighed. 'I'm sure you've read the literature, Ben. It's an attempt to create serious, useful technologies for the future while simultaneously leaving as light a footprint as possible on the poor bloody planet. We have small, versatile factories to help us produce the basics of life, we can combine those basics to make really quite complicated things with relatively few of us, and we have sufficient stores to provide anything else that might become necessary.'

'I see.'

'And as far as the need to be "out here" goes, I would say we are working on the model for another kind of life too, one lived in the natural world. People in the Villages get to live a better life and I'd like people in the cities to experience that too. I want to bring everyone with us. Unreasonable?'

'Not at all. But you haven't brought many people with you. To be honest, it feels to me like a larger version of a prepper place.'

He put his fork down, quite carefully, and I felt a sharp nudge in my leg from Bianca's side.

'Don't quite agree with you there, Parr.'

Perhaps the wine on the table had gone to my head, but whatever the cause, here I was, challenging Pemberley on his own terms, at his own table, and I felt confident in it. 'I don't see the difference. The preppers store things for themselves – you just said you keep stores here. They think the world might end. I'm sure the thought has occurred to you.'

'The end of the world.' He ran his tongue round the inside of his mouth. 'Funny phrase. Mostly people use it to mean a world without humans in it. So revealing. For most animals, what we think of as the end of the world would be a hitherto unimagined liberation. From being kept in a box, bludgeoned for your meat, having your habitat destroyed around you so some fool six thousand miles away can change his dining table. And we somehow define that as catastrophic.'

'That's as may be. But the preppers are doing the same as you. You're just operating on a bigger scale.'

'There is a significant difference.' Pemberley spoke softly. 'The prepper is retreating. This place is an advance. You see the difference?'

I shrugged, but he continued. 'The prepper hopes – pathetically – that if you store up enough supplies, you'll be able to just pick up your old life. Nobody has created anything like this place before. Nobody. You remember the people who ran to New Zealand during the last panic? Half of them died. One of them forgot the codes, locked himself out of his own fridge and starved six floors underground.' His cheeks had gained colour, and he took a drink of wine.

'Even so, you can see that—'

He cut me off. 'No, Parr, I don't see anything of the sort. There are men like me preparing their estates for the end of the world. They are preparing nothing but their own tombs. What have they thought of? A concrete bunker in some mountainside, living on tinned food, and then, after twenty years, you step out, to do ... what? Try to farm for the first time in your life? Repopulate the earth with your harem? Pathetic. Real wealth does not do that. Real wealth tills, and grows, and gardens, right now.' He looked around at the table, which had grown quiet, and moderated his voice. 'Real wealth works with others to produce something greater than any bunker. That makes sense, doesn't it?'

'It does. Yes.'

'Good. Because what you just said to me is an insult.'

I felt a prickle of unease, and was glad for the first time that Cara was not here to witness this conversation. 'I didn't mean to—'

'Forget it. Your first night here.' He turned to speak to Munro on his other side. The rest of the conversations around the table resumed, hurriedly, as if to conceal the fact that everyone else had been listening to Pemberley's speech.

I looked around me, alone suddenly. Pemberley was engrossed with Munro and Angela Knight. I was caught between mortification at how clumsily and needlessly I had offended him, and anger at his casual disrespect. Bianca avoided my gaze.

The long benches along the room cleared one by one, and eventually Pemberley stood. 'All right. That's enough for one night.'

Our party trailed through the hall behind him, as the table servants cleared the long benches. He moved past them, exchanging a joke or a comment here or there, and before long our group stood on the short flight of steps from the hall to the ground.

'All right, we're all accounted for. Goodnight, Munro. Francis, Joanna, such a pleasure. Look after that baby now. And young Mr Average' – he turned to me – 'where are you staying?'

'I'm not sure.'

'Well … Joanna, Francis, is there a spare room in your place? If you were originally allocated the cottage as singles?' They nodded with urgency; anything to help Sir John. 'All right, well, there you have it. You stay with these two tonight. Your things will be brought from the hospital.'

'I don't want to cause any trouble.'

'Bit late for that.'

I was still alarmed by the tension at dinner, and hoped I could improve matters with a few private words. I angled my body towards Pemberley, and he noticed and drew me back for a second. Angela Knight, on his other side, scowled.

'I really didn't intend to offend you earlier.'

'About what?' He was baiting me into apologising more explicitly. I reminded myself I was here to see Cara, not to sabotage her career.

'About the prepper idea. I clearly misunderstood the purpose of this place. I'm sorry.'

'Quite all right. Easy for false impressions to build up. Better to lance it now. Those people are my least favourite, you see.' His tone was calmer, and I felt confident.

124

'By the way, I didn't say before, but this building is beautiful.' I was minded to tell him I knew it, but Bianca was standing opposite us, and I remembered her frozen, horrified look when I had suggested mentioning Hillcrest to her father.

Pemberley looked at me. 'You like it?'

'I do. Is it based on anywhere?'

'My own invention.' There was a lie, and one I couldn't challenge him over.

'The mural at the end of the room is very striking.'

'The story of Fastitocalon. From the Book of Exeter.'

'I don't know that one.'

He looked towards the hall as he answered, and shadows filled the sockets of his eyes. 'A great beast. Lies in the sea looking like a spit of land, covered in weeds. Sailors moor their ships to him, and think themselves safe, and start a fire. And then he dives into the abyss, taking everyone with him, and swallows them at his leisure.'

'Not a very encouraging message for your residents.'

'On the contrary. It's something inevitable. It's like falling in love. No matter how something turns out, you must keep following the path you're on, into the abyss. You did that, coming here.'

'I suppose so.'

He turned back towards me. 'Cara didn't know you were coming, did she?'

'No. I feel pretty stupid now. Bianca said she's at the mainland estate. Is that right?'

'Where else would you imagine? I haven't sacked her, if that's what you're asking.' I felt great relief at that, and he continued.

'She'll be back before long. Why don't you take a couple of days here? Get that hand better. And then she'll be back and you can decide what to do together.'

If I had been asked earlier that day, I would have declined. I would have demanded to be taken straight to the mainland, to wherever Cara was, never mind my hand, never mind anything. But there was truth in what he said. By the time she got back here, I would be recovered. I might even have formed some kind of connection with Pemberley, the man she admired most in the world, and I could use it to regain her approval.

'That's a very kind offer,' I said.

'Then it's settled. Welcome. And Angela was wrong, you know, saying it was stupid to come here. It takes courage to do something like that.' He glanced towards the rest of the company. 'Goodnight, all. Angela, Munro: usual times tomorrow.' Then he turned and strode away, round towards the back of the hall, and was lost in the darkness.

12

At the cottage, I said goodnight to Francis and Joanna, suddenly feeling very weary after the sights of the day, and climbed the stairs to the plain bedroom they pointed me towards. I was exhausted, and my hand was throbbing under the bandages, but I lay awake for a while, thinking of Cara. I had to keep the sketch of her, the one now floating around the island's base, in my mind. I even found a plain notebook on a shelf downstairs and started drawing her anew, with my right hand. If I could re-create the original, I would be keeping her with me somehow. Yet no matter what I drew, no matter how many times I turned the page and started again, softened the features with the tips of my fingers, it seemed wrong. She was not there.

As I sketched, my mind slipped to the last time Cara and I had spoken. We had only had one conversation on the phone the whole time she was here on the island. I was in the flat, holding the phone with one hand and twisting the cord with the other, watching the steam rise off my coffee. The year had just begun to turn cold, and Cara had been with Pemberley a month. She had promised she'd phone within a week; I had been preparing angry things to say for another three. Soon enough, I told her she was abandoning the city, and she replied with anger.

'You're going to wait there your whole life, hoping things improve, even as you work for the people who have left. You want to stay where you are until you're the last person holding the country together.'

'I'm not the one who fucked up the country. He is.'

'Did he? Or did he provide a way out for a few people, people who—'

'People who could pay. Let's not pretend it's anything else, darling. He's a billionaire, and every year he grows richer, thanks to the underpaid people who service his bloody Villages and the wealthy people who buy in. It doesn't matter if he's nice to you. He's bad for the world.'

'That's absurd.'

'I mean it. He wrings everything he can out of tens of thousands of people on the mainland so he can play emperor with you and the rest of his staff. Why?'

'He has the willpower to change the world, Ben. You don't understand and I'm frankly not surprised. He's unique. But I knew you would disapprove.' Her voice shook. 'You disapprove of everything I do. Because you have the luxury of staying in your studio, painting away, creating art, while I'm out here earning, trying to create something meaningful. It's not fair. It's not *fair.*' At the last word, her voice cracked, but I stayed silent.

'Ben, you get to do work you love, and even when you think it isn't worthwhile, you're creating something new. When I'm working, it's usually for men who don't care about anything but themselves. But here, the man in charge is trying to do something good. He's built up all this money, he's changed the world, and now he's spending it keeping the world alive. And you *still* don't approve.'

I didn't respond for a minute, because there was nothing I could say. She was right. I just sat, thinking of the phone channel between us, the tiny thread linking me and her, and how nothing was travelling along it.

After a while, I heard the sound of the phone being muffled in her hand, and footsteps at the other end of the line. Eventually, after some indistinct words, she spoke.

'Sorry. That was the Knight woman again, reminding me of yet another mistake I've made.'

'She sounds difficult.'

'She hates me.'

'Really?'

'She wouldn't let anyone else see it, but I guarantee it. John's slowly appreciating that she's not fully capable of managing the business any more. He wants someone younger, someone who can run this place for years to come. She's started making mistakes, which is why she's trying so hard to criticise me. She's just Mrs Danvers, really.'

I wondered how much of this was true, and how much was her ambition speaking. 'So who does that make you? The new Mrs de Winter?'

'He doesn't fancy me, Ben. It's not even crossed his mind.' She sounded so tired of me.

'Of course. I'm sorry.' I wanted to say that I wished she wanted to be with me while she worked, but it had taken all my strength to build up to my earlier challenge, and it had come to nothing. She half answered me with what she said next, though.

'You know I've been waiting to find somewhere that might make the world a better place. This is it.'

'How can one man afford to do that?'

'You've seen the Villages, Ben. He's the wealthiest man on the continent. Maybe even in the world. The financial affairs are pretty complicated. But that doesn't matter. Angela is in charge of the historical stuff, and I'm helping with what comes next, with the future.'

'Won't he let you in on the past?'

'I've decided not to intrude, unlike everyone else. That's what it's like when you have someone this powerful. Everyone wants something from them.'

'I know I do.'

'What do *you* want from him?' She sounded surprised.

'You. I want you to come home to me.'

She laughed softly. 'I'll ring again in a week.'

'All right. Goodnight.' I added 'I love you', but too late, and it seemed probable she hadn't heard it as she moved to hang up the phone. She didn't call again.

The Sanctuary

I woke to the sun streaming through half-closed curtains. My second unfamiliar awakening in two days. Somewhere in the roof above me, baby birds were cheeping for their parents.

My clothes – my island clothes – were scattered on the floor where I had dropped them. My painter's roll was here, tucked inside the door. Someone must have brought it from the hospital. Apart from the bed, the room contained just a bedside stand, a wardrobe, a chair and a table. The table's drawer held a fresh bandage for my hand.

One of the room's doors led to a tiny bathroom; the other to the rest of the house. Through the window – the north window, I guessed from the sun – there was nothing but forest, larches and pines and aspens stretching as far as I could see.

The air was warm as I opened the window, and as I unwrapped my old bandage to change it, I heard the cries of birds unknown to me. No planes, no traffic, no swearing, no neighbours. I could be looking out over the world's distant past – or the distant future, when trees had churned the planet's concrete back to powder.

The cut across my palm was ugly, and it was uncomfortable to flex. I would soon be able to grip a paintbrush, though, and that was all that mattered.

After showering, I remembered my mainland clothes were missing. I thought of who I could ask – the staff at the hospital, maybe? – but when I looked in the wardrobe, I found it held more island clothes, in the same size as the ones I had been issued yesterday. They would do. What a very mainland concern,

I thought, to worry about clothes in a place like this. Then I reminded myself I *was* from the mainland. I'd be going home soon. With Cara.

There was a note pushed under the door, a folded square of cream paper. On the front someone had written, in a childlike scrawl, *We got this early. Hope you see it.* Inside was a note in a different hand – it looked educated, but slanted erratically back and forth.

Meetings literally all day so you'll have to amuse yourself. No more boat crashes, please. You'll be near top table for dinner tonight but probably not on it. See you afterwards. Enjoy the day. Not one person in a million gets to see this place.

   Bianca

Beyond the door, a woman's voice was singing an old song, soft and low. Joanna. She was sitting in a chair, folding a pile of clothes, and stopped to look up at me as I came downstairs. 'Good morning, duck.'

She told me where breakfast could be found – meals were provided over the road, in a communal kitchen for the eighty or so residents here. She said more, about what I might be able to get, but I had been distracted by the layout of the cottage.

Almost the whole ground floor was a single large living room. There were two armchairs, one on either side of a large fireplace, a few ornaments on the mantelpiece. The walls were covered in cream plaster interrupted by heavy wooden beams. The room had two staircases, each leading only to one bedroom, so there was no way of getting from my staircase to the other bedroom.

'Does everyone live in houses like these?'

'I wouldn't know, my dear. We've only been to a few hexes since we got here – visiting friends, you know how it is. But this seems pretty standard.'

'No kitchen?'

'No need. We have lots of shared facilities. We call it a library of rooms. Rather than eighty people each with their own laundry, we have a few machines. Rather than eighty kitchens, we have a hex kitchen. It lowers the costs, the space we need, all of it. Even the walls are bio.'

'Bio?'

'Bio-bricks. Made from the earth around us' – she patted the smooth plaster beside her – 'without cement or concrete. Just a chemical reaction to produce them. All designed to breathe with the world.' She beamed.

'It sounds very efficient.'

'Mostly it just makes sense. The place is so well insulated we don't even need to use the fire most of the time, even in winter. Imagine that.'

The only oddity in the cottage was a bulbous section on one side of the downstairs room, clearly a recent addition. It was a study, with bookshelves along one side and a desk and chair squeezed in with a low ottoman. A cold fireplace, clearly orna-mental, sat on the outer wall. The desk stood on a Turkish rug, pinning it down at all four corners – a curious placement – and there were notebooks on the shelves. It felt oddly like a city room.

'Is one of you a writer?'

She looked across at the study. 'That? Oh Lord, no. Not us, dear. That was the last fellow who lived here. Mad Thomas.'

'He sounds interesting.' I walked across to the extension and examined the bookshelves. This was the room I had stumbled into last night, where I had found the notebook to draw Cara. Every one of the notebooks I picked up was blank.

'Came here to produce a diary of the year, a guide to the island for residents. Lived with us for a while – this was his main home, but he moved around a lot, wanted to try every hex. John installed this office for him, trying to make him feel at home. Didn't work.'

'What happened?'

'Poor thing got sick and died.'

'He *died*?' I wasn't able to keep the surprise from my voice. Another death. I thought of the old man in Freborne, the man whose boat I had taken to get here. His son had died too. William Steensen, that was his name.

Joanna's mouth turned downwards as she spoke. 'Very sad case, Thomas. He was young – not more than thirty-five, I'd say. But he hadn't been happy here for a while.' She added the last thought brightly, as though it made things better, all things considered.

'Why was he unhappy?'

'He was a bit touched, if I'm honest. He would ask strange questions, like whether you ever noticed anything unusual, suspicious. Frank says he was paranoid, but that's not a nice thing to think of anybody if you ask me. He never liked anyone coming into the office, true, but we all need our spaces, I told Frank. That's perfectly natural.'

'Did he die in the cottage?' I thought of the clothes in my dresser upstairs. Had Thomas been my size?

'Oh, bless you, darling, no. He was off in the hospital for a while before that.'

'What did he die of?'

'Well, whatever it was, it wasn't catching. Doctors give you a really good look-over before you come, make sure you're as clean as possible. We hardly even have the common cold any more, Francis heard. Wouldn't it be something, if we had a world where nobody got colds any more because we were all here?'

I agreed it would be something.

'And they say we're going to be able to do wonderful things with genetics. Make sure we're as healthy as can be from the moment we're born. It's a hard life here – well, not hard exactly, but sort of tough, needs your effort and your love each day. But it's like there are all these advantages he's trying to put in – John, I mean – to make things easy along with the hard bits.' She gestured to her swollen belly. 'Do you know what I mean?'

I did, but I wanted to know more about Mad Thomas. Who had he been?

'Sure I don't know. Dead keen on his work, though. Arrived about a year ago, only lived with us a few months. But he couldn't see this place for what it was. Kept too many thoughts in his head, and then he'd let them out and start upsetting people. Everyone could see he wasn't happy. But it was a shame he got sick.'

'And you definitely don't know what of?'

'I know what you're thinking. You're worried about infection.' She nodded complacently. 'That bedroom, sharing it. Well, don't you worry. They did a sweep of the whole room. Went through all his notebooks too, just in case of any contamination. They said that by the time the next resident got here, there wouldn't be a single fingerprint.'

'That must have been very reassuring.'

'That's how we know Cara. She was in charge of making the hex safe to return to. We had to stay in a hex for over a week with some of the indoor farmers. That's when I was just pregnant. Often how it goes, someone dies as someone gets born. Although we're lucky. Most of us are so young, I haven't heard of any other deaths in my time here.'

'Did they bury him here?'

'Oh, I don't know. I didn't go to the funeral.'

'Why not?'

'They said they'd do it privately. Anyway, it wouldn't have been very joyful.'

When she stood from the chair she had been sitting in, folding, I saw for the first time how far gone she was, and when I asked, she told me seven months.

'Do they have provision here? For babies, I mean?'

'Oh, John's very good about babies. Keeps reminding us we'll have everything provided. The medical hex is half maternity as far as I can tell. That's what I mean about him doing everything to make us feel safer and happier. You see?'

I saw.

She told me to go and get breakfast over the way, and I did. At this hour it was still cold enough to see your breath outside; Joanna had been telling the truth about the clever insulation of the cottages.

This hex consisted of about forty similar cottages; in the middle was a grass area with a few communal buildings standing on it. One was a long, low canteen with glass walls. Francis was there, sitting at a crowded bench, but when he saw me arrive, he stood and showed me where to queue. The young woman behind the counter greeted me by name; Francis explained that he'd already told her about me. No payment was required.

Once I had my tray – thick earthenware mug of tea, plate of eggs and toast – Francis left his friends and sat with me. He was several years younger than me, I could tell, but stronger, more weather-beaten too. His face was almost split in three by a broad moustache cutting off the lower third and huge black eyebrows the upper. Beneath the brows his eyes looked sunken and hollow, like caves under a mossy overhang.

'All our food is provided. I know what you're thinking, it's probably all stew like you had last night. It's not. Jo and her lot in the kitchens help keep it varied. It's a marvel, what they provide with what we grow.'

'This place is very well thought out.'

He grinned. 'Don't be surprised. John spent decades improving his Villages on the mainland, and he doesn't even live in them. He spent two whole years just working on the design of the hexes, making sure they were right, before he started building.

And then once he'd perfected the design, all the homes were done in six months. He's a genius.'

'Does he live in one himself?'

A shake of the head. 'No. He lives apart, in the woods. Helps him think, withdrawing from the place. Sometimes goes missing for a few days, few weeks even, then he turns up again with fifty ideas. Makes us jump, I can tell you.'

I gestured around at the room, the lights, the ovens behind the canteen counter. 'How's this all powered?'

'Mix of things. Solar, wind. And they use the electricity for green hydrogen once they've done that. Don't ask me how. Not my line.'

'But there's a grid?'

'Course there's a grid. How do you think they got the power to cook that lot?' He nodded at my plate. 'It used to be powered by fossils but John stopped all that over a decade ago. Found it embarrassing, he said, being powered by the dead stuff. Says it's like spending the capital instead of the interest.' I thought of my schooling and the long-dead plants and animals that had paid for it, and I liked Pemberley a little more.

'Do you see him a lot?'

'He's always around here and there. Did a shift with us in the arables a couple months ago.'

'He works on island tasks?'

'Course he does. Spends a few hours each day doing some-thing, in the afternoons. Might be in the workshop, keeping the carts going; might be doing a shift in the design lab; might just be driving a plough. He loves it here. And he's very particular you just call him John. He doesn't want "sir", he doesn't want "Sir John" least of all.'

'Do you think I could join you for your work today?' I hadn't been told what I could and couldn't do with my time while I waited for Cara, and this might show me what life was like here. Either it would be as good as she had said in her letters, or – I found myself hoping – I would see what was wrong with it and persuade her to leave with me.

Francis looked at me with polite scepticism. 'Done any labouring before? Agriculture, I mean?' He added the last as though he thought I would be offended at the implication I might have never done a day's physical work in my life.

'I'm afraid not.'

'What about that?' He nodded at my bandaged hand.

'It probably rules me out for anything very difficult. Then again, I imagine you'd ruled me out for anything difficult anyway.'

He smiled, and evidently concluded that politeness trumped utility as far as I was concerned. 'Suppose you could come along. Not got much technical stuff planned this morning, at least. Yeah. Extra pair of hands very welcome.'

We went back to the cottage to get ready. I washed, quickly, at the basin in my little bathroom, and back downstairs noticed an old radio on the shelf.

'Does this work?'

Joanna was stowing the laundry in a low pine chest. 'I think so, my love, but don't tell me if there's anything upsetting. Bad for baby.'

I turned it on. It was one of the old-fashioned models with a dial, scaling and descending the wavelengths, stopping at outposts of civilisation along the way. I found some pop music and eventually some news, but the words came to me faintly: 'New queen ... urged everyone to remain calm ... duration of the difficult period, we will be introducing measures ...'

The static blew in again, like a flurry of snow, and standing in the cottage, watching the lazy motes of dust sinking through the sunlight, I realised it didn't matter too much whether I heard the words or not.

Francis was standing by one of the carts, keeping a space for me. The other seats were filled by more young men and women in practical farming clothes, and they talked to each other in low voices as the cart moved off between the trees. The forest blurred past, and the only sound apart from the whine of the engine and the quiet conversations was the birds chattering above us. Nobody else paid attention as Francis and I talked.

He explained that the outdoor and indoor farming operations were completely separate. Outdoor was for grain crops, and was designed to produce the maximum yield on a minimum of the island's land. Indoor grew a much broader range, mostly in oxygen-rich tunnels, warmed by hydrogen.

I still wanted to know more. 'But he – Pemberley – can't seriously hope to make the island self-sufficient. Surely you couldn't grow everything you need on an island this size? And what about all the stuff you can't grow? I mean – this cart. Rubber in the wheels, all the electronics ...'

Francis shrugged. 'He looks far ahead. He's imported a lot of materials we need in small quantities, for example. A few weeks ago he told us we have everything we need for the next ten thousand years. That's as long a time as has passed since people first started farming, ever. And he says we have the resources to live well in that time. I believe him.'

I asked a couple more questions about the practicalities of life here, with all the scepticism I could express without seeming rude, but he wouldn't be drawn.

As we moved, I saw a field covered by an array of translucent gleaming tunnels, tangled like dragon's guts. Francis pointed. 'The indoor lot. Growing hundreds of species over there, they are. No soil.' The tubes seemed to be writhing, until I realised they were full of figures in similarly pale suits, crawling around inside, looking no larger than weevils. 'They're the clever end of the game. But nobody's more or less important than anyone else here.'

'Apart from John.'

I was surprised to see Francis gesture, equivocal.

'He always says he won't be here for ever. He knows we'll have to be ready to take over some time. Hey, here's something you won't regret seeing.' He pointed out to the left, the southwest, and I leaned over to follow the line of his arm.

The structure was concrete, but it was coloured a gentle green instead of grey, and the harsh angles of its shape had been softened by the camouflage. It reminded me of ziggurats hidden beneath the rainforest, but this had clearly been built in the last couple of decades, designed to blend in. It must have been ten storeys high, and although oblong at its front, it bent at strange angles as it receded into the forest, so you couldn't easily tell how large it might be. There were no windows.

'What is it?'

'Seed vault. If there's a plant that grows on this earth, there is enough of it kept in there to restore it to life across the world, if we do it right. It's almost finished, too. Got two whole hexes of people just logging the things in there, keeping the temperatures right, humidity, soil content, all of it. Every time you hear about a plant going extinct on the mainland, you can be assured John's done his best to bring it here first.'

I had heard of these things before on the mainland, but for Pemberley to have one all of his own – a second copy of the world, all here – seemed too fantastical to believe. The breadth of his vision thrilled me against my will. 'Is it just plants?'

'This one is. There's one for animals over on the east coast. Not whole animals, you understand, but tissue samples and so on. He's got almost two million species in that one.'

The cart was slowing now. The road here undulated in and out, and we let a few people off every few hundred metres. Francis and I were the last ones off. Once we disembarked, we walked down a long tunnel of trees as the cart glided silently away.

The valley opened before us, and he pointed out the field we needed to get to. Above us, a bird of prey was gliding back and forth in sunlight clear enough to cast a crisp shadow on the ground.

'What are we doing this morning?'

'Stake-banging.'

Francis explained that we needed to fence off a particular field from another. The 'banger' was a huge metal canister, open at one end, with a handle welded on each side. I would hold the stakes at the right point in the ground; Francis would heave up the banger by the handles and hammer the stake home. He was polite enough to pretend he needed the help, and we talked as we went.

'Is there really enough food for you all here?'

'Nobody's starving, and we hardly bring any from the mainland. You heard John last night.'

I was so used to the news on the mainland – food imports rising, starvation threatened overseas, food airlifted in as a last resort – that the idea of this place being free of such afflictions felt magical.

'You see,' Francis said, grunting as he lifted the banger, 'the island has an unusually warm climate' – *bang* – 'so it's suitable for growing crops' – *bang* – 'and thanks to the tunnels, we're not dependent on outdoor farming anyway.' *Bang*. He hauled the canister off. 'And John says it's only going to get better as the century goes on. We use very efficient varietals. And we don't eat meat. That helps too.'

'It's amazing.'

We moved on to the next stake-hole.

'I know. Right now, we're technically in a phase that used to be called the Hungry Gap, not that it applies to us any more. A long time ago – centuries, I mean – that was the period when the previous year's fresh food had run out and the new year's hadn't come through yet. No fruits, no autumn vegetables. On the mainland, the gap gets filled with imports from other parts of the world, and you're careful not to ask what happens over there to the people whose food gets carried away. Here we have such a good tunnel system, it doesn't matter what time of year it is.'

'Does anyone ever get sick of life here? Does anyone leave?'

'Can't think of anyone.'

Immediately I thought of Cara – why had she left, then? – then of what Joanna had told me before I left the cottage this morning.

'I was hearing about your previous house guest.'

'Oh. Mad Thomas.' Francis grimaced. 'Yeah, he didn't get it. You have to remember we're all building it' – I recalled the phrase from last night – 'and he didn't.' He pursed his lips as if remembering the ingratitude of Thomas.

'What was he writing?'

'Dunno. He was a difficult customer. Kept claiming he'd help around the house, then disappeared back to his bloody hidey-hole to scribble. Stayed up late half the night rearranging the furniture. I don't mind the idea of creatives coming here, you understand' – Francis had clearly remembered, rather too late, the nature of my own work – 'but they have to contribute something.'

'And he didn't.'

'Never saw a word of it. More like a poser, if you know what I mean. He had a tattoo of a book on his wrist – wanted the look all right, but never had the guts to finish the work.' But if he had scribbled so much, where had the work gone? Francis finished another stake and heaved the banger onto his shoulder. 'Anyway. Enough on him. What are you here for?'

'I'm waiting for Cara. She'll be coming back soon.'

'She invite you?'

'Not quite.'

I explained the circumstances, and once I had finished, he turned to me, incredulous. 'You came all this way because she wrote short letters?'

'It wasn't like that. It was ...' It was hard to explain. It had meant a lot, standing in our flat on the mainland, to receive that note the week before our anniversary. 'It felt like she'd made a choice I thought she shouldn't make alone. She wasn't being honest.'

'Do you see now why she might not want to go home?'

I looked around. The sun was blushing through cloud to our south, and around us the valley was crawling with activity. Some distant figures kneeled in a furrow as if at prayer. There was a quiet hum from a large agricultural machine in one of the bigger fields to my right.

'I think I understand it better.'

'Probably wasn't anything to do with you.'

I understood now that the choice I'd been asking her to make – life here, or life with me in the crowded, difficult city – was stark. I couldn't see a way of persuading her that city life would be better, even with me; yet the prospect of returning to the flat without her, to spend my days painting alone, was unbearable.

'If you ask me, you'd be better off living here together. You never know, John might find a use for you. He did for me.'

'How so?'

Francis sighed. 'What I told you yesterday at dinner, about how I came here – it wasn't everything. At the time, I was …' he waved his hand in a vague swirling gesture, 'confused. Five years ago I was a very different man. I was twenty – servicing a Village farm, beets for sugar – but I was drinking. I was fighting. One night I got in the car and nearly killed a villager who'd left the walls for a walk.'

'Where did Pemberley come into it?'

'They fixed up the villager I knocked over, and the Tomorrow Trust told him they would deal with me. They brought me here, to see John. Just me and him.' He smiled at the memory of being the focus, just for a moment, of Pemberley's attention. 'He told me I had a choice. I could take my chances with the authorities in the city, and I'd never see daylight again, or I could come here and help him build this place.'

Francis paused, glanced at my expression, then continued. 'I know what you're thinking. He helped me avoid the justice of the land. But I never had much faith in that myself. And he made me into a better person. Look at me now. John told me the only interesting act of your life is the second one, because that's when you're responding to what you were before. So I owe him my life. And every good thing I do now is because I'm not rotting in some jail, or hanged.'

'Redemption on earth.'

'Call it what you like. He saved me.'

'Did you not' – I had to be delicate here – 'have any feelings about him or the company before?'

147

'Why would I?'

'He created these Villages. The inequality in your life was thanks to him.'

He looked blank, so I continued.

'Pemberley has earned a hundred fortunes from those places. And they're impossible to get into unless you're already wealthy. It's the comfortable class pulling up the ladder behind them.'

'I wouldn't have had work if it wasn't for the Villages. And we got paid fairly. Did you ever work in one?'

'I worked for the people who lived in them, and I was never very impressed. I didn't think much of the whole system.'

Francis shook his head, angrily, like I'd released a wasp into it. 'Clearly we disagree. Let's just leave it at that.'

I had no desire to seem like another Mad Thomas so early in my stay, so I changed the subject. 'The other people here. Did they all come here the same way? After incidents like yours?' The image occurred to me of an island of escapees, an entire population fleeing mainland justice.

Francis laughed at the question, sudden and loud, and kept laughing. Eventually he calmed down, and wiped a huge hand across his face. 'Seen my Joanna? Think she's a criminal, eh?'

'No, I wasn't implying—'

'And your Cara? She run anyone down?'

'No, I suppose not.'

'This isn't a prison island, Ben. Most people here have done wrong in their lives, but that's true of everyone in the world, I imagine yourself included. People end up here all sorts of ways. Some people are here because they messed up, like me. Some were victims, some just knew this was where they would feel most at home. Your Cara sounds like one of those people. The only common factor is that it's a place where we can try again.'

I thought of Cara, and wondered why she needed a second start in her life. And I thought of what I had achieved in my own life so far: the Bywaters with their new portrait, and the dozens of other paintings, of various degrees of dishonesty, around the country with my signature in the corner. A thought occurred to me: *you need that too.*

Francis had some more complex tasks he didn't need me for, so he told me to head north. I could make it to the point they called the Southern Summit – the highest point on the lower half of the island – and back, if I kept moving.

The valley was long behind me now, and I was back among thick trees, walking up a steep slope. To my left was a face of rock, folded over into enormous grey pillows, swathed with a veil of green. There were ferns tucked into any crack they could find, lichens covering the huge slabs, and even a hardy tree or two growing from the fissures between the stones. Everywhere life was hammering itself into whatever gaps were available.

The road was so narrow here, only one of the island's carts could move along it with ease. I kept my ears open for the sound of a quiet electric whine coming in the opposite direction, in case of accident. Every time I was unsure of myself on a road, I thought of my father.

I wished I could have told him about my journey here. He would have approved of the gesture – a daring rescue, an enjoyable tilt at a windmill too large to damage, and therefore safe in some inexplicable way. He might have thrived here. If anyone needed a second act, it was him.

So Pemberley supported lawbreakers; helped them escape their pasts. He had left poor Kevin Ladd's wife so traumatised she had lost her reason at the mention of his name. The old man in Freborne, Steensen, seemed to hold him responsible for the death of his son. He had wrecked the mainland with his Villages, so the only hope the young had was to serve the old.

And yet ... yet this place seemed so benign. He had saved the seabirds, created this world, was protecting animals and plants the world would have let die. And Cara had been so happy here. She wasn't the kind to be fooled by easy promises.

The summit was clear ahead of me now, and the vegetation had started to shrink from the winds that must whip the island's top. To my left was a winding stair up the rock, and a small wooden sign, with the letters SOUTH SUMMIT roughly chiselled out.

The steps were narrow and slippery; the ill-maintained stones had been worn down by rain, perhaps by feet too. Their age was indeterminate. This place was new and old all in one: Neolithic history, trees planted two centuries ago, and the new civilisation on top. I wondered which Pemberley valued most.

To the south, the hub was a distant matchbox; the seed vault was another. The hexes were tiny roulette wheels scattered across the view. I could not see the southern coast from where I stood. One lone wisp of smoke over to the east suggested something industrial, but I saw no wheels of hexes. In fact, on my tours with Bianca and Francis, the east was the one area I hadn't seen.

To the west was a miniature forest of turbines in the sea, as thin as razor blades. And before me, to the north, the island stretched out, even wilder than the landscape I had left, green and lush. I saw no signs of human life.

The only feature of the platform I stood on was a squat monument, a low stone obelisk positioned at the centre. Around the top there was a curved plaque of brass, and some Roman numerals, a date from nearly thirty years ago. It said: *WE SHALL INHERIT THE EARTH*.

I stood there for some time. All I remember thinking was that I could see why Cara had chosen to come here. Here, you could see the world might not be ending. Pemberley had created far more than I had given him credit for.

I remembered that my father's left hand had been injured in the accident that killed him. One more thing in common. I peeled off the bandage experimentally. The injury, a long cut stretching from one side of the palm to the other, had mended a little even since I woke. I left the bandage off. The island air would help me heal.

I didn't get back to Francis and Joanna's cottage until after five.

I washed in the bathroom, changed, and returned downstairs to explore the place in solitude. I looked at Mad Thomas's desk, then sat before it, experimentally, as if Thomas himself might emerge from a drawer to tell me the island's secrets. What had he been writing? I already knew the notebooks he'd left behind were empty. I felt the undersides of the shelves, the base of the bookcase, in case he had concealed something. No.

At least I could keep his paper to sketch on. I had already thought of asking Francis and Joanna to sit for me. Then I realised I had no idea what I would do with the sketches once I had returned to the city. Not just that – I had no idea what I would do at all if I returned without Cara. I had come here to find her, of course, but looking back now, I realised perhaps I had also come because my life in the city had lost its meaning.

That was the first moment I wondered whether I might stay on the island once Cara returned. It was absurd. There was no place for me here. But the residents I'd met so far were undeniably admirable. They were building a future together. Cara's notes had shared that tone too, of simple, radiant purpose. And what Francis had told me about Pemberley – the waifs and strays he took in – had impressed me, more than I wanted to admit.

I stood from Thomas's desk and left the cottage, to walk to the hub for the evening meal.

I saw Francis first when I got there. He was standing above Joanna, who sat on the grass slope of the hub, her hands on her belly. I wished I could paint them like that. He helped her carefully to her feet, and we went in together.

We were close enough to the top table to see who was gathered there; as Pemberley swept past us on his way to the centre of the room, I was sure he looked directly at me. There were no words of address to the room this evening.

I spent the meal – huge slices of pie, full of mushrooms and some unidentified meat replacement – talking to Francis and Joanna and their colleagues. The first was Anya, an engineer who had applied to stay on the island for six months in her early twenties. That was four years ago, and she was now involved in maintaining the road network. When I asked how they made the roads glow their gentle blue, she only smiled.

The others were Sumara, an irrigation specialist; Mat, a short but robust young man who worked shifts on security and ate with astonishing speed; and Shay, who worked in sanitation and told me she would only go into details of her work after dinner, for my sake. The four of them had all been put in a training cohort with Francis and Joanna recently, where island residents learned from each other's skills.

The meal passed quickly. Francis teased me about being a hope-less stake-banger, and then related the story of how I had asked whether everyone on the island was a criminal, to much amuse-ment. That turned the conversation to their stories of how they had come here. Almost all of them had a story of hardship followed by deliverance. Shay had been in an abusive relationship, living in terror of her husband; Mat had been addicted to gambling, tun-nelling into ever-greater debt; Sumara had become homeless after coming out to her family and had nowhere left to turn.

They had come from different countries, different backgrounds, yet in each case, they had made their way to Pemberley's firm, the Tomorrow Trust, via its web of charitable outposts, support groups and apprenticeships around the world. And Pemberley had personally saved each one of them. He had brought Shay's partner to the attention of the police; had helped Mat get clean of his habit; had found Sumara secure work in a Village before offering her a place here. Only Anya, the engineer, seemed to have arrived here free of any mainland trauma. But whatever the genesis of their journey, they all loved Pemberley.

After the meal, there was a moment where everyone fell silent, and in the gap Francis spoke again. 'You see what I mean about this place, Ben?'

I told him I thought I did, then turned when I sensed someone at my shoulder: Bianca. She greeted everyone by name, and traded a few comments with them before turning to me.

'Are you free for a drink?'

'I think so.'

'Great. Wait out front afterwards and I'll take you to the lodge.'

'We all invited?' This was Francis, grinning, and the others gave a little cheer.

'Sorry, Frank. This one's just for Sailor Ben.' Noises of mock-disappointment followed.

'Careful he doesn't drown you all.'

'The man's a liability.'

'All right, all right.' She turned back to me. 'Great. See you shortly.' And with that she was gone, greeting others as she returned to the top table. Past her, I saw Pemberley and Angela Knight deep in conversation.

'What did that mean?' I addressed the table in general; Francis was the one who replied.

'Very exciting. The lodge isn't for just anybody.'

'That's the home of the man who used to own the island. What was it, Francis? Effingham?'

'Fellingham. He built a home in the woods back when he was in charge, huge rambling place, and John lives in the surviving parts. He won't rebuild it, either.'

'I heard that too,' Shay said. 'It could be a palace if he wanted. But he doesn't want a palace. He wants to see us all living within our means.'

'Exactly.' Sumara's eyes shone. 'That's this whole place. Finally we're living within our means.'

At the front of the building ten minutes later, Bianca enjoyed hearing what the others had said about the lodge.

'Not far off, I suppose. Fellingham did build it and lots of it is pretty far gone now.'

I followed her. At the back of the hall, where the trees pressed up almost to the brickwork, was a slim path into the woods. It shone with the same faint blue light as the other roads, but this was narrower, a winding ribbon in the dark.

We walked single file, in silence. The woods on either side were thick, but occasionally I noticed another strip of pale blue leading off to the left or the right, and sometimes the trees receded a metre or two, to reveal a patch of gravel and a stone bench. The air was thick with the noises of insects and birds; frogs bellowed to each other across the path. It felt like we were approaching the island's heart.

After perhaps twenty minutes, the woods folded outwards on either side, revealing an open space of an acre or so, and at its centre, the lodge; John Pemberley's home.

Bianca stopped, gestured with a little flourish. 'What do you think?'

The Sanctuary

The lodge was an austere building of stone, two storeys high only, but those storeys were tall; the whole building looked like it had been stretched upwards by a giant hand. It was in poor condition – chunks of stone had collapsed from the exterior, and many lay on the ground in the moonlight as though the storm that had ripped them off had just abated. On the right was a low glasshouse, which seemed to have a tree bursting through the top of it. The building looked peaceful and overgrown; like the site of a battle a century on, if it weren't for the windows blazing with light, and the dozen faint conversations drifting to us across the grass.

'It's remarkable.'

A figure stood outside the building on the north side, lit from behind between the cool, dark stones of the porch, his breath condensing in the night air. Pemberley himself. He was holding a drink up to the light, looking through it towards the stars, and smiled at us as we approached.

'Good evening, Sailor Ben. Thought we'd better have Cara's friend here. Make sure he feels welcome so she doesn't give me a bollocking when she gets back.' To Bianca he gave only a nod.

We stepped through the enormous, heavy front door onto flag-stones the size of dining tables, and on through a high, empty corridor full of ancient-looking plants and ferns – some sprouting from thick terracotta pots as high as my hip, others apparently growing directly from the walls.

I was the first to speak. 'Fellingham must have loved this place.'

John replied swiftly. 'He hated it. Had it built then went back to the mainland after two nights.'

I gestured at the huge plants around us. 'These are striking.'

He ran a thick, loving finger along one of the giant fronds. 'Fellingham wanted a conservatory. I've turned the whole place into one.'

We passed more closed doors. Our destination was the glass chamber I had seen from outside the house. It was a huge room lined with floor-to-ceiling windows on two sides, warmed by a fireplace large enough to roast a boar, and filled with chairs of various degrees of decrepitude, around which twenty or thirty people were standing in twos and threes. There were more plants here, growing along the ceiling beams and up the window frames; the tree I had seen from outside had its own special pit in the brickwork. I walked with Pemberley towards the fire.

'Have a drink.' A tray appeared. 'You know everyone here.' Munro, the security head, nodded at me, as did Angela Knight. I found a seat at Pemberley's left hand.

'Father, I wondered if ...' Bianca hovered at his right shoulder, and there was an awkward moment when everyone in the circle except Pemberley himself knew she was there. Eventually he realised, and twisted in his seat. 'Father, I wondered if tonight the guests might like—'

'Bianca, for the last time, that's enough Father this and Father that. You'll make everyone think you're getting special treatment. Clear?'

Her voice dropped, and the light in her eyes dulled. 'Yes, it's clear.' In the background, Munro rolled his eyes at her sullenness, then caught Knight's eye with a smirk.

'Good. What was it you wanted?'

'Nothing.'

'Nothing what?'

She seemed to remember something just in time. 'Nothing, John.'

'All right then. I'll see you tomorrow.' He swivelled back to the rest of us, turning off her presence, and she hovered there a second before stepping back and leaving, her walk quite steady.

'Sorry about Bianca. Trying to drum the hereditary principle out of her. Only taken twenty-five years so far. She'll get the hang of it soon.' He barked with laughter, which the others echoed. 'Now. What are we talking about?'

'We're discussing a little thought experiment,' Knight said.

'Go on.'

'The oak trees on this earth are dying.'

'That's not a thought experiment. They are,' Pemberley said.

Knight nodded. 'Granted. So: here's a button.' Her hands twitched in her lap as though she really held it. 'The button kills almost every oak tree in the world. Only one oak in a thousand is left alive. But while the button does that, it also guarantees the ones that remain will survive, healthier than ever before.'

'It guarantees the survival of the species at the cost of the individuals.'

'Yes.'

'You're asking whether it's right to press the button. Guaranteed harm now, to stop a potentially greater harm in future.' Pemberley breathed heavily for a few seconds. That was something I had noticed at dinner yesterday; he breathed like a bull. 'You know what? Let's see what Ben here thinks.'

159

'Me?' The eyes of everyone in the circle swivelled to me; some bored, some scornful. Pemberley himself seemed amused.

'The floor is yours, Ben. Now that you've decided to stay with us a while longer, to see if you can stand the pace of life here.' He said the last words with gentle mockery.

'What's the question? Would I press the button?'

'I think the terms need a little definition. But we're talking about the principle. Yes.'

'Surely it depends on whether you trust the button-maker.'

Knight spoke up, disdainful. 'It's a thought experiment. Obviously you trust them.'

'Then I'd press it.' That surprised her and Pemberley alike, but it impressed him too, I could tell.

'Very cavalier. You don't know what invention someone might come up with in the next few years, something to save many more of the oaks currently standing. You limit your options dramatically by pressing the button now.'

'But the situation is truly grave. Ms Knight herself said so. And because she's asked me to, I trust her.'

She was frowning at me, and her next words dripped with dislike. 'Could you really cope with spending the rest of your life as the person who pressed the button?'

I smiled at her. 'My moral choice is a luxury in this situation, and it's one the rest of the world can't afford. Not after older generations have wasted so much time.'

Pemberley drank, then put his glass down and wagged his finger.

'Clever man. Cara chose wisely.' He leaned back, pushing himself further into the collapsed cushions of the sofa. 'You know, Ben, I was thinking about you today. About our conversation over dinner, about your work. Do you really think there's a point to it?'

'Of course I do.'

He was trying to bait me again, I knew, because he shrugged almost to the point of rudeness at my assertion. 'Well, what is it? Apart from cosmetic surgery on canvas?'

'As I said yesterday, you're showing people who they are. You're showing them an aspect of themselves even they might not have noticed before.'

'People ever complain?'

'It doesn't matter. History's full of people who have hated their portraits. Churchill disliked one portrait of him so much his wife burned it. Theodore Roosevelt did the same. Gertrude Stein hid hers away.'

'And I suppose you would claim these people were reacting to some truth about themselves the artist had spotted and to which they objected.'

'It doesn't have to be a great truth. It could be as simple as showing someone they're older than they think. Or not as benevolent as they seem.'

Pemberley met my eyes and held my gaze until I looked down, then spoke again. 'But beyond this mystical painter bond, I'm still stuck on what the point is, given that even the best paintings last only a few centuries.'

'We still enjoy Rembrandt, Leonardo, Caravaggio. Their works tell us about the deepest recesses of the heart from half a millennium away. Is that not long enough for you?'

'Not especially, no. Microfilm lasts five hundred years. Bianca told me that when she bought her bloody newspapers. Longer than most paintings have stayed the course. Anyway, it's not about whether your name is remembered or what you look like. It's about what you build during your time on this earth. Example: almost all the paintings of Fellingham are lost. Nobody cares. But this house should last another few hundred years, and the forest for thousands. Fellingham built something and it lasted.'

'I thought this place was all about not leaving an impact for centuries after we die. Isn't that the point of this whole society? Isn't that the whole point of all this composting and biodegrading and whatever else you're doing here?' My voice was a little louder than it should have been.

Pemberley smiled. 'That's a good point, except when you remember the impact doesn't have to be a painting, or a house, or any of these pointless baubles we surround ourselves with. Have you seen the rat traps around the place?'

'Bianca showed me one.'

'Well, knowing her, she probably forgot the main point of the story, which is that there are four species of bird alive today that wouldn't have been if Angela here hadn't done something about the rats.' He nodded at Knight, who gave him her twisted half-smile of acknowledgement. 'You know what proportion of bird and reptile extinctions are down to rats?'

'I don't.'

'Six in ten. And who spreads rats? We do. So taking them out of the equation somewhere . . . that's an impact for hundreds of years, right there. It's work that lasts. More important, it's work where nobody needs to remember the name of the people who did it.' If I had thought he was breathing heavily before, I had been wrong. Now he sounded volcanic. 'And there are thousands more species on the edge now, thousands more Nalas limping towards destruction. Do you see what I'm saying?'

'You're saying my work is pointless because canvases fade. But what if my pictures show people who they really are and inspire them to do this miracle work you're talking about?'

'I think it won't make one iota of difference. And another thing, I think you're only going to end up painting yourself. I don't think artists can help putting themselves into their work.'

'I'd welcome the chance to prove how wrong you are.' That pushed him back.

'How *wrong* I am?'

Knight appeared delighted at this misstep. Munro was giving me a parade-ground look of disgust.

'Dead wrong. There is always merit in showing a leader their own face.' There was a beat of silence. 'Why don't I paint you?' I didn't lower my eyes this time, and he kept his on me.

He laughed. 'I don't think you're serious.'

'You don't have to show the portrait to anyone. You can keep it locked away somewhere on this island. You can burn it if you like. But if I get it right, you'll see who you really are.'

Pemberley's whole attention was directed at me.

Munro interjected. 'Why don't we just have a break from this—'

'We don't tend to do very well with creatives,' Pemberley said. 'Ange, what was that writer fellow called? Hated it, went loopy, then pegged out.'

She almost glared at him. 'I don't recall.'

He shrugged and turned his attention back to me. 'Do you have a fee?'

'I do, but ...'

'... but I'm wealthier than the usual client. I know. You'll need to adjust upwards. Wouldn't be the first time.'

'It's not that. This place isn't about money and I don't want you to think that's what motivates me.'

He rubbed his jaw. 'All right. I think by now you know how much Cara loves working here. The fee I will pay is ... the cost of a permanent spot here, when she returns from the mainland. A cottage for you both, and work for you. If you're interested.'

'You mean that?'

'Of course. If you don't like it here after you've finished painting me, you can go home, first class all the way. Cara can go with you if she's so inclined as well. But I think there's something about this place you find very appealing, Ben. Correct me if I'm wrong.'

'It has a certain interest.' I hated that I couldn't contradict him. Because suddenly I wanted this, very much.

He shrugged. 'Take until seven tomorrow morning to decide. If you really need to. Come back here then.'

As I stood and left the circle, Knight and Munro watched me go with a mixture of disdain and amusement, like a pair of elderly relatives tolerating the foibles of the younger generation.

The Sanctuary

The air of the corridor was clear of smoke, and the huge stones of the lodge's wall were refreshingly cool after the wilting heat of the glass room. Before me, the chorus of insects and amphibians continued their nightly observances.

Pemberley was building a future here, the kind of new world that seemed impossible back in the city. His people here appeared to believe in it as much as he did. Life was so much better here than in the city, or his sterile Villages, the places that – I must keep reminding myself – had paid for this one. This wasn't real, I remembered; it was only the tip of a pyramid of inequality that Pemberley himself had constructed. And yet, and yet ... The air was fresher, the vegetation more green and lovely. Even the few drops of rain that brushed me as I stood there seemed somehow welcoming.

As I turned to pull the door of the lodge shut behind me, I heard a quick, small movement from inside, like the sound of light footsteps moving away.

I walked slowly, and somehow she was already ahead of me, lying on a low stone bench in a curve of the path. Bianca. As I approached, she sat upright and looked at me without expression.

'You're going to do it.'

'How do you know? You weren't there. Not in the room, anyway.'

'There's a spot on the floor above. It's easy to hear exactly what's being said around the fireplace if you lie in the right place.' I saw her then, lying on the floor upstairs at the lodge, just to hear a conversation she wasn't welcome at, and felt terribly sad for her. 'Going to be the court painter?'

'I would have thought you'd be glad. Maybe I'll paint you.'

'I doubt it.'

'Why's that?'

'You'll hear soon enough. My character is difficult.'

'Doesn't seem like it to me. But if they think so, why not leave?'

She laughed shortly. 'Yes, why not leave? I hope your paintings aren't as simple as you are.'

I ignored that. 'Perhaps he's harder on you than he is on other people. It's often the case with fathers. I expect you'll be in charge one day.'

She shook her head. 'He doesn't want me inheriting.'

'Why not?'

'Because this place would turn into just the hippy commune it gets caricatured as.' Her voice was deeper, and I realised she was imitating her father. 'The crops would rot, the lights would go off and we'd revert to the status of animals. We need competent people running this place. People who can adjust to all the disasters you get when you're trying to establish a civilisation.'

'Is that what he's doing then? Establishing a civilisation?'

She looked at me as if deciding whether it was worth explaining anything more, and clearly opted against it. She stood.

'My cottage is through here.' She gestured along a narrow path I hadn't seen before.

'That's good to know.'

The Sanctuary

'Come for a drink?' She started along the path, and then turned back to look at me. The light of the moon was in her hair, and gleaming on her cheek. She was quite beautiful in that moment, a breathing thing of dark marble; but she was not Cara.

'I think I'd better be heading back. A long day tomorrow.'

Before I'd even finished speaking, she had gone.

15

When I awoke, the sun was filling the room, cheerful and bright as soap. Cara had been next to me as I slept, I had been sure of it, and yet there was no dent in the mattress, no sign of her.

I looked at the clock, and was startled; just twenty minutes until I was supposed to meet Pemberley. I rose, washed, dressed. There was nobody else downstairs in the cottage; the other bedroom door stood ajar. I drank water from the tap, checked my appearance in the glass of the front door, and left.

I found the path I had stumbled along last night, the one leading back towards the lodge, and passed the bench where Bianca had interrupted me. I could not help wondering what other journeys the path had seen, which other configurations of the island's residents moving through the dark.

Anyway, I thought as I moved, I was no longer leaving immediately. I would wait for Cara, and until then, I had a commission. As for the island, it might be innocuous after all. Mad Thomas might have lived up to his nickname; the old man's son might have drowned by his own efforts. The more I saw of this place, the more I understood Cara's love of it.

The door to the lodge was unlocked, and the plant-lined corridor was empty. I moved quietly along it, fearing I would disturb any sleepers left after last night's revels. One door, halfway along the corridor towards the glasshouse at the back of the building, was ajar, and two voices were discussing something on the other side of it. I leaned closer.

'... certainly approaching full readiness. I'd say we're there.' A woman's voice. Not Cara's – it was older, and sounded Californian. Much more American than any other voice I'd heard here so far.

'God. How long have we been waiting for this? It would be nowhere without you, you know. Absolutely nowhere.'

'Nothing a small band of the dedicated couldn't do. Now I simply wait for your authorisation.'

'I want us to hold off for a bit. I'd rather get it right than do it now. We only have one chance at it, after all.'

'Of course. But you know as well as I do how positive the early trials have been. In my opinion we could action it today.'

'Well, I'm saying we wait a little longer. I have some final elements to consider.'

'Anything I should know about?' The woman's voice was tense, and his reply curt.

'Legacy.'

'There's something you're keeping from me, John.' He made no reply. She continued, frosty now. 'You can't seriously be thinking of changing your mind. Munro would be perfectly—'

'I'll think what I like. These decisions are too important to be set far in advance.'

'You don't want to listen to my opinion?'

'He did well, making his way here. Better than I would have expected.'

'Who did the work underpinning this place? Who's been helping you here for thirty years?'

'I do not need lectures about loyalty from you or anybody else.'

'I'm not giving you a lecture. I'm giving you the best chance you'll ever have to change the world.'

'You know how much I think of you. I'll be taking that chance soon, despite the consequences for us.'

'Whatever these final elements of yours are, whatever impetuous thing you're thinking of, it could ruin everything if you don't tell me. If we don't plan for it.'

'That's enough for one day. I'll take no more instruction from you.'

'As you wish. The project is ready, if you ever decide you are.' These last words were clipped with disdain, and furniture scraped on the floor. Someone was about to enter the corridor I stood in.

I just had time to move back to the front door, as though I had only just opened it on my way in. The door halfway along the hall swung open, and Angela Knight walked out.

'Good morning.' Her voice had changed between leaving the room and speaking to me. It was almost unrecognisable. She did not regard me with suspicion – hardly looked at me at all, in fact, and ignored my flushed greeting before proceeding through the front door I still held open, as if I'd been waiting for her.

I walked back along the corridor into the house, making myself louder this time. When I got to the room I knew Pemberley was in, I knocked, and in response to his muffled word, lifted the latch and entered.

The room was high and airy, with three large arched windows. It faced east, and the early sun streamed in towards me. It seemed to be a chapel of some kind – a small lectern at the front, three long high-backed pews on either side. Pemberley was sitting on one of them, facing away from me. 'The thing is, Ange, it's not you who's pulling the ...'

He turned as he spoke, and for a few seconds surveyed me as if he was unsure who I was.

'It's Ben,' I said. 'You told me to be here for seven.'

'How long have you been here?' His tone was sharp.

'I got here just as Ms Knight was leaving.'

'Good.' He nodded. Several seconds passed like that – me standing at the border of the room, him lengthways on his pew.

'I came to accept your offer. Your portrait, for a place on the island. With Cara.' Until that moment I hadn't been sure of it; saying it now, I knew it was what I wanted. The island felt like home, a real home, in a way nothing else had for a long time. Not the flat, not school, not even Florence.

Pemberley merely nodded, and rose to his feet. 'All right.' He paced past me into the corridor. 'First, let's get out of this morgue.' He closed the door behind us and locked it, producing a key from nowhere and palming it again.

'I didn't know you had a chapel.'

'Came with the building.' I found it interesting that Pemberley, with his evident mania for changing things to just the way he wanted them, had maintained a religious room. 'Let's talk in the garden.'

He led me towards a low oak door at the back of the building, to the left of the glasshouse. Some debris from last night's gathering was still around – cigarette ends, a few empty bottles, a smashed glass. He picked up a butt and surveyed it.

'Aren't humans amazing? You buy an island, you create an entirely new way of living, you fill the place with the brightest young people you can, and some people will still find a way of smuggling in fags.' He threw it to one side in disgust.

I told him how long the sittings would take, what would be required of him. He questioned me closely about the style of the painting, although from the nature of his questions he seemed already familiar with much of the process.

His whole demeanour had changed since last night. Then he had been overbearing, argumentative, a caricature of a plutocrat. Now that it was just the two of us, he was quiet, focused, determined. It was like talking to a different man.

'Any particular touchstones in your work, Ben?'

'Touchstones how?'

He sighed, impatient. 'References. Key influences. Deepest impressions. All that.'

'Well, if we're talking paintings, probably the depiction of Judith and Holofernes made the deepest impression on me. The one by Gentileschi. It's a story from the Book of Judith, in the apocrypha. Biblical books that—'

'I know the Book of Judith.' He said it quietly.

'Then you know the story. A widow steals into the tent of a monstrous invading general at night, after he's drunk too much wine, and carefully beheads him, with the aid of an old serving woman. Extremely violent. You can see the sword in his neck, and yet she stays so calm.'

'And it moved you because ...?

'It's like David and Goliath, but far stronger, I always think: sex, as well as power. And justice defeating brute strength.'

He grunted, and I continued. 'Gentileschi returned to the theme a lot, actually. There is a later portrait of Judith and the servant leaving with the man's head in a basket. But she's looking off to one side, as though she's about to be caught. Or as if she's just realised something. I prefer that one.'

He smiled, thin and brief. 'Where will the sittings happen?'

I told him that for the best results I would need something like the studio I had in the city. A small space only, but well lit.

'We'll think of somewhere. What about equipment? Paint and so on?' He listened as I told him what I needed. 'Yes, fine. Speak to Knight. She'll ask one of her people to arrange it.'

'How many people does she have?'

'Lots.' He surveyed me blandly and looked at his watch. 'When can you start?'

'As soon as I get a canvas.'

'Tomorrow, then.'

'There's one other thing.'

I told him about the final element of my Village commissions – shadowing people, being near them in social settings, building up my impressions of their faces until I knew them as well as my own. I may have overemphasised how necessary it was, but I wanted to see how he spent his days.

'You want to follow me round to see if my face does anything interesting, so you can put it in the painting?'

I shrugged. 'Francis has established I'm no good at farming. I don't have anything better to do.'

'It's not your time I'm interested in.' He looked at his watch. 'I'm driving to the stones in a bit to check on their progress. You can accompany me there. Anything else?'

'One thing, actually.' I cleared my throat. 'Cara. When is she coming back? I don't think it would be right to accept a place while she doesn't even know I'm here. She doesn't know, does she?'

He put a hand on my arm. 'She knows you're on the island, Ben. She was a bit surprised, but she's pleased to hear it too. She'll be back in a few days, once she's finished a project for me. Does that sound all right?'

I nodded. For a moment, the thought of being with her here, the two of us young, starting again in this place – making our life together, just like Francis and Joanna – was so overwhelming I did not trust myself to speak.

Pemberley smiled, and told me to wait outside the house while he gathered a few things from indoors.

Once he was gone, I wandered to an iron table and chairs behind me, and sat admiring the lodge. The building had an air of peaceful permanence; it seemed almost older than the trees that surrounded it. Pemberley clearly enjoyed manipulating people's sense of how ancient or modern everything here was.

After about fifteen minutes, he emerged, alongside Angela Knight. I thought she had left the building earlier; clearly I had been wrong, and she had merely retreated to a different part of it. Pemberley was still speaking to her, urgently, as they reached me.

'... not nearly fast enough. Understood?'

'Of course, John.'

'Good. Ben, there you are. Let's do this. Angela, you got the files through?'

She offered him a folder she held, and he opened it up and laid it flat on the table before me.

'Right. Which men, Ben?' There was a grid of faces in front of me. 'The men who extorted you outside Freborne.' I looked at him blankly, and he explained: 'Angela told me about them.'

'I didn't expect ...' I was about to say I hadn't been trying to get anyone in trouble. That would have been a lie, though, and he picked up on it.

'What, you didn't expect consequences? We need to know who. Without integrity, the firm is nothing.'

The grim faces stared up at me from the glossy sheet.

'This one, this one and ... I think this one, but I'm not entirely—'

'Good. They'll be let go immediately. Angela?'

'I'll have it done in ten minutes.'

'That's the stuff.'

I started saying some words of surprise, or gratitude, but the matter was clearly closed.

'Ben, this way.' Pemberley moved round the building. I followed him.

At the front was a standard electric cart. It seemed like he really did treat himself as an ordinary resident, at least some of the time. We got in; the engine whined, and the green flicked past.

'So many trees here,' I said. 'I'd have guessed the forest was more than a couple of centuries old.'

'It's why I bought the place.' His voice changed. '*Wer mit alten Bäumen zu sprechen, ihnen zuzuhören weiß, der erfährt die Wahrweit.* "He who knows how to speak with and listen to ancient trees shall learn the truth."' He glanced at me.

'Is that Hesse?'

'Goodness. What a little scholar we have here.' He snorted. 'So how does this observation process work?'

'You just have to go about your business. I'll see you as you move, the way your face changes, the muscles in it. It all helps.'

'Good luck getting anything out of me.'

'Oh, you'll be an open book.'

He didn't smile. After a few minutes, he said, from nowhere: 'Wonderful woman, your Cara.'

'She's been looking for an opportunity like this her whole life.'

'Exactly what kind of opportunity would you say that is?'

'An important job in a place devoted to the future. But one that pays enough to live. Maybe even enough to get a place in a Village, though that sounds rather silly now.'

'Not at all. They're good places to live. Although you clearly don't think much of them.' He spoke casually, but glanced at me as he said it, gauging my reaction.

'What makes you say that?'

'You're not the only one who observes the human face. Every time the Villages come up in conversation, you flinch. Why don't you like them?'

'Really?'

'Really.'

'All right.' I chose my words as carefully as I could. 'I spend my time working for the people who can live in your Villages. And I'll never, ever become one of them.'

'You should have chosen better work.'

'It's not just me. Most people can't. That's why I don't like them. The young work for the old. Only the old can afford Village life; only the young have the skills to make them work. People literally live outside the walls, like servants, running the place.' I paused. 'It's medieval.'

He smiled, as though I had revealed something without knowing it, but I went on.

'When this happens – a caste of people cut out of their own future, people who could have made something of their lives in another system – you get riots.'

'Slave uprisings?'

I shrugged.

'And yet here, Ben, is an island of youth and opportunity.'

'For a chosen few. Chosen by you.'

'Is that why you're so critical? Because one person's in charge?'

'It feels like a rich man's toy. I know you think it's a serious prospect for the future, but the whole world couldn't live like this.'

He paused, and I could sense him choosing his words. 'I think they could, Ben, if they only saw. This place provides the essentials people need – food, shelter, stability, energy, the essential ingredients of civilisation – and it adds the things we've been missing in the West for two centuries. Nature. Peace. Society. If we had done this a hundred years ago, Nala would have been one of a million elephants on the planet. I suppose that doesn't matter to you.'

'Of course it fucking matters.' I hadn't meant to lose my temper, but he carried on as if I hadn't spoken.

'That word you used. Toy. It's interesting. People love to trivialise toys. I think they're the most important things on the planet. Children invented the wheel, did you know that? They played with little toys with wheels, and later they grew into adults who remembered their childhood games and created full-sized wheels. The world today runs on a child's toy.'

'And the island is your toy?' I sighed. 'Forgive me. I just think I'm predisposed against ... against the extremely wealthy. It's too easy for people with your resources to do damage, even unwittingly.'

He laughed. 'You think it's enjoyable having this kind of money? You think anyone's built for it? I can assure you they are not. Drives most people mad. Completely mad.' He shook his head. 'Most wealthy men have no idea what they're doing. They can't see what their responsibilities are, they can't see they're meant to be grabbing the wheel, showing the way. So they buy another yacht, or another house that takes the space of a thousand trees. They don't look out of the private plane and see the earth below. They only look in.' He spat out of the side of the vehicle. 'Billionaires.'

'Then what good do the Villages do?'

'There are tens of thousands of young people working in the Villages, Ben. Young people who now have all the skills needed to run the world. That's not worthwhile?'

'Not if they never get the chance.'

'We'll see.' He braked suddenly. We had been climbing for a while now, but here the path broadened, the grass at its sides well trodden as though crowds sometimes passed this way.

He stopped the cart and turned towards me. 'We're here.'

16

'Here' was a broad green bowl beneath us, finally free of the trees, overlooking the sea but far above its noise. At its centre were two circles of yellowed megaliths, aged and weathered but massive. The smaller inner circle was intact; the huge stones further out had collapsed at a couple of points. Around them, at our feet, was a stone amphitheatre descending in layers towards the central circles. I looked out beyond the cliffs and saw a dozen pillars of rock, as tall as the island itself, ridged a hundred times and impossibly gnarled. Pemberley followed my gaze.

'Like those? The Devil's Chessmen. Phoney name, of course, but rather striking in their way.'

'What is this place? These circles, I mean?'

'Made by the initial inhabitants, whoever they were, for religious or theatrical purposes, or both. Unique, as far as anyone knows.'

'It's remarkable.'

'Mm. Here's Latham. Our man in the past.'

A hunched figure was sitting at the base of the steps, measuring a seat and writing something in a notebook. As he heard our footsteps, he jumped up, stashed the book safely in an inner pocket and buttoned his tweed jacket. He was younger than me, I reckoned, but looked older, prematurely aged.

'Morning, Victor.'

'Good morning, John.' Latham moistened his lips as if to oil them up before attempting a smile. It was a brief smile, jerked upwards like a marionette's string and then dropped just as quickly. If I could have identified a reason, I'd have said it was nerves.

'Quick progress report from you, please, Vic, on our options for this space.'

'Of course.' Latham's looks were well concealed by his beard and his comically tiny glasses. His hair was a vague brown, and I thought how easily he could lose himself in a crowd.

'Ben?' I had been asked a question without hearing.

'Sorry?'

'Vic here was wondering if there was anything you wanted to know.'

'How can there have been the population to create a theatre this size? It looks like it could fit over a thousand people. Did the island support that many?'

'There's a lot we don't know. The forest cover makes excavations very difficult, you see.' Latham added, with a nervous glance at Pemberley, 'Not that it's a problem, of course. The island probably didn't support nearly as many people as it does now. Although they would have had millions of seabirds at their disposal. Flesh to eat, fat to burn as fuel, feathers for bedding and warmth. A whole society just based on eating the birds.'

Pemberley interrupted him. 'Vic knows my theory – this is where the last remnants of the Greek Empire fled as their world ended, and where they desperately tried to re-create the things they had known. Hence the theatre.'

Latham's face twitched, as though he had heard it before but must raise a smile somehow, and I drew Pemberley's attention with my next question. 'What could have killed them off?'

'Murdered by their own slaves, I expect. Quite right too.' Pemberley gave me a look. 'Excuse me, Ben. Private meeting.' He and Latham walked off, around the seating, pointing at bits of them as if planning to install more.

I couldn't believe I'd spoken to him that way in the cart. All the things I'd wanted to say, I had said. And he had ... not accepted them exactly, but he'd listened. I was trembling just thinking about it. What had I done? He could send me away now, no question. Perhaps he'd been waiting for just this moment. I'd be sent home, without Cara.

Without her. Back in the city, by myself, where I would live, and work, and age, all without her. My throat squeezed shut; my skin prickled. I focused on the stone seat in front of me. The shape of them was curious – each one was uneven, but in almost the same way. I could hardly breathe now, or so I felt.

'Ben?' Pemberley was next to me. Latham was nowhere to be seen.

'Sorry. I'm just ...'

The Sanctuary

'You're breathing very fast. Regulate that. Take a big deep breath in. In. That's it. Now let it out. Slower. In again. That's it. Look at me, Ben.' I looked, and there he was, the man who had built this little kingdom, sitting next to me like a bull beside a lamb.

'There, you're doing better already.' I did feel calmer. 'Keep it up, and cool off. Come to the cliff when you're ready.'

I sat in silence for a few minutes, and my panic ebbed, leaving behind a wash of shame. I approached him as he looked out over the edge.

'Feeling better?'

'Yes, much. Thank you.'

'It's an adjustment. A lot of people get a bit alarmed after a while here.'

'The thing that made me panic wasn't the thought of staying here. It was the thought of going home.'

He nodded, understanding. 'You can stay, Ben. We've agreed it. You, plus Cara when she gets back. She's important to this place. And as for you – I'm not put off by you talking back to me. We need people with courage, Ben, people who ask difficult questions.'

'Really?'

'Really.'

I had been thinking of saying my next words for a couple of hours now, in spite of Bianca's warning. 'The dining hall reminded me of somewhere, actually.'

'And where was that?' He was looking down towards the sea below, and I said the next word quickly, before he made eye contact again.

'Hillcrest.'

That got his attention. His head snapped upwards, and his whole face changed. 'You went to Hillcrest.'

'I did. Seven long years.'

'I asked you the other night where you were educated, and you said some school in the south. You lied.'

'I wasn't sure you wanted me to say in front of people that I knew the building. So I made up something else.'

'A *lie*, on this island. At my table.' His voice was low. I would have preferred it if he'd shouted. 'Who else have you told?'

'Nobody.' I thought of Bianca, the closest person I had to a friend here. 'Nobody at all.'

'I should send you back to the mainland for your deceit. Perhaps I will.' He was breathing heavily, as if barely keeping himself under control.

There was only one thing I could say to improve the situation, something I had divined from his tone.

'I don't know if you enjoyed Hillcrest as little as I did, but if I had the money, I must say I wouldn't have rebuilt it.'

Pemberley shook his head, irritably. 'You don't know what you're talking about. You can't stop the past growing out of you. It's like trying to stop your fingernails.' He paused, then looked at me sideways. 'You disliked life there?'

'I hated it.' It was true enough that I could say it with conviction. 'If it wasn't for the art, I'd have run away. But it gave me a sense of purpose, and something in this world to defeat.'

'Being what?'

'The people around me. The complacent people who didn't have that purpose and didn't have to struggle.' We looked at each other for a few seconds; I resolved not to drop my eyes first this time.

'I'm very disappointed about this deceit of yours, Ben. Very disappointed indeed.' He moved close to me, close enough for me to feel his breath. If he wanted to push me off the cliff right now, there would be no witnesses – none but Latham, and he would lack the nerve to tell anyone. Absurd thought. Disregard it, I told myself. Breathe.

'I think there are similarities between us,' I went on. Don't look away, I told myself. Don't look away. 'I think I see the world the same way as you.'

'Do you now?'

'Yes. I don't think you like the Villages either, actually. Or the people in them.'

This was the moment of supreme danger. Pemberley's eyes widened, and yet he kept control of himself. Then he let out a long, slow breath. The moment had passed. I had seen something true and he had acknowledged it. And this time, he was the one who looked away first. The tension in the air slackened.

'I'm sorry. I miss painting. I haven't painted for days. My hand is practically twitching.'

'We can do something about that.' He paused. 'Have your observations this morning gone as planned?'

'Not exactly.'

'I thought not. I'll show you one more place here, and then you can get to work.'

We stood, and Pemberley waved farewell to Latham, who was standing a hundred yards away. We were almost back at the cart when Pemberley's head swivelled round. 'Hear that?'

I had heard nothing, and he stood poised for a second, as pointed and still as a gundog, before he heard whatever the noise was once again, and started moving quietly towards it.

It was at the edge of the treeline, sheltered and hidden among a tangle of roots: a small bird, not one I recognised, badly injured. Its wing had been crushed somehow. It gave another cry as we approached, high and small.

'It's a greenshank chick. Poor thing.' Pemberley knelt and picked it up. 'You're a long way from home, aren't you?'

'What hurt it?'

'Probably one of the predator species. Or there are a few traps still around, metal ones. Might have caught itself in one of those and crawled far enough away to die. Might have just lost a fight.' He gently ran a finger along its back. The creature was terrified, but too close to death to twist round and defend itself, and he kept speaking to it, in the same slow, cooling tone of voice he'd used on me a few minutes earlier.

'There you are, my girl. There you are. Not long now. Very soon, you'll see, all of this will be gone away.' He gathered his thick fingers into a ring, and pinched the bird at the base of the neck until there was a tiny crack and it went limp.

It may have been the right thing to do, but I could not keep the note of accusation from my voice. 'Why did you do that?'

'It wasn't going to live, so I helped it die.'

'Yes, but you could have—'

'I could have nursed it back to health, yes, and in the time it took, another three entire species would probably have gone extinct. It takes courage to end something. Most people don't have the strength to administer the final twist. But the world owes a lot to the few who do.' He stood, and brushed from his knees the clinging earth.

'Are you going to leave it there?'

'Of course. Food for something. Look at how much life there is around it already.'

Beneath the little body, a grub was passing it by, a small red thing, and Pemberley leaned down.

'See that caterpillar? Rebel's large blue. *Maculinea rebeli*. You know what they do? They are liars. They make the noise of an ant – specifically, of a red ant queen. The ants nearby hear its song, pick it up, take it into their home and feed it, all the while listening to the wonderful regal noises it's making. They do absolutely everything for it. They make its life as easy as it can be.'

'Does it always work?'

He gave me a sidelong glance. 'Not always. Sometimes the caterpillar picks the wrong kind of red ant. It gets taken into the nest and devoured. Very dangerous life, going somewhere full of your enemies.' He bared his teeth a little. 'But if it gets it right, it gets everything it needs until it's finished growing.'

'And what happens then?'

'It erupts through the side of the ant heap, destroys the place that gave it life, and escapes.' He paused. 'Moral or not?'

'I don't think morals apply. I find it a little shocking.'

'I think it's wonderful.'

We walked back to the cart and he started the engine.

'Where now?' I asked.

'Further north. We'll see the birds.'

'Must be quite a life for Bianca, seeing all your plans, helping them to fruition.' I paused. 'But it must be daunting for her too, thinking of everything the island needs to keep it going.'

'Why's that?' We hit an incline, and he jabbed at the gears.

'Well, she'll have a role here one day, I presume. I mean, as your daughter ...'

For several seconds the whine of the cart was the only sound around us.

'Ben, were you paying no attention last night? The hereditary principle, that assumption – look where it's got us. It's another natural principle we've warped beyond recognition. Nobody is well adjusted enough to spend their entire life getting ready to inherit what I've put together. And I wouldn't put Bianca through that. She's had a difficult life.'

He seemed angry to even be discussing this, but kept talking. It was as if I had knocked a hole in a barrel. 'And even if I wanted to hand the place to her, it would be against everything I've worked towards. This idea of the son or the daughter, everything passing to them automatically ... it's what's wrong with the world today.'

'I wouldn't know. I inherited nothing.'

'But that's how it should be, Ben. These empires we've built up over the years, these huge pyramids of wealth' – he gestured at the passing island – 'they're what has brought this world to the edge of ruin. Wealth and luxury. It all comes from inheritance, from the piling-up of things, the hoarding old age allows. What we need is youth. Young people who know how the world works, who can run the place free of the generations above them. You understand me?'

'I think so.'

But it seemed he could not help returning to the subject of Bianca. 'All I will say is, my daughter suffered terribly at her mother's hands. It's taken years to return her to the healthy, happy young woman I always knew she could be.'

I remembered his cruelty to her last night in front of everyone, the injured eyes she had cast around the circle, the thought of her eavesdropping on us from the floor above, the sight of her waiting on a darkened path to proposition a man she hardly knew.

I realised Pemberley was waiting for a response from me. 'Of course.' And on we drove.

17

We drove north in near silence for almost an hour. At one point we skirted an enormous lake; the eye in the centre of the island, Pemberley said. Huge birds I did not recognise stood by its edge, as immobile· as ancient gods. I found myself almost wishing I was a landscape artist instead of a portraitist.

We reached the northernmost point of the road; beyond here, Pemberley explained, the terrain was kept wild so the birds would go undisturbed. We were at the top of a range of hills that fell away northwards to the sea, and the plain between us and the ocean was crawling with life – thousands upon thousands of sea-birds. The white and grey of their plumage shimmered back and forth, and above them hundreds of minuscule specks wheeled against the iron clouds.

The Sanctuary

'When I first came here, there weren't one fiftieth of the birds you see today. Not one fiftieth. We made this happen. All of us living here. This is what the energy of youth can do.' There was moisture in the corner of his eyes as he looked out.

'This is all thanks to getting rid of the rats?'

'Entirely. A lot of people disagreed with me about it, told me the place was too far gone for salvage. You'll find no end of people willing to tell you to give up. Makes them feel better that they're not doing anything themselves.'

'Why did you do it?'

'Oh, the urge to create, I suppose. Mixed with the urge to destroy. Both crop up in equal measure.' He wiped his face with a sleeve.

I wondered what else there was to be destroyed, now the rats had gone, but I kept this thought to myself.

'Seen enough?'

I nodded, and he got back behind the wheel. We drove on, but the silence was broken now, and there was so much more I wanted to know. 'What about the government? Are there inspectors? Who checks what the children are being taught?'

'We had a lot of government inspectors in the early days. They thought I might be raising a private army, something daft.' He shook his head. 'Then they realised how harmless I was and they've left me alone. Paying taxes helps, of course.'

He seemed friendly enough now, just about. I judged it was time to ask about Ladd.

'I heard there was going to be a biography of you.'

'Then you were wrong. We get about one request a week for an authorised biography, long interview, broadcast debut. I turn them all down.'

'Why?'

'Ben, this place is the most wonderful environment on the planet and they want to focus on the life of the owner. What I drink, what my life was like before I came here, the colour of my shoes. Christ. Spare me. That stuff – people's love lives, their family, all that rubbish – it's just a way of distracting from the things that matter.'

'This one sounded like it would have been more about the things that matter, I think. A man called Kevin Ladd was behind it. A journalist.'

'Ladd . . . Oh, come to think of it, yes. I have a vague memory of him approaching. He was a bit more persistent than the others. Bit more serious too, which is usually code for wanting to go through your finances.'

'But it never happened.'

'Great reprieve for the reading public, I'd say.'

'Do you know why not?'

'You'd have to ask Angela. She dealt with everything back then.' I had the distinct impression that, again, Pemberley was lying to me. 'I'm sure Mr Ladd has had a wonderful career without having to bother with me.'

'He died, actually.' I realised the stupidity of giving this away as soon as the words were out of my mouth.

Pemberley kept steering, looking straight ahead. 'Been doing your homework on me, Ben?'

'I'm sure you would do some homework if the person you loved had gone away and not told you whether they were coming back.'

'That's just it. I have no need to do any homework.' He took his hands off the wheel for a second, spread his arms. 'Everyone I love is here.'

The drive back south took longer than expected. We made several stops along the way – mostly to greet workers in different hexes. Everywhere Pemberley went he was treated like a gentleman farmer doing the rounds of his property, greeting his tenants, receiving answers to technical questions he'd asked on his last visit, asking new ones. He changed again, becoming more charming, less menacing, but always obviously in command.

We visited the solar hex and the glassmakers, as well as a little mill that wove the island's crops into cloth. At the edge of each one, the thick line of trees waved their branches in gentle benediction.

Between stops, I had a chance to ask Pemberley about how the hexes worked. 'Do you recruit people who know all about these areas already?'

'Half and half. There are experts and there are apprentices. We try to make sure the apprentices have the potential to learn the skills of each place and pass them on. But we also try to keep it balanced.'

I remembered the discussion at the dinner table the other night. 'Do you only recruit people who've had trouble in their lives?'

'Everyone's had trouble in their life. There just happens to be less of it once people get here.'

We drove on. I could tell from the sun that we were moving south-west in a rough parabola, skirting the edge of another area. Thick trees blocked the view, and I saw some fencing too – the first since I got here.

'What's over there?'

Pemberley waved a hand vaguely. 'Biosecurity bit for the non-native plants. We can't have any getting out, so the protocols are strict.'

'Of course. Francis mentioned that.'

Pemberley seemed surprised. '*Francis* told you?'

'We're talking about the seed vault, aren't we? That's the same thing?'

'Ah, the seed vault. Yes. Well, that's in a different part of the island, but it's the same sort of thing. Got to keep the biosecurity high.'

'So we're the only invasive species with free rein here.'

He gave his short barking laugh, and we drove on, curving south then tending west.

The way back took us to Francis and Joanna's hex, and Pemberley stopped the cart before we entered. Above us, the light was starting to fail.

'*Entre le chien et le loup*,' he said.

'Pardon?'

'The hour between the dog and the wolf, where you can't tell which is which. Just another way of saying dusk.' He nodded. 'So? Seen enough of my face? For the painting?'

'Oh. Oh, yes, of course.' The day had been so long, had forced so many new sights and impressions on me, I had almost forgotten the painting. But Pemberley himself probably couldn't have known that from the conversation we'd had, and I had been observing him, after all. 'I think I've seen a lot of aspects I can draw on, yes.'

I was telling the truth, at least. His face was, if not mobile, then versatile. When he had calmed me by the amphitheatre, when he was challenging me about the Villages, when he was furious at my questions about his family – all those moments had prompted expressions new to me. I just had no idea which of them, if any, was the real man.

'Excellent. I'll drop you here.'

He pushed the cart's starter button and drove us into the hex. As we passed the threshold, a much larger vehicle, like an elder sibling to the carts, was coming the other way. It looked like a construction vehicle of some kind, with a revolving cylinder at the back of it, and Pemberley lifted a finger off the wheel in salute.

The hex looked the same, but as I climbed out of the vehicle, Francis and Joanna's cottage seemed different somehow. I couldn't work out exactly what had changed about it, but Pemberley was already speaking.

'So. You'll come to dinner tonight – and you start your portrait tomorrow. Yes?'

'Yes, of course. There'll be supplies?'

'We'll arrange it.'

I was still distracted by the cottage. 'Has something … changed here?'

He shrugged. 'You tell me. You're the close observer.' And with that he accelerated away.

I looked at the cottage for a while before realising what it was. The brick bulb on the outside that had contained the office space for the previous resident, Mad Thomas, had been swept off the building, as if a giant hand had batted it away. In its place was another extension, the same width but rather higher, plastered white on the outside.

I entered the cottage. The double doors between the office – the former office, anyway – and the rest of the cottage were closed. I crossed the room and opened them, and felt for a moment as though I had travelled in time; that I had just got home from the Bywaters' Village a week previously.

I was in my studio, the studio from our home in the city. Not merely an approximation of it, either; exactly my studio, its dimensions, its walls. It was painted in the same white, had the same skylight in the same spot. The curtains, the furnishings; everything in it was identical. Even the brushes and easels and pots I used for my work had been placed here. I feared for a giddy second to look out of the windows in case they suddenly opened onto my usual view of the city, in case they revealed that the last week had been a dream.

My paintings were there too, the completed ones as well as the half-finished ones sitting there for lack of time or inspiration. Were they really mine? Had they been couriered up here, carted through the stone tunnel from the harbour, or were they merely imitations, printed out in some undiscovered hex and stretched across a canvas of exactly the right size?

The Sanctuary

There were only two things there that had not been in my city studio. The first, on the wall, was a perfect copy of Gentileschi's *Judith and Holofernes*. I looked at my watch; just six hours or so since we had been discussing it. I wouldn't have put it past Pemberley to secure the original.

The second new thing was a white envelope resting against one of my easels. I opened it; in a simple, masculine hand two words were written. *Welcome home.*

The flooring was the only thing not altered, but the floors in the two rooms were very similar, and presumably the island builders Pemberley had asked to complete the job had decided to leave it be. Of poor Mad Thomas's possessions – the bookshelves, the desk, the sofa – there was no sign.

I left the cottage and walked the edge, examining the new room from the outside. The only sign of its construction was a thin white seam of plaster, a ridge running from top to bottom, very slightly damp, which must be part of the building process here. I went back into the cottage, to the office – now the studio – and sat in the wicker chair I'd had back in the city. Or in a copy of it, I could not tell.

If Pemberley could create the island itself, of course he could create this, but his ability to reach into my life robbed me of my balance. I looked around the room, dazed. The great hall at Hillcrest, my studio – what else on this island was an artful copy? Was Pemberley himself a clockwork man, a facsimile of an earlier model?

Clearly, as well as the ability to create, he could destroy. First the rats, and now this. This had been the room of Mad Thomas, the writer, and now it was the room of Ben, the painter, and Thomas had been washed away in a single stroke.

The patch of floor the wicker chair was positioned on was darker than the rest, less bleached by sun, and I recalled there had been a rug over it, on which Thomas's desk had rested. I had noticed the awkward arrangement, the desk pinning the rug, on first arriving, then forgotten it. But I remembered what Joanna had said about Thomas – *Frank says he was paranoid, but that's not a nice thing to think of anybody* – and I wondered why one would go to such trouble to keep a patch of floor covered. Francis had said something too: Thomas had *stayed up late half the night rearranging the furniture.*

I examined the floorboards more closely, from end to end, and – *there*. One of the boards had a gap at one end, just wide enough for an inserted tool to prise it upwards. I looked at it more closely. A fine shape had been carved at the corner, a curved and elaborate T.

My painter's roll upstairs contained a metal ruler, thin but strong. I retrieved it, and inserted as much of it as I could along the length of the board, then levered upwards. It didn't move. I tried again. At last it came up.

There was an alcove beneath the board, long and slim. It held a bizarre collection of jetsam – one of the metal snares Bianca had shown me in the tunnel, a few feathers, some dried flowers wrapped tight in waxy paper. A single glove, hand-stitched from animal skin. And beneath all these was a tall black notebook, like those I had seen on Thomas's shelves on my first morning in the cottage. My scalp prickled.

The Sanctuary

I opened the notebook. Inside the cover, in scratchy, uneven writing, was a name – *Thomas Candler* – followed by an address. He had lived in the city too, I noticed. The pages were lined, full of writing in the same hand. The notes began neatly marshalled, but as the pages went by, the discipline of writing within the lines seemed to have proved too much for him, and the writing had broken out, started occupying double heights or spinning off into elaborate diagrams sketched in rough ink.

I took the book back to my chair in the corner, and began to survey it in detail.

The notebook itself was ordinary. The paper was of a quality one rung above pulp, and seemed almost to be waiting to return to the gloop it had come from, once the owner of the book had finished with it. I had owned a couple myself.

Nobody could ever have filled a notebook with quite such a bizarre assortment of words and sketches as Thomas had. The first fifty pages veered apparently at random between diary entries, detailed sketches of flora and fauna (with the word 'Native?' next to each one), aphorisms and scraps of verse, all cross-referenced to each other in the margins. Two questions began to dominate the book as I read on:

What is in 41?

Where the rats?

There were other phrases in here, phrases that made me question the author's frame of mind. The words 'island within an island' had been scratched on several different pages. There were references to 'SJ' scribbled throughout, sometimes 'JP' or just 'J'. There was a list of 'Key Players' inside the back page. One of them, at the bottom of the list, was 'New Handmaiden', with a little pencil sketch of her – Cara. She must have arrived here soon before Thomas died. It was strange seeing Cara sketched by someone else, and yet the sketch was accurate enough to make my heart lurch.

Halfway through, there was a rough attempt at a complete map of the place, which included the label '41?', with an arrow drawn to a spot of land in the south-east of the island.

The number seemed to have had a significance for Thomas. It was scrawled repeatedly throughout the margins. In one place, fifteen consecutive pages had all been neatly numbered '41' in the upper corners, in a range of different styles, from Gothic to an etiolated copperplate. The notes grew personal. The diary entries, initially in neat sentences, declined to scratched half-lines. One read, in its entirety: *Followed again today. I dare not write more.* Another said: *A man must hold close the present and future who does not have a past.* A third, rambling one described *the living manifestation of the suicidal instinct of the species.*

Another pair of pages contained sketches of Pemberley – competent ones too. The following spread had more of the same man, but his features were twisted somehow, leaves writhing up his neck. A few pages on, his head was peeled open to reveal a monstrous flower. The final drawing in the series was only of a huge and ancient-looking bloom, with a suspicion of human features remaining.

Francis and Joanna were right. Thomas had clearly had some terrible breakdown during his time here.

The Sanctuary

At that moment I heard footsteps pass the window – close by – accompanied by voices I recognised. Francis and Joanna were outside. From where they were standing, they couldn't see the floorboard, and as they moved around to the front door, there was just time to push it back into place, shove the notebook into my pocket and pretend to be looking at a nearby canvas before they came through.

They were excited about the change to their home, thrilled apparently to learn that the room would be used again – 'It was so creepy when it was all abandoned, wasn't it, ducks?' – and, according to their eagerly matched accounts, used by someone who wouldn't waste the opportunities of life on the island. I smiled awkwardly, and showed them a few of my completed paintings without admitting I was unable to tell whether or not Pemberley had cloned them. Neither of them seemed to notice my perturbation.

The pair assured me with warmth that the installation of the studio was a mark of great favour from John, that I couldn't be luckier. 'You'll be running the place this time next month,' Francis smiled, and Joanna laughed and patted my arm. I knew Pemberley probably only wanted me here if it would make Cara happy, but it gave me great pleasure. Clearly I was a better neighbour than the unhinged Thomas.

They had come back to prepare for dinner. Joanna ushered me and Francis upstairs, telling me to dress smartly ('in case your Cara's suddenly back') and Francis to wash the fields off his hands. When I got back downstairs, I just had time to turn on the radio and tune it until I found a familiar station. The noise seemed fainter than it had done when I last tried it. The presenter was saying something about restrictions, about the need for vigilance, about the short order in which normal life might be restored.

But Francis was tumbling down the stairs, and Joanna donning a cloak against the cold, and I switched the radio off. Whatever was happening on the mainland was unimportant here. Francis had stories from the day's work, and Joanna an encouraging report on the baby, and the sky above us was high with orange shreds of cloud. We found a cart out at the front readying itself to leave, crammed ourselves in with the others and sped towards the hub along quiet roads.

John had been sincere in his invitation to dinner; I was greeted warmly at the door, and led once again to the top table. I recognised a few faces from the day as I passed along the aisles, and smiled and nodded my way to the dais. When I arrived, two other residents I hadn't met were already standing there, looking even more terrified than Francis and Joanna had done on my first night.

The notebook was in my pocket still: I feared that if I left it at the cottage, someone might search my room in my absence. It felt uncomfortably large against my thigh. Even having it felt like an act of betrayal against Pemberley and the island. It had been written by a clearly paranoid man. Then again, was I equally paranoid to worry that someone would search my studio?

I was between one of the newcomers and Bianca that night. Pemberley had Angela Knight at his right hand and Munro at his left. I had no chance to thank him for the studio before the meal began, but he gave me a brief look and a raised eyebrow, as if acknowledging his sleight of hand.

From the lectern, he warned the assembled islanders to return tomorrow, adding that there would be an announcement made, 'a substantial one', about our future here. His closing refrain of 'We're building it' was followed by a buzz of conversation. As he said those three words, I could have sworn he glanced at me with a flicker of delight, as if only he and I knew he might have been alluding to the studio.

I spent most of the meal talking to Bianca. In response to an enquiry about how she had spent her day, she replied vaguely that she had been doing some reading. I again received the strong impression that there was almost nothing here for her to do, and I remembered thinking the other day that her decision to spend time giving me a tour had mostly been a relief to her.

Not that she was difficult to talk to – quite the reverse. She had a powerful curiosity about my life on the mainland. How many homes there were in my building, and how many people in those homes; what my parents had done, how I had come to discover painting ... on it went. She gave the impression she hardly knew how life functioned on the mainland – but as Pemberley's child, of course, she could hardly be expected to know very much at all about normal life. Every so often I noticed Pemberley surveying us with amusement.

There was little group discussion tonight. The two islanders to my left sat enthralled, and said nothing unless spoken to directly. Knight stayed moody and silent. Only once did a single subject dominate the table, and when it came, it came in the form of a sentence spoken by Pemberley.

'You don't know that.'

The words were loud enough to temporarily silence all other conversation. He was addressing Bianca, who had clearly said something to displease her father. I had been speaking to one of the newcomers, and had missed the comment that riled him.

'And even if you did know,' he continued, 'what gives us the right to wipe out every last fish and bird and mammal and crawling thing? What makes that the right thing to do?'

'I simply meant it doesn't seem likely to me that everything would be wiped out. You yourself said how resilient life is.'

'Bianca, there is so little we know about the situation. You remember Cuvier? Angela, have I mentioned Cuvier at this table before?'

Knight nodded, surveying Bianca mildly as she did so. 'I think you have, John.'

In that instant I saw Knight's unforgiving side, the part of her that would earn and keep her place in Pemberley's company no matter what it required.

'Cuvier was the French scientist who invented extinction. Invented the notion of it, I mean. Before him there was no idea it could ever happen. We drove whole species from this earth before we even realised we were doing it. When he first proposed that you could delete an entire animal, he was mocked. But he was right. And now you suggest this earth needs none of our help?'

'I'm terribly sorry, John. I must have misunderstood.' Bianca's face was a mask of pain. For a moment I found myself thinking, *How foolish of her to displease him*, before wondering where the thought had come from.

'It's not a question of misunderstanding. It's a question of possibility. We – our whole species – stand on a bridge so terribly precarious that the chances of our making it across are almost none. The worst part is, we ourselves wore away at the supports as we crossed. And now here we are, standing in the middle, surrounded by a peril we created.' The table had fallen silent.

'If our species survives just one more century without killing everything off, then a great upland of potential awaits us. How short a time a century is. A fraction of a heartbeat in the life of this world. And yet right now, we are at the point of the very great-est danger. If we keep hacking, we will all drop into the ravine of our past. And the worst part of this is, we are not crossing this bridge alone. We carry with us the fate of every other living thing on earth. You remember last week, what we said about the elephants?'

Bianca nodded, still clearly mortified at having ruined the mood, apologising with the gift of her full attention.

Her father continued: 'Fifty years ago, nobody thought the elephants could die. We were wrong. So that's the work of this place: to find a way for all of us to cross the bridge together. This is our task, and I will continue even if it kills me.'

'How does that fit with eradications like the rats?' I hadn't intended to ask, but I knew, somehow, he would have an answer.

'You're a creative, Ben, are you not?' I nodded. 'Have you ever made a mistake on a canvas so grievous you had to start again from nothing?' I nodded again. 'Do you think there is inconsistency in your approach and mine? Man made a mistake by transporting animals to places they would never have reached. When we settled the Pacific islands, a tenth of the world's bird species were driven to extinction. Thanks to us.

'Think of the earth we could have had. And look at the world now. We botched the canvas. Now we can mend it. Hence the destruction of the rats. Does that make sense?'

'Yes. It does.'

'They came back, though.' Bianca was speaking, obstinate despite her earlier reprimand. 'They came back two years ago.'

'We got rid of them again,' Knight said.

'I just don't understand how they got back in,' Bianca replied, mildly. 'It seems so unlikely to me, given how strict things are here. Almost as if—'

Angela cut across her. 'Rats are clever. And sometimes invasive species are given a tiny foothold and work their way in.' She looked at me. 'And it takes a lot of effort to root them out later.'

Pemberley spoke again, calmer now. 'Angela's right. We got rid of them again. And in future' – he waved his fork – 'how much we will be able to do. How much.'

There was a general sense of a sermon ending. Most people went back to their own conversations, but for a few minutes I could not help observing how he and Angela Knight talked, almost conspiratorially, their heads together. I wasn't the only one. Bianca was observing them too, and the corners of her mouth were dark with wine.

The rest of the meal passed without incident. Afterwards, Pemberley excused himself to walk among the islanders still at their long tables. Knight drifted away too. Bianca leaned in towards me.

'Come for a walk. There's something I want to talk about.'

Outside the hall, groups of residents were gathered beneath bulbs that glowed a gentle blue. The sky had darkened almost to night during the meal, and Bianca and I slowly walked the perimeter.

I spoke first. 'What was that argument really about?'

'I was trivialising the situation on the mainland. Or in the rest of the world, really. I don't blame him for pointing out how silly I sounded.' *At least she saw sense eventually.* There was that small, calm voice again, the one that had sided with Pemberley against his daughter during the meal.

'We'd been receiving dozens of ships a month,' Bianca said. 'It's not surprising one of them could have had a pair of rats on board. Anyway, it's all just ego stuff. Angela's meant to be in charge of biological control.'

Knight had taken the opportunity to belittle Bianca during the conversation, I remembered, subtly enough that others might not notice it.

Outside the hall there were stone seats, massive granite rocks with their innards scooped and smoothed to convert them into comfortable hollows. We sat in one, and I spoke first. 'This place just seems to work. It's extraordinary.'

'It's not so hard when you divide up the labour. The first main responsibility is the general smooth running of the place from day to day: ordering new solar cells, supervising shoring-up work at the docks, arranging welcomes for new residents. Cara's been overseeing all that.'

'Sounds like an enormous job.'

'She's very talented.' I felt pride then, pride in Cara's knowledge and her work. 'The other thing is overseeing the final progress of the bio-vaults and making sure they are paid for. That's Knight's job. The job of her life, really. It was finished a couple of weeks ago.'

'The bio-vaults?'

'The stores of life. Every single species of flora and fauna on the planet; preserved, logged, you name it.'

'But that would take thousands of people to do. Surely.'

'John *has* thousands of people. Most of the work happens either on the mainland or in the international branches. But it's all been leading here.'

'How can he afford it?'

'He's even wealthier than you imagine. And he's willing to spend it all to make this place self-sufficient. Once he's done that, it won't need wealth. It will stand on its own. He says it's the equivalent of spending your fortune educating a child so they can live for themselves.'

'Did he do that with you?'

Bianca looked uncomfortable. 'I would have thought you'd be happy to learn that. He's a self-destructing billionaire.' I had to admit that the idea of a great well of money being emptied and spread across the island was beautiful, in a way.

But my question had made her look miserable, and I changed the subject. 'Knight doesn't like me, does she?'

'She doesn't like many people. She and John had some big dispute about the direction of the company recently, but neither of them is talking about it. But he's in charge, not her, and she's coming to the end of her work now. He wants someone with energy. Someone other than me.' She sighed.

'Is there something he's going to be launching soon?'

'Launching?' Bianca looked guarded suddenly. 'Like what?'

I told her what I had overheard of Pemberley's discussion with Knight in the chapel this morning. *Legacy, early trials* ... I wished I remembered more of it. 'And is it connected to what he said tonight, to this big announcement tomorrow?'

She shrugged. 'No idea. Any more questions?'

'I mentioned my schooling to him. At Hillcrest.'

'Christ, Ben. Why?'

'I didn't see the harm. Is it really that private?'

'His childhood is off limits, even to me. God. It's like you want him to evict you.'

I wondered whether she was protecting her father's childhood the way he must have protected hers. After a minute of silence, I remembered she had brought me out after dinner for a reason. 'You said you had something you wanted to discuss.'

She paused, and then spoke in a rush, as though forcing the words out was the only way to get them said.

'Cara's not on the mainland.'

'What?'

'I phoned the mainland estate this afternoon. She's not there, according to them. Not at any of their offices, and she wasn't reported to be in the field either. The company over there doesn't know where she is.'

'That's impossible. Your father said ...' What had Pemberley said?

'Did John ever actually say she was on the mainland estate?'

'He said she'd be back soon. Where else would she be?'

'I don't know, Ben. But they checked the manifests of ships for me. There's no record of her disembarking in the last several weeks, not in the time since I last saw her on the island. Maybe she's still here.'

'She can't be.' I looked out at the dark trees. Was Cara there, watching us even now?

'I don't know, Ben, I just wanted to tell you. You have a friend in me.'

'If she's not here, or on the mainland estate, then …' Then where was she? I felt so exposed in that moment, so keen not to think about Cara being missing, untraceable, that I had to change the subject. I would think about it when I was alone.

'There's something I want to talk to *you* about.' I dug in my pocket and held the journal out to her. 'It's a notebook belonging to the man who lived here before me. Thomas, I think he was called.'

Bianca's expression changed. She grabbed the book from me and leafed through it. 'You shouldn't have this. The maintenance people cleared his possessions.'

'Well, he hid it. Why would they do that?'

'Whenever someone leaves, their remaining belongings are removed.'

'Did you know Thomas, Bianca?' She did not look up, but she nodded slightly. I reached out and took the notebook back from her. 'It's pretty strange stuff. I don't think he was entirely stable.'

It was the wrong thing to say, because she seemed upset. 'Of course he wasn't. He had a lot of odd ideas. God knows where they came from; perhaps his disease was kicking in early. It was sad, really. He was so convinced this place was malign, it drove him out of his wits.' She reached out. 'You shouldn't have that, Ben. I knew him. I can take it.'

A deep voice cut across our conversation. 'I hope you don't mind me joining you.'

Pemberley had appeared by the bench, the round filament from the light above making a reflected halo on his shining head. We stood. I held the notebook in my hand, unable to conceal it.

'Bianca, I'm sorry for speaking intemperately in there. I just thought I'd been making such progress in articulating why this place matters. And …' He shrugged, as though he couldn't be responsible for losing his temper when a disciple or a daughter proved blockheaded.

Bianca was all forgiveness, blushes, apologies herself. She clearly didn't get such attention from her father often, and a corner of my mind wondered whether the scene of a father caring for his misguided daughter was being staged for my benefit.

Pemberley turned to me. 'Like the studio?'

'I'm speechless. I don't know what to say.' *Cara's not here. Cara's missing. Where is she?* But I kept silent, and he did not notice the look on my face. 'How did you do it? Get into my home, I mean, in the city?'

'We have ten thousand people working in the city, Ben. We can take the best of the old world and graft it straight onto the new one.'

'It's remarkable.'

He shrugged, clearly delighted by the praise. Then he leaned over and, before I could tighten my fingers, plucked the book away from me. He turned it in his large hands, feeling the ersatz leather it was bound with. 'What's this?'

I swallowed. 'I would strongly prefer you not to look into it, if that's all right.'

I must have put a bit of authority into my voice, because he paused, his hands folded around it as if in prayer, thumbs poised to open it.

'And why not?'

'They're … very rough preliminary sketches. Blame an artist's superstition. It's bad luck for a subject to see himself before it's finished.'

Pemberley paused for a second, then glanced up at me through his thick eyebrows and grinned. 'I wouldn't want to place a curse on your portrait. Here.'

'Thank you.'

Even when the book was stowed, I worried Pemberley would turn and insist on seeing it after all. When I examined my feelings later, I realised I had been afraid not that he would see the scrawlings of poor mad Thomas, but that he would send me away; away from him and the world he was building here. Even then, even in a new fog of worry about Cara, the thought of banishment had filled me with fear.

Pemberley ignored my sickly look. 'Well, we can improve on sketches, I'm sure. First session tomorrow. Seven all right? Good.' He turned, and the cool white of his shirt bobbed away through the gathering dusk to the edge of the open hub.

Bianca let out a breath I hadn't realised she was holding and nodded at the book in my pocket. 'I'd get rid of that if you want a future here.'

She walked away after him, and my fingers tightened around it.

Back at the cottage, I fell asleep almost immediately, but my dreams were disturbed, and I woke after a few hours and crept downstairs, trying not to disturb Joanna and Francis. I poured myself water, and looked out over the island from a side window on the landing outside my bedroom. From this aspect the island was mild, and the trees above the hex were as still as a landscape painting. The cry of a distant animal cracked the air.

For a moment, a strange sensation came over me, as if I was looking down on myself from a great height, many miles away. I saw myself standing on the outer rind of the planet, kept on its surface by the most casual of forces, the coincidence of gravity. I sensed the silk-thin layer of the atmosphere, the layer that contained every living thing we had ever known, and how far we had gone towards its destruction.

How odd that I had ever considered the city the best place for me. And what strange joy in the prospect of a life here with Cara, painting the most important group of people in the world. If only I knew where she was. She was missing, she was not on the mainland – if Bianca was to be trusted, at any rate – and I had not taken the chance to ask Pemberley about it. Why not?

Pemberley had explained about Ladd, the journalist, after all. Ladd's widow must have mistaken my innocent enquiry for something more menacing. And Pemberley himself cared for my welfare so much he had summarily fired the men who beat me on the road here. Better still, he was starting to see the purpose of my work; I could tell I had intrigued him with my conversation today, and I knew that over the coming weeks I would prove to him what a painting could do.

Yet still I didn't know where Cara was.

Enough. Time for sleep, to be fresh for tomorrow's painting session. If Cara came back tomorrow, she would find me restored by the spirits of the island.

There was no thought back in the darkness of the bedroom, but I did see something else after a while: an anthill as high as my head. A stream of shining black carapaces circled it, collecting food for their queen. I leaned towards it and began pulling it away, chunk by chunk of wet, dark matter, until the colony was exposed before me. There, in all its pomp, surrounded by devoted attendants, was a beast I had never seen before. It was no ant, nor was it a caterpillar or a grub. It was new, a circular beast with a hundred tiny arms, and when I tried to pinch out its life, it sank its small teeth into the tip of my thumb and made me another of its slaves.

My fears had faded by the morning, and the night's dreams had gone with them, driven back by the soft, warm light flooding the room. How easy it is for gentle sunlight, birdsong and fresh morning air to reveal that all the terrors of the night before were nothing but shadows on the wall.

By the time I got downstairs, Francis was already lacing his boots, and Joanna was stirring something in a glass, a drink she had been prescribed by the doctor here; the vitamins she needed for pregnancy. They wished me luck as I left.

I hitched a lift back towards the lodge and was dropped next to one of the footpaths leading there. The forest on either side was bursting with the energy of spring. A few of the trees that had seemed leafless just a few days ago were packed with tightly folded buds: one tree had exploded into blossom already, like a firework frozen at its most beautiful moment. I counted nine different bird calls as I went.

Pemberley was sitting outside the lodge, alone this time, and in a better mood.

'Sailor Ben! Today you become Painter Ben.' He was sipping coffee from a small cup before him. 'Drink?'

I accepted. It was good coffee, dark and bitter. 'From here?' I asked. He nodded, and I marvelled that this island could support so many wonders.

'Come. I've got a room already set up.' He stood and led me inside, along the corridor, then upstairs. The walls were lined with dark, shadowy portraits I presumed had been Fellingham's. Pemberley himself was certainly uninterested in telling me anything about them.

Halfway along the landing, he opened a door.

'Here all right?'

The room was a stone cube about thirty feet on each side. The walls were grey, and it would have been a dark and forbidding chamber were it not for the fact that at the far end, the roof had been torn off from left to right, stretching about ten feet into the room from the far wall. Three unadorned pillars stood at the open end, supporting nothing; one had a determined green frond climbing towards the top. The floor at that end of the room was stained with rain, and – even more intriguing – there were drains where it met the wall, and a slight tilt halfway across, as though the place had been built to remain open in all weathers.

The room's inhabited half held a case of books, a dresser, and a small, spartan writing table with a chair. As I looked round towards the door, I noticed a bed in the nearest corner. Not even a bed, really – a thick tatami mat on the floor, with what looked like a hard block at one end of it. Beside it was a long, plain broom.

'Is this …?'

'I sleep here, yes. But it's where I think, too. You did say you wanted something that got to the heart of the painting's subject. This room fulfils the brief nicely. Something new made out of something old.'

'Do you sleep here through the winter?' It didn't seem possible.

'The trees bring the island the warmth it needs, Ben. Besides, it very rarely snows more than halfway into the room.' By now I could hardly tell if he was joking or not. I wouldn't have put it past him to have dragged the mat in here from a luxurious chamber down the hall, just to amuse himself or fool me. 'Anyway, I like it. Will it do?'

I looked around. 'Well – yes, this will be fine in the mornings, with the sun on the other side of us. Enough light, none of it direct.'

'Where do I stand?' I showed him a spot, pulled a chair to it and gestured him to sit, and told him the easel would sit on the flagstone next to him, here.

He expressed surprise that it would be so close, and I told him the name of the method I would be using to paint him.

'Sight-size?'

'Exactly. I view you and the painting side by side, from a distance. You sit here, with the easel just beside you. Then I move back to here' – a spot a few metres towards the door – 'to see the overall look of you from there. Then I return to make my marks on the canvas. I'm viewing you and the painting side by side at a distance. It gives me an impression of the whole painting at once.'

'And this helps you how?'

'It gives you a picture very true to nature. So often clients think they want an exact portrait. If I did that, I'd end up with a hyper-real painting but I might lose who you are. But if I translate what I see from over here into the terms of the painting, I get an image that is impressionistic but alive. It's more really you than a photo.'

'So it's a trick.'

'It's the real you from a distance, but a trick up close. Close enough, and it dissolves into chaos.'

'Sounds like most of us.' He barked with pleasure at his insight.

'I'll need to leave the easel in the building so I'm not carrying it back and forth.'

'You can leave it in the corner. Let's start, then.'

'Today I'll just sketch, if that's all right.'

'Thought you already had sketches. In that little book of yours.'

I swallowed. 'Formal sketches.'

'Fine. Where did you learn this stuff, anyway?'

'Florence.'

'Lovely place.'

'I met Cara there.' He had naturally adopted a rather striking pose in the chair, leaning slightly forward, and I requested he hold it. He did so, but asked me to tell him about the circumstances of our meeting.

That meeting in Florence had been chance, but at the end of the first evening Cara had told me how much longer she was staying in the villa on the city's outskirts, and we arranged to meet the following night. Her aunt was visiting for her health, and she was happy to let her niece have the run of the city after an early supper.

We spent our evenings walking up and down the narrow streets, trading comments with the wandering salesmen, admiring their goods. Sometimes we would stop in one of the cramped bars for a drink or a game of dice, but whatever we did we were constantly talking: about art, about work, about the shape of the world to come. If this sounds serious, it wasn't: we were coining new jokes and in-jokes all the time, building our love like a stack of cards.

She was on the verge of graduating, and her plans then were chiefly about her ambitions in life. She spoke of climbing through the world, climbing to safety. It was the image that told me most about where she had come from. Pemberley grunted with approval at that.

Cara had had no parents since the age of five, and I always assumed this had been the motor that powered her worldly ambitions. She had grown up with her aunt, poor – very poor, she had hinted – and when she had been old enough to start working, she had worked. The trip to Florence had been paid for entirely by her.

Cara had stayed devoted to her aunt until she had died, a few years after Florence, and since then her ambition had been boundless. My own diagnosis was that she was out for revenge on a world which had treated her only family so poorly; but whenever I asked, she insisted it was simply a matter of security.

That was the dominant difference between us, I explained. It didn't matter at first, because we each wanted the other to succeed and we both dreamed of a world greatly improved. But our methods of getting there seemed different. Cara was searching for a unique, elite project like the one she'd found here; I wanted more of a collective struggle, although I was careful not to criticise the island as I had yesterday – I understood it so much better now, after all.

Later, after leaving the room, I was not sure how I had been induced to speak so freely, but I felt safe, as though I was with a friend. Pemberley kept his face perfectly still as I spoke, but he maintained an air of intense curiosity, and I saw again what Cara, with her hopes for the future of the world, saw in this man and this place.

It seemed to me that elements of my own face entered the sketch I produced; I drew Pemberley's eyes rounder, his cheekbones more prominent. When I looked at it later, I felt our two faces had become muddled somehow, that I had produced neither of us faithfully but a third person, borrowing DNA from both. It was a mistake I had never made before, and it was oddly discomfiting.

Once I had finished speaking, Pemberley waited a minute or two, then spoke.

'You know, the work we are doing here is for the young. They're the only generation who have ever mattered. As a species we're not good for much past the age of thirty-five, I'd say.'

'Thirty-five? You can't mean that.'

'I'm quite serious. After that, we amass, we hoard. We become dragons, sitting on piles of gold and denying those who come after us. Age is detestable, Ben. Don't ever get old.'

'It's surprising to hear someone older speaking that way.'

He shrugged. 'All my most important work I'd done by thirty-five. If I'd died then, it might have made the world a little less unequal. But here we are.'

'I'd better do my most important work quickly, then. I'm thirty-three.'

He shrugged once more. 'You have time.'

'Do you ever encounter hostility from older people for that attitude?'

'I don't meet any. The island is too young. It's getting younger all the time, too. We've had so many births, the average age has come down in the last three years.'

I couldn't help remembering the last old person I'd seen, in Freborne. 'You've reminded me of someone I met on the way here.'

'Oh yes?' He was looking down at his fingernails, distracted momentarily, and as I recounted the story, trying to seem nonchalant about the old man's account of his son being killed on Pemberley's soil, he kept on examining his hands. Once I'd finished, he merely shook his head sorrowfully.

'The young man was poaching the birds. One of my rangers gave chase and the young man fired at him. The ranger had no choice but to shoot back. The poacher was killed, of course, and the ranger handed over to police. They decided there was no case to answer. A great waste.'

'I suppose when you're doing something as ambitious as this, not everyone is going to like it.' He nodded, and I was emboldened. 'It seems a shame Thomas didn't like it either. The writer.'

He nodded again, grave, then returned his head to its former position, making sure I could keep sketching him. I found that very considerate.

'Poor, poor Thomas. He had the best possible treatment in his final hours. Nobody could have been tested, examined, monitored more closely, but by the end he almost seemed not to want to live. Problems from the mainland following him here, perhaps. We can't save everyone.'

It was no good. He was so convincing, but none of it mattered except my next question. 'I was wondering if you'd heard from Cara lately.' I paused to control my breathing. 'I haven't seen her. She hasn't phoned the island. I know you said she knows I'm here, but ...' I paused, unwilling to directly accuse him of lying. 'I just want to speak to her.'

'She sends me a daily digest, Ben. Would you like to see it?'

'I ...' He was so convincing. I was on the brink of saying *No, that won't be necessary, I believe you, of course*, and I had to force myself not to. 'I would, yes.'

'Wait there.'

He left the room, came back with a pile of memos in his hand. I looked at the topmost one – dated yesterday – and recognised her handwriting, her turn of phrase. He reached out a thick finger and turned the page over. There was her signature.

'She's looking forward to seeing you, Ben, very much. I don't think you're in trouble especially.' He smiled, lupine. That was it, then. Bianca had been lying to me, trying to deceive me for reasons known to herself. 'What did you think was going on?'

'I don't know. I just had this mad fear' – *it wasn't mad, it wasn't* – 'that she was missing.'

'Are you sure someone didn't suggest that notion to you, Ben?' There was an edge to Pemberley's voice, and I understood from it that if I named Bianca, she would be in deep trouble. I would ask her about it later.

'No. Nobody at all. Purely my paranoia, I assure you.'

His face cleared, and he ditched the pile of paper on the desk and resumed his seat before me. 'How's the process going, then? Getting cramp yet drawing these features?'

I told him it was going well, and thanked him for his consideration. But I was so awash with relief, and we were on such good terms now, that I felt I could ask for something different, and here I made my mistake.

'I was wondering one thing. Do you have any pictures of yourself, maybe as a young man, even as a boy, that might show me how your face has developed?'

'No. I don't.' In an instant the set of his features – that confident, stern mask – vanished, replaced by a curious blankness.

'Is there really nothing? It can be anything. A family photo is best, of course, because then we can see how your parents shaped you.' If I was honest, these were not strict requirements for a successful portrait, but I felt emboldened to suggest it by how enjoyable our conversation had been so far.

'I don't have any.' That was all he said, but the tone in which he spoke made it clear he would discuss the matter no further.

A few seconds later, he surveyed his watch and stood. 'I think that's all we have time for today. Come back in a couple of days. Maybe you'll be able to get painting then.'

Before I could adjust or even apologise, I had been ushered into the corridor, and the door was firmly closed behind me.

As I left the house, my face hot, I replayed the moment of clumsiness again and again, cursing myself, and as I went I risked a look back at the lodge. In the room I now recognised, open to the sky, I thought I saw a glimmer of movement, a retreat behind one of the cool pillars. But I could not say for sure.

When I reached the hub I moved to the library, up a short flight of steps and into shadow.

Like so many other buildings here, it seemed to have been designed to sprout from the earth. The entrance hall was high and spartan, and contained nothing but a central desk surrounded by empty marble floor. The lighting was gloomy, and had no visible source. The only sign of the place's function was a tall glass deck around one of the upper storeys, beneath which I could make out shelves of books, but even the windows up there had been topped with a roof overgrown with greenery, tendrils of it tumbling over the edges and swaying against the glass in the breeze.

Behind the desk stood a woman. She was young, with soft auburn hair and gentle, round features, and wore a deep blue set of overalls.

'You must be Ben.' I was starting to dislike the way every-one here knew my name. 'Is there anything in particular you're seeking?'

'Not really. I'm just looking around.'

'Well, we have a section for general readers here.' The librar-ian turned sideways to retrieve a map, and I realised she was pregnant, like my new neighbour Joanna. I thought so, anyway; there was just enough looseness in her clothes to leave the fact in doubt.

'Can I search myself?'

'Of course.'

The means of searching was the microfilm. These were the newspapers Bianca had been proudly explaining about, her own contribution to this place. The librarian gave me brief, uninter-ested instructions in the use of the machine and keyed in a code to unlock the huge aisle of reels before returning to her desk. Ordinarily, she explained, I would ask her what I wanted, but her condition ... She gestured to her distended stomach. We assured each other I would manage without her.

The reels were stored along one of the building's long, high aisles, stretching back hundreds of feet into the gloom. There was a huge book of yellowed paper, a guide to which papers were stored where.

From long experience on the mainland I knew 'John Pem-berley' would bring hardly any results. But now I had two new names to research. Neither of them might be here, of course: Bianca's purchase of the archive might not include more recent copies. But she had said it had only been imported in the last few months. I checked the notebook, still in my pocket, for Thomas's surname.

Thomas Candler. Thomas Candler writer. I tried hunting for him in one of the city's main papers, remembering the address in the front of his notebook, and the rough date he must have come here. Missing people of his class usually made at least a few headlines. Before long, here he was. He had written a couple of books on the world's last wildernesses; had worked for anti-capitalist groups, protest organisations too. Around seven months ago he had been reported missing. His friends and family had issued tearful appeals. He stared out from the screen, arrogant and youthful. None of the people wondering about him on the mainland knew he was dead. I could see why he would have applied to live on the island, hoping for a scoop. He must have run away from his old life and come here. I felt a prickle across my neck. Hadn't I done the same thing?

William Steensen. This time I searched the yellowed book for one of the papers local to here, then went into the long, dark alley of reels again. If he really had been a poacher, there would have been some record – an arrest, a charge. Unless he had been entirely beyond the law.

When had Steensen died? The old man had said it was a couple of years, and the local paper only published once a week. This search was faster, and before long, a second face looked out at me from the page. According to this report from the time of his death, two years ago, William Steensen had been no poacher, but an ecologist and ornithologist, killed in a boating accident about fifty miles from here.

Of course, Pemberley's account made sense if Steensen's ecological work was a front for poaching. That certainly made more sense than anything else. And if the rangers had been fired on, what could they do but fire back? Perhaps the location of the death had been changed to cover things up, give him and his family some respectability in death. I was inclined to believe Pemberley's version of events, to give him the benefit of the doubt. He was frightening, imposing, but no murderer.

'Can I help you further?' The librarian was at my side, soundlessly.

'I was just trying to find out a little more about this place.' A foolish lie, given what she could clearly see on the panel before me.

She smiled: a beautiful smile really, one of great innocence. 'I'm sure John will tell you anything you need to know.'

I spent the afternoon walking in the south-east of the island, near the area Thomas had marked in his notebook as being the site of '41', whatever that was. I found nothing that justified his paranoia. The path twisted around at various points, but it was merely following the landscape on either side. The trees overhead scattered the sun and made navigation difficult. At the point he had drawn, the woodland was impenetrably thick, with sharp thorns. I thought I saw a fence in the distance once, but it might have been nothing but a curtain of creepers.

The rest of the day I spent sketching in the studio and leafing through the notebook. The more closely I examined it, the less I trusted Thomas. He had written a list of Pemberley's benefits and kindnesses, then undercut each one with baseless speculation about what Pemberley might have wanted in exchange. Mad Thomas: Francis's nickname for him seemed fairer than ever.

When it was time for dinner, I travelled to the hub alone, and – after my stupid, tactless questions to Pemberley this morning – was unsurprised to find myself off the top table again. There was no announcement from Pemberley before the dinner, except a few words asking us to wait afterwards so he could speak at greater length. I sat quietly with residents I didn't know. I had been here three days now. And Cara was still not here. Shouldn't she be with me to hear whatever this announcement was? If she was on the mainland, why hadn't Bianca been able to find her? And why was she in touch with Pemberley and not with me?

'Good evening, everybody.' The meal was over, I realised, and Pemberley was at the podium. 'Everybody present in this room; everyone watching from nearby, via the links we've set up. Welcome to the end of another day in our sanctuary. Another day in paradise.' He inhaled, and his whole frame swelled.

'We have achieved so much here, my friends. So much. We tread lightly on the earth. Our farming teams grow extraordinary foods from the air itself; the planet's beleaguered species flock here for safety. I'm proud to say that, thanks to the remarkable efforts of Angela Knight, we have completed our biodiversity bank of almost every species on this earth.' A cheer at this. 'We have destroyed the parasites our forebears introduced here.' Another cheer. 'We have done *so much*. There have been doubters. Cynics. But we have proven them wrong.'

Once again I was aware of Thomas's notebook in my pocket, and felt great shame to have entertained those thoughts.

The Sanctuary

'But it is not enough. You know that. Each day the planet hastens towards its grave. Many of you have asked what more we can do. We advocate, we publicise, but the fact remains: each day, countless more of our fellow beasts die, thanks to one species.' There were some boos at this, at the mainlanders shipwrecking the entire world.

'So tonight I want to tell you about the next phase. For us to show the world what we can do. I want us to prove this community can stand by itself – that we can live good lives, abundant lives, without destruction. Where they see limitation, we will approach the truest possible manifestation of life on earth. So this is my announcement. In two weeks' time, we will close the gates of this island, and we will become truly self-sufficient. No new imports; no extra resources pillaged from elsewhere. Just us, together, making it work.'

He was talking about closing the tunnel Bianca had shown me on my first day here; about closing it for good, truly cutting the island off. I looked around, startled, hoping to find some of the confusion and shock I felt reflected in the faces around me. I found none. The eyes of my dining companions shone, and they cast disbelieving looks of happiness at each other.

Pemberley continued. 'Now. We can only do this with everyone's consent. If anyone here wants to leave, then you may. Crowns for convoy will be put into your purse. Many of you may have reasons to want to return to the mainland – although I confess I can't think of any.' A ripple of laughter. 'This is a trial, too – we are going to do it for a short spell, and then, if it works, carry on. But if you do stay, I promise you this: we will create a new world on this ship of stone, and you will inherit it sooner than you think.

'And now, ladies and gentlemen, if you step outside, I will show you the proof that we can do anything.'

He stepped down from the podium, and the gleam of the spotlight vanished from his polished scalp.

Applause flooded the room; then chatter. I listened to my neighbours eagerly asserting that they would stay here no matter what. The doors at the end had opened and we streamed out, into the fresh evening air.

The central space of the hub was filling. The island's residents covered the grass slopes and the surrounding plateau, but the middle was left empty, with a path leading through it to the edge. Pits of fire stood around, ready for the cool of night. For a second I remembered being at the circus as a boy, and thought of the ringmaster, sinister and brilliant.

I walked to a point at the top of the circle, where the path met the hub. Pemberley was already there with Angela Knight and Munro, the head of security, as well as Bianca. He nodded at me.

'That was a wonderful speech,' I said.

He looked sideways at me. 'Hold your praise, Ben.'

There was a pause, then Munro spoke up.

'Are you going to tell us what we're standing around for, John?'

Pemberley merely grinned at us, and let Knight speak for him. 'You'll see, Alun.'

The circle fell silent. I looked around. There must have been four thousand of us standing there, experts and apprentices and healers and engineers, all the people who had made this place real. And me.

John stepped forward, into a patch of light, and raised his hands for silence. Unseen microphones amplified his voice.

'My friends.' He had spoken these words loud, for attention, and lowered his voice again. 'My friends. I promised you remarkable sights if you stayed with me. As those of you who have been with me for some time know, I like to make good on my promises. Please, if you will, welcome the newest recruit to our island life.' He turned and gestured past us, into the darkness.

Something was approaching down the marked-off path to the middle of the arena. There were a few screams of shock and delight from the people right by it, but nobody else could see what it was before it passed the fire pits at the end of the path. Then and only then did the rest of us see what was walking into the centre of the circle. At its side, dwarfed by it, were two attendants, who gently tugged it with the aid of ropes, and spoke to it in a language I did not know.

It was young, I gathered later, although I can't imagine how much larger a fully grown one would be. Female, too; I learned later that these ones all had tusks, whether male or female.

It stood there and issued a small cry, then the only sound in the entire circle of four thousand people was the flickering of the flames around the edge.

Bianca was the first to speak.

'Is it real? Is it ... made? What is it?'

'We made it,' Pemberley said. 'We made it and it's only the beginning.'

That was when the cheering began, a great ragged cry from four thousand throats, and as it looked warily around at the throng beyond the fires, the elephant raised its trunk and joined the chorus.

Later, a bonfire was lit in the spot where it had stood, and we gathered near the flames in the dark. I felt drunk.

'How, how did he do it?' I asked. 'Either he bred it and kept it secret on the mainland estate, or he's cloned it, or ... or something else. But how did he keep it secret?'

'I have no idea.' Bianca was the only one who had not remained astonished for long by the sight of the elephant. She had seemed almost repelled by it, in fact.

'How is it being raised?'

'Animatronic costumes, I guess, or disguises. It probably thinks it's being raised by more of its own kind. It thinks it has proper parents.' She shrugged. 'Probably for the best it doesn't know.'

'A secret elephant. He really is a god.'

'Don't let him hear you. It'll go to his head.' I laughed, and Bianca glanced at me. 'It's a choice, being here. You do know that, don't you? You have a choice.'

I couldn't see that I did. I had to wait for Cara. Pemberley had said she would be back before long, after all. As for Bianca's phone call to the mainland – she simply hadn't phoned the right office. She was unworldly enough to get the wrong impression and cling to it. I could not dispel those doubts entirely, those shreds of cloud on the horizon, but I had been wrong about such feelings before. I would be wrong again this time. I must have faith that I was wrong.

The fire in front of us was burning higher than ever, and as the breeze shifted, its heat was driven towards us. A small team of islanders were feeding it with broken planks of wood, and new tongues of flame jumped up to investigate them: bright, and welcoming, and obliterating. I had a momentary vision then of the whole island in flames, I couldn't say why, and shivered, even in the driving heat.

In my pocket, the notebook Thomas had kept felt as leathery and rough as the elephant's skin had looked. This place was perfect – the evidence of my eyes was all around me – and yet here I held the one piece of solid evidence from someone who had believed it to be hell.

Book III

Sea-Change

Annihilating all that's made
To a green thought, in a green shade
Andrew Marvell

21

Ten days had passed since we had seen the elephant. There had been further wonders since, but that was the point at which I had finally realised how much more *real* this place was than the poor carnival of shadows that had preceded it. The mainland killed elephants; this place made new ones.

Spring had advanced in a rush. The sun pitched higher in the sky each day, and across the island, life had surged from the earth with the confidence of an invading horde. The conifers were lush, their branches heavy with deep greens, and the deciduous trees stretched towards the sun. The air was sweet with new scents and washed with torrents of birdsong.

A line from an old play, or perhaps a poem, kept recurring to me: 'Be not afeard; the isle is full of noises'. I couldn't remember where it was from – the works of the mainland had faded in importance by now – but it felt true. It had rained for three days a week ago, yet the paths underfoot had stayed well drained, and we had been warm and dry within our homes. Everything was for the best, and the world was grown new again.

It was hard to remember the cramped, ageing mainland without a shudder. I remembered how I had thought the world's future could only be secured by the millions of people in my country and the countless millions more around the world; it was embarrassing, now that I had seen what a few thousand could do with determination and true leadership.

My mornings were spent painting John. My hand had recovered fully, meaning I could accompany Francis in the fields once the day's sitting was over. I had been to the polytunnels, where you felt nourished simply by breathing in the scent of a hundred different species. Some afternoons, I would wander the island, introduce myself to a different hex each day and learn whatever I could. I felt like the reverse of Mad Thomas. Where he had found pain and suspicion, I had seen the good written through this place.

After dinner – several times a week I would sit with John and his companions, not that that mattered – I would often be invited to a gathering at John's lodge. I laughed sometimes, thinking of my cramped home back in the city, compared with the life I led now.

All I needed was Cara – and John had assured me several times that her work on the mainland estate was almost complete. There were still five days until the island's closure. She would be back in time. I had not told him what Bianca had told me, but

John seemed far more reliable on this matter. I worried, of course, but I had faith too. What is faith if unaccompanied by doubt?

I had mapped almost the whole island now, barring the tangled corner of the south-east that held the biological vaults, where naturally strict protocols applied. I was luckier than most of the workers; I had more time free to make myself useful or increase my knowledge of the place. In this, I seemed to have John's tacit approval.

My main work, the painting, was nearing its final stages. In the sessions, out of them, as I woke and before I slept at night, it was the only thing I cared about. I had felt more purpose, more creative spirit, in a few weeks here than in ten years on the mainland. Finally I was carrying out the labour I was meant to fulfil.

John was sitting forward in the portrait, his hands before him, fingers interlocked. He wanted a pose that suggested energy, potential. Now, so many of my previous pictures seemed dull in comparison – those families with their perfect lives, their dogs. He had asked to see some of them, and I had shown him a few. He had not said anything critical, but I had blushed as he surveyed their flatness, their lack of life.

This, however ... John's was a portrait where energy and truth jostled in equal measure, a picture that would inspire its viewers with the dynamism of the man it showed. The base layers were long complete, the background painted in (a single ivory column from his bedroom, mirroring his strength and solitude), and the clothes and hands were finished too. I was building up the layers of the face slowly. But I was struggling. How could one depict energy like his in a still image? Some mornings I doubted whether the entire medium could contain him.

To be painting a man like John in such close proximity – and, of course, in solitude – was giddying sometimes. He was like a young morning star, a bringer of light, and he exerted an almost physical pull on everything and everyone around him. It was evident at dinners, or when I accompanied him on journeys around the island – his people wanted to be near him. When he and I were alone together, I felt a curious power, as though I had temporarily borrowed some of his gravity. Approaching the canvas standing at his right hand was invigorating and terrifying, every time.

John himself did little to alleviate the difficulties in my work; painting him was like depicting a landscape in all four seasons at once. My former clients had usually arranged their features into whatever shape they thought made them look best. John's own emotional state each day encompassed the pensive, swaggering, thunderous, humble, solemn, bombastic, and dozens more. Perhaps an outside observer would say his expression looked the same from one day to the next, but I could tell the different states within him. I told him sometimes I felt like I had to paint a crowd, and he snorted and told me it wasn't his fault I couldn't hit a moving target.

The whole island had a feeling of expectancy. In the wake of John's announcement a few residents had left, with our good wishes; but once they had gone, we who remained had acknowledged that we had never been entirely sure about them. When the small party of leavers had departed by boat – a modest ceremony was held at the harbour – the rest of us had surveyed each other with excitement. We were the remaining crew of the ship of stone, and we would guide its course through the months and years ahead.

This approaching change in direction – this moment of embarkation – gave each day on the island a frisson. Each night at dinner John announced how many days remained, and we all applauded the progress. There was an extra pressure in the air, the kind the city felt before a riot – but benign, of course, wholly benign. John felt it too, and called it 'the electrical charge of the future, calling us towards it'.

The practicalities were being dealt with now. There were a few final consignments of goods to arrive – mostly raw materials the island lacked in sufficient quantities – but they would be here in a day or two. Some of us had heard that the mouth of the tunnel was being fitted with explosives, to be detonated on the day of closure; the stone umbilical would be severed at last, leaving us free. Cara would be back in time for that, I had to keep reminding myself, and we would watch it together.

Two people alone remained curious bruises in this place. Angela Knight had lost status even in the short time since I had arrived here. Her look at the dinner table most evenings was abstracted, as if she was striving to remember something just beyond her memory. She was out of favour, and clearly felt it.

When John spoke to her to cajole her, she livened immediately, but as soon as the beam of his attention slid off her, she lapsed again into a torpor veined with bitterness. Our dinners were not seriously inhibited by this – she had never contributed much in any case – but it was enough to cast a slim, mournful veil over otherwise cheerful proceedings. Occasionally John lost his temper with her – justifiably, in my opinion.

Bianca Pemberley had worn a similar air of sorrow these last weeks. Although we still had enjoyable conversations at dinner, it was clear to me that John had been right – she was somehow damaged beyond repair. I had less time to spend with her, of course, given the demands of my work. But I worried for her. She had picked up a habit of breaking off from the conversation and looking down at her lap. If you were next to her, you could hear her crooning gently, blocking out the world.

I was concerned about her not least because of the terrible effect her behaviour must be having on John. She and Knight were two of the three people closest to him – had been, at least, before I arrived – and their inability to enjoy life here after all his work must have weighed on him heavily. Whenever possible, I cheered her up, and in just the last fortnight I suspected I had become one of the people here she trusted most.

John and I talked a great deal in our painting sessions. Sometimes I would pause my work for minutes on end while we spoke, then feel the time escaping and reluctantly ask for silence for the next few brushstrokes. We talked about everything: the extinctions on the mainland, the vault of life, how the island's climate would shift in the decades to come. I asked after the elephant, too, and John told me it had been transported to the mainland. Soon it would be taken onwards to a more suitable environment, in one of his substantial overseas estates. More would be created to follow it, he said, although he refused to reveal how the work had been done, taking refuge in the idea of himself as the island's resident magician.

We even – and this is when I knew I had truly gained his confidence – spoke a little about his early life. It had begun with shared reminiscences of school, of which buildings had changed, and when I mentioned my own family, he listened with patience, trusting I was not soliciting information about his own. Occasionally he seemed to suggest that his parents had been in the law, or business, or perhaps politics. None would explain his extraordinary wealth, of course, but I guessed he had inherited a small amount and done the rest on his own. And if I felt curious still, I had to remind myself to be satisfied with the completed man before me.

We spoke about the world outside, too. John received digests from his offices on the mainland and would disseminate the relevant parts to us. I had not appreciated before what a burden it had been back there, being caught in a drift of news, a fresh trough of mud to wade through each morning. Here we had the perspective of distance and saw the world for what it was – a distraction from our work.

I was moving from my position at the canvas, right by John, to my spot a few metres away, to get the perspective for my next strokes, when I thought to say it.

'May I ask ...' I did not know how to put this, given the argument during our first ever conversation. 'I know this is nothing like a prepper's home. But is it partly designed to carry things forward? If it all goes wrong elsewhere?'

'You could put it that way.'

I was abashed to say what I said next, fearing laughter, or freezing silence. 'Like an ark.'

But he was gentle in his reply. 'That's one way of thinking of it, Ben. And I see why you think that. We have several thousand species here that are now found almost nowhere else. Thanks to Angela's work, and of course to Cara's great efforts too.' He paused. 'But it does nobody any good to think of it that way. If the people here knew the weight of the burden they carry – protecting so many possible futures – they might not be able to stand it.'

'Why tell me, then?'

'Because you are one of the people who will take this place forward, Ben. By helping Cara – once she's returned, of course. You must see that.' I had thought of it before, imagined I was being prepared for a greater role here at various points over the last week, but to hear John say it now brought a great warm feeling to my face, my chest, the palms of my hands. He carried on. 'She has practical skills, and you have the vision to support her. And you had a wonderful anger in you when you came here, because you thought I'd made the mainland what it was.'

I looked down at my palette, embarrassed. 'Yes.'

'That's all right, Ben. I understand it. You wanted change. But the mainland will always be like that. We'll never change its rules, so we're making new ones here. And you and Cara have the courage and the youth to carry it forward.'

'But you're not ... going anywhere, are you?'

'Of course not.'

'And ...' I hesitated to ask my next question, knowing how private he could be, but I thought I was secure enough to take the risk, 'why not Bianca?'

He sighed, moved his shoulders. 'Expected inheritance rarely works. You know the idea of the *novus homo*?'

'The new man?' He nodded, and I felt relief. 'Someone who goes into a field untainted by a family history within it, not receiving advantage.'

'Exactly. Look at the leaders who tried to create something new, then rowed back and handed over to their children. Napoleon, Cromwell, a hundred dictators. It never worked. Why not?'

'Because their children were expecting to inherit.'

'Exactly. They may have had the raw material, but they never had the chance to create themselves first. I love Bianca very dearly. But she carries too much of her mother, and her expectations have warped her too far. You have noticed her frailties, I'm sure.'

The conversation lapsed, and I painted in silence for a few more minutes until the close of the session.

That afternoon I sat in the studio at the cottage, trying to understand what John had told me. He had as good as confirmed me and Cara as his heirs here. It seemed fabulous – although of course, it would not be relevant for many years to come. And yet, when I looked at it again, why should we not be? Cara had the skills, as he said; I was temperamentally suited to help her, in his judgement. It made perfect sense.

My reflections were interrupted by a knock from beyond the cottage. Francis and Joanna were both out – him in the fields, her in the island's kitchens – so I left the studio and opened the door.

Beneath the porch, dark-eyed and shivering, stood Bianca Pemberley.

She was wearing jeans, and a thin T-shirt not quite warm enough for the day. Her hair was wet, and I saw the gooseflesh on her upper arms. Her face was blotchy and scrubbed; she seemed to have put on some make-up in an attempt to conceal the discoloration, although she looked as if she had never worn any cosmetics before in her life. She was nervous too, and glanced around at the empty hex behind her as though she expected to be stopped and dragged away any moment.

'Can I come in?'

I moved to the side and gestured to the main room. She walked through it and into the studio before I could stop her.

'I think Munro's following me.'

'Why would he do that, Bianca?'

But by the time I had finished asking the question she was leafing through a stack of canvases brought over from the mainland.

'These are beautiful.'

They were some experiments in landscapes I had made a few years ago, of the city's wild places – a tree bursting through an abandoned railing, a library giving itself to the ivy.

'Is everything all right?'

'Of course. Just coming to see how you're getting on.'

I nodded. The real purpose of her visit would doubtless emerge before long. She leaned the stack gently back against the wall.

'And these . . .' She looked through some preparatory sketches I had made of her father's head, then shifted them beneath some other works, as if to hide from him. She turned to me. 'Do you think you could sketch me?'

'Of course I could.'

'Today?'

'We can start now if you like.'

I arranged her seat so she would be comfortable, and as I stood near her, I noticed a series of scratches running along her right arm.

I began to draw. She seemed more fragile than she had on my first day here. The features I recognised from her father's face – her chin and the set of her eyes – were still there, but they were disguised by the cosmetics, as if she was trying to make herself look as different from him as possible. She had been slender before; today she was almost gaunt. But she still managed to ask the occasional question that made her sound like the lady of the island.

'How have you been spending your days?'

'The painting is taking most of my spare time. That and touring the island, trying to understand how it all fits together. It's wonderful.'

'Very wonderful.' She was looking away from me, at the painting of Judith and Holofernes.

'The things I've seen here could fill a book.' I wished I hadn't said that as soon as the words were out. I thought of Kevin Ladd, the last man to try writing a book about Sir John, and felt annoyed with myself for even thinking of him. John had assured me of the truth there.

'Thomas was working on a book.' She spoke softly.

'I'm not sure Thomas was completely well, Bianca.'

A pause after that. She seemed to be screwing up her courage.

'There's something I'd like you to do for me.'

'Yes, of course. Anything. What is it?'

That seemed to be the wrong answer, because at that moment she burst into tears – not quietly, not modestly, but in a great torrent of misery. The tears ran down her white cheeks, and her eyes reddened afresh. I stood, abandoned the sketch, fetched water from the main room, but by the time I got back, she had slid from the stool to the ground and was folded there. I sat beside her, murmuring various soothing idiocies without knowing what would help.

After a few minutes, she stopped and pulled herself back.

'My father ... I know you won't believe me, but ... he killed my mother.'

She must have seen my expression, because she carried on, bolstering her statement. 'He did. As good as. He took me away from her and left her alone. He took everything from her, all her hope and her happiness, and she couldn't survive for long after that.'

I remembered my misgivings about John before I had arrived here; the embers of feelings I had struggled with and finally overcome now glowing again as she breathed on them. I could not pretend I didn't want to know more.

'That doesn't sound like him, Bianca. Why do you say that?'

'I know what happened to my mother. He separated us. He brought me here when I was one year old and I've never been anywhere else.'

'That's not what John says.'

She was clearly in a state of some fragility, because that angered her. 'Oh, and what does he say? That I spent years on the mainland, suffered from my own weakness there, with men and drugs and God knows what else? That I had to come back for my own good, that I can't bring myself to remember those times? None of it's true, Ben.' Those were, indeed, exactly John's intimations, which disturbed me a little. 'And you believe everything he tells you? Bianca L. Pemberley, the island's resident monster?'

'I'm not qualified to—'

'I believe you could see him for what he is if you bothered to try. He is …' Her hands flexed, trying to summon the shape of him before her in the air.

'Why me, Bianca? Why tell me this?'

'Because you still seem like a human being, more or less, even though he's got his hooks in you. I can't talk to Angela. Munro would run straight to John and tell him. The rest of these people are fully paid up. I had to tell someone.' She breathed deeply, and began.

Her mother had been a model on the mainland, she told me, twenty-five years ago, the same age as John. Her name was Persephone. They had met when he was new in the city, setting up his first batch of ten Villages, still in his early twenties. They had become close; she was his first ever lover, and – from what Bianca intimated – his last. Part of me wanted to hear none of this personal information about my benefactor; another part fed on it with great relief. Another element in me, far below the surface, rang in sympathy, as if I had always known it.

Persephone and John had had their baby, but Persephone's health suffered terribly, and after a year of pain, she was no longer capable of looking after the infant alone. John had brought Bianca here, lamenting only that she was not a boy. There was a dispute in the courts, and Bianca's mother was crushed by the weight of the law. Now that John had ensured his genes survived, he had no use for the human vessel who had made it happen. Custody of the little girl was granted to him.

From then on, Bianca's mother had lived no life at all. She would take a portion of her remaining money from the bank to the nearest bar, every day, back and forth, back and forth, and the drink had robbed her of herself, had made her flat and empty inside and out.

'How do you know all this?'

'She wrote to me, sometimes. Angela took pity on her, and brought her letters when she could.' So that had been it – Bianca's mother had lost her in court but found a conduit to manipulate her daughter for years after that. I was surprised to hear about Knight, although I would not put it past her to maintain her influence in the family's next generation in case it proved useful one day. What Bianca was describing sounded like abduction, and I told her so.

'It's not abduction if it's your child and the world thinks her mother is unfit. Then it's good parenting.' All the tensions I had detected in her in the last weeks, the sorrows, the purposeless-ness – they made sense now.

'Do you want me to talk to John about this?'

'No. That's the last thing I want. Please. You mustn't ever tell him I've told you. Swear it.' I did so.

'Why would he do any of this?'

'It's more a question of why he would have had a child in the first place. You've seen the way he talks to me sometimes. It's like he's talking to all the bits of her he couldn't stand.'

I recalled occasional moments of strictness on John's part, but I had hardly thought of them as cruel until now.

'You've seen how he hates age and wealth. Passing things on, concentrating them, growing old and rich, your children spending their whole lives waiting to inherit, growing slack ...' Bianca gave a short bark of a laugh, sounding for a moment like him. 'I'm just the unlucky one who happens to be his family.'

'You said there was something you wanted me to do.'

'He's closing the island in four days. But there's something else going on beyond that. I'm trying to find out what.' I thought of the conversation I had heard in the chapel between Pemberley and Knight in my first days here.

'I don't know why you think I can help especially.'

'You went to the same school as him. You told me that when I showed you the hub. I want you to find out what he did there.'

'What he did at Hillcrest?'

'Maybe they have records of his behaviour. Maybe his parents' names. Something. Anything.'

'Why do you want that?'

'Nobody knows anything about him before the age of twenty, when he turned up in the city, rich as God. You're the only link I have. Nobody even knew the hall in the hub was based on the school until you arrived. I can't go there myself. So I'm asking you to find out.'

'Why now?'

'Because I need to find out what he's going to do next, and it's tied to the island closure. I have no idea what it is, but I want to know.' She met my eye. 'I think you do too.'

'How do you expect me to find anything out?'

'There are phones in the admin hub. You could use one of them.'

I nodded. My former teacher, Fentiman, would probably talk to me. She had been at Hillcrest for decades before me, although there was no guarantee she was still alive, let alone that she would remember John.

'Will you do it? Say you will.'

'I'll think about it, Bianca.'

'You're worried you'll never finish your precious painting.' She had her father's gift for finding points of leverage.

'It's not so simple.'

'Yes it is. You think you're on the brink of creating something special, a real work of *art*, and you think that means you can blind yourself to everything else here.'

'My job is to complete the painting.'

'I thought your job was to see him accurately, and show what you see to the world. Clearly I've made a grave error.'

A third voice, high and harsh, speaking from the doorway, cut across the two of us. 'What's this?'

Angela Knight stood in the gloom of the cottage. I had left the front door open, partly so I would hear anyone approaching; Knight had clearly moved more subtly than I expected. What she thought when she saw us, I have no idea: Bianca on the floor, her back to the wall and her legs stretched out, her face still blotchy with tears, and me standing at the other side of the room, arms crossed, biting my thumbnail. Bianca broke the silence.

'Munro took a while to track me down this time.'

'Don't be paranoid. You were seen coming this way. Your father wants you.'

She got to her feet, thanked me for my time, and walked past Knight out of the cottage, looking once more like a china doll.

'What was going on?' Knight was looking at me with her usual dislike.

'Sketching session.' Although I realised later that by the time Knight had come in, I hadn't even been holding my pad.

Dinner began quietly that night. John was late. Bianca was as subdued as usual. Munro, the security chief, rearranged his cutlery and made little passes in the air with his knife. Our guests at the table – Yshani, who worked in the engineering hex, and Mat, my friend from security who I'd met on my third night here – picked up on the mood like nervous pack animals, and stayed quiet. Knight arrived late too, and sat herself next to Munro. The pair of them kept up a muttered conversation, one the rest of us were not party to.

Only John's eventual arrival, one course in, managed to raise our spirits. He seemed to sense the collective depression and responded to it – cajoling, hectoring, teasing and declaring, until gradually we warmed and became malleable under the beam of his attention.

My own attention was distracted by Bianca, spearing her asparagus, her eyes low. How could she live here thinking such things about her father? Had she been lying or exaggerating earlier on, or did she really believe he had caused her mother's death? My desire to contact the school and enquire about John weakened in his presence, but the choice before me was still stark: I could explore his past and risk my entire future here, or refuse and earn Bianca's lasting contempt.

John, of course, skated over the tensions around the table, and as I listened to him speaking, I was reminded again that everything would be all right just as soon as Cara returned. My thoughts drifted, and I only paid attention when the conversation turned once again to extinction. Knight was speaking.

'... fact is, species are resilient, but only when they get a chance to be. If we were cleared away, they would find the entire place serviceable. A bit shabby, a bit battered, but essentially quite liveable.'

'You're right,' John said, 'but that doesn't answer the essential question.'

'Which is?'

'How you create that space on a large scale.'

'Like the rats.' I remembered that from a couple of weeks ago, and wanted to contribute.

'What's that, Ben?'

'The rats. They got a foothold here a few years ago, found it was a perfect space for them, then had a resurgence and had to be wiped out all over again.' Knight rolled her eyes, and I remembered too late that she had been furious with Bianca for bringing it up last time. But she couldn't know what I had read in Thomas's notebook. *Where the rats?*

'Yes, it's true. They must have made it to land on one of the containers, improperly screened. Or they escaped the biobank. It won't happen again. There are new protocols in place, thanks to Angela.' John grinned at her, and she smiled back. In the candlelight of the table, she looked almost maternal.

'Did they multiply so fast because the island was ready for them?'

John glanced at me, on the edge of irritation. 'Of course. Empty territory. Conditions ripe. It's meant to be a sanctuary, after all. The tragedy is, so many species around the world are waiting for an opportunity to spring back. But we're not giving them one.'

'Did you have to make a new lot of traps?'

'Actually we found another way of doing it. Very clever way. Isn't that right, Angela?' He smiled again at Knight, who acknowledged it with another small twist of the cheek, less friendly this time.

'And what was that?'

She cut across me almost before I'd finished the sentence. 'Proprietary information, I fear.'

'Angela's right. Can't have you running the whole place just yet, Ben.' Beyond him, Knight's smile was replaced by a blank expression. I felt sorry for her in that moment, but not too sorry. She had hardly been kind to me. I doubted John had told her his intentions for me and Cara, and felt unconcerned whether he broke the news gently or not when the time came.

It was Francis who had confirmed Bianca's claim about the rats coming back. We had been at the roadside a few days before, erecting frames for new polytunnels. As we walked, he found a collection of small bones tucked in an alcove beneath the road's surface, and he told me the story. I related it now, leaving his name out of it.

'Someone told me they ran rampant for a few months, then all seemed to just drop one day. As if the entire species had been poisoned in one go.'

'Wouldn't that be nice.' John guffawed, and the conversation turned again. But I noticed Knight's knuckles were white as she gripped the stem of her glass.

After dinner, I excused myself from attending the lodge, pleading exhaustion after the day's work, and told John I could not paint him first thing. He swore, but laughed as he did, and told me to paint him at noon instead.

It was that conversation that decided the matter. I found Bianca before I left, and together we made our plan for the following morning. My night's sleep was going to be a short one. Perhaps that's why my first dream stayed in my mind, and woke me with a start under the moon's cold light: I had seen a rock in the ocean swarming with rats, and John, benevolent John, standing astride it, as large as a house, laying about him with a mallet and laughing as he did.

The number for Hillcrest would be the same as it ever had been. I remembered it partly because the school wrote to me each autumn, each time on cheaper paper, making appeals for roofing work, new science centres, everything bar food and teaching. Cara and I called them 'organ donation' requests, after the time they had written asking us to sponsor a pipe.

Their desperation was understandable. In the years since I left, fewer and fewer children attended private schools; for most Village parents, the internal system of education laid on was more than satisfactory. Even during my days there, Hillcrest had been suffering due to the Villages, like a tree choked by the ivy using it as a support. Funny to think that the school's most successful alumnus had been the chief cause of its decline.

I had never woken this early on the island, but as soon as I had shaken off sleep I resolved to rise at this hour every day. The air was cool, the landscape wreathed in drifting mists that robed the trees. Birdsong cut through the thick dawn air.

Bianca was waiting for me outside, and we took a cart for ourselves. It was early enough that even the administrative hub was almost totally dark as we approached. It was a long, low building with a roof that gradually sloped upwards; some workers had a huge airy space above them, and some were in a space no taller than they were. Bianca went to speak to the solitary figure of the night manager. A few minutes later, she came out and hurried me through to a side room at the lower end, to my relief; a room almost empty barring a desk, a chair and a phone. She seemed agitated.

'What?'

'We left it too late.'

'You said this time would be safe.'

'They've brought the shifts forward an hour each day as they prepare for the closure. You don't have long to make your call before the first team arrive. They won't need the room, but it's best for you not to be seen making the call.'

'Can the lines be recorded?'

'This room is one of the off-grid ones. I arranged it with Harry last night.' Bianca nodded at the distant figure of the watchman who had let us in. 'There are still one or two advantages to being John's daughter here. But I'll go and talk to him now, just to make sure.'

She moved down to the other end, where the columns supporting the hub soared up like a cathedral, and spoke to the watchman, then gave me a quick nod and a thumbs-up.

I dialled the number for the school without thinking; my fingers knew the pattern better than my mind. A voice answered, glazed with sleep. I could picture the porter's lodge the phone had sounded in, jerking him awake, a cosy den with small windows and a smaller radiator, crammed with paperwork and all the paraphernalia required to keep the school in motion.

It was strange to be speaking to the mainland. The people there had faded from reality somehow, and when I looked at the half-completed canvases in the studio, they seemed to me like elaborate fabrications, pictures of people who did not really exist. Yet here the mainland was, answering my questions in a tired northern voice. Fentiman had retired; Fentiman still came in to the art department sometimes, like an honorary colonel inspecting her regiment; Fentiman was living in a care home, and yes, he'd give me the details.

I dialled the number, explained the hour of my call by saying the matter was urgent. Eventually Sarah Fentiman was brought to the phone, or it to her.

'Hello?'

'Dr Fentiman. It's Benjamin Parr.'

'Who is this?' She mumbled those words, and I felt a moment of dread. She had lost her memory, or her clarity, and I felt a wash of disappointment that I would find out nothing further. Maybe it was a sign that my errand was a foolish one. Perhaps I should simply return to trusting in John and his works.

'It's Ben Parr. The artist.' I was speaking louder, in the patronising way of the young towards the old. At the other end of the line I heard a door thud shut, and at my end I heard a momentary quiet on the other side of the partition. I lowered my voice. 'I was at Hillcrest.'

Fentiman spoke again, sharper this time. 'Ben Parr – yes, I remember you. I was just waiting for them to leave the room. None of their business who phones me.'

'How are you?'

'Still here, and I mean that' – she took a breath – 'both as a positive and a negative.'

'Have you been living at your current place long?'

'About six years. The food's appalling, but I give them a good thrashing about it in the meetings, and one of the nurses buys me cigarettes.'

'I hope you're still painting?'

'I am, but it's an uphill struggle. Half the people here don't recognise themselves, so a portrait is a bit of a waste, and we're all looking past our best anyway. I've even started classes, would you believe.' I murmured admiration, but she merely grunted in reply. 'So *stupid*. Passing a skill around my generation is like throwing a ball back and forth on the edge of a volcano. But that's not the point, I know.'

'You always told me the point is to keep doing it.'

'Did I? How perceptive of me. I hope you listened. How's your career?'

'It's fine. More than fine. I'm sorry, I should have written and told you, but I've stayed in it. I paint a lot these days.'

'I should think so. There were four or five pupils in my time at Hillcrest who I thought might show a bit of promise, and you were one of them. You know what you're doing, of course?'

'Tell me.'

I heard her chuckle. 'You're using your wits to defeat exactly the sort of people you were schooled alongside.'

'Actually, Dr Fentiman, that's what I wanted to talk to you about. I've had a bit of a change in my circumstances.'

'Yes?'

'I've ended up working not so far from the school, actually.'

'On an island?'

'... Yes.'

'An island owned by another former pupil of this school?'

'Yes.' My cheeks felt hot. 'How did you know?'

Another throaty chuckle, which transmuted into a hacking cough. 'Well, well. I wouldn't have put you two in the same space. But there we go. I hope you're being treated well.'

'Very.' I allowed a little coldness into my voice. There was an oblique criticism in her tone, of John or of me, and much of me was still clinging to the hope that everything might be resolved.

'What do your family think of the choice?'

'I have none to tell, I'm afraid.'

'Shame. I remember meeting your mother on several occasions. Jennifer, yes?' God knew how she had remembered that. 'A lovely woman. I'm sure she'd be very proud.' This seemed manipulative, as though she was trying to remind me of the world I'd left behind, but I murmured thanks.

'Not at all. I'm sure she's in a better place, although goodness knows almost everywhere else seems better at the moment. So are you ringing just to tell me your news, Ben Parr?'

'No, I'm not.'

'You want to know something.'

'I do. Whatever you can tell me.'

'About your new patriarch?'

'I wouldn't call him that.'

'Nonetheless, you knew who I was referring to, didn't you?' There was her sarcasm again. I had missed it. 'Anything in particular?'

I looked at the partition wall in front of me. 'I'm just trying to fill in the details.'

'You sound worried. Do you think you're being overheard where you are?'

'It's possible.'

'Well, I'll talk then, and you can shut me up if you need to.' She sounded jolly, almost, as if she had been waiting all this time simply for someone to ask about John.

'You must remember this is over thirty years ago. I was middle-aged then, if you can imagine such wonders now. And you must understand none of this came via me. We were placed under dire injunctions of secrecy after he left, by that worthless head we had, Muir, and although I think they'd struggle to lock up an octogenarian in worse conditions than I'm currently in, I dare-say they could take my brushes away and we don't want that. All right?'

I told her, all right.

'He came to Hillcrest one morning. October, it was. A month after term started. He had no luggage, but clothes were sent for. That happened back then. Parents would send their children to the school with expense accounts for the tailors in the town, and the teachers were expected to arrange it. Fourteen years old, he was, but there was already a quality to him. Something had been … cut off. A terrible thing to say of a child, but it's true.

'We were briefed about him, which was uncommon, and we were left with no illusions how much more important his happiness was than ours – or rather his comfort, I should say. His happiness seemed a bit beyond us. We all assumed some deal had been done. Don't let anyone tell you the people who run private schools aren't gangsters. We're all just looking for protection money really, and for the right sum we'll … Well, anyway.

'He wasn't unhappy. But he arrived after the start of term, so he found it hard to make friends. And he had this ill-fitting quality about him. He felt like the loose element in a painting, the one you can always identify immediately. For the first year he excelled at biblical studies, I remember, and struggled with everything else. Had half the Bible in his head, but could hardly read. His painting was intolerable. He looked at me like I was mad to even suggest it. I let him sit and daub, and that kept him quiet enough.

'The other thing he was really obsessed with was gardening. In his early years he spent all his free time following the gardeners, asking them questions, taking cuttings. When not in lessons, all he did was tend however many pots he was allowed in his room. There was some incident where another boy smashed up his collection of greenery, and Pemberley beat him senseless. Smoothed over, I believe, with a poultice of money.

'He never went home. Never. We're used to putting children up over some holidays when their parents have forgotten them, or they've decided their offspring would be an inconvenience because they're starting a new affair. I do think it's miraculous we turned out so many people who were basically functional after the experiences they had outside the grounds. But we never had another pupil constantly on school premises for four years.

'I was driving back after a holiday once, and as I came through the gates – you remember that amazing view opening up? – there he was, straight ahead. He was the only figure on the whole wide lawn, playing some invented game with a pair of sticks. He stopped as I went by, as if embarrassed to be caught in a moment of play, and then went back to it as soon as I had passed. I must say I pitied him then, for all his wealth.

'Anyway, there was a fair bit of curiosity about him, you can imagine. We were used to the maladjusted children of the rich, and usually the problems increase with the wealth, but it was as if he'd been raised in a desert. Paul and I – you might remember him as Mr Jacob, if he ever taught you, biology teacher – tried to find out who he was in that first year. We were an item at the time. He's dead now, poor thing. Anyway, we looked in the bursar's office at Christmas – Terry was always terribly lax with his keys, especially after a party.

'You might imagine he was the son of someone fabulously wealthy, some prince or shah. Well, the only entry for a parental contact was a number – a long string of digits, looked like a phone number. I took it down, didn't really know why, but it gnawed away at me, and a year or so later I phoned it out of sheer curiosity, anonymously of course, from the pub in the village. Now, what was the name they gave when they answered?' She paused for a long time. Please let her remember, I found myself thinking.

'Aramanthe. That was it. Aramanthe Partners.' She spelled it out. 'I sent it to a friend of mine, a journalist. Kevin, his name was. He told me they were a law firm, based in the city. He looked into it, years later, but I doubt anything ever came of it.'

I tried to sound casual. 'Was that Kevin Ladd, by any chance?'

'You always were clever, Benjamin. Yes. Kevin Ladd.' She kept talking as though it was natural I would know him. 'How is he?'

'Same place as Mr Jacob, I'm afraid.'

'Oh, what a shame. Well, it's the time of life for that sort of thing, especially the men.'

As she spoke, I had imagined myself back in the school, walking the corridors John had walked a few decades before, playing on those lawns. But my own outsider status had been thanks to my comparative poverty. John's had come from some-where else entirely.

'What happened to him in the later years?'

'That's the most interesting thing. He woke up, rather. After two years as this odd little drifter, he suddenly started paying attention. It was like he had been activated, like a bulb waiting for spring. And from then on he was very nearly a prodigy. Dropped biblical studies like a hot potato, even dropped most of the plants, and started with everything else. History, government – I always worried about the children whose natural urge was to study government, instead of something normal like French – all the structural things that showed how the world worked.

'He was very adept at the life sciences too, I recall. Paul said he was obsessed with heritability, the perfection of the human form. You wouldn't think it, from someone who went on to make all his money from property, would you? But that was his obscssion, once the plants thing had died down a bit. Paul ran out of things to teach him.

'His character changed, too. All of a sudden he was charming, self-assured, firm of handshake, smooth of brow, all that stuff. He developed a way of looking at you when you addressed him, confident but inviting. It felt horribly *learned* to me. Mechanistic, as if he had read a paper informing him of the exact angle to hold your head to seem empathetic. But the other teachers quite disagreed; they said it was proof we had succeeded totally in turning him around from whatever circumstances he'd escaped. I had my doubts, and I have to say the other boys seemed to agree with me. He left with as many friends as he had when he first came. But then, as you know, he started building, and that was it.'

'Why didn't his friends ever talk to the press about him?'

'He had none; it was that simple, I'm afraid. He didn't cultivate people his own age. The social act was all with the oldies. And as for the teachers, we were under very strict instructions never to talk about him. You know, I sometimes wondered if young John hadn't bought the headmaster.'

'Did you ever find out where he'd come from?'

'No. The law firm was very quiet, I remember Kevin telling me. Global clientele, all keeping their money in sunny places where nobody could get at it.'

She chuckled again. 'John Pemberley. It's not his real name, of course. It was chosen for him on his arrival by the headmaster. He had clearly tried to come up with the most solid name he could possibly think of. I never knew the boy's previous name, and I'm quite sure that was deliberate. We taught him the novel, Austen's novel, when he was a little older, and he was delighted by it. He liked it so much that he instructed one of my colleagues to buy a first edition of it.'

'A first edition, at his age?'

'He was wealthier than you or I could imagine. You can see why he liked the notion, of course. Unimaginable riches, manicured gardens and forests, the perfection of the human form, and a background clear as tar. Not a bad model, although we chose better than we knew. Remember where Mr Darcy's money really came from?'

'Can you remind me?'

'The servitude of the poor.'

24

I said farewell to Fentiman without revealing the reasons I had wanted to know about John, although she chuckled again as if to suggest she knew far more than I did about the matter.

As I left the admin hub, the first batch of administrators were arriving at their desks, still yawning. I moved past them swiftly enough, and the nightwatchman Bianca had been speaking to gave me a nod. He looked at me curiously, as if my face was arranged in an unusual manner, but there was no need for that, because I felt quite all right, and there was nothing wrong. Nothing at all.

Bianca and I had agreed to meet back at the cottage, but when I got there, I found only a note, wedged into the door frame where anyone could read it: *Come to the s.c.* The writing was a scrawl, quite unlike Cara's beautiful copperplate, the product of long hours of calligraphy in girlhood, the toils that proved she would make something of her life. That Cara had made the time to improve herself, to lay her own path upwards, while Bianca had retained this scrawl – it reaffirmed what I thought of both of them. For all her friendliness, Bianca had the carelessness of the rich, had not inherited her father's diligence. I wondered whether Francis or Joanna had seen the note.

The cool air of the early morning had burned off by now. My journey to the stone circle was long, nearly two hours of walking, and I could feel myself sweating whenever the path was not shaded by trees. When I arrived, Bianca was already there, lying along one of the central stones in the sun, sinuous and feline, still as a sphinx. She did not move at the sound of my footsteps, and I had another momentary sensation of having rounded a corner and arrived suddenly on a scene from the deep past, this time the scene of a sacrifice.

I thought of the archaeologist John had introduced me to on our visit here. 'I'm not sure Latham would approve of you being up there.'

'Let him disapprove. He's a fraud anyway.' She twisted her legs round and pulled her body upright. 'Did you phone?'

I told her what Fentiman had told me.

'Aramanthe Partners.' She rolled the words around her mouth, with wonder, and her face broke into a bitter smile. 'Well done, Ben. I didn't really think you'd make contact.'

'I'm still not sure it tells us anything useful about him, or anything damning.'

'You're very trusting. Ever since you arrived here, you've let this place weigh you down, feather by feather, and now you're too comfortable to move.'

I approached, and squinted up at her silhouette. She reached out for me to help her down, and I offered her my hand. The skin of her hands was softer than I had anticipated, perfectly smooth despite the rocks she'd scrambled up. I had hardly touched anyone in my time on the island; she and I were very close to each other now.

She turned my hand over in her own. 'Look at that. All healed. Healed by the magic of Sir John.' She smiled at me.

'What you just said wasn't fair.'

'No?'

'No.' I pulled my hand free. 'I made my way here through a difficult land, and I've been free to make up my mind about what I've found. I've experienced both ways of living, and I can tell you it's better here than on the mainland.'

'You wouldn't mind never leaving? You wouldn't mind if the tunnel closed for ever?'

'It's hard to imagine anything the mainland could offer me now.'

'What about everyone you've ever loved? Your family, your friends, all the rest of humanity, struggling along together.'

'I have no family. And the rest of humanity are just like the people here. Except they don't have a plan.'

'Did you phone the mainland estate too? Did you ask about Cara?'

'He showed me messages from her, Bianca. Letters and memos. She's coming back any day now. He promised.' *She still hasn't written to you, though*. The small voice mocked me.

'Oh, sweet Ben. He can make an elephant, but you think he can't mock up a letter?' She was manipulative, but she was right. I was spared the need to reply – not that I could think of a fitting response – when she turned on her heel. 'Come with me.'

She crossed the bare earth and left the stone circle on the path north, parallel with the island's cliffs. After half a mile or so, she turned off into the woods, picking her way through the underbrush towards the cliff edge, stubborn as a mountain goat. Eventually I saw the treeline that meant the cliffs were just ahead. She stepped out, a few paces before me, and gestured for me to come closer and look at something at her feet.

The air was much colder out here beyond the trees. To our left stood the Devil's Chessmen, impossibly ancient; to our right the cliff extended away, dwindling to nothingness. I advanced slowly, unwilling to stand so close to the island's edge, and looked down. Before us, cut into the side of the rock, was a stairway. The steps were steep, of uneven heights, and coated with slime and mould. But they led down, down out of sight, towards the blackened sea that lapped at the shore beneath.

'What is it?'

'It's the only other way off the island. Leads down to a rock beach. Sheltered, too, and not too difficult to get out to sea. There are caves at the base.'

'How did you find it?

'About ten years ago, I was walking the whole edge to see if I could. I don't think anyone's done it before. I doubt it was Fellingham's people who built it, it seems older than that. Maybe it was the original inhabitants.'

'Perhaps it was sacred.'

'Or a last resort.'

I looked down the stair again, to where it rounded a huge boulder and disappeared along the wall of rock.

'Who else knows about it?'

'Nobody. Nobody else knows the island like I do.'

'Why are you showing me this?'

'Because I think you might need it one day soon.'

I thought of Cara and the decision this place was slowly revealing to me. I could stay here, part of the world to come, but in a world that would be meaningless if I didn't have Cara; or return to the mainland, to the decaying world I knew. I wanted to stay here, to turn my eyes away from everything I had seen that didn't fit; and yet I knew I could not leave Pemberley until I had pinned the real man to the canvas.

'I know why I want to know more about John. But why do you, Bianca? Why's it so important to find out about his childhood?'

She looked at me directly then, and I saw a little of her father's stubbornness and strength.

'We all have a right to know where we came from. What we are made of, and what we are capable of. Being created and then denied an explanation, with no more sense of yourself than an animal ... I feel no better than that poor elephant.'

I sighed. 'Well, we have the name of the law firm, but they won't tell us anything. I imagine he owns them too.'

'What if you had his real name?'

I thought of Fentiman's comments about John's surname. 'How do you know Pemberley isn't his real name?'

'It's one of the only facts about him my mother told me. She wrote it in one of her last letters. As I was born, he told her he wanted her to have something of himself. His real self. God knows why – just a moment of weakness, I suspect. Then he got a grip on himself, and she never learned anything more of his real life from then on. But he told her the name he was born under. She tried to find out more, but even that was protected. Something to do with his childhood. She never found out anything else.'

'What is it?'

'Jacob Mann. It's from the Bible. Jacob was the son of Isaac, born holding the heel of his brother Esau.' She glanced over the edge of the cliff, down to the rocks below. 'It means "he who supplants".'

When we got back to the stone circle, I offered to walk back with Bianca, but she declined with a sudden hauteur, and scrambled back up her rock, resuming her former pose and stillness. She did not look at me as I left.

I drove back in the cart she had brought, at her instruction. The morning was high now, and I did not want to miss today's painting session.

I had told Bianca I would look into the matter further, despite my loyalty to John. If asked about my state of mind then, a few days before the island's closure, I would have said that I simply wanted to find any additional connections between John's past and my own. His childhood sounded just like mine – an absent father, a constant worried search for meaning, a talent that only reached fruition in his teenage years. The more I knew of our common history, the closer we would be. It was, even then, all about John.

Driving these paths, hearing the birdsong etched on the air around me, it still felt impossible that the presiding genie of this place had any malice in his heart. Yet Bianca's comment – *He can make an elephant, but you think he can't mock up a letter?* – would not leave me alone.

John was waiting outside the lodge, sitting in one of the pine chairs he had spent the last week working on. Munro was there too, and they were looking over blueprints of some kind. I felt great relief on seeing him. He was still the solid, strong body of the present day, a man of action and of ideas combined, not the weak, lonely, childish spectre Fentiman had raised. As I greeted him, I had to struggle not to call him Jacob, and I wondered how he would react if I did. As it was he merely turned, cursed my lateness, then dismissed Munro and climbed the stairs to the studio.

During that morning's session, I managed to raise the subject of our school again. Fentiman could have been lying about her acquaintance with him, of course, could have been confusing him with someone else. I should test the matter, at least, and he need never know I was doing it. I told him about how my career had started, and it was natural to bring up my first significant teacher, cautiously.

'Sarah Fentiman?'

'Yes, she'd been at Hillcrest for decades. Had probably been there since ... Forgive me. I didn't mean to mention it.'

'No, that's all right. Describe her.'

'A tall woman, quite broad as well. Wore glasses with those large teardrop lenses, or she did when I was there anyway. Curly hair, quite short and close, I think probably brown when she was younger.'

'Fentiman. Fentiman.' He frowned, and I could tell for a second he had never met her. She had been making it up. It was all a fabrication and I could let the matter rest there. Then he spoke again. 'Yes, I think I knew her. Quite funny, wasn't she? Sarcastic. Got the sense she felt herself a cut above the place.'

'That's right.' I felt a terrible disappointment. But I had prepared my next question and I couldn't avoid asking it now.

'She was very friendly. A bit overfamiliar. Tried to make friends with my mother, even when she was just dropping me at the start of term. She used to sit by the gate all day and have a chat with everyone as they arrived and left. Did she do the same with you?'

'Yes, absolutely.'

'So annoying. It held up the queue for ages. I remember sitting about five cars back, seeing her have her little leaving chat with each parent. Do you remember that, waiting in the queue and seeing her talking to everyone?'

'Yes, absolutely.' But I didn't have to tell him not to smile at the recollection, because his face had not moved a bit.

'Did you have to travel far each term?'

'Not far, no.' An edge had entered his voice, and I let the conversation lapse.

There were lots of reasons why his parents might have never removed him from the school. He might have been a simple orphan, looked after by the law firm Fentiman had mentioned. The firm might have arranged for him to stay over the holidays. And those sad memories would provide a perfectly reasonable explanation for why he would lie to me, why he would prefer not to tell me anything meaningful about his years at Hillcrest.

Even as I tried to think all this, moving back and forth between the canvas and my spot near the door, I knew I was struggling to believe it. But even if I wanted to leave, I could not. I had a more important question I wanted to ask.

'John, I need to know. Cara will be back in time, won't she? Before the island's closure?'

'Of course she will. I spoke to her this morning, Ben. If you'd been here on time, you could have spoken to her too. Her boat is booked. She's looking forward to seeing you.'

'You're kidding.'

'I assure you I'm not.' He smiled for a moment, pleased by my shock. 'It's going to be tight, but there's no way we'd leave her off the island.'

I was struggling to keep my composure. 'Well, that's wonderful.' I didn't voice the treacherous thought that followed: *it's only wonderful if you're telling the truth*. But if he was, Cara knew I was here, and my troubles were as good as ended. 'And she'll definitely be back before the closure?'

'Ben, if she's not back by the day before the closure, I will personally see you onto the last boat returning to the mainland. I'll reunite the pair of you if it kills me.'

My heart felt lighter than it had done for days. I felt guilty about the call I had made to Fentiman earlier this morning, about my collusion with Bianca. Cara's return was guaranteed. John himself had said so. All would be well.

But for the rest of the session, as I observed the way the light fell on him and on the twin image by his side, I saw discomfort on both faces. The man I had built up layer by layer upon the canvas was in pain. But that pain was not the only new element present. There was malice there, too, and deception, and vengefulness; but all showing in their slightest aspects. Like minor chords, or the faintest ripples from a pond-dropped stone.

I spent the afternoon walking the island, dazed by its beauty. I had painted few landscapes before, yet everywhere I looked I saw vistas any painter would dream of depicting. And one phrase kept returning to my head, over and over: *when Cara is back.* When Cara is back, we will walk this path, and if she has not noticed it before I will point out this view to her and bring her delight. When Cara is back, she will tell me the truth about Bianca; whether she's honest or whether her stories about her father are the lurid concoctions of a troubled girl who never grew up. *When Cara is back.*

The prospect that Cara was not coming back, of course – that she had chosen to stay on the mainland, had outgrown this place or the prospect of spending her time here with me – was not one I allowed myself to think about.

The Sanctuary

I managed to make myself late for the evening meal, and once I reached the hub I hurried to the top table. John was deep in conversation with Munro. Knight was talking to tonight's guests, and Bianca was gazing down into her bowl. My place had been cleared, and for a lurching second I thought my deception, my phone call to the mainland, had already been discovered. I had been uprooted from the island; all that remained was the removal of my body. The image of my predecessor, Thomas, lying in the cold ground wherever these people kept their human remains, recurred to me quite beyond my choice. Then John spoke, and removed my doubts.

'Ben! We were practically sending out search parties.' He waved a hand. The cutlery that had been removed from my space was replaced in a few seconds, and a plate – scallops, still steaming from the kitchens and topped with fragrant slivers of sea herbs – followed it. 'You're worrying yourself to death over this painting, that's why you've lost track of time. For God's sake, I'm not getting older that fast. If you don't like this one, we don't have to put it on display at the closing ceremony. Or we can position it so far from the crowd they don't see it and take my word it's a work of genius ...'

He rattled on, and I realised I was in no trouble. He was warmer than his usual self tonight; the fierce edge he carried with him most of the time was sheathed. The idea that he could have anything sinister planned seemed so stupid, most of the time. But the doubts of my first days here were back, and now at least I had more to find, much more. I would search tomorrow. *Aramanthe Partners. Jacob Mann.* I must not blurt any of those words out, no matter how much they filled my head.

From two places over, Bianca gave me a long, enquiring look, and I smiled, tried to be normal, suggested with a look that I would talk to her later.

There was a lot of discussion that night of how the final preparations were coming along. Our guests – a metalworker and a clothier – had a great deal of insight into the process, into how long the final few consignments of raw materials could be recycled for and how many years' independence from the mainland they would buy us.

'The big question, of course, is what comes next.'

'In what way?'

'Well.' John stabbed with his fork for emphasis. 'Who develops faster, of course. Us or the mainland.'

'Surely it's them?' I had spoken rashly, too interested in what he was saying to filter my responses, and his attention turned to me immediately, hawkish.

'Why's that?'

'I would have thought ... Simply that if they have millions of people and we have a few thousand—'

'Irrelevant. If you have a smaller number of people who have expertise and motivation, you can innovate much more. Especially if you're not constantly patching the problems of a hundred years ago.'

'I suppose so.'

'I guarantee it. Look at Jason and Helena here.' Tonight's guests looked up, young and confident. 'Helena has completely changed the way we recycle our clothing. Now we have machinery that cuts the cotton we need by four fifths. Jason is a metallurgist – an alchemist to you and me. His work on titanium fracturing will keep our factories working far better throughout the winter months. And these are just two of the people here. A few thousand people, trained right and with the proper apprentices, can provide the seed for an entire population.'

'Toba,' Knight muttered.

'Quite right. Exactly right. Any of you familiar with the Toba eruption?' I shook my head, as did our guests.

'Seventy-five thousand years ago, a volcano in Indonesia explodes. One of the largest explosions in the history of the planet. Sun blocked out. Humans are reduced to just ten thousand individuals. Maybe even fewer.' He tipped one of the empty bottles on the table over and tapped on the slim neck with his knife. 'An almost random reduction to almost nothing. But look what happened once they got through.' He waved a hand in the air. 'The greatest civilisations in history, just a few tens of thousands of years later. Lesson?'

Knight spoke. 'It doesn't matter if you have a bottleneck as long as the right people get through it.'

'Exactly. This place is the seed for a whole new way of living. Because at the other end of the bottleneck ...' he smiled, 'paradise.'

He beamed around, and we beamed back. The only person who didn't glance up at him or smile was Bianca, and I saw a muscle twitch in his cheek as he looked at her surveying her plate.

'Don't you think so, daughter?'

'I was just wondering what would happen if this cataclysm comes to the rest of the world, like you love predicting so much, and it comes here too.' She looked down as she said it, meaning John had to lean in to hear her, and kept her eyes fixed on her plate once she'd finished speaking.

'Well in that case, Bee, we're all in big trouble. But I think you knew that already. It'd be like working hard to bring a child into this world who doesn't appreciate anything you do, or the efforts you make on their behalf.'

Bianca's only response was to rise from the table. As she stood, she gave me a brief glance. Then she turned and walked slowly away along the aisle. John gestured as if he wanted to rise too, but Knight very gently placed her hand on his arm as if to dissuade him.

He looked round and smiled. 'Very unusual medical trouble there. Adolescence extended to the age of nearly thirty.'

The weak joke broke the tension, and the conversation turned. We kept it going until I realised with some relief that the meal was over and the others were standing to leave.

As I walked through the darkness towards the cottage, I reflected on what I had learned. All I knew was that John's education had been funded by this law firm, that Bianca claimed he had been called Jacob Mann at birth, that he had deceived me over his schooling. Of course, Bianca might have been misinformed by her mother, and her mother might have been misinformed by John himself; he could have set her along the wrong path, deliberately made sure the only clue to his identity was a dead end. It didn't seem too paranoid at all for a man who could create this kind of distance between himself and the world.

The Sanctuary

What was ahead of me? The cottage again. Francis and Joanna and their ostentatious happiness, the sound of them moving around preparing to sleep on the other side of the wall, and for me nothing but an empty bed. No, I could not face returning to the cottage yet. I would walk on and return later, once they were asleep.

Where, then? Further into the dark. I turned back and looked for the narrowest of the paths leading from the hall. The path towards the lodge was too well known to me; I searched again around the edges and found another worm of light at my feet, almost extinguished by the vegetation on either side. This would do. This was a path obscure enough that I would meet nobody else on it.

As I moved, I heard Cara's voice, reproaching me. I had been doing this more and more in the last week or so – conjuring her up. It was a way of staying sure of the details of her; keeping her bright and clear in my mind, not letting her fade away. But even the Cara I summoned to myself was unwilling to comfort me, or tell me only what I desired to hear.

You don't know anything about John. But you love him anyway.

'I'm finding out more every day. I bet you didn't manage to find out his original name.' I spoke the words out loud, to nothing but the trees around me, and still heard her reply as clear as if she stood before me on the path.

You don't even know what he's working towards. You're helping him build his world with no clue what it's going to look like, and you think somehow you're going to fit in.

'You did the same. And I know why I'm doing it. He's given me the chance to create a work that will last. That's more than any of us can hope for in this life.'

She's flirting with you, you know.

'Who?' I kept speaking to cover the sudden silence, muttering my way through the darkened woods. 'I don't know who you mean.'

But I heard no more from her.

I was starting to lose my reason here. I knew the voice I was hearing was nothing but my own refracted fears of Bianca's claims about this place. And yet wherever that voice had come from, wasn't it right about my own feelings for the island, and for John? It was impossible not to admire him, to want to work for him, to want to learn the way he thought and develop my own thoughts in that direction too. My feelings about him were so confused I could hardly keep the two sides in my head.

As to the other point … Bianca may have flirted with me a little, in her naïve way, but nobody who had seen us together could possibly think I returned those feelings. And Cara was the one who had come here in the first place, had brought everything of herself to the service of this man, only to vanish again. She had disappeared, failed to return, failed to call, and yet I was the one responsible when someone took an interest in me? Nobody could blame me for the way things had developed since I arrived. I wasn't responsible. *You never have been*, whispered another voice – this time my own.

Whenever I came to a junction between two paths, I took the less used of the two. Narrower, narrower still, until all I could see was a tiny wriggle of light at my feet, interrupted by the leaves growing over it. I was totally lost now, the woods thick around me, yet I felt I was no more than a mile from John's lodge.

I stopped when I saw a solitary cottage ahead, one I had never seen before. It was a squat building, almost totally overgrown by the trees crowding in on it, and its windows were suspicious, squinting eyes. One of them was lit, and inside stood a familiar outline. I recognised the short hair, the bulk of the torso at once.

If my thoughts had been clearer, I would have waited, calmed myself, repaired my dishevelled appearance. Instead, I approached. My feet crunched on the gravel, and Angela Knight opened the door before I could even knock. She wore an austere wrap with one end trailing down, giving her the look of a half-undone mummy.

'Good evening, Ben.'

'What happens after the island is closed?'

She sighed, and turned.

'Come in.' She shuffled down the narrow corridor onto which the front door opened and pushed aside a curtain leading into a low-ceilinged and cramped parlour. It felt like a room from a century ago. Framed photos clustered on small polished tables; a fireplace held a vase of artfully arranged leaves; above the fireplace, a portrait of some moustachioed ancestor kept watch, frigid and disapproving.

'What is this place?' I knew how rude I sounded, but I could not stop myself.

She shrugged. 'It's my home. There are some benefits to long service with Sir John, although I dare say you'll never find out.'

I repeated the question I had asked on the doorstep, and she sighed again, as though speaking to an elderly relative asking a question for the twentieth time.

'After the island is closed, we carry on as before. I don't know what kind of lurid answer you're expecting, but there will be no sacrifices before the standing stones, no maypoles. We will take no money. Quite the opposite, actually. Sir John has beggared himself making this place proof against the world.'

'Why have you all been preparing the island as if it's about to be besieged?'

'We are simply laying in supplies like we have done every year for almost three decades. This time we will merely attempt to survive without depleting our resources. Sir John thinks we can do it and I'm inclined to agree. Those who doubt him have seldom been proven right.'

'Is that why he treats his daughter like that, because she doubts him?'

'I don't know what you mean by "like that". I haven't noticed him treating her any differently from the rest of us.'

'The way he addresses her doesn't seem strange to you? Unkind, deliberately so?'

'He's put up with so much from that girl. She's not even a girl, she's your age, and she's repaid him with nothing but pain.' Knight sniffed, as if even discussing Bianca was beneath her. 'In any case, I'm not surprised you feel like that, given ...'

'Given what?'

'She's just showing off to impress you. Trying to show you how independent from her father she is. It's a kind of primitive attempt at seduction, I suppose, although I don't think you'd be wise to reciprocate.'

'I'm here for Cara.' I was; but saying her name made me think of the madness of this place, and Cara had seldom seemed as far away as in that moment. I had to remind myself of the bigger question I needed to ask. I thought of Thomas's notebook, of his desperation, and said it:

'What's in the forty-first hex?'

Knight smiled, uncertain, as though wondering the best way to humour me and my stupid question. 'There is no forty-first hex, Ben.'

'You know what I mean. Whatever you call it. The bit that's cordoned off. Is it something to do with the rats?'

'It's no great secret. There's a biosecure storage facility for the millions of species samples we have. It is the pride of my working life. It's staffed by a small team of islanders, who observe strict safety protocols. And that is as secret as we get. If there is something else, I would know about it. Your lovely wife-to-be would know.' She smiled again.

I was feeling increasingly unsure. 'People have said it exists.'

'It does. The facility is where we store our samples. What extra, mysterious thing is meant to be there, Ben? I know every man and woman who works there. I could name every one to you now.'

'Then what did . . .' I didn't want to say anything about Thomas's notebook. 'Why is nobody allowed to go near it?'

'Because to release an invasive species here, without the proper planning, would destroy the balance of life, quite destroy it.' I nodded, and she carried on. I hadn't realised before how soothing her voice was. 'Is there anything else you want to know? You must feel comfortable on the island, Ben. John values your work here.'

'What does he want? Do you know? Does anyone?'

'Of course I know, and if you look in your heart, you do too. John wants peace on earth. He wants to halt the suffering we see around us, day after day – the slaughter of everything not human, the pillaging. Even all his resources are nothing but a tiny candle against the darkness outside. But he is trying to show them the writing on the wall.'

She looked at me closely. 'I think you're terribly tired.' Her voice was soft, and I was grateful for her tact. 'Do you think you should maybe go home and rest?'

I did feel exhausted in that moment. 'Perhaps I should.'

She led me to the door, but before I had a chance to step through it, she gripped my arm tight and leaned close.

'Don't you trust him, Ben? Do you really not believe Sir John has your best interests at heart?'

'Of course I trust him.' And for a brief moment, I did. I remembered all my previous suspicions and doubts, and how each time my worries had been smoothed away.

'That's good, Ben. I do too. I know he wants the best for all of us. He's the presiding spirit of this place. And that's why you must have faith in what he is doing, just like I do, and Cara does. He is doing something so precious for us and the rest of the world, although they don't know it. He is a wonderful young man.' Her eyes shone. 'Goodnight, Ben.'

The Sanctuary

I bade her goodnight and left, down the path again until it rounded a tree. I felt her eyes on my back with every step I took, and for a few minutes I kept walking, on the path that would take me back to my own cottage. Then I stopped, and quietly doubled back until Knight's home was just in sight once again, through the trees. The woods were dark enough that just four or five feet away from the path, a prone body could not be seen by anyone passing.

I lay down in the dirt among the ferns, smelling the rich crumbling loam beneath me, and before long I was rewarded by the sight of Angela Knight, her face blank, leaving her cottage and moving swiftly around its side.

For a second I faced a choice: whether to follow her or to try and enter the cottage somehow. I followed. I wasn't sure I trusted John any more; but even if I did, Knight was another matter entirely.

Knight had made her way round to the back of her home, then taken another path at its rear. There was a third path leading away from her cottage, heading off to the side, but I had seen her take the broader one at the back. The night was so dark that all I had to judge my movements was the slim strip of light at my feet. I had to guess her speed, hang far enough behind that my own progress could not be heard.

Twice the path forked or wavered, and I lost her; twice I found her trail again, after an agonising minute of stumbling in the dark, trying all the time to stay as quiet as possible, avoiding anything that might snap or crunch beneath my feet. My body was in an agony of tension; my breaths sounded like bellows in my ears. Eventually the treeline opened and revealed, across a hundred feet of lawn, John's lodge.

The chapel on the ground floor had a light burning in the window, and I saw bodies moving behind it. I moved a quarter of the way round, concealed by the trees, then approached across the lawn in an area with no lit windows overlooking it. Finally I crept round until I was beneath the chapel.

'. . . knows about it and asked me directly.'

'An enquiring mind.'

'He can't be let alone.'

'On the contrary. He must be.'

'Why?'

'You wouldn't want my portrait to go unfinished, would you?'

'John.' She sounded like a schoolmistress scolding a naughty charge. 'I thought you'd learned seriousness. He should be removed.'

'Thank you, Angela. I learned a lot of seriousness, in the same place he did.'

'Your chief duties are to me and this island.'

'That's true. But he's no risk. And he has potential.'

'For this place? You must be joking. We had our disagreements about her, but even I saw the use. You can't really mean the same about him. An artist.'

'We're all artists. *You* are, Angela. Think of the things you've created here. And I think he'll surprise us. I surprised you once.'

'You are made of quite different material. You know that, John. You are the only one who could have done all this.'

'Flattery. You know we did it together.'

'His age ...'

'Young enough, just about.'

'What if he starts contacting people?'

'It's too late, even if he does.' I heard the smile in his voice. 'My word on the matter is final, Angela. Do not waste your time or mine arguing.'

'Very well. As you're in such a decisive mood, I would like to know your thoughts about the release. There is almost no time to do it before we seal the island.'

'It's in motion.'

'I *beg* your pardon?' She sounded scandalised, like a maiden aunt.

'It's in motion.'

'Without my arranging it?'

His voice was closer now, and I sensed him standing at the window, facing out. The scene would make a wonderful picture, I realised, to anyone observing us from across the lawn. Me crouched beneath the window in darkness; him standing in it lit by the taper before him, the bearer of light.

'I'm afraid so, Angela. I want control over this, because I want to carry the responsibility.'

'You really mean that? You've done it?' Knight's voice had changed, become almost afraid.

'You lit the torch, I carry it. Someone wise once told me about the paramount importance of the first incision.'

'I remember that well.' Her voice was low.

'Goodnight, Angela.'

I had slipped away from the lodge as soon as their conversation ended, back to the treeline and the nearest path. The journey back to the cottage took another hour of walking. The occasional late-night cart passed me on the road, but whenever the driver greeted me, I smiled and declined a lift, claiming insomnia. I needed time to order my thoughts.

I felt guilty. To hear John defending me like that against Angela showed he must have my best interests at heart. But it did not shake my resolve.

I had come here chasing Cara alone. Yet the spell of this place – why lie to myself: of John's company – had descended on me like a veil, one that grew steadily heavier, and I had sunk beneath it to the ground. I had found room in my heart for more than Cara, and she had clearly felt the same about me in the months before I arrived here. Where was she? And what had John set in motion?

If she would just return for a day … If we could spend a day with each other, nowhere, to clear the island from our veins and remember what it was to simply be together against the world … A faint hope, and I doubted now what good it would do. Things had grown more complicated since my arrival, since I had been gently brought into the small group of John's closest associates. How had it happened so fast? Yet here I was, on the verge of making something truly meaningful, and it was all thanks to him.

The Sanctuary

The last few weeks seemed to break over my head then. I thought of the strangeness of this place. There were so many young people here; so many of the women were pregnant. There was the elephant with its artificial parents, my re-created studio. Fentiman's account of John's schooling, Jacob Mann, Bianca's treacherous hidden path down to the shore, the extra hex lurking in the woods ...

I had reached Francis and Joanna's cottage. The empty bed, deferred for a few hours, met me again, and I lay in it as still as if I was in my own grave.

John was quiet this morning.

The island was being scourged with rain. Even on the tree-covered paths it was coming down hard, the drops swelling fatly on the leaves before they fell. I had woken after only a few hours of broken sleep, and hurried back to the lodge. I was relieved to see the rain had battered any footprints from last night out of existence.

All that mattered was to stay here until Cara was back, to cling on a day or two longer to ensure I didn't miss her. The thought of leaving the island and John was terrible, but the idea of being sent away just as she was on the brink of returning, our paths crossing as the island was closed – that was worse. I would find out just a little more about John, find out the truth about this firm, Aramanthe, and then she would return and we would carry on with our life together. All would be well. All would be well.

There was nobody on the lower floor of the lodge, as far as I could tell, so I made my way upstairs. I heard nothing in response to my knock but words being spoken aloud, so I opened the door thinking I was being summoned.

My eyes met an extraordinary sight. The back half of the bedroom floor was slick and dark with rain, which ran down towards the guttering by the wall in dancing rivulets. Just inside the dry half was John's table, strewn with papers covered with tiny annotations. And in the open half of the room, facing outwards, stood John himself, fully beneath the downpour, wearing a plain shirt and trousers slick to the skin. Standing there between the stone columns, his head glistening in the rain, he looked like a sorcerer, something far beyond a normal man.

I must have made some noise, or perhaps the door closed too loudly behind me, because he turned then. I saw he was holding one of the pieces of paper even as it disintegrated in the rain. His face, lost in abstraction, became a mask of anger when he noticed me. He gestured to the door, and swore, loud enough that I heard him over the noise of the elements. In a few seconds I was on the other side of the door again, hurrying back to the stairs, stumbling down them into the corridor of ancient ferns.

I waited downstairs, reflecting on what I had seen, wondering what it could mean, panicking. He had never sworn at me like that. My footprints must have been found; I had been seen last night. Had John spotted me at the window, had Knight followed me back through the dark? Had Bianca told him I had phoned the mainland, to finally win his favour? She was so maddened by his withheld love, I would not blame her especially. But I could not be sent away from here, not from my painting, not as Cara was on the brink of returning. I would lie, denounce the others, do whatever was required.

There was a noise on the stair and John stepped into the room. Gone was the madman, standing beneath the open sky. He had dried himself, changed his shirt, looked normal once more.

'Ben.'

'I'm so sorry for interrupting you, John. I didn't mean—'

'Forget it. Come.'

Back in the room, the desk had been stowed against the wall and the papers had vanished. What had they been? I had hardly seen him with paperwork before. He prided himself on his ability to get by without it. But these papers had looked old and yellowed, personal somehow. I wondered if I had yet again stumbled over one of the fissures between Jacob Mann and John Pemberley.

The rain had quietened by now, but it would still have been enough to ruin the painting in a few seconds. Thank God it was tucked in its usual corner well under the roof, far from the elements. Even so, for the morning's session I had to bring John and the canvas towards the door to make sure it stayed dry. That didn't matter; the background was complete, and all I was focusing on today was his face.

I moved backwards and forwards, observing and dabbing. In the last couple of sessions, John's expression on the canvas had been slowly evolving, and although I could not tell how it would look at last, I knew I had to trust my hand and eye.

He interrupted my thoughts. 'Do you remember the thought experiment from your second night here? The one about the oak trees?'

'The magic button Angela offered me.'

'Exactly. Would you still press it? Damn the species to guarantee healthy individuals?'

'I hope I would. But you never really know with these questions of principle, until you have to actually do it.' I was standing right by him, close up, making a tiny adjustment to the line of his brows.

'You are right, Ben. It depends who you are. Or who you have been forced to become.' He paused. 'Anything else worrying you?'

'Cara.' The name had forced itself out. 'I'm starting to really worry. If she would only contact me … If I could just hear her voice once.'

'Christ, Ben.' John's brow furrowed. 'She hasn't been spirited away. She's still on the fucking payroll. She will be back tomorrow – a full day before closure – and if she isn't – although she definitely will be – you can leave without so much as saying goodbye. All right?'

'You said it would just be a few days until her return when we first spoke. That was two weeks ago.'

He frowned again, and I saw once more the twist of the features that had startled me when I first entered, the sorcerer's glare. 'Honestly, Ben. You should know by now we don't throw away our most valuable people. And you and Cara are valuable to us. She'll be back. I think you're simply worried she won't want to talk to you when she gets here, that she's still angry with you for bringing yourself here without permission. Is that it?'

I nodded, swallowing the lump in my throat, unable to speak.

He was right. I was worried about how I stood with Cara. That was all it was. I must keep reminding myself of the truth. I took a long breath, 'Thank you, John.'

'Forget it. Let's continue.'

At that moment, I stepped away from the canvas again, back to my usual point near the door, and looked, really looked at it for the first time this morning. I must have stood there too long, surveying it, trying to remain calm, because John made some comment or joke, and I hastily resumed the work. But there was no denying what I had seen.

Under my hands, the face I was painting had taken on an aspect of menace. The benevolent command was replaced by grim authority; the wisdom had become low cunning. The corner of the mouth bent with wry humanity had now been supplanted by a sneer of base cruelty. And the worst part of it was that as I looked from the canvas to the subject and back again, I thought I had done my job faithfully and well.

I ended the session abruptly after that shock. The thought that returned to me as I put away my brushes was of the sight that had greeted me this morning: of John pacing around his room in the storm. What had he been reading? Was it the paperwork of his forgotten life, or his plan for the world to come?

The Sanctuary

There was so much to do. I had to learn more from Knight somehow, without arousing her suspicion. I had to talk to Bianca. But first and foremost, I had to know about Jacob Mann, and the firm that had paid for his childhood at Hillcrest.

The rain had slackened during the sitting, and I arrived at the library of the hub hardly damp. The librarian there was unsurprised to see me. She was more obviously pregnant now, and moved slowly and with difficulty as she took me to the information bay.

When she was gone, I found the yellowed concordance of papers again, and wondered how I was going to do this. I had the name of the law firm: Aramanthe Partners. I had John's real name, or what Bianca believed to be his real name: Jacob Mann. And running away into the murk, I had a thousand newspapers from the last century, miniaturised. He must have left a mark somewhere.

But where? Kevin Ladd, the journalist I had tried to phone on the way here – he might have found out about the firm and investigated them too. But he was dead, his papers burned, and his widow wasn't talking.

Kevin Ladd. Aramanthe Partners. Jacob Mann. It wasn't enough, not nearly enough, to narrow the search. If I started at random among these papers, I'd be looking for a hundred years. I buried my head in my hands.

After a while, I rose from the desk and wandered the rest of the library, hoping for something that could help me. Did they have such a thing as a directory of companies? That might help. The reference section was a tall room off to one side containing a hundred dictionaries and encyclopedias. High up on a shelf, another collection caught my eye: a lengthy series of volumes, half falling apart. A list of firms, a guide to company registrations in this country and a few others.

The hunt paid off; Aramanthe Partners was listed in there. *Ownership: private.* Of course. There was no way a firm this secretive would let its real owners be known. But there was a list of associated firms too, threads to elsewhere in the huge series of books. I pulled several off the shelves.

Twenty minutes later, I found one lead, and it looked strong: *Insula Inc. Founder: Mann I. Location: Eugene, Oregon.* It was followed by a date of incorporation from half a century ago. The initial was clearly an I, not a J, and I was looking for Jacob Mann. Then again, Jacob Mann wouldn't be the name I needed. I needed his parents' generation. Bianca had said something about her father's name, something biblical. That was it: Jacob had been the son of Isaac.

This could be a firm founded by John's father. Insula, based in Eugene, Oregon. I knew nothing about it. But that was a start. Back to the microfilm.

As I reached the microfilm bay, I risked a look back at the librarian at her desk. She was reading, lost in a world of her own – I could see from here it was some obscure work by Shelley – and paying no attention to me. A search for local papers in Oregon could hardly attract attention.

Each of the newspapers miniaturised and stored here had a location on the shelves that I could navigate to with the paper guide. The city of Eugene had had one local paper, which was stored in a couple of reels halfway up one of the ladders, a long

way back. The building had sensors installed to track movement, and the shelves around you lit up with a gentle glow as
you approached them, as if conscious of your proximity. I found
the reels I was looking for, removed them from their holsters
and loaded the first in the machine. I knew the date of the firm's
incorporation and guessed the following couple of months might
be the likeliest to yield results.

Twenty minutes later, I had found no mentions among the
thickets of headlines. Eugene was a quiet place; the decade I was
searching through had been a turbulent one for the world, but
it seemed to have passed the city by. The cluttered paraphernalia of the past – sports fixtures, local politics, the life of a small
city – spun by beneath my fingers. How many of the babies in
the births column had led the lives their parents had imagined in
this foundering world?

Physically, I began to suffer. Crouching on the bench to look
through the metal goggles was starting to fold my spine, and the
harsh light behind the blown-up screen below was making my
eyes stream. I carried on.

I stopped at one article, I could not tell why. The headline
ran, *NEW CHURCH SUBJECT OF LOCAL COMPLAINTS*, and
I would have passed it by entirely, except the word 'Insula' had
been lurking in the first sentence and it must have caught my eye.

This was it. This was the company John's father had built. Not
a company, but a church.

*The residential community known as Insula and located
on the Greenmartin plain, ten miles outside the city limits,*

has in recent weeks been the subject of complaints from local farmers, who say it has become a residential area without adhering to the local regulations controlling such. The number of people living there is claimed to be beyond five hundred, all housed, fed and working on the site, when not travelling around the state and beyond, recruiting new members to join them. Founder Isaac Mann explained to our correspondent that the land, being legally his and not registered as arable, is exempt from the rules his neighbours are obliged to observe, and any further complaints would naturally be dealt with in the open and positive manner he is instilling in his flock ...

That was John's father. Even seeing him reported indirectly in a local paper from fifty years ago gave me a low, deep thrill, like an archaeologist who had found the fossilised outline of some monstrous ancient creature until now only hypothesised.

Even better, I knew now to look for any mention of a church, or a new church.

The next came a couple of months later. The church had been recruiting aggressively, some locals claimed, not just from other churches but from cities across the region. They were taking anyone they could, enlisting people from the streets, sucking up heirs and orphans and anyone with trouble in their life, giving them purpose, a mission, unending acceptance from the highest power imaginable. The numbers had swollen to a thousand. The place was described by Mann as 'a community for the further revelation of the messages of God', and many of the residents there were paying to take courses. If you had no money, the church would accept your car, or urge you to start applying for loans.

Mann himself was travelling the country raising funds to spread the word. There were other outposts being built around the country, it seemed, more starter churches, which took their lead from him and paid their tithes, but they all led back to the Greenmartin plain.

The headlines multiplied, telling lurid stories of disturbances out in the darkness. Each time, Isaac Mann appeared in the paper to respond, explaining away whatever state of affairs the newspaper had alleged, expertly sanding the corners off the story, making everything sound reasonable once more. That was not his only tactic. The newspaper began to hint at legal threats against it for asking these questions, then at blatant intimidation. There were photographs of notes its reporters had received, a picture of a car smashed into a lamp post with a rock through its window. The newspaper seemed uncowed; editorials asserted the truths the paper's staff would not flinch to investigate. Nevertheless, the bylines on the stories changed, as if multiple reporters had been scared off the story.

Then, for six months, the church was absent from the headlines. There were no mentions. Perhaps the threats had worked. I wound through and through, losing all track of time, forgetting the strain on my eyes, my back, my fingers aching as I hauled at the machine's iron spindles to turn to the next week's edition. And then, after nearly a year without any mentions, the front page ran a headline I couldn't miss: *RAID AT GREENMARTIN.*

Thirty-four years ago, the state authorities, accompanied by federal troops, had launched a raid on the church in response to claims of abduction, abuse, even torture inflicted by senior members on their flock. The action had been prompted by the parents of a young woman there, who had arrived, tried to see her, and been denied access. They were told she had rejected them and the world outside. They had managed to persuade a single state trooper to take an interest. When he had arrived, there was no chance for Isaac Mann to smooth things over. His followers, taking matters into their own hands, had attacked the trooper. He had barely made it back to his car alive.

This skirmish had set a course that Isaac Mann had not anticipated, but relished regardless. The law had arrived in greater numbers, and been fired upon. After the loss of several officers, reinforcements had arrived. After much debate about what to do with the children present, the place had been stormed.

Isaac Mann spent the siege in a white stucco tower at the centre of the compound, commanding operations, calling the children of the Lord to defend their kingdom. The newspaper contained a photo of his body, hunched and circled, a tangle of limbs arranged into a ghastly mandala on the floor. A leak from the coroner noted that, as well as the bullets in his front, he had been wounded, once, in the side with a large knife, but speculated no further.

Children had been found there; dozens of them. The place had specialised in fertility. Church members claimed with pride that many had been fathered by Mann himself. Apart from a few bricks of banknotes, there was no sign of the dozens of fortunes his followers had poured into the church.

The Sanctuary

The people of Greenmartin were distributed and filtered to their various fates. Some were held, pending prosecution; others were kept under armed guard in hospital. The children of the place were not mentioned again.

And at the end, as if in rebuke to the violence and chaos of the preceding few pages, there was a black and white photo of a sunlit group, staring at the camera. The clothes were simple, and the twenty or so people framed were smiling. At the centre of the shot stood a man, hirsute and beaming, in a robe. The structure of his bones looked very familiar. Before him, at his right hand, stood a boy who must have been in his early teens, squinting into the light, a gap in his teeth. *The Last Happy Time at Greenmartin*, the caption read.

One other aspect seemed oddly familiar. Standing at the back of the shot, looking with a dazzling smile at Isaac Mann, stood a young woman who half a century on, with the coarsening mantle of time gathered around her, might have come to look remarkably like Angela Knight.

'We are closing now. May I take these for you?' The librarian had approached me softly, and her voice had come as a shock. I glanced at her belly, and she smiled. 'Don't worry, I won't be climbing any ladders. I'll keep them safely under the desk and my assistant will return them tomorrow.'

'No.' I did my best to sound normal. 'No, that's fine. It won't take me a minute to return them. Thank you.' She smiled on me, and waddled to her desk.

Across the room was an ancient machine to copy the photo, to restore it to life-size, and I did. It was a little grainy, but the faces were still visible enough, and that was all that mattered. Proof. I tucked the copy into the back of Thomas's notebook.

One other thing disconcerted me. When I got to the top of the ladder, and returned the reel to its shelf, I could not help noticing the layer of dust along the front of it, interrupted where I had pulled the canister out. But beside it, on a part of the shelf I had not touched, was a set of small finger marks in the dust. Someone else had been here before me.

Another islander? The marks were far smaller than my own. It did not look like John himself had been here. Knight? Someone else? A treacherous voice whispered another name to me: *Cara*. She had looked these up and been spirited away. It could not be. It could not. I drove the thought from my mind.

I stumbled outside to the hub, where a crowd was arriving at the hall for the evening meal. After a minute composing myself in the shadow of the library, I entered the hall, and remembered as I approached the table the previous night's interview with Knight at her cottage. Bianca was to my right, and yet I could not stutter out more than a few words of awkward greeting to her before we were standing, and John was arriving, praying us to take our seats, taking his usual stand at the dais.

'Two days, my friends. Two days until we enter our next phase. All of us together are like a great grub, entering the chrysalis. We don't know what the conditions will be like out there when we emerge. We only know that we will face that world – whatever it contains – with unity and purpose.' Cheers at this.

Then came dinner. John seemed aware of some friction around the table. Bianca was not meeting my gaze. Knight was smirking at some secret known only to herself, occasionally flicking a small confiding smile in my direction. Only John, Munro and our guests seemed relatively normal. John, as usual, led the conversation.

'So. Two days. You ready for it, Munro?' His personal bulldog smiled, instantly and solely his creature.

'I can't wait, sir.'

'Hear that, Ben? Six years here and still he calls me sir. Special dispensation for former squaddies. What about you, eh? You ready?'

'Of course.'

He gestured at me with his fork. 'That's what I mean, Ange. Those who shall inherit the earth. Not the meek, I would say, but the people who are willing to do the work.'

She nodded, and smiled at me again.

At the end of the meal, as our whole group was moving towards the door, I found a moment to mutter to Bianca.

'We have to speak.'

'Everyone's going to the lodge. We can speak there.'

'Not there. Now. Privately. Please.'

We waited as they set off, telling them we would catch up, and strolled to the edge of the hub, to the circular path that stretched round its edge.

She stared across the hub, and in her glistening eyes I saw the reflections from the evening's fires.

She listened, expressionless, as I told her everything from the last day – my meeting with Knight, Knight's meeting with John. Finally I told her about this afternoon's discoveries in the library.

'You see? Nobody recovered the church's money. Isaac Mann was killed in the raid. The children were taken into care. One of them was clearly the favoured one. He must have been designated the sole recipient. His name would have been changed. He would have been sent overseas, educated. And after enough time has passed, he inherits his fortune and starts to build this place. The Villages on the mainland, everything here ... they're all the same thing. The only reason it looks normal to us is that we don't know what prompted it.'

'The authorities would never have let him inherit. Not if it was the proceeds of crime. And enough people would know his identity to monitor him as he grew up.'

'Would they? Or could he have slipped through, ensured his real identity was lost, quietly paid off the only people who knew it?'

Bianca said nothing for a few seconds, and we both looked out across the hub at the buildings and the tangle of lights beyond.

I broke the silence. 'This whole place is founded on a wound.'

'We still don't have the proof we need, Ben. You have a name I gave you, which is worth almost nothing. No, don't interrupt me. I'm just trying to lay out how flimsy it would sound in court, especially if it was us doing the talking. You have the name of a law firm from your elderly teacher, who might have forgotten or made it up anyway, a firm that has hundreds of clients around the world. And you have this church, where someone happens to have the name I gave you. How do you know I didn't find out about the place and build it from there, fabricate a link between Jacob Mann and John Pemberley? That's what they'd say.'

'There was a photo. I made a copy. Look at it.' It was in my pocket still, and I showed it to her.

Bianca glanced at it briefly, then looked back out across the hub. 'That could be anyone. Cameras were worse back then. You can barely see his face in it.'

'How do you know? You've hardly looked.'

And then, a realisation. 'You've seen these files before. It was you who looked them up. Those were your fingerprints on the shelf.' She did not seem embarrassed to hear it, nor did she deny it. 'How did you manage it?'

'I guessed the biblical link. Jacob, son of Isaac. There weren't many people called Isaac Mann from that time, not with his money. And I had time to do a lot of searching.'

'Why did he let you install the newspaper archive if he thought these papers might lead back to him?'

She shrugged. 'He didn't know I knew his real name. He probably forgot he'd ever mentioned it to my mother. And I suspect he didn't imagine I was capable of doing the work to find the handful of articles leading back to him. You just happened to have one extra strand I didn't have.'

'Fentiman.'

She nodded. 'It's still not provable, of course. What would we rely on? The word of an unstable girl, the vengeful, disturbed daughter of the philanthropic billionaire, plus a retired teacher and a jealous young man worried about his missing girlfriend?' She laughed. 'Do me a favour. Show me how this stops him. It doesn't even slow him down.'

'You know the boy in the photo is your father. You do. You saw Knight standing behind him, I take it? She's been with him since the beginning.'

She shrugged. 'What can we do about this even if it is true?' I had no answer, but I spotted then a little of the cautious determination I had seen so much of in her father. 'John will argue it's all untrue. And even if true, it's not relevant.'

'You don't think it might be relevant to this place that he grew up in a death cult?'

'He'll say it was a religious community.'

'One that ended with violence. Murders.'

'He'll have a back-up identity ready. Or ten. We won't pin it on him.' I realised she had hoped for some unassailable evidence, far beyond the few facts I had been able to present her with – facts she already knew – and now she was demolishing everything I had discovered to punish me for not finding what she needed.

'Jesus, Bianca. He's literally re-created the place he grew up in. He used the church money to build this place and we know nothing about what he's really doing. Nothing at all.'

She was trembling, and lowered her head so I could not see her face.

'Bianca. It's me. It's Ben. I haven't changed. I think you believe the worst about this place, and I'm saying I understand why. All I can do is offer to help you.'

She turned to me, and her face was streaked with tears. I felt relief, relief that she was suffering just as I was; and shame too, at the joy I felt in knowing it. And then I remembered.

'There's something else I saw today. Something I think might help us.'

'Where?'

I nodded along the path, towards the lodge.

We had spoken about how we would do it as we walked, in low voices. The daylight had faded as we moved; we arrived in darkness. The lodge lay ahead of us.

'Ready?'

'Not really.'

'If I'm found and kicked out, you'll at least be able to go back to normal life here, without an idiot painter causing trouble, won't you?'

'Normal was awful. I'd rather not go back to that.' She smiled at me, and I thought for a second how beautiful her mother must have been, to so overwhelm even John's strong features.

The room was crammed as usual with smoke and conversation, a mix of island types filling the armchairs, standing in corners, enjoying intrigues. As we passed them, I glanced at their faces, suddenly more lupine than I had ever noticed before, and wondered – had they always looked like that and I had been too blinded by this place to see it, or had they changed in the last few days, as the island approached its closure from the world beyond?

At the heart of the room, surrounded by all of it, sat John.

'The young troublemakers return,' he boomed, and I realised he had enjoyed the wine at dinner.

'Angela,' Bianca began. 'I wanted to ask you something about the biobank.' I could see Knight was flattered, and Bianca launched into such a technical question that John groaned and interrupted.

'None of that, none of that. Take it outside.'

Bianca led Knight away to the back of the room, the opposite direction to the corridor. My turn.

'John, I'm really sorry. I left a brush in your room after today's session. Do you mind if I go up and get it?'

'It can wait, can't it?'

I shook my head, anguished. 'It's a brush I really need for the fine details. Stupidly forgot to take it away to clean it. Already it might be half ruined.'

'Paint with a tuft of hair. Or get some bristles from Munro here.' He cackled at his joke. Munro – as hairless as Pemberley, but less drunk – tried to laugh along.

'Is it all right for me to just pop up? I won't be a minute.'

He waved a hand. 'Forget it.'

I sighed, looked anxious, knitted my brow, and eventually, after a couple of minutes, John swore at me and fumbled in his pocket for a key, which he handed to me.

'Christ. Song-and-dance show. You know where it is.' As I stood to leave the circle, I spotted Bianca, keeping Knight facing the other way; her lips were pressed, her forehead corrugated with worry. Her eyes flickered to me for a brief moment, before she returned to keeping Knight's full attention.

The corridor was cool and quiet, and as I went, I checked again that the brush I had put in my pocket earlier in the day was still there. A flimsy alibi, and useless if I was interrupted, of course, but better than nothing.

John's room was as I had left it earlier. The canvas was in the corner, covered so he would see nothing of the painting until it was ready. I pulled it out, turned it so it faced away from the door, and took the cover off. If anyone came in, I could claim to be working on it. Next to it was the bookcase, which I hoped would contain the bundle of papers John had been reading earlier.

There was no time to look at the books now. A couple of titles jumped out at me: tomes on the future, on forestry, on acid seas and hazy skies, and, incongruous among them – so Fentiman had been telling the truth – three simply bound volumes with *Pride and Prejudice* in tiny neat writing on their sides. I couldn't see a bundle of papers.

But one volume, lower down, wasn't a book at all. It had a spine, but the top was smooth lacquer, painted to look like gathered pages. It was a beautiful box of sweet-smelling maple wood, the corners real leather rubbed with age, and as I pulled it out, I saw that the front bore a symbol, an impossible knot, futuristic and ancient.

There was no lock, and inside were the same papers – now stained with rain – I had seen earlier.

They seemed to form a collection of speeches. They were annotated in the hand I knew as John's from seeing him sign documents. The dates at the top proclaimed them to be twenty-five years old – from his early twenties. I replaced the box on the shelf, placed the papers on the easel, and read.

Were we created stooped and haggard, creatures who only consume the earth's resources? We were not. Were we created to rob the future from our children? We were not. We were created with youth, with health. We were created to create more – something almost all of us do at the start of life, not its end.

The Sanctuary

For ten thousand years we have been working with our forefathers, a great collusion stretching backwards from our modern catastrophe. What success we have enjoyed. No need to invent the plough, or the spade, or the gun with each passing generation; we have been holding hands in a great chain stretching back to the earliest days. And where has this great chain led us? It has let us build ourselves up into countries, with governments, with bombs, with limitless resources for our own destruction.

I say again, this great chain will destroy us. It has brought us medicines, inventions, a thousand novelties to give our lives ease. Yet look at the suffering the chain has brought forth. Look at the squalor and the pain of most human lives. For every perfect life in this new world, there are a thousand lives of poverty and indignity in our own species, let alone the billions of animals that suffer for us. Look at the fortunes built and left in vaults, unshared. The men who created those fortunes have denied them to the world. They pass the wealth on to their children, and their children's children, and the wealth and the corruption have thickened like tar.

The world has grown old, and before long we will all be dependent on the few young people remaining. How are we to recover? There is only one answer, my friends. We must make the world young again.

I will not rest until our whole species is one of young, strong gardeners. It is worth launching a lifeboat if your ship is sinking. And it is worth sinking the ship to ensure the lifeboat gets away.

319

Steps approaching the door. No time to put the papers back in the box, no place to hide them, only a few seconds to gather them into one pile, resting on the easel.

'John?'

The word had been whispered. Knight was standing in the doorway with a look of hesitant expectancy; half hope, half doubt. When she saw me around the easel, standing at the canvas, it was replaced by her customary look of frost.

'You shouldn't be in here.'

In reply, I gestured to the canvas before me. Thank God I had moved it so she couldn't see it from where she stood.

'I just came in to fetch a brush. And I got distracted looking at the painting.' The papers were in front of me, resting on the bottom of the canvas. As long as she didn't approach, she couldn't see them.

'May I see?' She started moving around towards the canvas.

'No.' I spoke with an authority I hardly felt, and she stopped. 'The painting can never be seen until it is finished. Not ever.'

'It would be a gross invasion of privacy, would it?'

'Yes.'

'Almost as great as you loitering in this room without John's consent.'

'He told me I could come in. But I'll leave.'

'You should.'

Under her eye, I put the cover back on the canvas, concealing the pages as I did so. I could only hope John wouldn't open the box again before I returned tomorrow for our final sitting.

As I left, Angela spoke softly. 'I'm sure it's a wonderful picture, to justify you spending your time up here looking at it.'

'It's one of my better ones.'

'That's good. He deserves the best, you know. He's suffered so much for us all.' And to accompany these words, she gave me a perfectly innocent smile.

As John said goodnight to me, back downstairs, he stood and clasped my hand as I offered him the key.

'Did you get it?'

'Get what?'

'The brush.'

'Yes. Yes, I did.' I fumbled in my pocket to show it, but too late; he had already turned to the others.

'The painting is saved. The artist has recovered his sacred object.' He lapsed back onto the sofa to argue something with Munro, and I quietly left. As we went, Angela Knight was standing at John's shoulder, waiting to speak to him, and she glanced at me with malevolence. I was glad the cover was secured over the portrait.

Bianca was outside. 'I'm sorry. I kept her as long as I could.'

'You did well. I had lots of time before she got there. I would never have managed that without you.' We walked in the crisp, hollow moonlight, and I told her about the speech I had read.

She thought for a while after I had finished, then spoke. 'There used to be something called the dark green groups. I read about them in the library. They were operating around that time. I've often wondered if he would have been tempted to get caught up with them. But I had no evidence.' She paused. 'That idea of breaking the chain with everyone above us … he's talked about it before. He is fascinated by the idea of new men. I dare say he's asked you about your father.'

'I told him the truth. My father died when I was young.'

'No wonder John likes you.'

The cottage was in sight now. The studio Pemberley had built on its side was paler than the rest of the building. I had thought it looked benign in its first week. But with the dimples on its surface, the streaks left by raindrops on its white round wall, now it looked like a monstrous fungus.

'What do we do?' I said.

'We could leave.' She spoke the words quickly, as though she had only been waiting for me to ask. 'There are container ships going until the day before the closure.'

'You'd never get on. You're too recognisable.'

'So I smuggle myself on. Go in a disguise. Go in a sack of potatoes.'

I laughed, and she joined in, but I knew she was serious. 'I don't think we should, Bianca. Not yet.'

'No?'

'No. For one thing, I wouldn't finish my painting.'

'You're not serious. Fuck the painting.'

'I mean it. It doesn't matter whether John's a good man or not. It's a good painting. My only good one, perhaps. I want to finish it.'

'Ben, you can't commit your life here to one day's work on a painting. If you're saying he's not a good man, then we have to leave.'

'No. We have time. I know we have time. But if I don't finish this, I'll regret it until I die.' The old man in the harbour at Freborne spoke to me again out of the darkness. *Because he's the devil.*

'You keep giving him the benefit of the doubt. Time and again he relies on that from people, and they give it to him. It's like magic.'

'I'm just saying, the speeches of a man at twenty—'

She turned to face me. 'Christ, Ben. Open your eyes. There's no difference between this John and the man who delivered the speeches you found, except he's now found a way to conceal his ideas until he acts on them. You've seen this place. It's a cult of youth. It's designed as a rebuke to age. He still believes all this.'

I conceded that, and she continued. 'And what about this thing he and Knight are talking about? This manoeuvre, this operation, whatever it is?'

'I'm not sure. I think it's something to do with the rats. God knows what. But Knight seems twitchy about that.'

'Well, if you're still painting away, I'll have to be the one to find out about it.'

'What are you going to do?'

'There's a lab where Knight goes in the daytime, under the biobank. I'll bluff my way in, tell them there's some emergency, that I need access on her behalf. You've seen how the other islanders treat me. They think I'm his heir still, whatever he says.'

'Are you sure you can do it?'

'I've had quite enough experience of pretending to be something I'm not, Ben.'

There seemed to be little use talking her out of it, and I could actually imagine some of the islanders letting her through on the strength of her father's features – unless, of course, Knight had explicitly instructed them otherwise – so I merely nodded.

She turned to go, and as she did, I could not help asking the question I had been thinking of since I left the library earlier in the day. 'Do you think she's alive?'

She looked back. 'Cara?' I nodded again. 'Yes, Ben, I do.'

'Why?'

'John cares about you. So I think he'd preserve something you wanted. I'm sure she's fine, Ben, wherever she is.' Her face was half in shadow as she said it, and I saw that just as I had encouraged her despite my doubts about her chance of success, she had reassured me about Cara solely to please me, no matter how deluded she thought I was.

I was woken by the sun and resolved to move early this morning, to fix the situation with the papers I had left on the canvas. Yet by the time I reached the lodge, John was already standing outside in sports clothes, stretching, and Munro was moving away across the grass – they had clearly been exercising together. When did he sleep?

'Painter Ben.' He threw me a key, the same one I had used yesterday. 'Go up and prep. Still finishing up here.'

I tried to hide my relief that it would be so much easier than I had thought. I climbed the stairs, entered John's room, took the cover off the canvas – and discovered the canvas alone, nothing else on top of it. The papers had vanished. Had he found them? Had he taken the cover off to see the painting and discovered them, realised my betrayal?

I heard his tread on the stair, too fast and light for me to do anything about, so I merely stepped back and stood in the centre of the room, waiting. He poked his head around the door frame.

'Everything all right? You look exhausted.'

'I didn't sleep much. I'll shake it off.'

He grunted. 'Give me a minute. Shower.' He disappeared again.

When I heard running water in the room next door, I risked going to the shelf and pulling out the box. The papers were back in there, on top as they had been before. I returned the box and crossed the room to look out from the open half. It was a beautiful, clear day. A wash of green before me. Feet in the corridor once again.

'Here I am. Let's get on.'

I smiled as we assumed our customary positions. He could not have seen the papers. He would never have greeted me like this if he had. I had been saved. How? Knight would have told John immediately – unless, of course, there was a way she could store up the revelation and use it to damage me.

It could have been Bianca. Could she have returned, stolen John's keys, seen the papers and returned them to his box? It didn't matter. All that mattered was that the session would go ahead as normal. I would finish the painting.

Since yesterday's sitting, I had found out about John's childhood – or what appeared to be his childhood – and his life as a young man too, or the sliver of it I had read in his speech. I looked from the image on the canvas to John himself and back again. I saw it now. His face was a balance between all these forces. The adjustments the painting required were minimal, could be made in this session. They would make it an honest reflection of the man I saw.

'Going to make a mark, or what?' I must have been staring down at the image of him for a while.

'Sorry. Of course. When you're this close to the end, you can look back and see what has crept in along the way. It's the last chance to make adjustments that can change the whole picture.'

In the first few weeks, I had always felt a pull towards John, and when I moved to my position by the door to consider him and the canvas next to each other, I had been eager to hurry back, to be closer to him. Today I felt no such pull. I saw him as he might have looked in the aftermath of his days in the church, as he might have looked leaving Hillcrest – a hollowed-out boy inside a man's frame. I must keep painting. I didn't know what I was liable to say if I didn't.

'You're quiet today, Painter Ben. Having second thoughts?'

'About what?'

'About staying on after we close up shop. A couple of days to go now. Still plenty of time to have the unveiling ceremony tomorrow and leave the following day.'

'It's not that.' There was something squeezing at my throat, and if I wasn't careful to remain calm, it would stop me from speaking at all.

'Ben, stop for a second. Stop, stop, stop. Hey, move this thing out of the way. Don't worry, I'm not looking at the bloody picture. There. Look at me. Look at me.' He hadn't been this close to me since we had been out at the stone circle, and the touch of his hands on my shoulders prompted a great rush of feeling.

He was provoking me, I could tell. He knew he was tormenting me. Or had my mind been turned against him by my discoveries about his past – the facts of his life that weren't his fault? 'Tell me what's in your heart, Ben. Be honest.'

I took two deep breaths, his hands still resting on my shoulders, and met his eyes. I had to say something, any lie.

'I'm just trying to paint. And going through all this without Cara, feeling so important to this place and not knowing whether I'm worthy of it …' *And I'm wondering whether you still believe the things you said in those speeches, and whether your childhood bent you out of shape. I wonder whether these emotions you prompt are solely because of the tricks you learned in a cult, or whether there's a real connection between us. I wonder who I'm talking to.*

He squeezed my shoulders, and kept my gaze. 'You're fit for this place, Ben, I assure you of that. All I need is your trust for a little longer. Do I have it?'

My breathing had regulated again, under his eye, and at last I was able to nod. 'Of course you do.'

He returned to his chair, and resumed his portrait face, so I moved the canvas back into position beside him and kept painting, saying nothing. It seemed to be the right decision, as he spoke again.

'Ceremony tomorrow, then. And closure the day after.'

I nodded. His eyes tracked me as I moved back and stood by the door, examining him and his twin, the portrait before me.

The Sanctuary

John spoke again. 'How do you think you'll be judged, for what you've done?' I was startled, and I even glanced at the box in the bookcase before I realised he was referring to the painting.

'To be honest, this work is better than almost any I've ever produced. This and one or two others get close to honesty. But sometimes the reputation of the artist can depend on what the subject goes on to achieve, and most of my subjects – people in the Villages – are there because they've already finished their life's work.'

'Those places ... they're a mortuary of achievements. Don't shake your head. I know you think it because I think it too. Whatever hope there is, it's in the service hubs. That's where the future lies.'

'Either way, the work I'm finishing now' – I dabbed at the palette, adjusted his brow – 'might be the only one of anyone really substantial. In terms of their potential, I mean.'

'Flattering to hear I still have potential. If you paint Cara after her return, that tally would increase. I have high hopes of her.'

'I'll never paint her.'

'Why not?'

'A silly superstition of mine.' I explained it.

'So you think I'll pass out of your life as soon as this portrait is finished?'

'Seems unlikely, I know.'

He laughed, and said nothing more for the rest of the session. At the end, I stepped back and took a long, final look at the canvas before telling him it was done.

'Can I see it, then?'

'Not yet. At the unveiling tomorrow.' The island's closure ceremony would take place in the great bowl of the hub, and John's portrait would be projected onto a huge screen so the whole population could see it.

'As ever, I bow to the artist's demands.'

I thanked him, and had already put the protective cover back on, half an inch above the painting's surface, so it would dry perfectly.

'What do you do now?'

I told him I would go for a walk.

'One last look around before signing in blood. Very wise.' I turned to leave, and he spoke again. 'It won't be paradise at first, Ben. You do know that, don't you?'

'I don't think paradise exists.'

'Actually, I think it will. It simply isn't finished yet.'

As I left the building, Bianca was moving towards it, across the open land, and I intercepted her as she came. She looked dazed, and I had to repeat her name before she turned to me.

'Ben. Sorry. I was thinking.'

'You're here to see John?'

'Yes.' But she made no move towards the house. She just kept looking at me. 'There's something we need to talk about. Something I've found.'

I looked back towards the house. 'Can you tell me?'

'Not here. He'll be watching.'

'But ... briefly?'

'He's done it. They did it together. He's watching. I can't say any more. But you were right. It's too late. I've wasted my time here. All these years, I could have done something, and instead I've …' She broke off, and I twisted to follow her gaze. John was out at the front of the house, waiting for her, his expression forbidding. 'I've got to go.'

'Tell me tonight. We'll work it out,' I said. 'We will. It's possible it's nothing. This whole thing.'

'I guarantee it's not.' She broke away from me, and headed across the lawn, towards her father.

I spent the day walking north, like my first day here. It was hard to remember now that that had been just a couple of weeks ago. Life back on the mainland, grubbing for commissions, hoping to build a reputation among enough Village-dwellers to earn a place among them, dreaming of escape … all of it might have been a book I had once read. The people I passed were happy; they had not felt the need to look beneath the surface of this place. If I had not also been educated at Hillcrest, if I hadn't spoken to Ladd's widow, found Thomas's notebook, I could have been happy here too.

After a couple of hours I reached the standing stones, and passed them through the woods to see the stairway Bianca had shown me. At least that was still there, had been no fantasy. The stair itself, sprouting from the rock and covered with a glistening sheen of slime, still horrified me and attracted me in equal measure. As I stepped closer, a low, moaning wind from its base cooled the sweat on my skin.

I moved back to the stone circle and took a seat in the low amphitheatre around it. The age of this place calmed me greatly. I pulled Mad Thomas's notebook from my pocket. The sketches of John in there, of him mid-metamorphosis into a grotesque carnivorous plant, seemed as real as the painting I had just finished. But I had finished my depiction of him nonetheless, formed my own impression, and I could think freely now. If I challenged him, I knew what he would say.

'Was it my fault I grew up in a cult, Ben?' He would give me a look of wounded puzzlement.

'You hid it from the world.'

'Is it hiding from the world to simply keep my childhood private? Do I have a duty to inform everyone of the pain I escaped? Perhaps you would like to see the wounds it left on me, poke your fingers into them?'

'But the place you are creating is identical to the one you left behind.'

He would raise his hands, spread his thick fingers. 'Is anyone here being relieved of their money, Ben? No. Are the people here abused, cowed, imprisoned? No. Are they forced to worship God in the way I was forced to as a child? They are not. So why this talk of uncanny similarities? Is it because this place has a leader? Perhaps because everyone here is working for a better world? You do me a grave injustice.'

'But your father—'

'My father's house was ruled by fear. This place is ruled by hope.'

'You're closing the place off. The rest of the world needs the help of somewhere like this.'

'The rest of the world is dying, Ben, dying of us. But here, here we have reached the bottleneck. We are in the precious age where an individual, one man alone, can take decisive action. Once a good man has the power to take action, he must, because if he does not, who knows who will seize it from him?

'I know nobody should have the power to do what I have done here. I know that. Yet if I have this power, I cannot renounce it. I must do the right thing.' Tears glinted in the corners of his eyes, and he smiled suddenly, a smile that creased his face into a hundred new wrinkles. 'We are just before the change, Ben. The world will sink into a boiling sea, and only a few of us will survive to make the world anew.' He was growing ancient before my eyes, and white hair sprouted from his skull.

I woke at that moment, startled and sweating. The sun had drifted down the sky, was only a few thumbsbreadths above the horizon. I was stretched out along one of the stone seats, my left shoulder buried in the moss at the back.

I twisted my head sideways, out of the light, and as I did, I saw something strange in the seat that rose behind me – a curious ridge, or seam, running from the top to the bottom in the corner, almost impossible to spot from an upright position. It was identical to the seam on the new studio at my cottage. I sat up, and shuffled along.

The next slab had one too. All the stones on this row had the same join along one of their edges. I went to the centre of the circle, and examined the smaller and then the larger stones. Every one, every single one, had a similar seam, facing away from the audience, out towards the sea.

These stones were new, then. It took me a few minutes to fully understand that, dazed as I was after my sleep. They had been made, or moulded, fabricated somehow in the island's workshops. More of John's endless creations. Just like the studio, and the elephant, and the Villages. Did the islanders know? Had the men and women who made these stones stayed here? Had they been allowed to live? I started to doubt the earth beneath my feet, before another thought occurred to me.

I set off, walking at first, then breaking into a run as I reached the darkness of the treeline. Behind me, the sky was tangerine, and the ageing sun lowered itself gingerly into the sea.

Past the cottage, ignoring the few people who greeted me as I went; past the hub, skirting its edge, stumbling with haste; back through the woodland the way I had taken last night.

The cottage Knight lived in – dark now – had had a slim glowing path leading to it from the hub, and another one at its back, leading towards John's lodge. But there had been a third gleam of light in the darkness, a third route away from it, one that led south-east, to the corner that had rebuffed all my attempts to find it.

I took that third path now. It was hardly visible, but it was there, and after ten minutes following the strip of light at my feet, the trees fell away. Here, improbable in the wilderness around me, was a gate, flanked by a dark green wire fence stretching into the darkness on either side. The gate hung ajar, wide enough for me to squeeze through it. I didn't touch it as I went, and held my breath as I moved as if it had been dipped in poison. Once I was through, no alarms sounded, no watchdogs barked. Nothing.

This was the 41st hex.

It was a site a couple of acres across – industrial in nature, and abandoned. The sheds in one corner sat with their doors open like slack mouths. Here was the residue of a fire on the paving, now just a skeleton wreck of whatever had been burned; in another corner, a few empty barrels had been scattered, a blue liquid dribbling from their tops and leaching into the ground. Across the empty ground at the back was a larger-looking exit for vehicles – not a road, but a tunnel mouth, a miniature copy of the route leading to the harbour.

The atmosphere here was not like the clean air of the rest of the island. It tasted scorched. Near me on my left was a long, low building that looked faintly like a barracks, and another that must have been a mess hall. The barracks was empty, from a tiptoed look through the small windows; the beds were stripped. There was even a half-abandoned mug of coffee on one narrow bedside table. This place was not like the other hexes, which had the feel of the Villages on the mainland – this was a place spartan and withdrawn.

At the far left corner by the sheds was a short row of earthen mounds, about eight feet long. There were markers in the ground, with dates on them, and the most recent one was dated to a few months ago. A digging machine lingered in an open shed nearby, traces of earth in the bucket at its front like a mark of guilt.

I could never operate a machine that size. I looked round the corner, into the darkness of the shed. A pair of gleaming eyes resolved themselves into the shape of two broad shovels. One of those would do.

For a few moments, back at the darkest mound of earth, shovel in hand, I thought of the taboo I was about to break. Yet the markers were not headstones; I would pretend I was merely digging without knowing what was under there. I had disinterred the rest of John's past with less compunction.

The soil was not packed tight, but any soil is weighty, and my time on the island had required little heavy lifting. After the first twenty minutes I was sweating, and I had to strip off the outer layers I had been wearing and work in my T-shirt. It took a couple of hours to get through the mound, even though it was far shallower than I had thought – it was only a few feet before the spade hit wood. Until then I had been deferring the thought of what was in there, but the sound of the shovel biting into the plank broke down the defences I had erected within myself. They had fabricated her messages to me. She couldn't come back from the mainland because she had been here all this time. Keep digging. Don't let that thought in. Yet that was the only thought that would explain it all.

By the time I had finished unearthing the length of the box, the darkness was long since complete. I had received a shock earlier on when all the lights in the courtyard snapped on simultaneously, and wheeled round in surprise, but they were simply on a timer nobody had bothered to deactivate. No Knight stood there to interrupt me, no John to take the shovel from my hand.

The coffin bore, on its side, a date matching the marker above ground, carved into the wood in a plain font. The lid was secured not with screws but with easily opened clasps, and I realised with horror it had been designed to be opened again. That was why the body had been buried shallow – to allow further study. I undid the clasps.

Inside the coffin, his head turned to the side as though seeking comfort or shelter, was the body of an aged man. Relief washed through me. This was not Cara.

I took a minute, straightened my back and felt the sweat cooling on me. Once my breathing had slowed, I examined the body more closely. I thought it was William Steensen at first, the son of the old man at Freborne, the man whose boat I had travelled here in, but this was a far more ancient face, and there was no family resemblance.

It seemed impossible that a normal body would last several months in such good condition, yet here it was. The skin had tightened to parchment and the lips had pulled back, gently parting over the yellowed teeth, but the shreds of white hair were neat. They blew a little in the breeze as I watched. This was – could it be? – the first truly old person I had seen since my arrival here, unless you counted Angela Knight.

The body was wearing the remains of a rough suit too small for it, and just at the point where the fabric ended, I saw a hint of blue on the skin. I managed to nudge the cloth back up the cold, unbending arm, and uncovered a picture: an opened book.

The Sanctuary

I remembered Joanna describing Thomas Candler, Mad Thomas, on my first morning in the cottage. *He had a tattoo of a book on his wrist; imagine liking the things that much.* What else had she said? *He was young – not more than thirty-five, I'd say.*

But this could not be Thomas. It could not. This, as anyone could see, was the body of an old, old man.

The body was back in its coffin, the lid restored, and although the earth on top of it was shallow, it was closed, and safe enough from wild animals. From above it must look like a giant had spilled his snuffbox. I was patting the final spadefuls down when I heard the voice.

'Drop the shovel, Parr.'

The words were spoken quietly but clearly through the empty night air, and they startled me. But I had the presence of mind not to follow the instruction until I had turned around, slowly.

Munro stood behind me, halfway between me and the gate. My back had been turned as I dug, and the sound of the shovel had masked his footsteps. He held a stubby pistol, short enough to be inaccurate at some distance, but as I straightened up, he walked towards me until he could be sure not to miss. The gun's mouth was a perfect O.

'You shouldn't be here, Ben.'

'I think I should, Munro. What is this place?'

'It's your ticket to the bottom of the sea. Drop the shovel or I shoot.'

I lowered it gently to the ground. No sense dying yet.

Munro was nervous, and as he covered me with his gun arm, he wiped sweat from his eyes with the other. I guessed he hadn't had to make many arrests lately. 'Over to the shed.'

'Don't kill me in the shed, for Christ's sake.'

'Nobody is killing anybody. I'm going to lock you up in there, nice and secure, and we're going to bring Angela back here and work out what we do with you.'

'That sounds very sensible.'

We started walking.

'Do you know what's been going on here? Do you know the full extent of all this?'

'I don't know anything about this. I look after the perimeter. That's my whole job. I keep the place safe.' He was unhappy, I could tell, and while I kept on at that part of him, opening that uncertainty further, he probably wouldn't snap and fire. Probably.

'Something bad has been happening here, Munro – look at these piles of earth – and it's important we find out what it is before the island is closed. Do you understand that?'

'I understand you're not a proper islander, that's what I hear.'

'I spend hours of every day with John. You think he's going to be happy to hear I've been injured, or worse? I'd pray for mercy from Angela, because you won't get it from John.'

We were almost at the door now, and thank God, Munro was careless, letting me get closer to that darkness inside. I just had to stay slow. I knew what I was heading for, and there it was, just inside on the right.

The Sanctuary

'Stop.' I was in the doorway. 'Turn around.' I turned to face him. He'd realised his mistake. The gates of the shed were big, and he would have to walk away from me to haul them across and seal me in. 'Get down on the ground there where I can see you.'

'Anything you say.' And with that I dived backwards, into the darkness, and rolled to the ground.

He fired then, and the bullet pierced the iron wall of the shed, agonisingly loud. He fired twice more, but the shots just showed me where he thought I was, and he was two feet wrong. He paused for a second, not wanting to take his chances coming into the darkness, and I could practically hear him thinking of the best next move. He unhitched the door, breathing fast, just a foot or two from me on the other side of the iron, and as it swung slowly round, I pictured where he would be, following its path. The bar of light from the lamps outside started to grow slender as the door covered it. I backed up. Nearly, nearly: and then I began my run. Just as the door met the wall, right at the point where Munro would be fumbling for the latch cover, I hit the other side, shoulder first, and the entire sheet of metal boomed as it struck him.

As I stepped outside, he was on the ground, his nose bloody, and it was little work to kick the gun away from him. I hit him with the shovel – not hard enough to do serious harm, just enough to stun him further. By the time he knew what was happening, I had dragged him inside the shed and managed to find a length of rope to lash him to a barrel inside a metal cage they had in there.

'Ben, don't hurt me. I know you're a good man.' Coming from someone who had just tried to shoot me three times, this was too much.

'Why wouldn't I hurt you? Now breathe out. No, out, properly, or I'll hit you with the sharp edge next time.' He breathed out, and I tightened the rope around him. 'For what it's worth, Munro, I don't think you do know the truth about what's been going on here. Because if you did, I wouldn't leave you alive.'

The night was dark, and I heard the cries of unknown birds as I made my way back towards Francis and Joanna's cottage. I was no longer comfortable thinking of it as mine.

Knight's cottage had been dark as I passed it. Vivid, ugly premonitions had bombarded me as I approached it, but there was no time to try to leave by the road route out of the new hex and make my way the extra miles round. Munro was sealed as tight as I could make him inside the cage; the cage was locked, and the shed too. I had not had the stomach to knock him out, reasoning it would buy me only a few extra hours, so I had settled for emptying his pockets and clearing everything within six feet of the cage. He could make a lot of noise in there without being heard.

I had missed the whole evening on the island. If I was lucky nobody would be looking for me – or Munro for that matter; if our absence from the table had been noticed, there might be a search abroad. I thought of faces seeking me in the darkness, half lit by torches, glowering like characters from a Caravaggio. Every new lamp along the path looked like a searchlight at first, and whenever I paused I could hear my heart beating loud enough to summon anyone nearby.

Eventually I drew close to the cottage. There was a figure in the downstairs room, sitting upright in one of the armchairs. As I entered, as silently as I could, the figure raised a hand, and for one glorious moment I saw Cara there. She had returned to me. The nightmare was over; this had all been a mistake. John had been telling the truth all this time.

I was wrong, of course. Bianca leaned and turned on the lamp next to her, before putting a finger to her lips and gesturing to me to stay where I was. She moved past me, out of the door, and led me away.

Outside, fifty metres along the path towards the next hex, she stopped. The moon was behind her, and her hair was silver in the light.

'The walls in there aren't soundproof. No need for your cottage-mates to hear this. Where have you been?'

I ignored her question for a moment. 'Was anyone looking for me after dinner? Did John ask anyone to look?'

'No. I told him you felt unwell, nerves before the unveiling, that you would be eating in the hex. So?'

I told her everything I had seen – the extra hex, the empty yard, the grave, Thomas, Munro. It seemed like a nightmare now. As I mentioned the body, she shuddered, and looked at me with horror, as though she knew something I did not. When I finished speaking, I remembered our meeting earlier today, outside the lodge, and how frightened she had looked.

'What was the thing you wanted to tell me earlier?'

'It's how they killed the rats.'

'At a time like this?'

'Just listen, Ben. It's important. You told me what was in the notebook.'

'Thomas's notebook?'

'Yes. He kept writing about rats. He was terribly preoccupied by them. Knight always looked uncomfortable when they were mentioned around her. I thought at first she was just embarrassed – that there had been a security breach at the biobank and she was responsible – but the way she spoke about it made it seem like more than just an error. It seemed like a test.

'So early this morning I went to look in the biobank files. They're kept below the main building, but I told the staff there it was an emergency. I pulled rank as John's daughter, and it worked. They were worried about getting into trouble with Knight, but they let me in.' She took a breath. 'And I found it. Have you heard of telomeres?'

'I've heard the word, but not much more than that. They're something genetic.'

She nodded. 'They're sections of DNA found at the end of each chromosome. They control the ageing process. As you age, your telomeres shorten. Eventually, when the telomere is short enough, the cell undergoes senescence. They call it apoptosis.'

'Meaning?'

'Removal. Programmed cell death. Clear?'

'All right.'

'For a long time, people thought that if you could somehow stop those telomeres fraying, you could stop the ageing process. Create bodies that have eternal youth.'

'They can't have managed to do that.'

'They haven't been trying to. The reverse is true as well. If you shorten the telomeres, you shorten the life. Several years ago, Knight and a couple of her team had a breakthrough. They came up with a process called telomeric abrasion. And they created a chemical to trigger it. If an organism is introduced to this chemical, it prompts a chain reaction through its entire body, affecting none of the cellular function except the telomeres. You understand?'

'It makes animals age?'

'It's a way of shortening the internal fuse of the entire organism. You can set the length you want the telomeres to abrade to. If you set them to abrade beyond the point they have naturally aged to anyway, the organism dies.'

'And what if the organism is young still?'

'Then it introduces a new point at which rapid senescence sets in. Do you understand? Let's say the rat lives to four years normally. You can set it so the rat dies at three years, two years.'

'So then you have only young rats.'

'Or you could adjust the structure so it shortens the telomeres and prompts extreme senescence at five weeks – in other words, before the rat becomes sexually mature.'

'No more rats.'

'No more rats. That's what they did. They released rats across the island for a year, let them get a foothold, and then they released bait laced with the compounds that cause telomeric abrasion. The rats died before they got to the point at which they could breed.'

'But you'd still have to bait each one individually.'

'That's just it, Ben. They've had another breakthrough since then. They've created a way of passing it from creature to creature, so it could spread without anyone needing to put down poison.'

'You're saying they could do it with other organisms.'

'Theoretically, yes. It would take a huge amount of work, of course.'

'You're saying maybe that's what they did to … Thomas.' It felt too big, the line we were about to draw between the rats and poor dead Thomas; between the way John thought, his childhood, and the course it had driven him onto.

In the bushes there was a small disturbance, some little struggle of life and death between two rival species. The sound ceased after a while, and we heard the victor dragging its prey away from us through the undergrowth.

Bianca spoke next. 'We don't have conclusive evidence.'

'Don't we? There's a whole industrial site. There's the body of a man who was our age a year ago, looking ancient.'

'It doesn't prove that John has definitely adjusted the telomeres for humans. Or that he'd do anything with it.'

'The rats alone prove he's willing to exterminate.' I thought of the mural at the end of the hall, of Fastitocalon waiting to drag the unlucky sailors down and down, and thought: we are on the long descent now.

Bianca still couldn't face the fact. 'It would affect John too. Him and Knight. If they set the barrier anywhere near where we're thinking of.'

'I'm not sure they're planning to live.' I realised something else, too. 'Think of the service hubs on the mainland. They're the people he wants to survive. All this time people have been thinking about the Villages. It's never been about them. Never. It's about ensuring a core of people have the skills to make the world new. Young people. That's why he gives all those apprenticeships. They are the ones who will inherit the earth.'

'It could be Knight, Knight acting alone,' Bianca said. 'She's the geneticist. She would know how to do this. She's had the apparatus all this time, and the authority to do it. It's her cottage that leads to the extra hex.'

'The project they were discussing together – it could have been this. And when I last overheard them John was saying the release was under way.' I thought of Cara. Had she known about this? Or was she one of the bodies in there, in one of the pits I hadn't dug into?

Bianca nodded slowly, then blinked and shook her head, as if throwing off water. 'I'm sorry, I can't believe this. I just can't. He wiped out the rats to save the birds here. He's just found a clever way to do it. He's my *father*.'

I thought of John, the man I had known such a short time, the man who had moulded this island to the exact shape he willed, who had reformed the mainland and this place alike. The man who had always prioritised the small tribe over the mass movement; who had written the speeches I had uncovered in his room; whose eyes glowed when looking at the birds and beasts of the field. Yes, he was capable of this.

Bianca kept talking. 'He's a good man. He's a great man. I shouldn't have gone looking. Stupid of me, really. I've always been prone to getting hysterical like this. Maybe we can forget it.'

'Bianca—'

'I'm serious. I know he doesn't like me, I know I've let him down. But I can't believe he's capable of this. He must be acting for the good.'

She looked down, twisting her hands, and I felt a great pity for her. She had taken on every sneering comment her father had directed at her, every put-down from Knight, every patronising remark from Munro, and driven them so far into herself she could no longer tell they weren't a part of her.

'Maybe he believes he's acting for the good, Bianca. But the very worst acts in history have been committed by men acting for the good.'

She nodded. She looked beautiful, in that light, with the moonlight catching the edge of her cheek, and her mouth was now a hard line.

'What time is it?' I asked.

'After four. Not long till dawn.'

'I'm going to go and see him.'

'Ben, if you say these things to him, there's no telling what he'll do.'

'If they're true, then it doesn't matter what he does to me.'

'I want to come with you.'

'It's not safe for the two of us to travel together if we're the only two people who know about this. Did you take a copy of this information? Do you have a file, a drive, anything?'

Bianca shook her head, miserable. 'I was too shocked. I left.'

'If you can find a way to get back in there and make a copy, that would be very important once we've left the island. But don't do it if the risk is too great. Don't cross paths with Knight. And if you do get it, go walking all day. Don't go near anyone.'

'All right.' She hesitated, then spoke again. 'What if he's already done it? Released this thing?'

'We can't allow ourselves to think that. Is there nothing scheduled to leave the island? No shipping or consignment?' I remembered the last conversation between Pemberley and Knight I'd overheard. *It's in motion*, he'd said to her, and she had sounded shocked to hear it.

Bianca sounded uncertain. 'This thing would need infrastructure, wouldn't it? Surely? They would need a lot of it?'

'We don't know that. It might need a teaspoon.'

'Christ.'

We turned and held each other for a moment. She felt slight in my arms, and I realised how close the stress of her life here had come to unravelling her.

'We can still choose,' I told her. 'You know that. We can travel back to the mainland somehow. We'll expose him, and we'll stop this. You'll make a life there.'

'I believe in this place, Ben. I know that sounds stupid, because of Thomas, because of everything, but I wanted to stay believing in it.' Her face was wet against my shirt. 'I was still trying to believe in it until you got here. And now the whole thing is falling apart.'

'It's not me that changed it, Bianca. Nor you.'

'I know.'

'We're going to work out what to do between us. That's the real unit here. Not the Villages, not the hexes. You and I will work this out together.' We released each other. 'It's possible we're wrong about all of it. It's possible he created this technology just for the rats. But there's no harm in making as sure as we can.'

'I know.'

'Get some sleep if you can. I'll be back at nine. If I don't come back then ... I don't know. Try to tell someone else. Someone on the mainland, perhaps? Maybe the authorities could blockade the place?' It all sounded fantastical, the sort of thing that would happen to other people.

We had shifted position as we held each other, and I saw her face clearly now. She looked sideways at me, with a little of her father's cunning.

'If you don't come back, Ben, I think I know what I need to do.'

31

There is a light before dawn, a gentle glow that spreads across the landscape like a blush, the first indication that night will end and daylight return. It rarely appears in portraits, but it is one of the most beautiful hours of the day. As I reached the field surrounding the lodge, that light was arriving, and it gave me a sliver of hope. It was just before five in the morning.

The ground floor of the house was open, as usual, and the enormous entertaining room was cluttered with the rejectamenta of the previous night's revelry. More than usual, too. Something had been celebrated.

On the corridor upstairs, the door to John's room was ajar, and as I approached, the sound of his breathing, stertorous and regular, reached my ears.

The Sanctuary

The heavy door made no sound as I nudged it – slowly, slowly – and I felt for a hideous moment as if I were looking in on a sleeping infant. As it opened, I saw his body stretched out, half covered by a single sheet. He lay on his back, his only movement the slow rise and fall of his chest, and the faint dawn breeze from the open roof stirred the thick black hair on his arms. One arm was thrown across his face, covering his eyes, so all I could see was his nose and the line of his mouth.

There was a folding knife in my pocket, the one I had put there yesterday with the intention of trimming the canvas. It was in my hand before I knew it, and as I looked down, my fingers seemed to take the initiative from me and gently, silently eased it open.

If we had left it too late, then any action I might take now would be superfluous, and we might never learn the truth about this place. But if what Bianca and I had uncovered was even one tenth true, one life didn't matter. If there was even the slightest chance of changing things here, then the duty on me to take this step was overwhelming.

At that moment, John's breathing stopped, and he spoke.

'In this life, Ben, you must act when it occurs to you. Or you've already lost.' He shifted his arm. I saw his eyes glitter in the dark, and I knew he had won.

'I came for the painting.'

He glanced at the foredawn light outside. 'At this hour? I don't think so. What's troubling you?' His voice was low and confiding, and he made no reference to the blade in my hand. Here was the John of old once again, the one who had built these wonders, the one who had won my trust, and it was all I could do not to blurt everything out there and then.

'John, I have a task in life, or I had one, at any rate, and that was to produce art. I understood it. It didn't make me happy all the time, and I didn't always succeed at it. It made my life harder in many ways. But this island has changed me. I don't know what I should do any more.'

'A sea-change.'

I knew the reference well enough. 'I don't feel like I've become something rich and strange.'

John sat up. 'Is there something in particular on your mind? Tonight's unveiling? Tomorrow's closure?' He paused. 'Something else?'

'All of it. It's all overwhelming.'

'You must trust me. Look at the things I have shown you already, and imagine what you will be shown in the world to come.'

'I do trust you. I truly do. But … you keep hinting that Cara and I are important to the future of this place.'

'All right, Ben, if you want the chapter and the verse – I want you and Cara to be my heirs. I want you to run the island once I am dead. Clear enough for you?'

He kept his eyes on me as I groped for a reply. 'Why?'

'I knew Cara was right for it as soon as she came here. She has the will to continue the species. She may think she wants a career, or wealth, but I see what she really wants. Then you came. Someone who understood being an outsider from their early days, who didn't grow up thinking everything would come to them. Someone unimpressed by money. Someone with anger. You have exactly the virtues this place requires.'

'You've only known me a few weeks.'

'Feels longer.' He bared his teeth in a smile. 'Everything will be plain tomorrow evening. But I need to know you see the truths I have shown you. Don't doubt me now.'

I could do nothing in reply except nod. 'Thank you, John. My mind is clear.'

'When we started this process, you said you wanted to see the reality of your subjects, show them something of their own self. Do you feel you have seen me? Will you show me who I am?'

I met his clear, unclouded gaze. 'I will.'

The smile reappeared on his face, like a card reappearing at the top of a magician's deck.

'Then take your picture, and prepare for tonight.'

I arrived back at the cottage just as Francis and Joanna were leaving for work. Joanna was moving much more slowly now. Their baby was due in a few weeks, and she seemed to have passed into a mood of permanent, placid acceptance, as though she had retreated from the world in preparation for the most important event of her life. It was strange to witness, yet comforting too. I didn't think any external event could affect her now, unless it had some bearing on the health of her baby. I was glad of that, for her sake.

My final adjustment to the portrait of John didn't take long. Then I placed the cover back on, screwed it tight enough to deter casual viewers from removing it, and put the canvas in the corner of the room. It would shortly be transported to the venue for tonight's unveiling.

With that done, I packed the brushes away in my painter's roll, smallest to largest. The other tools of my trade, so expertly re-created or mimicked or cloned by Sir John, went in their allotted places too. I imagined the brushes being displayed in a museum one day as relics of John. If what Bianca had discovered was true, of course, maybe the age of the museum was coming to an end. Maybe John's new remnant of the species, fresh and young and needing only to survive, was the answer. We would have no time to learn complicated skills, only time to grow and fruit and die.

And yet, and yet ... What if I was wrong, or Bianca had mis-interpreted what she had seen? What if I demolished my future here because of some combination of circumstances the two of us had completely misunderstood? Yet always behind that thought came the next question: what if we were right? Inheriting the island would mean nothing if what we had found was real. And in that event, the most important thing was keeping the island in safe hands.

I knew things about John he couldn't have worked out I knew yet: his youth, his schooldays. I knew his parentage, even. I must have the advantage over him.

My painter's roll was tightly wrapped; the sketches I had pro-duced during my time here were neatly packed away on a shelf. I took a final look around the studio, wondering when the doors would next be opened, and then left to spend the day in preparation for the evening to come.

Spring was well advanced by now. The few trees not yet in leaf at the time of my arrival had shaken themselves out, like birds of paradise startling in their plumage. The birds themselves seemed dazzled by it, leaping from branch to branch, calling to each other with joy. Even now, in the late afternoon, the sun still stood above the horizon.

Before the evening meal, there was an all-hands gathering planned in the arena outside the dining hall. The portrait, now with a ceremonial cover on, had been moved to a chamber beneath the hall. Once everyone was present, it would be brought out and its image cast onto a large screen erected for the occasion, visible to everyone. I realised, looking at the screen now, that it covered exactly the spot from which the elephant had emerged a few weeks ago.

John had asked me to say a few words, and I had assured him I would. The unveiling of the portrait, however, was just part of the evening's events. Afterwards we would eat together, the last dinner before tomorrow's closure. I wondered if he could still believe I thought Cara was coming back; I felt a wave of grief remembering how long I had clung to that belief.

A crowd had gathered on the slopes of the hub, around its edges; and in the central area, long pine benches had been set out for whoever might need them. The children of the island were here too. The youngest were strapped to their parents' chests, the older ones gathered at the front. I couldn't help wondering how my actions tonight would wrench their lives onto a different course; and then I thought of John in his own childhood, himself just a boy in a closed world about to be torn from seam to seam. So many people depended on this place and this man, and I wondered again whether my plan was wise. It didn't matter now, in a way. I had gone this far. Part of me thought the younger John would approve.

The screen was at the far end of the hub, cutting one end off. We were standing at that end, behind part of the gantry that held it up – Bianca, Knight, John and I. There was no sign of Munro. Had anyone missed him? I wondered. I wished I had left him some water. Bianca and I avoided each other's gaze. The last thing we wanted was someone to see our expressions now and realise what we had planned.

'So. I go out, Ben. I say a few words, introduce you. You say a few words. You press the button in front of you, and the painting will appear on the screen. Everyone claps. Then you hand over to Angela and she wraps up. We dine, we celebrate, and in the morning you wake up to half the island wanting you to paint them too. All right?'

'All right.'

'Good.' He stepped out to the centre of the stage and breathed in the applause, seemed to swell up with it like a hothouse flower in the sun. Eventually he raised his hands for silence.

'I know how unusual it is to have every one of us gathered here at the same time. Nonetheless, here we all are. The hospital beds are empty, the security towers too. The chefs have assured me dinner will be served at the usual time, and they've guaranteed it won't burn.' Laughter at this.

'It is amazing, isn't it? All of us, this whole society, together. Every one of you here is an expert. You know everything about a hundred arts – feeding people, clothing them, housing them. Sanitation, medicine, engineering. All the vital arts of modern civilisation are preserved here, ladies and gentlemen, and in a crew gathered from so many different corners of the earth. We are here. We have made it. I love to say we're building it – I tell you now, we have built it.' The crowd gave a collective sigh of unspeakable content.

'Some of you have been with me from the start; some of you I have known a few weeks. But I know you all. I am so proud of you. I have only been blessed with one child, wherever she's got to – Bianca?' There was laughter at this. 'But I feel like a parent to all of you. This island – this sanctuary – has been our creation, between us, and I feel proud, too, as any parent, of the great things that will happen here. We have the world's flora and fauna safely stored, waiting for the madness out there to end. Here, *here* is where the decline stops.

'More important, we have the finest four thousand people in the world. Four thousand two hundred and sixty-one of you came here. When I made my offer a few weeks ago, just thirty people departed. No more than thirty decided they couldn't cope with paradise. They were taken back to the mainland and I wish them luck there. Not too much luck, of course' – a grin – 'because I know they have turned their back on the greatest luck of all. They and their skills shall be replaced with ease. Already there are dozens of new lives among us, lives that will grow and strengthen and maintain this place in years to come.

'We have planned no great ceremony. All that remains for me to do is this.' He clapped his hands, once. A few seconds later, the crisp, flat sound was answered by a distant rolling boom of thunder, which crackled on for twenty seconds before dying away. 'That noise, ladies and gentlemen, was the sound of the tunnel's ceiling being detonated at two points. It would take a good while to clear that lot for anyone either arriving or leaving. We are, all of us, now officially in it for the long haul.' There was a pause as the audience took in his meaning. Then the applause returned. Slowly at first, but it built and built to a roar, clapping and cheering too, and the crowd held that note for an age, as John stood before them and raised his hands. He had tricked us all, and they loved him for it.

In that lasting roar, he glanced towards the side of the stage, where we few were standing. He caught my eye, and there was a look of glee on his face. The island's god had closed us in prematurely, had lied again and again, gulled his chosen people into staying. Then he was looking back at the crowd again, basking in the light. I leaned towards Bianca.

'Does this change anything?' She had to speak loudly over the crowd's applause, but Angela was standing far enough from us that she would not overhear.

'I think it does.'

'I can go now, start things earlier,' she said. 'You'll have to talk for a while, though. Try to keep them going until you see the sign.'

'Go, then. I'll find you.'

The Sanctuary

She slipped away. Not a moment too soon: the roar was dying down now, and Pemberley began to speak again.

'There is one more thing to show you. A month or so ago, you may remember we took in one of our most recent recruits here. A young man called Ben. He is an artist, a prodigiously talented one, and for those of you who know her, he is also engaged to be married to our own most precious Cara.'

Another squall of applause, and an answering stab of fury inside me. How dare he mention her name to these people?

'Ben has just finished his first commission for us here, and we thought the unveiling might work well tonight too.' He looked sideways at me again. 'Ben told me soon after he arrived here that a painting is a way of looking at a person, of truly seeing them. In the months ahead, we will see the truth about each other as never before. I trust that Ben has seen the truth about me. And in him, we will keep one of humanity's finest art forms alive. You'll all be seeing a lot more of him over the coming months and years, and he'll be seeing all of us right to the heart. So please, welcome him now.'

I took one last look at Angela, standing with a smile plastered to her face, and stepped out. John and I crossed paths as he returned, and he leaned in and took my forearm.

'They're all yours.'

I could not tell whether he heard my reply over the noise of the applause, but I think his expression changed a fraction as I spoke. 'This is for Thomas Candler. And for Cara.'

And then he released me and I was at the centre of the stage. As I glanced to the side, he seemed to be muttering something urgent to Knight.

Once I reached the lectern, the lights on me from each side were bright, and it took a while for my eyes to adjust. The brightness helped to calm my nerves, but my hands still shook as they rested on the lectern.

'As you've heard, I'm Ben. I'm a painter. I think you're all doing something remarkable using the skills you've learned. You're the ones who have made this place. My skills are more limited. But I do think paintings are important, for just the reason John said.

'The great artists a few centuries ago painted stories – moments of a battle being won or lost, acts of mercy, or heroism, or vengeance. That isn't quite what I've done. But I think you need to know the background to this image before I show it to you. So I want to tell you about a young boy. His name was Jacob Mann.'

I couldn't see much in the light, but at the side of the stage, I was aware of Knight starting. She did not move, though, because John had laid a hand on her arm. He was watching me with care, and with something almost like a smile on his face.

'Jacob was born half a century ago, and he grew up a long way from here, in a community like this one but much harsher. The people living there were stripped of their goods like sheep being shorn bloody. They were in thrall to the man in charge. He was Jacob's father, and he brought his son up to expect greatness.

'But eventually his outrages and his abuses grew too great to ignore. The world came knocking and the place fell apart, and young Jacob escaped, an orphan now. His name was changed, and he moved across the world, came to this country. He was educated, and when he reached his majority, he inherited his father's money and started to spend it, building the world to come. But he had remembered the lessons of his childhood. He knew the old world, the weak and decayed world of the past, would be ending soon, and it was his duty to help bring that end about.'

I looked sideways again. John had not moved, had not even taken his hand from Knight's arm. He was watching me as if in a trance. The crowd was motionless, so still they looked like a painted backdrop.

I took a deep breath. 'Eventually his practice was finished, and he gathered his chosen people on an island and prepared to close the barrier between them and the rest of the world. If that was all he had done, it might have been an end to the story. But he had created one other trick as well. A new technology, if you like, a way of shortening life. It would make sure that nobody lived past a certain age. He would cut the human lifespan in two.

'After lengthy trials, his new technology was complete, and all he had to do was release it, let it be carried on the air. In future, he thought, nobody would live long enough to create the kind of fortune that had destroyed the world around him. There would be no elders ruining things for their inheritors; only children, and their parents, working to survive and build a new world. A simpler world, humble before God, and a small group of the select, in a green garden.

'He tried out this new invention on a few people on the island. One was a man called Thomas. Thomas was exposed to this invention, and he died. Now our leader is about to try and release this creation further. That's why you're all here. You're here because you're young. You will live long enough to keep this place going, to pass on your skills and your genes, and then you will drop before you are forty.'

They were murmuring now, in consternation, but they listened still.

'This is his vision. Humanity reduced once again to its proper state. He loves his father's God, and he loves nature, and yet above these two feelings he hates you all. This permanent reduction of us is what he wants. But it's not too late to stop this invention from getting out. I know we can prevent it.' I knew nothing of the sort, and I felt sick wondering if John's poison was already spreading across the world. But I could not let them see that.

'I've spoken too long. But I wanted you to know the kind of man whose care you have placed yourselves under. He once said it was worth launching a lifeboat if your ship was sinking. He even said it would be worth sinking the ship to ensure the lifeboat got away. Behold the man.' I moved to the side, removed the cover from the easel and pressed the button on the lectern.

The crowd fell silent as the image swam onto the screen. I looked up and around. There he was, leaning towards the viewer, his hands locked like a magician halfway through a trick. He was giving his customary look, both searching and accepting, human and diabolical. The light gleamed on his bare head and reflected off it, forming a fractured halo in the air above him. And in his face was everything I had seen in him: my scepticism, my love, and the fear I had of him now. There was compassion, ambition, monstrosity, charity, the greatest virtues and the most wicked vice, all I could summon onto the canvas and everything he deserved. The skull sitting on a surface behind him was painted from memory, a late addition. There had only just been time to add it and let it dry before this moment. Its empty eyes watched the living man.

John was next to me now, and I took a step backwards. He raised his voice.

'Stop, stop. My friends, I wanted to let Ben here say his piece. Suffice it to say, none of what you just heard was true. As I think is obvious, he is not well.'

'No.' I was not speaking into the microphone any more, but I knew what I had to do. I had to stay on the stage, not lose my liberty. Just a little longer. I could tell people were approaching me from the other side too, but with caution, and I kept my face towards John in case he rushed me.

I heard a crack in the distance then – *finally* – followed by a shout from the crowd, and turned in the direction people had started to look. There was a plume of smoke in the darkening sky, thin yet, but swelling, and not in the south-west, not where the tunnel had been detonated. It was further round than that – by the site of the island's seed vault. People were pointing it out to each other now, and there were more shouts as the plume thickened, and began to billow. Then a great roar, as one of the oxygen tanks went up. Thank God. That was my cue to leave.

John turned back to me. 'What have you done?' He was speaking just to me, but the microphone caught his words, and his voice had lost its gentle tone. 'Did you do this?'

'Not alone.'

He glanced at the side of the stage again, and seemed to notice for the first time that his daughter was missing.

I stepped backwards. A party of Pemberley's men had gathered at the other end of the stage, waiting for me. There was only one gap left I could see – beneath the screen, along the long green path south of the hub.

I turned back to John and gestured past him, to where Knight stood at the side of the stage.

'She was at Greenmartin too, wasn't she? It's always been the two of you together.'

The name of his childhood home did not provoke him to fury. He turned to look at Knight, then back at me, his face a total blank, and that was my moment to run.

As I moved, I saw a small detachment of people streaming towards the source of the fire. Pemberley's men at the end of the stage had clearly decided to take no part in that endeavour: I heard feet behind me, and the whine of carts suddenly in motion, and I left the path, curving back around the edge of the hub and heading north. I knew exactly where I was going.

My lungs were about to burst, my skin was on fire, but I had outpaced them for the moment. I was alone.

Perhaps an hour and a half had passed as I made my way north and west. Bianca had done her job well; as I ran, I looked over my shoulder and saw the flames starting to build. One or two of the hexes I passed seemed to have blossomed into flame, too. The supply pipeline she had found to set alight must have led there. I skirted them as best I could, and the few islanders running back and forth among the burning buildings seemed not to have noticed me.

Bianca hadn't intended to burn the interior of the biobank: just the outside, she said, to draw as much attention as possible. But it had clearly spread. The other thing she said was that the hydroponics had always been a fire risk. Water, electricity, oxygen ...

there was a surprising amount to burn. The dragon's guts Francis had shown me during my first days here must have looked wonderful blossoming into flame.

A siren had blared for a while, harsh coughs of noise that seemed to be coming from every tree around me, but eventually I had run beyond the sound, and here, arriving at the stone circle, there was almost perfect peace.

Darkness had fallen as I ran. The iron light of the moon lay on this empty arena, and the usually white stones were now pale grey. No birds sang, and although I knew now that the place was nothing more than another of Pemberley's fabrications, I could not help pausing, taking in the magnificent bleakness one last time before starting out across the plateau.

The woods opposite me were empty at the moment I stepped into the cold, bare arena, and nobody stood along the path behind me. But almost by a trick of light, when I looked round again twenty seconds later, I was no longer alone. Ranged behind me was a band of a dozen islanders – part of the agricultural crew. A few more moved round to my right, far enough to block off my exit if I turned and tried to run north. One or two were familiar to me; one especially so. But the gathering night seemed to have changed them into a gaunt, unemotional hunting pack. They fanned out around me, and Francis stepped forward.

'Come back south, Ben,' he called softly. 'There's nowhere else for you to go.'

I stepped backwards. Francis and his men took another step towards me.

'He murdered the man who lived in your cottage. He killed Cara too. You don't know what he is, Francis.'

'Thomas fell ill and died, Ben. I don't know what you think you saw, but I assure you John has no harm in him. Look at this place.'

My folding knife was in my pocket still. I tried to look casual, slipped my hand inside and pressed the button to release the blade. I risked another step back. They took two forwards.

Francis spoke again. 'Don't do this, Ben. You can have a fine life here.'

Another voice – higher, older – cut across him, and I paused, on the verge of pulling the knife out. 'You're wasting your breath, Francis. He's quite deluded on this point.'

A few of the men shuffled aside and revealed her standing there. Angela Knight, looking serene in the frosted light of the moon. Her grey hair matched the standing stones around her, and something within her seemed to resonate with them too. 'Bring him to me.'

Francis started towards me, a man on either side.

I called out to him as he approached. 'Francis, John is a killer. Anyone at our level, anyone who asks questions, they're disposed of.'

'I'm sure he's made mistakes. He still created this place. He's in charge here, and you'll have to answer for what you did tonight.'

But I had found a point of leverage in him, and I spoke faster as he neared me. 'Francis, listen to me. You never told me what Thomas's tattoo was, did you? You told me he had a tattoo of a book, but you never said which one. It was called *Nostromo*. Do you remember? I only know that because his body is still here. I saw it yesterday.'

Francis paused, held a hand up to the men on either side. He was within a few feet of me now.

'They've aged him, Francis. He looks ninety. And the same thing is going to happen to you in a few years – to all of you – unless you listen to me. You'll never see your child grow up.'

'Just take him, will you?' The noise was followed by a metallic click. Knight had produced a stubby revolver from somewhere, and as Francis turned, she kept it pointing somewhere between me and him. It was her only mistake, really, but it was enough to provoke him.

'I take instruction from John, not from you.'

Her reply was crisp. 'I assure you that John takes instruction from me, and you can take instruction from either of us. The island has plenty of bone-headed farmers.'

I spoke next. 'Angela, don't do anything rash. He's about to become a father.'

'Not if he doesn't do as I say.'

Francis looked at me, a long, appraising look. He muttered something under his breath – I could not swear to it, but it sounded a little like *Nostromo* – then, curiously, he gave me a wink and the ghost of a smile before turning towards Knight – but slowly, far too slowly.

There was a roaring noise, and he stumbled backwards towards me. As he looked down at his chest, at a small rosette of red growing there, another bullet caught him and spun him the other way, whirling him onto the ground like a blown leaf.

The third shot found no home, nor the fourth, but a fifth and a sixth found the men on either side of him, and the group erupted in confusion. Half the men were moving towards Knight, half were scattering, all of them shouting. I was forgotten for a moment, and in the tumult I turned and fled onto the road north; away from the circle, away from them all.

There were yells as I went, but no more shots, and I could not tell whether Knight had carried the rest of the group with her.

I sprinted along the path that twisted through the woods, astonished that I had the breath to run. My legs were cramped, my shirt soaked, but I knew what I was looking for, and I could tell from the lack of immediate pursuit that Knight's authority over the remaining men had not been established yet. I risked a look back, and although I heard crashing noises a way behind me, nobody was directly in sight. Keep going, keep going, until … there it was. A log off the side of the path, fallen, big enough to shield me from view.

I vaulted straight over it, down a short drop on the other side, and then into the hollow, as far as possible into the soft, cool dampness, dislodging worms, burrowing in like a desperate animal, a fox reduced to the base panic of the hunt.

The noise of pursuit passed me, faded to nothing. I even glimpsed one or two of the men through the trees, heading north, but they did not turn back, and within a minute they were gone. Still I waited, and a few minutes later I heard quiet steps on the path. I knew they were Knight's somehow. I did not move, and the steps faded, following the main party that had been looking for me. I was alone again.

I stood and started moving west, towards the coast. I reached the cliffs before long, and after only a minute or two found the staircase, in the darkness twice as alien and unforgiving as before. It was lit only by the stars above, and by the wavering half-moon, occasionally shrouded by clouds. After a long, careful look around to make sure I was alone, I began my descent.

The journey down would have been treacherous even with proper equipment, climbing shoes, ropes; I had nothing, and so had to move with a tortuous slowness. Some of the steps had worn away almost completely, so smooth and weathered they had lost any purchase, and I had to stretch myself to step over them. Even on the intact ones, the carpet of slime covering them like a skin robbed them of almost all the grip they might have had. Every step felt like the beginning of a disastrous drop.

Now and then I slipped, and scrabbled desperately for purchase on the damp rock. When I found stability again, I froze for a few seconds, as though that might help me stay inconspicuous. At one moment, an unseen bird cried out by my ear, and if I had not flattened myself immediately, it would have startled me from my position and sent me plunging down to the rocks below. After that shock, I paused again, and in that pause I thought I heard a tiny noise from beneath me; although it stopped after a second, and it might have been my imagination.

Down, down, down; for an age I descended, sometimes backwards on all fours as if descending a ladder, sometimes slithering down on my back, jabbing sideways for purchase like a strange insect. There was no shape the staircase didn't demand me to assume at one point or another. It felt like the island was enjoying one last game at my expense, forcing me into strange new contortions, testing my desire to leave.

It was endless, and added to the exhaustion of last night, I felt more than once as though I had slipped out of the living world and into a kind of purgatory. There was only the staircase dropping away ahead, and no matter how long I crawled for, the ground seemed no closer than at the start; I had been descending for ever, through an eternal night, and if I tried to climb again, I would surely grow exhausted and fall.

Eventually, the ground beneath looked a fraction nearer, and another age after that, I was finally upon it, my muscles racked, my clothes soaked from the damp surfaces. I looked primal, like the first man, born from the mud. But I was here, and past the worst. I thought of John's words about the bottleneck, and wondered if the island had started through it yet.

Here, then, was the bay Bianca had directed me to this morning. The walls of rock on either side were sheer and forbidding. Behind me, the top of the dark cliff was hardly visible, although there was a slim line of total darkness beneath the stars that marked where it ended. Before me the ocean lapped at small, rough stones, and a narrow pass led to the open sea outside. Beyond that, standing pale in the moonlight, I could just see the sea-stacks, the Devil's Chessmen. In my addled state, I wondered if John had built them too. And scattered around me on the sand were a dozen wrecks, boards and engine parts and rudders strewn as if they had just crashed here.

More pressingly, and closer: Bianca had promised it, and there it was, bobbing in the water, tied to a stake buried in the rocky shore. A boat, smaller and slimmer than the one I had arrived on, without an engine. Its oars were tucked into the bottom.

There was a sound over to one side in the darkness, like the one I had heard before during my descent – a little shift of the rocks. That must be her.

I started towards the overhang at the side of the bay. She might have been injured setting the fire, or since then. At least she had got here; she could not have been too badly hurt. What if she had fallen, had only managed to crawl here? But there she was, in silhouette, hunched over a weak light, facing out to sea. I breathed out in relief. We would be able to haul ourselves into the boat and find the route south, away from here, back to the mainland, to sanity. We could still stop this.

'Bianca?'

But as I got closer, the silhouette unfurled and rose; taller than me, and broader, and topped by a shining dome. Sir John.

I had known he was a large man, but to see him now, I realised that the veneer of civilisation had concealed his strength. His feet were bare, and the clothes he had worn to the ceremony had been stripped back to only an undershirt and trousers. His face seemed a little scorched on one side, as though he had been singed by the fires his daughter had set before making his way here. He stepped towards me, and I moved back. He looked like a burned god.

Neither of us spoke for a second. Words seemed unnecessary. I had said everything I needed to earlier. Then he opened his mouth.

'I thought my daughter might do something this stupid. But I expected better of you.'

'I'm happy to have let you down.'

'You came down here, though, didn't you? I had enough sense to predict that. You people, thinking you know this island better than me.'

'I know some things better than you imagined. I know about Greenmartin. I know about your father, and about your life at Hillcrest.' His face was quite still in the moonlight reflected off the waves. 'I know about telomeric abrasion, too.'

'You've done wonderfully, Ben. Looks like you've found every fact about this place but the most important one.'

'What's that supposed to mean?'

'Oh no, Ben. You tell me. You're the great investigator.'

'All I want to do is leave.'

'You think we haven't prepared for fire?' He laughed. 'We've prepared for everything. This place will survive.' He glanced up at the cliffs, and there seemed to be an orange glow there. Perhaps the fire had spread further, faster than I had anticipated.

'Now the islanders have heard the truth about you, they won't stay. They'll find a way off. Knight has started shooting people.'

'They won't. They're tied to the island now. You've changed nothing.' He sighed. 'It's such a shame, what you've tried to do. You would have been a good steward of this place. But not now.'

'It's true, isn't it? What I found. The extra hex. The rats. Thomas.'

'It's not my job to tell you the truth. All I have been doing here is suggesting another way forward.'

'Jesus.' Somehow I still had the capacity for shock. 'Bianca was right.'

'You have gone quite mad. Either that, or you've let my daughter infect you with her own madness. You have no proof of any of this. The extra hex, as you call it, was a place for our trials. All we wanted to do was extend human lives and wipe out invaders. Thomas was a terrible mistake. And now you threaten me. You try to burn my food. You kill my islanders.'

I was moving slowly towards the far wall of the bay, away from him, and I passed into the shadow of the rocks as I stumbled back. Not much further to retreat.

John's voice was sorrowful. 'You could have had this whole place. You could have built your home here, had a family. And you threw it away.'

'Cara believed in this place when she came here, John. She believed in this place so much she left me behind. She left everything behind because she thought you wanted to make the world a better place. But you killed her. I don't know how, but if she was alive, you would have produced her by now. I'm surprised you didn't try to rustle up a copy of her.'

'You fool. Your Cara is on the mainland, alive yet. You would have seen her soon. She will be at the coast shortly, and tomorrow your time here would have begun.'

I shook my head, but he kept talking. 'As for the world . . . All I have ever wanted was to create more life. My whole work here has been to do that. Look at what we have made here. Look at this place.' He waved an arm. 'It is garish with life; pure, super-abundant life. Then you came, without knowing why, without knowing anything about me, or about your own self. You tried to destroy my vision. And now you think you can simply leave.'

He stepped towards me again, then paused. I took the moment to glance down, and snatched up a spar of wood that lay before me on the ground. It felt uncomfortably soft as I hefted it.

John kept speaking. 'You'll have to kill me with one blow, because by the second one I'll be on you. And I'm willing to bet you can't do that.' He took another step, his shoulders tensed and ready.

He moved towards my left first, towards my painting arm, and knocked the plank from it. I should have grabbed a stone next, tried to stun him with it, but there was no time for that, none at all, because he leaned forward with a shoulder and bulled straight into me. I fell backwards, scrabbled for purchase, kicked out at his descending head and hands, but he absorbed the blows almost as if he had not noticed them, and kneeled on my legs, holding them down with the weight of his body. Then he delivered a single blow to my face, hard enough to stun me, for my nose to pop in pain, and before I could recover, his hands were around my windpipe, squeezing so hard I felt my head would burst.

I looked up at him in that second. The only thought I was conscious of as I beat vainly at his head and neck, prised at his unyielding arms, was that I would die as I had lived, staring at his face. My portrait had needed more of the animal in it. The veins stood out on his arms, and in his eyes there was only the look of a beast intent on the single task of subduing its prey. I could not stay conscious much longer. The stars above him swam in and

377

out, and the sound of the sea merged with the blood roaring in my ears.

And then, after a few seconds, the pressure of his grip released. He must have relented. I heaved for breath, and twisted to the side, pulling in air – wonderful salt-laced air, never sweeter. John had changed his mind, was about to forgive me and explain it away again. He was the benevolent man I had imagined after all. Bianca and I had made a mistake; Christ, the whole thing had been a mistake.

But I was wrong. He had pulled back from me and was kneeling on the sand, looking directly ahead of him. His neck had something growing out of it, like the stem of a sapling; a knife handle, thick and malevolent, and swelling with dark liquid at its base. And holding the other end of the handle was Bianca Pemberley.

He tried to turn, to swipe at her, but she was holding it firmly enough to resist him. The line of her mouth was grim, and she looked with concentration at the task before her. She twisted the blade and levered it sideways. He fell backwards, sitting upright and feeling the side of his neck as if in a trance. He looked at his hand, back at her, then to me, and managed to speak somehow, although I could not tell who he addressed.

'Just like . . . your father.'

Bianca stood, patient, the muscles of her arm taut, until she judged the moment was right and withdrew the blade. Sir John Pemberley toppled onto the sand. He did not move.

I left Bianca by her father, stumbled to the waterline, dipped my head in the freezing salt. My face was in agony, and my neck too, from the imprints of his great hands. I drenched my head and looked down, trying to find my reflection. Whenever the water was still enough for me to see myself, the pain grew too great again, and I had to disturb my reflection to get more. The image of my face in the water was a collection of shards.

Bianca was behind me now, over my shoulder. Her voice was different down here, more confident.

'I knew he was strong enough to subdue the two of us one by one, so I had to wait for his attention to be drawn.'

I pulled up from the water and turned to her. It felt as if the consequences of what we had done were spreading outwards from us like crystals forming in a dish, and as I looked up at the night, they seemed already to be assuming huge and monstrous shapes in the air around us.

'Let's get you away from here.' Bianca helped me stand and walked me carefully back to where the boat lay.

'How did you manage all this? How did you get the boat?'

'It was washed up here. A little damaged, but mendable.'

'You repaired it alone?'

She nodded at her father's body. 'Being his daughter left me with a lot of freedom. Enough to learn everything he would have taught me if he'd ever considered me his heir.'

'Why didn't he?'

'It feels like he was waiting all his life for someone else to turn up. And he settled on you.'

'Why me?'

She shrugged. 'I have no idea.'

We hauled the boat towards the water. Bianca had already stashed my painter's roll in the bottom of it, I don't know when, and seeing it brought a lump to my throat. I waited for her to get in, assuming I would push the boat down the shingle. But when I gestured for her to do so, she stepped back and gestured with her hands: go.

'I'm not coming, Ben.'

'What?'

'You heard me.'

'You've been waiting for this freedom your whole life. You don't want to see the mainland? Really see it?'

'Of course. I want it so much. But there's a lot to change here.' She rubbed her brow, and for the briefest moment I saw in her face a shadow of her father.

'You're sure about this?'

'Yes. I want to bury John. And besides, you know as much as I do about this thing he was creating. If there's time to stop it, then that's what you have to do. And if there isn't, someone should be in charge here.'

'You'll make it back up the cliff all right?'

'I brought equipment.'

'What about Knight?'

'I'll deal with her.' She nodded, and her father's face recurred again in her own, like the chiming of a distant bell. 'You sure you know which way you're going? After the fifth chessman, steer south, past the harbour. Then keep going due south for a mile. That should carry you into the old postal current towards the mainland. It's strong, and it'll do most of the work for you. Just use the oars to keep yourself in the middle of it and you'll be back on land by dawn. There won't be anyone coming for you.'

She nodded towards the boat. 'There's a bag of supplies down there somewhere.'

'How is the island going to survive?'

'Either I'll run it by myself, my way, or it won't survive. I haven't decided yet. Perhaps you'll find a way of contacting me once you find out what's happening on the mainland.'

'Thank you, Bianca. For everything.'

'Forget it.'

'He said I'd found out every fact about this place but the most important one.'

'He had a knack for saying things like that. You can forget that too.' She smiled at me in the moonlight. 'Anything else?'

'The painting.'

'I'll look after it, Ben.' She paused. 'But not because of who it shows.'

I looked back at the lump on the ground that had been her father. 'Were we right about him? He said ... he said he just wanted to create more life.'

She shrugged. 'We'll know soon enough.'

I nodded. 'When I get to the mainland ...'

'If you can raise the alarm, halt the release somehow, then do so. But try not to tell them about here. You can leave me to worry about straightening things out. We're set for the future, once I've brought them to heel.' She nodded towards the clifftop. 'There was a lot of good in what he was doing.'

'Goodbye, Bianca.'

She turned towards me, and for the first time she looked as if she belonged here. We hugged, awkwardly, and yet even in that moment of warmth, of human connection, I shivered. There was something about her that was alien and familiar all at once, and all I could think to explain it was her father's blood.

I climbed into the boat and left her there on the beach, kneeling beside the body, as the tide climbed towards them.

33

I rowed backwards from the moon through the cool night air. The stars shifted above me, and I could feel the current beneath. The air was almost still, and my sweat had long since dried on me. My face was a mess, but I would tidy myself up when I got back to land. I couldn't credibly raise the alarm looking like this.

For hours, the island had been a lump on the horizon, slowly diminishing as I headed towards the mainland. It seemed impossible that the single dark swell hosted the miracles I had seen in the last weeks. An entire little world lay there, jewelled and perfect, once prepared for whatever storms lay in the centuries ahead, now on the brink of unravelling, thanks to Bianca and to me. I felt like the only survivor of the sea monster in the hall at the hub.

Eventually the island was out of sight, and the mainland ahead of me too. The only thing left was the boat, and the current I sat in. No seals accompanied me now. The sea around me looked like a desert.

I spoke, and my voice was flat above the gentle ripples of water about the boat's hull. 'He had the means to do it. He wouldn't invent something like that and not use it.' I sounded as if I was trying to persuade myself.

He'd clearly used his new technique on at least one human, of course; on Thomas. But what he had said about that on the beach, that it had been a mistake, that the whole aim was to extend life … that felt as if it could have been true as well. Perhaps he really had intended to help Thomas. Perhaps he had meant to use the technology to wipe out other invasive species, become the gardener he always dreamed of being. Wasn't that more likely?

I was desperate, I knew, and I remembered the documents Bianca had found. Why defend him further? His final lie about Cara being alive, being on the mainland now … I wept then, wept for knowing I would never see her again. The island had swallowed her, and the vengeance gained with Pemberley's death had not filled the hole an inch.

John had been turning into a kind of island god. *Maybe islands need gods*, a rival thought whispered to me. No, it was no good; he would have killed me on that beach if Bianca hadn't been there, and then returned to running his sanctuary without another thought.

The portrait remained in my mind even as I wept, and the benevolence stitched through John's face, tangled with the power and the cruelty. Those doubts, that memory of his face with its impossible combination of gentility and evil, stayed with me for a long time, as I sat and pulled at the oars, gently keeping the boat in the current carrying it to shore. The memories lasted until long after the grey hour had lifted, and the sun had broken through into a dawn of unexpected, sparkling beauty.

I rested the oars beside me and took the notebook from my pocket. It held Thomas's hideous drawings of John, and I felt great disgust. I stretched back my arm to throw it as far as I could into the sea. It was the final bit of evidence of the place I carried. And yet … I lowered my arm. It might prove useful back on the mainland, might show whoever I could speak to that things had been seriously wrong there. From the pouch at the back I took out the photo I had copied from the archives, the photo of the community at Greenmartin.

What had John said down at the beach? *Looks like you've found every fact about this place but the most important one.* I looked closely at the photo again, in the early morning light, for some time.

Isaac Mann stood in the centre. John stood before him to his right, his young double, recognisable even with a mop of hair, together with a woman who looked enough like him for me to guess she was his mother. Angela Knight also stood at Isaac's right. But John was glancing sideways in the photo, and I followed his eyeline. There was a young woman standing on the other side of Isaac Mann. She had her hands crossed before her stomach, as though hiding it from view.

It's not easy to see these things, close up. Children can look nothing like their parents. It had been many years since her death, of course, and her photo was not before me now. But as the boat bobbed and creaked in the current, I saw that the girl standing on the edge of the picture looked remarkably like my mother.

The sound of the waves against the boat's hull drained from my ears, and I did not feel the breeze.

My mother had always said she had me young. I counted back. The date in the newspaper, when the community at Greenmartin had fallen apart, would have been about six months before my birth.

It couldn't be. My father – the man I had thought of as my father – what about him? Another thought occurred to me, the way I had described him to others: *a minor fraudster. He'd do anything for a little money.* Including, perhaps, pretend to be my natural father.

I had been sent to school at Hillcrest – how, and with what money? With the money from my uncle, of course. We had visited my uncle, hadn't we, at his home? He had been away at the time. I had never actually met him face to face. Then whose money had paid for my schooling? Who had ensured I was given a start in life? The same man who had done all that had also ensured that I would be given the opportunity to get close to him, and that when that opportunity arose, I would seize it. The man who wanted an heir and an innocent at the same time.

John Pemberley. A son of the community at Greenmartin, but not the only child of that place. John Pemberley. My half-brother.

I leaned over to the water, and half the face of Isaac Mann looked back at me.

I had heard that conversation in the chapel, between Pemberley and Knight. *He did well, making his way here. Better than I would have expected.* He had insisted that whoever should inherit the island wouldn't have been groomed to it their whole life. He had never wanted Cara, I understood now; he had never cared whether she succeeded in her work here or not. Cara had merely been a way of getting to me.

I twisted in my seat. There was the mainland, at last. The boat was coasting towards the land ahead of me, the current still carrying me towards it. I hardly needed to row. A few shreds of cloud had drifted across the sun, and as they moved its light broke through again, stronger now, and dazzled my sight.

This was a bay, and from the structures scattered around its edge, I knew it must be the harbour of Pemberley's mainland estate. No living person was there to greet me. None, at least, except a lone figure standing at the dock, with the rising sun behind her. She wore a long, dark dress, and as I drew closer, she grew familiar, greatly familiar to me. Hers was a face I had never painted before, out of a childish superstition.

Yet as the boat approached, as it drifted towards the concrete harbour and her features grew clear, I saw she was strangely aged, a decade older at least than when I had seen her last, her eyes creased, her hair quite grey.

The creation that Knight had built, that Bianca had discovered, that Pemberley had wanted to release on the mainland ... it was already here. The trees around the edge of the bay danced in the breeze, echoing with the sounds of birds and insects and small wild things. And Cara, my Cara, stood on the shore watching me approach, like the first angel outside Eden, waiting to see what would happen next on this sunlit and reborn earth.

Acknowledgements

I owe a great deal to everyone who helped *The Sanctuary* up off the slab and set it lurching out into the wide world.

My agent Peter Straus gave me superb feedback about which bits were (and weren't) working in the early stages, and his colleague Jon Wood provided some highly astute insights in the closing stages of the early stages too. Everyone else at RCW has demonstrated what a wonderful agency they are – always enthusiastic about authors, and always keen to usher the next book into the world.

Selina Walker has once again proved an editor *par excellence* – with a keen nose for the most important elements of a story, the determination to keep going until it's just right, and an absolute ardour to spread the word once it's finished. Her colleagues – including Joanna Taylor on the copy-editing front, and many more – showed themselves more than equal to the challenges this book threw up. Ceara Elliot designed the fabulous and intriguing cover and Jessica Pilling produced the brilliantly eerie hexes which slowly crumble through the book's interior.

The joint work of Najma Finlay (Publicity) and Sam Rees-Williams (Marketing) spreading the word has been invaluable – and Mat Watterson and his team in Sales have also done a marvellous job, as ever. If you've heard about the book at all – and I'm not sure how you're reading this if you haven't – it's because of the efforts of this team.

Early readers and cheerleaders: the steering committee of Maisie Glazebrook and Katherine Rundell (plus a cast of dozens more) did great work talking me up when I had doubts, and occasionally talking me down off the ledge when I had more substantial doubts. Thanks too to Gill Hornby and Robert Harris, for their huge generosity and hospitality to the scruffy hermit who would occasionally appear waving his hands and shouting about plot holes. Lastly, to Molly, for your wisdom, for your patience, for reading the thing more than anyone has a right to ask, and for all the tea and sympathy (followed by more tea) … thank you.

Bringing a book from manuscript to what you are reading is a team effort, and Penguin Random House would like to thank everyone at Hutchinson Heinemann who helped to publish *The Sanctuary*.

PUBLISHER
Selina Walker

EDITORIAL
Sophie Whitehead
Joanna Taylor
Jane Selley

DESIGN
Ceara Elliot

PRODUCTION
Nicky Nevin

UK SALES
Mat Watterson
Claire Simmonds
Olivia Allen
Evie Kettlewell

INTERNATIONAL SALES
Richard Rowlands
Maddy Bennett
Laura Richetti

PUBLICITY
Najma Finlay

MARKETING
Sam Rees-Williams

AUDIO
Meredith Benson